PAPER TARGETS

PATRICIA WATTS

PAPER TARGETS

A NOVEL

atmosphere press

For every woman who has ever been silenced.

A slurp and a gulp. The knock of something solid against the surface next to the phone. Common noises on the other end of the line—she's taking a drink, setting down a glass.

Then—the ear-splitting boom of a gunshot, the shallow thud of a weight hitting the floor.

I scream her name.

No noises now.

My best friend is dead.

———

At Roanne's funeral reception, the eagerness for answers was thicker than the abundant short ribs set out next to the potato salad and baked beans. The guests had no appetite. They wanted to sink their teeth into why Roanne chose to die the way she did. And they were all looking to me, her closest friend for fifty years.

People had driven to Round Rock from other parts of Texas or from farther away to spend the morning at the church, midday at the cemetery, and the afternoon gathered at the home of Roanne's sister, Darla.

They leaned out and asked, "Why, Connie?" as I walked through Darla's living room, taking small, deliberate sips from a glass of iced tea, avoiding eye contact, unable to respond.

Roanne had called me that night, at three minutes after eleven. I'd hit the TV "off" button, was headed to bed; I had stayed up too late again, hooked on my latest Netflix binge. The words we had exchanged played back to me with every shiver and stab to my heart that I had felt then:

"I got the bastard," she said. From the hollow sound of her voice, I knew her phone was on speaker. "Straight through the balls." Her words shook.

"Ro? You're scaring me, girl," I said. "Got who?"

She was breathing hard, with a sharp, staccato, "Uh, uh..."

"Is someone with you?"

"Not anymore. Just me, myself, and I," she said between a snicker and a sob.

"Are you at home? I'll come get you." My adrenalin was pumping. Something terrible had happened or was about to happen, but what? I could make the ninety-five-mile drive from San Antonio to Round Rock in an hour and ten. I switched my phone to speaker and pulled a pair of leggings on under my nightshirt.

"Don't bother, I'll be done soon." She breathed in, a deep reverse sigh, like she was struggling to find the strength to get the words out. "The anger. You take it and take it, and one day you see there's no way out. You're trapped."

"You're angry? With whom?"

"With Johnny, with the whole goddamn male establishment, my daddy, the school bullies, the boss, the superintendent, the judge, the lovers, husband, ex-husband, the smartass at Home Depot, the whole lot of 'em, every Tom, Dick, and Harry."

Her words seemed silly and frightening. "That's a bunch to take on by yourself. Why don't we talk about it, regroup?" I needed to get between her and whatever it was that was galloping, like my heartbeat, toward her. Couldn't you find someone's location on a cell phone? But you had to set that up, and I had had no reason to before.

"Now what would Judd do?" she said.

I pulled the name from the past through my memory to the present. It didn't fit in the moment. "Judd? Mr. Asher from senior social studies?"

"You know what I really liked about Mr. Asher?"

"He looked like David Cassidy?" Giggle, Roanne. Be okay, Roanne.

"Exactly, that too." I pictured her smiling through the pain in her voice. "He seemed to have all the answers, didn't he? Only he wanted us to figure things out on our own."

I stepped into my running shoes, left the laces untied. "What does Mr. Asher have to do with—"

"Figure it out for yourself. Speak up, Con. Don't let them have the final say." Roanne's words slurred and trailed off. "It's too late for me, but—"

"Hang on, it's never too late." I could feel the bad ending like the anticipation of an icy finger about to touch the back of my neck, raising goose flesh. I picked up my keys and purse. I headed for the garage. Keep talking, Roanne, please keep talking. "Tell me where you are, sweetie."

Another intake of air. A gap of silence. A gulp. The boom.

"Roanne!"

———

My iced tea sloshed onto Darla's living room carpet as a hand reached out from the sofa and snagged my elbow.

A thirtyish, delicate-looking man in a dark suit and ostrich cowboy boots balanced a paper plate of untouched food on his lap and looked up at me.

"Connie?" he said, his pained frown making his wire-rimmed glasses slip off the bridge of his nose.

I had met him before, the assistant manager at the Hallmark shop where Roanne had been employed for the past sixteen years. What was his name? Something French. Jacques. Jean. Didn't the ladies at the shop call him Jay?

"How could she do that to her daughters?" the young man pleaded. He didn't seem to expect an answer. "You can't blame them for not coming to the funeral, can you?" He picked at the food on his plate.

The coroner's report had said the bullet that Roanne sent from the pistol into her right temple killed her instantly. Johnny, her ex-husband, had died more slowly, bleeding out on the garage floor from a gunshot to the genitals.

"How are you holding up?" the man on the sofa asked. "You must feel so...you were so much closer to her than any of us. Did she give any signs?"

Across the room, I caught Darla's eye. Her hands fretted with a napkin. Her look beckoned me.

"Oh, I don't mean you were to blame in any way," the young man said. "Of course there's nothing you could have done. She was obviously very disturbed. You just wonder after something like this, don't you? Was there some clue you missed, we all missed?" He slapped his forehead with the flat of his palm. "I'm going on, aren't I? It's how I deal with something so, so...so sorry." He caught my hand and squeezed it. "Connie, I'm so sorry for the pain you must be going through."

His words brought back the image of a man I had passed in the back of the church as I was leaving the funeral. He had spoken to me, with the same words, even my name. I hadn't recognized the older gentleman in a tweed coat with thick white hair swept back off his forehead, but something about him had been familiar, the eyes that smiled in spite of his somber words. I had thanked him and continued to the exit.

"Excuse me," I said to Jay-Jean-Jacques, "I'm going to check on Darla."

Darla greeted me with a stoic smile and a long hug. We had rarely seen each other, even on my trips to Round Rock to see Roanne, but death can pull together what life has not. She was younger than Roanne by five years, a shorter and forty-pounds-heavier version of her statuesque sister, her blonde bouffant stiff with a generous application of hair spray.

Tears had washed pale streaks through her makeup and smudged her mascara. Her pink lipstick was faded and revealed a speck of dried blood on her lower lip where she may have bitten it. A smear of barbecue sauce stained the front of her navy crepe dress.

"Sit with me," Darla said and steered me to chairs near the sliding glass doors to the patio. She pulled a shoebox from under her chair and handed it to me.

"What's this?" I asked.

"Some old photos I came across. I thought you might want them. Remember all those pictures taken of us kids every time our families got together?"

I cradled the box on my lap. "My mom was a crazy woman when she had a camera in her hand."

The Slaters and the Canellis had been close ever since the Slaters moved in three houses down from ours on Pecan Street in Austin, the year Roanne and I turned fifteen. My dad was an aircraft engineer at Bergstrom Air Force Base. My mom stayed home, mothering and housekeeping. Mr. Slater owned a roofing company. Mrs. Slater mostly kept out of sight, more often than not just a voice from the back bedroom, "under the weather."

"Weather," Roanne would say, "is Mommy's favorite brand of vodka."

Darla threw up her hands. "What am I gonna do with all that food?" She burst into tears and covered her mouth to stifle the sound.

The table in the center of the room groaned with Darla's culinary handiwork, which on any other occasion would have been picked clean by now. I set my glass and the box on the floor and put an arm around her.

"I've prayed and prayed, 'Lord Jesus, help me understand,'" she said, "but I just don't. Thank God, Mommy and Daddy have passed and don't have to deal with this. How could she do it?"

I patted her shoulder. "I don't understand either, hon."

Darla turned to me. "Have you talked to the girls?"

"To Stella. She flew back to Virginia right after Johnny's burial service. Zoe won't take my calls. She hasn't spoken to Roanne in years and now... I don't know how an orphan

7

adopted from the other side of the world processes losing a second set of parents."

"No one's touched your angel food-orange cake. It was so sweet of you. You shouldn't have gone to the trouble." Darla looked like she might cry again.

I gently squeezed her upper arm. "It was no trouble. You know me. I always bring the cake, whether I'm asked to or not."

"And how are you coping, dear?" she asked.

I hesitated. I was expecting the "these are the times you need faith" talk from Darla. What I needed, according to other well-wishers over the past week, was community, routine, counseling, or hot yoga.

I wasn't falling apart. I had taken to scrubbing my bathtubs more than normal, but, otherwise, I did the usual, watered and weeded my tiny garden enough to keep most of the plants alive, went to the grocery store once a week. I put in a minimum of four hours of writing daily on my latest book and kept my author website up to date. My blog posts had become sporadic, but I still made an effort.

I still volunteered every other week as a docent at the Witte Museum, and, although I had temporarily misplaced my motivation to move it or lose it with Wednesday senior water aerobics at the YMCA, I planned to restart the class sometime soon.

I still talked as usual with my neighbors whenever we crossed paths while checking the mail or taking out the trash or on early evening walks, though they tended to stay inside their air-conditioned spaces most of the year. We were a loose community who mostly minded our own business.

But I couldn't avoid thinking about the times I would have called Roanne or driven up to see her or met her somewhere in between, and sleep had become a nightly torment.

Movies had played in my head for the past week. They came up out of the blue at any time of the day. Roanne and me, little scenes from our lives together. They came with a distinct memory of when each had originally occurred, the year, sometimes the exact date, scenes from several months ago or when we were young wives and moms or girls in high school. Each time, I was there, and she was there, like it was happening in the present. Each morning, I would awake after barely nodding off, rattled out of my sleep with tremors in my hands, furious with Roanne and missing her like crazy at the same time.

When it came to sharing feelings, Roanne and my sister had been my tiny comfort zone for a long time. I didn't open up to Darla. "I'm okay," I said. "Some days are harder than others."

"I pray for you, and I pray for Roanne's immortal soul, that she had the time to accept Jesus as her Savior and ask Him for forgiveness before she...she spoke to you before she... What did she say?"

"She wasn't making sense. She mentioned a teacher from Bonham." I paused to rerun from memory Roanne's other ramblings. "She said anger was a trap, and I should speak up. Gibberish, really."

Darla stared at me. "She was angry at a teacher from high school?"

"No. Just angry."

"That doesn't sound like Roanne. I know she took it hard when Johnny left her, but, my God, that was almost twenty-five years ago. For all her failings, and, of course, we are all in need of God's mercy, no one can say she wasn't a cheerful person."

That was true. Roanne had lifted me out of the dumps with her smile or a clever word more times than I could remember. Our lives had run parallel in many ways—college right after high school, marriage soon after college, both to military guys who served in Vietnam. They were best buddies like us, her Johnny and my Scott, two daughters for her, one son for me.

Both divorces were ugly events that seemed much longer than necessary compared to the marriages of nineteen years for hers, mine after twenty-four.

"Lord Jesus, help me understand," Darla repeated. "Scott was a jerk, too. You divorced him. You didn't do...that."

"My life didn't splinter into bits around me. She lost everything she cared about because of those rumors."

"Her and that student."

"She always blamed Johnny."

"She couldn't prove Johnny had anything to do with those rumors," Darla said, irritation in her voice, or maybe just fatigue.

"You can know something's true even if you can't prove it."

"Still, you move on, don't you? You're not going to go over to Scott's house with a gun and—" Darla's volume went up a notch, her tone bitter. "'Domestic violence,' that's what they said on the TV news. Roanne wasn't violent. She was a nice lady, just like you and me."

"Maybe there was a part of her we didn't see?"

"Nonsense. Roanne was transparent as a picture window," Darla said. She put a hand to her mouth. "Oh, my, the boys will be disappointed there are no bones for them. After the guests finish off the ribs, I always give them the bones."

"The boys" were Darla's two Cairn terriers. Roanne and I had concluded long ago that the dogs were substitutes for Darla's sons, the one who had died as a child and the one who stayed far away on one business assignment or another.

I touched her hand. Distraction had always been Darla's way of coping. She was stuck in her living room full of grief with no immediate escape route, no place to secretly wolf down a pint of ice cream or a pan of brownies.

She curled away from me and pulled her hand out of my reach. "It must have been an accident. I refuse to believe she could have..."

"Shot Johnny, then turned the gun on herself?"

Darla shook her head and waved her hand in a dismissive motion, like she was trying to erase my words. "No, I've read about this kind of thing. Women don't do it."

I caught her hand and patted it. "But she did do it, hon, she did."

Darla abruptly stood up. "That potato salad won't keep."

- 2004 -

"I bought a gun," Roanne said as she emptied a grocery bag onto the kitchen counter in her new apartment in Round Rock.

I had pulled up in her guest parking space just after she had carried her shopping through the front door, right on time to give her a hand. I stopped in the middle of stacking the frozen vegetables in the freezer.

"What? You were in Walmart and all of a sudden between the pork chops and the crinkly fries you decided 'I'll buy a gun today?'"

"Actually, you can't buy a handgun at Walmart. I went to Academy Sports. It took all of thirty minutes. Simple." She smoothed a strand of hair behind her ear, tucked it into the platinum-gray knot twisted on top of her head, and handed me a bag of peeled shrimp.

"You don't even like being around guns." I put up the seafood, closed the freezer, pulled out the crisper bins in the bottom of the refrigerator, and waited for her to unload the fresh produce.

"That's you, not me," Roanne said. "I've just never felt the need."

I put away the broccoli, lettuce, radishes, and cucumbers, and shut the fridge. "You've lived fifty years without a gun, why now?"

"For protection. You heard about Janelle at the store?"

"Oh. Yeah." Roanne's coworker at the Hallmark shop had been sexually assaulted three weeks before while unlocking her car in the mall parking lot. "How is she?"

"She's not coming back, too traumatized. I don't want to live in fear like that. Walking to your car after a six-hour shift selling greeting cards should not be a risk to life and limb."

"Such is the world we live in. Isn't mall security stepping

up its game?"

"If you mean we have the option to wait an extra hour after we get off to get an escort to our cars. So, no, security is not doing enough." She opened a cupboard and put away breakfast bars, a bag of rice, pasta, a two-and-a-half-pound bag of M&Ms.

She didn't even stand on tiptoe when I would have needed a two-step stool to reach the shelf. Her lifted arm raised her loose, plaid shirt to expose a love handle edging over the waistband of her jeans, a little extra weight put on in the eight years since her divorce. A half-empty bottle of Jack Daniels stood against the back of the cupboard. Since when did Roanne drink whiskey? Whatever gets you through the night, I supposed.

"What about these?" I asked, pointing to four eight-count boxes of canned tomatoes.

"Leave that," she said. "It's for the food bank. I've started volunteering, every other Wednesday."

"I should do something like that." I folded the grocery bags. "A gun is your only option? Really?"

"Exactly. You think I'm going overboard, but I'm not. All of us, the other ladies, we now have a little something extra in our purses."

I stared at Roanne's red leather bag on the counter behind me, imagined a loaded pistol shoved in with her lipstick and hairbrush and her new reading glasses that she neglected to wear. "Would you, could you really shoot someone?"

"I can picture a situation where I might, could, yes, if I had to. Haven't you ever fantasized about pointing a gun at Scott and pulling the trigger?"

"No, well, yeah, but I could never actually do that."

She took a plastic pitcher of lemonade from the fridge, retrieved two glasses from the dish drainer, filled them, handed one to me, and snagged some paper napkins. I grabbed a Tupperware container filled with homemade poppy-seed pound cake that I had brought from San Antonio, a kind of housewarming present for my first visit to Roanne's new digs. We walked into the living room with our refreshments and sat at opposite ends of the burnt-orange, microfiber couch.

"I like the new pad," I said.

The two-bedroom on the first floor of a gated complex was more spacious and secure than the run-down studio apartment Roanne had lived in after she moved from her home in Pigeon Creek. The new place smelled of recently installed carpet, the dove-gray walls looked freshly painted, and the front bay window let in plenty of afternoon light.

"I'm moving on up, making more than minimum wage now." She took a bite of cake and flicked a crumb from a corner of her mouth with the tip of her tongue. "So, what if you were shooting at human silhouettes, just pieces of paper, that you had to put names on?"

"Oh, we're back to that?" I sipped my lemonade.

"Yeah. Who would you pick? Name five people."

"I don't know."

"Come on, you know, Scott..."

I thought for a moment. What would be my answer if this was a question on a game show? Name the top five people you would like to use for target practice.

"Okay, Scott, for sure," I said, imagining putting a shot through a drawn-on heart on a black outline of a man.

"And Joey?"

"Yeah, probably my twin brother."

"Who else?" Roanne asked, shoving a last bite of cake in her mouth and taking another piece from the container.

"I don't know, maybe that meany manager at Winky's car wash."

"Really? The Winky's guy? That was ages ago." She narrowed her eyes. "Who else?"

"No one. Stop."

"Someone who really, really did you wrong?" She drew

out the words, like she wanted me to think hard about my answer.

A vise squeezed my upper arms; my body was pinned to a flat surface, weight pressed down on my chest. "Brent. Put him up there."

"Brent, the guy who—"

"Yeah, that Brent," I cut in.

"That's only four. Why do I get the feeling you're holding out on me? I thought we told each other everything."

I fought the urge to tell her she hadn't said anything to me about her plans to buy a deadly weapon before she made that rash decision. "That's enough. It's only pieces of paper anyway. I wouldn't really shoot anyone."

"I don't plan to either. But I feel better that I can take things into my own hands, that I can stop someone if I had to. It gives me a kind of confidence in the way I carry myself."

I rolled my eyes. "Wow, if only you had picked up a hunk of lethal metal earlier, high school would have been a breeze."

"What are you saying?" She put a hand on her hip. "I was a wallflower?"

"No. You were a rose that bloomed before its time."

"Jealous, were you?" She wiggled her shoulder at me.

"Yeah." I smiled and threw a balled-up napkin at her. "You were Barbie. I was Midge."

She tossed the napkin back at me. "We were both Midge."

"And now I guess you're what, NRA Barbie? It scares me that you may have a false sense of confidence. Do you even know how to handle a gun?"

"I had a lesson at the shooting range," she said with a smug look.

"What if it goes off in your purse?" I looked over my shoulder where only the handle of the red leather bag was visible on the other side of the bar that separated the kitchen from the living room. "You or someone else could get hurt, or worse."

"It won't go off. I know how to put the safety on."

I took a bite of cake and let it soften on the roof of my mouth. "This is just temporary, right? Until mall security gets up to speed?"

Roanne dusted the crumbs from her hands onto a napkin in her lap. "I'm not holding my breath. I could get killed waiting for someone else to save me. You said it, 'such is the world we live in.' "

– 2019 –

After the funeral reception, I headed south on I-35 back to San Antonio from Round Rock, the driver part of my brain on autopilot. The sky was overcast. The evening light would be gone in less than two hours.

The shoebox of photos from Darla had spilled onto the passenger seat next to the angel food cake. Most were of the Slater kids, Roanne, Darla, and big brother Chip, together with the Canelli siblings, Frank, who was a year older than me, my twin brother Joey, and little Christine. In the faded images, our younger selves played football in a backyard, mugged at a birthday party with cake-smeared grins, splashed in a municipal pool.

One picture showed Roanne and me the summer after high school graduation on a hiking trail in Big Bend. The flame-colored hair I had inherited from my mother was pulled into bushy pigtails. I wore a gingham shirt knotted at the waist and rolled-up jean shorts that displayed my overflowing thighs. Roanne stood eight inches taller than me, almost six feet, her long, blonde hair tucked under a pink baseball cap, a tank top and gym shorts exposing her long, slender limbs. She made a goofy face that wrinkled the peeling, sunburned skin on her nose.

Roanne's last nonsensical words, before the gunshot, ran through my head like a hamster on a wheel. My arms trembled. I struggled to stay in my lane. She was angry? Well, so was I. She wanted me to speak up? I'd speak up, all right, and give her a piece of my mind.

I passed the exit for Kyle, fifty miles south of Austin, and pulled Mellow Yellow, my fifteen-year-old VW Beetle, off the highway. I drove a quarter-mile along a dirt road lined with prickly pear cactus and Burr oaks, stopped, and got out. I stared at the scaly bark of an oak that stood about thirty feet away. One of its lower branches was splintered and hung down, grazing the top of the surrounding brush.

I spied a pile of stones, picked up one, cocked my arm, lined up my aim with the oak.

"Okay, Roanne, if you were so angry, why didn't you let it out?" I yelled. "Go to counseling. Climb up on your roof and scream your fool head off. Sue the pants off the school district. Fight tooth and nail for your kids, no matter the fallout. Anything but—you killed two people!" I shouted at the oak. "Who the hell do you think you are, telling me to figure it out, leaving me to pick up the pieces! I hate you!"

I let the rock fly. It careened into the brush. I picked up another and chucked it at the tree, then another and another and another.

I threw the rocks until I had perfected my technique and they struck their target, pinging off the bark of the oak. My shoulder ached from the repetitive motion. Sweat dampened my forehead and made my underarms sticky. I didn't care. I was laser focused on those rocks hitting that tree.

Before I noticed, a Williamson County Sheriff's car had pulled up, and the deputy was beside me. "Ma'am? Is this your property?"

I jumped at the sound of his voice and whirled around.

The deputy towered over me, a muscular young man in a wide-brimmed, gray hat with his uniform shirtsleeves rolled above his biceps. He wore mirrored glasses that reflected the image of a woman with hair frizzed into a wild, silver cloud in the humid air. Her face was flushed, her brows pulled into a frown, a pink bra strap strayed down her upper arm from under the sleeve of her dress. A rock was clenched in her fist.

"You want to put the rock down, ma'am?" the deputy asked.

I dropped the stone. It bounced off the toe of my black pump. I shoved the bra strap up to my shoulder.

"Is this your property, ma'am?" he repeated, more forcefully but politely.

"No. I live in San Antonio."

"What are you doing out here, ma'am?"

"I was throwing rocks at a tree."

His eyebrows arched from behind the shades. "Have you been drinking, ma'am?"

"What? No. Why would you ask such a thing?"

"You're pulled off the road throwing rocks at a tree."

"I can explain that."

"Ma'am, you want to step over here and show me your license and registration?"

I nodded, complied, and tried to sound as reasonable as possible. "You see, I was upset because—"

"Ms. Canelli," he read my name off my documents, "I'll have to check your record. I'll be right back."

While he was in his vehicle confirming, I supposed, that I wasn't a fugitive from justice, I realized I needed to pee. I wondered if he would wait while I ducked behind a tree. My cell phone, on my front passenger seat, vibrated, and I reached into the open car door and snagged it.

"So sorry I didn't make it to the funeral." My sister Christine's easy cadence reached my ear. "I was elbow-deep in frosting at the shop. "

"I know, the day before Valentine's Day. Cupcake craziness, I imagine."

Twenty-one years ago, Christine and I had opened C is for Cupcakes in Austin in a strip mall between Patty's Liquor and Larry's Patio Oasis. She had stayed in the city of our childhood, married a pilot, and raised two daughters there. Our business took off like a rocket, a spectacular launch that slowed into a steady arc, and six years later we opened a second location in San Marcos in between Austin and San Antonio.

After Scott and I had moved to San Antonio, I drove up to Austin on weekends to give Christine those days off. Now, dependable seconds-in-command were in charge of day-to-day operations. I visited the shops sporadically, but Christine was still a hands-on owner three days a week and every day running up to a holiday. She had the energy. She was ten years younger than me.

Christine was stuffed full of common sense that made her seem like the older sister during my occasional emotional outbursts. She talked less than me but somehow said more. Side by side, we were celery and apple. She was long and lean with an angular face, her dark hair cropped close to her scalp. It was funny how Christine and Joey shared the same features, although he was my twin. I looked like our older brother Frank: short and round, red-haired, although now he was nearly bald and I had let my untamed, shoulder-length waves go to silver.

"Are you home already?" Christine asked.

"No, I'm pulled over near Kyle."

"Why?" Her pitch rose. "Are you okay?"

"I will be as soon as the cop lets me go on my way." I leaned my hip against the side of my car and craned my neck toward the deputy.

"Speeding?" Christine asked.

"Chucking rocks."

"What?"

The deputy exited his car and walked toward me.

"I'll fill you in later." I ended the call.

"You were upset, ma'am?" The deputy asked, his eyebrows raised again. He handed me my documents.

"Yes. I usually don't do this kind of thing. When I get upset, I scrub all the bathtubs." The deputy looked unimpressed. "With bleach. But, obviously, there was no bathtub available." I swallowed hard and blinked back the tears balancing on the edge of my lower eyelids. "My friend, my best friend, died. I'm coming from her funeral."

The deputy stood as impassive as a statue. "I'm sorry for

your loss, ma'am. I understand you may be a little emotional."

"Deputy, I—what's your name?"

"Deputy Trujillo, ma'am."

"Deputy Trujillo, I don't think you understand at all."

He held up his hand. "Ma'am, it's my job to protect your safety. You can't be out here throwing rocks on private property. I wouldn't want an armed property owner to take you for a trespasser."

I got it. It wasn't about me. Deputy Trujillo had a job to do, and I was the one who needed to be understanding. "Do you really think someone's going to shoot a gray-haired lady in her mid-sixties for throwing rocks at a tree?"

He tightened his lips, apparently miffed at my comment. "You never know these days, ma'am. I'll wait for you to get into your car, and I'll follow you out to the highway. Do you have yourself under control enough to safely operate your vehicle? Do you need a moment?"

"I'm not hysterical if that's what you mean," I said in an agitated tone.

"No, ma'am, just trying to be sensitive to your situation."

I felt a twinge in my bladder. For a half-second, I reconsidered asking if I could take a quick pee behind a tree, if he could be sensitive to that situation. The urge to get away, to be home was stronger.

"Yes, I'm fine, perfectly calm." I measured out each word in a flat, soft voice.

He tipped his hat. "You drive safe now."

I mustered my best in-spite-of-everything smile. "Thank you, Deputy Trujillo."

He followed my Bug for two miles before he peeled off to exit the highway. I drove three miles farther before my palms relaxed their grip on the wheel and stopped sweating.

I kept my eyes riveted on the traffic, back on autopilot, and talked to Roanne.

"Hey, girl, you know I didn't mean what I said, about

hating you and all. I get it. You were angry. You had a right to be, without every Tom, Dick, and Trujillo patronizing and scolding you your whole life. You needed to get their attention, grab them by the balls. You had the final say."

Tearful frustration welled up in me. I was not in understanding mode. I was in blessing-someone-out mode. "Well, bravo for you, Roanne Slater. So, you think you're one smart cookie. But, let me tell you something. You did not figure it out. Mr. Asher would not be happy with your answer. He would be so sorry to hear that you—"

"So sorry." That's what he had said to me. The white-haired man in the back of the church. Mr. Asher.

- 1972 -

"Welcome to Bonham High School Career Day, ladies and gentlemen," Mr. Simpson announced from the auditorium stage.

The rumble of talk and the fidgeting of my fellow senior classmates in our thinly upholstered theater seats faded. Our science teacher wore his trademark tweed suit and bowtie. The stage lights bounced off the bald portion of his head above the white tufts of hair that stuck out over his ears, a la Einstein.

We seniors had looked forward to this seventy-five-minute assembly all week. Last period had been canceled, replaced by guest parents who would give presentations on their careers. In Roanne's and my case, we would avoid the sixty minutes of Mr. Simpson's nasal, droning lecture that was a minefield of information guaranteed to show up at random on the next physics test.

The five speakers, four dads and one mom, would each have ten minutes to speak and three minutes to take questions. Dr. McKenzie, an orthopedic surgeon, kicked things off, followed by Judge Martin and Mr. Peterson, an oil company executive. Roanne and I had positioned ourselves in the second row for a good view in the two end seats closest to the exit. Francis Canelli, my dad, the aeronautical engineer, was up next.

"You've all heard about NASA and the astronaut program," Dad began.

He stood tall and trim in his dark suit, trousers perfectly creased. His Roman nose, which I was glad I hadn't inherited, looked manly on him. His hair was full and wavy like Ted Kennedy's and was just starting to show gray at the temples.

Roanne elbowed me, and I beamed with pride. I had

watched Dad rehearse at home, talking about how aeronautical engineers helped support the space missions. His work was much more mundane and in the background, but focusing on the astronauts, who were national heroes, was a good attention-getter for a roomful of teenagers. He projected on a screen mug shots of all the men who had gone into space since the 1950s and told funny stories about John Glenn and Gus Grissom. The talk didn't have much to do with his daily work, but it got the loudest applause.

"Any questions?" he asked as the clapping died down.

Roanne popped up from her seat and waved her hand.

"Yes, young lady," Dad said, like she was any interested student rather than a frequent visitor at our house.

"Thank you, Mr. Canelli," she said with formal politeness. "My question is: Are there any women astronauts?"

Dad chuckled, although I didn't think Roanne was making a joke. The representation of moms with careers did seem lacking. Last year, after Frank's career day, he had said no moms were on stage, just one of the math teachers, Miss Adolphus, who had talked about her job. I remembered because Frank and the other boys in his class called her "Adolf," due to the unfortunate combination of her last name and her hairy upper lip. My school counselor had recently mentioned that an early childhood development degree was becoming a popular choice for college girls who imagined themselves in the fast-growing field of childcare workers.

"Well, no women yet," Dad answered Roanne, "but if you study math and science diligently, you might be our first one."

Applause broke out again, and Mr. Simpson made his way back to the mike to introduce the last speaker, Mrs. Carrington, a nurse.

Behind us, a male voice said, "She fills out that white uniform real good. Ooo-wee."

Jimmy Hollister sat directly in front of Roanne in the first row, flanked by a couple of his buddies. They jabbed each other and, judging by their snickers, shared something funny in each other's ears.

Then Jimmy turned around and leaned toward Roanne. "That was a stupid question. Everyone knows girls can't be astronauts."

"Why not?" Roanne snapped.

"Because if they got on the rag in space, they might go loony and push the wrong button and never get back to Earth."

The three boys broke out in stifled giggles. Roanne's face turned red as a beet.

"You're a retard, Jimmy Hollister," I whispered through gritted teeth. "The Russians have already sent a woman into space."

From the other end of our row, Mrs. Griffin, the biology teacher, leaned forward, turned our way, and frowned with a finger to her lips.

As soon as Mrs. Griffin leaned back, one of Jimmy's buddies turned to Roanne. "Hey, Roanne, when you get on the spacecraft, don't forget to bring your Kotex."

Roanne was wearing a skirt, but she hiked her knees up to her chest and slammed the bottoms of her shoes hard into the back of Jimmy's seat. Jimmy went flying forward, the cushion banged against the seat back, and Jimmy hit the floor and came up on all fours with blood gushing from his nose.

It happened so quickly, for a split second I didn't believe what I had seen. It wasn't like Roanne at all. Jimmy's buddies ushered him out the exit, and three minutes later, Miss Perkins, the assistant principal, motioned for Roanne and me to join her in the hall. Silently, we shuffled to her office.

We sat in stiff chairs for ten agonizing minutes waiting for what would happen next, like prisoners at the foot of the gallows, while Miss Perkins talked on the phone in a serious tone and then went out to bring in two more people. One was Jimmy who had white spongy things shoved up his nostrils.

His eyes were puffy, like he'd been crying, and blackened underneath. His face was as red as a boiled lobster. He looked like he might have a cow when he saw me and Roanne. The second person was my dad, who had not left the school quickly enough, complicating things for both him and me.

"She did it!" Jimmy yelled and pointed his finger at Roanne. "She kicked the back of my seat."

"No!" I yelled back. It was a gut reaction, but I knew what I was doing. Sometimes Mr. Slater would give Roanne and Darla licks with a belt. I had seen the welts on the backs of her legs. If she got suspended from school, no telling what her dad would do. My dad, on the other hand, would wag his finger and get all blustery, but that would be the extent of his outrage.

"Now, Connie," Miss Perkins said, drumming her fingers furiously on her desk. "Jimmy didn't just spontaneously fall out of his seat with enough force to cause that horrific damage to his face."

"It wasn't Roanne," I explained. "It was me. Jimmy's back was turned. He couldn't see who kicked his seat."

"Is that what happened, Roanne?" Miss Perkins asked, an eyebrow raised in suspicion.

Roanne looked at me, confused. I cut my eyes hard at her to let her know I had a plan.

"Exactly, ma'am," Roanne said.

Dad leaned forward, his jaw hanging. "Connie, what do you have to say for yourself?"

"I didn't do it on purpose, honest."

Miss Perkins's suspicious cocked eyebrow was back.

"I had a muscle spasm in my leg, and my foot jerked out and hit the back of Jimmy's seat. I had no control over it. I swear to God." I turned a pained look to Jimmy. "I'm sorry, Jimmy. It was an accident."

Jimmy gritted his teeth like he was about to blow again and narrowed his eyes.

"Connie, I don't have time for any nonsense. Are you telling the truth?" Dad asked with as stern a look as he could muster while he checked his watch.

I sat back wide-eyed and shrugged like I hadn't a clue. "Dad, why would I want to kick the back of Jimmy's seat on purpose? That makes no sense."

Dad nodded reluctantly, Miss Perkins's eyebrow relaxed, Jimmy fumed, Roanne shrank into her seat, trying to disappear. Miss Perkins lectured us kids about safety and respecting others while Dad looked at his watch some more and muttered about getting back to work. No one was suspended.

Roanne and I rushed to our lockers to retrieve our social studies books and binders. Finals started the next day.

Peeking at Roanne around the metal doors, I whispered, just in case anyone else was looking to get us in trouble. "Jimmy Hollister got beat up by a girl." I waited for her to return my coy smile of victory.

Instead, she pinched her brows together, gnawed her lip, and whispered back, "Do you think his nose will be all right?"

– 2019 –

My phone's ringtone pulled me out of unconsciousness. The cell time display told me I had fallen back asleep for two hours after I had been jolted awake, my arms shaking atop the bed covers, by dreams I couldn't remember. Those unawake travels had left me disturbed and thinking about Roanne's final phone call. I peeled my face from where it was smooshed into a pillow.

"Hi, Claire," I said to my stalwart agent-editor of twenty years. The latest chapters I had sent for Claire's review three days ago had come to me in a burst of inspiration, and I could hardly wait for her feedback.

If it hadn't been for Claire beating the publishing bushes, my Maxie Dallas mystery series would have died in obscurity long ago instead of finding its way to bookstore shelves and the top bookseller websites. The series was a modest success, and I was in the midst of writing the fourteenth installment.

I had created my traveling cake decorator-lady sleuth while following Scott around the world as an army wife. The writing gave me a productive purpose in places like Panama and Delta Junction, Alaska, where it was hard to make friends or find a job. In those days I had also freelanced for travel magazines, putting my journalism degree to use, but the work and money were few and far between.

Maxie Dallas had starred in unpublished short stories or stand-alone scenes until I seriously began work on my first book, *Death by Devil's Food Cake*, many years later after Scott had retired from the army and we had settled back in Texas.

When I hooked up with Claire, she had landed me a contract with Diamondback Press, a Texas publisher, for the first three books, one every eighteen months; which grew to ten books; which grew to thirteen.

"Hey, girlfriend," Claire said with an unusual trace of concern in her casual lilt. "Just a question for ya. Are you absolutely positive you don't want to take some time off after the loss of your friend? I'm sure Diamondback would push back the deadline a bit."

"No. I need to write, it's the only thing that keeps me from thinking about how much I miss her." Claire was going somewhere with this, but I couldn't figure where.

"Hmm. Seriously, precious, you need some take-care-of-Connie healing time. You shouldn't be staying in the house and wallowing. You need to get back in the swim."

"How did we go from writing to wallowing?"

"Bad choice of word. I mean pump up the activity, girlfriend, step away from the keyboard, get out there and move, do something to get the endorphins going."

"I do get out. I do move. I take a walk every day, almost every day, at least once a week."

"You also need to talk to someone. After a person suffers a loss—"

"I do talk. I talk to my sister. I talk to you. Are you my editor or my shrink?" I took a breath. I couldn't help sounding annoyed. "I'm getting you the chapters on time. What's the problem?"

"That's the problem. The chapters you sent me. It's like I don't even recognize Maxie. I understand you're trying to be contemporary. You've brought in this take-no-shit attitude about women's rights. But Maxie, she's an established cozy mystery character. She slays with her genteel ways."

"And?" The annoyance crept back into my voice.

"The pineapple scene. Our Maxie, whom we've known and loved through thirteen books, picks up a pineapple and hurls it at Clint, the big-city detective, narrowly missing taking off his head. What has gotten into our heroine?"

"That asshole Clint has been undermining her investigative process and taking the credit for every lead she gets. She's pissed, and she's not going to take it anymore."

Claire breathed out a long, heavy sigh. "Yeah, not going to happen, girlfriend. Maxie is not going to throw a pineapple at somebody's head, no matter how obnoxious he is. She would more likely kill him with kindness, make him a pineapple upside-down cake."

It was my turn to sigh. "Look, Claire. Maxie has already smiled through thirteen books. Her facial muscles are seriously fatigued. She's been fighting injustice, not least of all the injustice of not being treated with respect by her male colleagues. I think, in number fourteen, it's time for an update of the nice Maxie."

Claire smacked her lips. "See, that's the tricky thing. Nice Maxie is our bread and butter, so we're stuck with her. We don't want to risk losing our core audience. Those nice ladies just below the country club set who meet at the coffee shop next to the bookstore once a week. We've never established this feminist activist background in Maxie. You can't spring it on them now. The readers are going to scream, 'Where did this come from?'"

"Any of them over thirty will know where this came from." My voice rose. "They've been stockpiling rage since the first time they were told 'nice girls don't act like that' or 'you're prettier when you smile, honey.'"

"Yeah, but the thing is—"

"They've, we've, all been victims of the constant favoring of the brothers, the deferring to the husband, the praise of the male coworker for your great idea." My voice picked up speed and volume. "The endlessly hearing you can't do this, you can't be that because you have a vagina." I breathed hard. My speech had tired me out.

"Okay, pull it in, sugar buns. We can't go off on that man-bashing tangent. Your male audience is small, but mostly older white males who are going to run, not walk, away from that kind of stuff. And those nice, suburban ladies who make up the majority of your readers? They have older, conservative husbands whom they depend on, in many cases, for financial security and social status. They will not take kindly to an attack with a pineapple or otherwise on their knights in somewhat tarnished armor. Bottom line, I can't sell this to Diamondback, and they have the rights to the series."

Her slightly lecturing tone softened. "So, please, sweetums, take a month or so off—I'll clear it with Diamondback—say you'll kick it into double time by April 1. Recharge, unload on a grief counselor, work out, whatever it takes, and get back into that Maxie groove. Okay?"

"Whatever it takes as long as I don't come back with any hurling pineapples, I suppose?"

"I love it when we're on the same page."

"I'll work on that."

I took some of what Claire had said to heart and left my house for the pool at the St. Mary's Y to hang out with a half dozen active sixty- and seventy-year-olds in unstylish tank suits. The brave souls, some in cue ball swim caps, exposed various stages of crepey skin, bat wings, and saggy chests and buns.

I breathed in the muggy, chlorine-scented air and the lemongrass aftershave that made my nose itch and that telegraphed the proximity of the only man in my senior water aerobics class. Two women at poolside called out "Hey, Connie!" and "Good to see you back!" My next-door neighbor Lillian and Janet...Janice...no, Jeanette. Three others splashed in the shallow end, Concepcion and the two Marians.

I fidgeted along the pool edge. Tiffany, our cheery, young instructor, was uncharacteristically late. While I pondered whether to lower myself into the water, the lemongrass smell wafted stronger.

"Hi, Cupcake!" Howie called out as he ambled toward me, his flip-flops slapping and squishing across little puddles. He was a retired dentist, tall, thin, shirtless, with heavily freckled skin, and barely enough ass to hold up his baggy blue trunks. A yellowish dye made his thinning hair less attractive. He had often reminded me he was sixty-nine with a creepy chuckle like he was hinting at something sexual.

"Howie," I said without enthusiasm. "I've told you not to call me that." Howie had a habit of giving people creative nicknames. The other ladies thought that was cute, but I regretted telling him about Christine's and my cupcake shops.

"Is that a new suit?" he said with a wink. "Marilyn Monroe pink?" He stared; I supposed he was giving me time to get the reference. It didn't click. *Gentlemen Prefer Blondes?*"

I stared down at my bright pink one-piece stretched over my extra-round hips. "Pepto Bismol pink. Stomach distress commercial."

Howie gave me a thumbs up. "Ha! That's a good one." I peered over his shoulder, trying to look like something else had gotten my attention. "I haven't seen you in a while," he said, adjusting his waistband which had slipped a couple of inches below his navel. "Where've you been?" He moved closer, almost bumping my shoulder. His aftershave made my nose run.

Howie's other annoying habit was prying into other people's business. I took a step back and avoided eye contact. "I had some family issues to take care of."

He grinned, displaying his perfect set of dental implants. "Whew! I was afraid you'd run off with some handsome, young man."

"Like there's a chance that you and I..." I rolled my eyes.

My little insult went right over his head. His eyes were flitting around. Howie also had a habit of listening mostly to himself. He tapped my arm. "Are you out there?"

"Out where?"

"You know, dating."

"No. I've found dating to be a huge investment with very little return. All that figuring out who is supposed to say what or do what when."

"Me? I don't worry about what's 'appropriate.' " He made air quotes around his last word. "I just jump in, and the water's fine." He winked. "Hey, how's that long-legged, blonde friend you brought with you a few months back? Ruthanne?"

My brain collided with an image from last fall of Roanne sitting on the pool edge in her shorts and tank top, playfully kicking her feet in the water. She had come into town unexpectedly, I had invited her to the aerobics class, and she had played the good sport although she hadn't brought a swimsuit.

"I thought she and I really hit it off," Howie rambled on. "Sure would like to see her again. Where is she these days?"

I gritted my teeth and glared at him. "She's dead."

Howie stepped back like I had pinched his too-close arm. With seeming effort he squeezed his face into a look of concern. "Cancer?"

I glared again. "No, men."

Howie froze, then busted out laughing. "Ha! Dead. Ha! Men. You're pulling my leg, aren't you? You're one funny lady, Cupcake!" He leaned over and slapped his knees.

I grabbed his shoulder and hip. "Jump in! The water's fine!" I shoved him into the pool.

He landed, arms and legs flailing, his mouth and eyes like big "O's" before his head went under and he came up choking and spluttering. I suddenly remembered that Howie was a non-swimmer and was always careful to keep his head and shoulders above water. He yelled at me, red-faced, his lips pulled back in a snarl. "What the hell?! You're nuts!"

I stabbed my finger at him while my female classmates stared. "Well, you're...you're not appropriate!" I yelled back.

"Good morning, everyone!" Tiffany's voice burst like sunshine from the poolside entry. I stomped off toward the exit. This was not the day for me to get back in the swim, but Claire had given me some good advice.

When I got home, I found Megan Greenleaf, specialist in grief counseling, on the Internet. Her credentials were impressive: forty-nine years old, master's degree but no fresh-out-of-college youngster, twenty-two years' experience. In her photo, she appeared pleasant enough. Her smile was soft, not toothy, her lipstick and blush a tasteful rosy pink, her ash-blonde hair swept gently atop her head. I made an appointment, 10:30 a.m. the next day, not a lot of time to chicken out.

In the meantime, I'd take another look at that pineapple chapter. While I waited for my manuscript folder to open, Megan Greenleaf stared back at me from my computer screen.

The counselor looked different on second glance. Antiseptic. She would have cookie-cutter answers. She would suggest antidepressants or antianxiety drugs or both. The longer I looked, the more her smile seemed a know-it-all smirk. I didn't want to talk to that woman, bare the depths of my soul about the loss of Roanne.

But, yes, I would talk to someone, someone who cared and who had known me and Roanne and had known we had been best friends since we were kids. I hadn't had any contact with him since high school graduation, but I figured he had stayed close by if he had heard about the funeral. I started my search on Google, phone directories in Travis County, Facebook. How many Judd Ashers could there possibly be?

– 1971 –

"You don't really believe all that stuff Mr. Asher says, do you?" Roanne hugged her history text and notepad against her chest.

I gathered up my book and binder and slung my purse over my shoulder. We left homeroom for our next class to part ways until last period in geometry. "That we have the power to change history?"

"Exactly. Okay, so he has this simple little process, the what, the why, the what if." She stuck out her forefinger. "What? Six million Jews killed." Her middle finger joined the first one. "Why? Hitler was greedy for power, and the Jews were an easy scapegoat he could use to whip up a following." Her ring finger went up. "What if? The Germans had refused to buy into his crap."

We navigated the crowded hallway; the chatter of students echoed off the walls; tennis shoe soles squeaked against the gray tile floor.

"Yeah, what if they stood by the Jews instead?" I said. "And Britain and France and the US had stepped in instead of ignoring what was happening?"

"But they didn't, so it's too late. The Jews got gassed. We can't change that. We don't have any power, see?"

"What he's saying is that it could have turned out differently, and if the situation arises again, like in our lifetime, we could handle it differently."

We reached her locker, and Roanne turned the combination dial. "That's not going to happen. Another Holocaust is not going to arise."

"Why not?"

"Because the world is different now. People wouldn't let it."

"They would handle it differently. Which proves Mr.

35

Asher's point," I said.

"You know, that's very astute." She jerked her locker open. "Judd, I mean Mr. Asher, would be very proud of you."

We busted out in giggles. We referred to Mr. Asher by his first name whenever no one else was listening. Judd Asher. It was a name straight out of a soap opera. Roanne and I had a massive crush on our social studies teacher.

"Do you suppose he has a girlfriend?" I asked. I went to my locker, which was three down from Roanne's. The bell for the next class would ring in two minutes. "I mean, a serious girlfriend."

"I've never seen him with anyone." Roanne took a handful of M&Ms from a bag she kept in her locker, tilted her head back, and let the candies trickle from her fingers into her mouth.

"We don't ever see him except in class and in the parking lot when he leaves."

"True," she said through a mouthful of chocolate, the molten brown obliterating one of her front teeth. "But, what if he's still available in a few years, and I have my teaching degree, and we work at the same school? We would be on the same level, a woman and a man, professionals, then, who knows?" She cast a dreamy, faraway look over my head and pulled a strand of blonde hair from where it had stuck to her peach-colored lip gloss.

"Do you think he's going to wait for you for five more years?" I asked.

A girl on the other side of the hall cackled in response to some crack made by a passing boy. Roanne tossed her book into her locker while I fidgeted with the combination on mine.

"I guess he would be kind of old by then, in his thirties," she said.

"The age difference would be the same, silly." The door of my locker rattled as I yanked it open and set my book inside.

"What if I could freeze him until I caught up?" she said.

"Like on *Star Trek*."

I pointed to the corner of my mouth to let Roanne know she had a smear of chocolate there on hers. "Well, Lieutenant Uhura, maybe in the future freezing our heartthrobs will be one of the powers women will have."

She poked the tip of her tongue into the corner of her mouth, and I nodded to indicate she had cleaned off the chocolate. "Let's get to class before Mr. Day starts harassing us," I said.

"Wanna come over after school?" She closed her locker and spun the dial on the lock. "My dad has to check on a job site in Bastrop, and my mom is having a bad week, so I have to stay home with pain-in-the-butt Darla."

"Can't." I shut my locker. "Rehearsal for *A Midsummer Night's Dream*. I— Helena—will be chasing her true love through the woods."

"Oh, yeah. Way better than babysitting." She glanced over my shoulder and pointed her chin in that direction. I turned my head and spied Mr. Day's squatty shape at the end of the hall. "He's so ugly," Roanne said. She pulled her hair back off her forehead and screwed up her face to imitate the scowl of our least favorite hall monitor. "He looks like—"

"A Klingon."

"Exactly."

– 2019 –

Blue and red lights flashed against my living room window. The squawk of a radio was followed by the whine of a siren that was abruptly aborted. I had fallen asleep on the couch the night before, and, on a day when I had meant to get up early, I had overslept. Maybe my new messed-up sleep pattern was moving into another phase.

I peeked through the blinds. Four police cars and an ambulance were stationed directly across the street. I spotted half a dozen officers on the lawn of the pink-brick house that faced mine. A couple of the cops were taking photos at the side of the house. Paramedics rolled a stretcher toward the front door.

I ran a hand through my tangled hair, slipped on a pair of walking shoes, grabbed my phone, and went outside. It was almost eight. I had intended to be on the road to Pflugerville no later than seven, to arrive by nine. When you showed up unannounced, you were more likely to catch the person you were visiting at home earlier in the day before their errands and appointments.

My neighbor, Lillian, stood on the sidewalk at the bottom of her yard, holding a steaming coffee mug.

"Hey, Lillian, what's going on?"

Up the street a dog barked. A few other neighbors watched the police activity from the tops of their driveways. The stretcher reappeared at the front door. A paramedic held an IV aloft as he rolled the gurney out onto the sidewalk.

A woman in her thirties stood on the opposite sidewalk and gesticulated while she talked to a police officer taking notes. Her excited tone, but not her words, traveled from across the street.

"Home invasion last night," Lillian said. She pointed to the woman talking to the officer. "The Goldbergs' daughter came by this morning and called the police."

"Oh, no. Are Jacob and Rachel all right?" An exclamation more than a question. I could make out a head in a cervical collar on the stretcher as it was slipped into the ambulance. I couldn't tell if it was Mr. or Mrs. Goldberg. At least it was a live body.

Lillian shrugged. "We can only hope."

"This is crazy," I said, shaking my head. A car approached from the corner, then slowed to a creep as it passed the clutch of police vehicles. The ambulance pulled away from the curb with its light strobing and siren squealing. "Nothing like this has ever happened around here before."

"You didn't hear about Mrs. Bushnell two blocks over?"

"That sweet little lady who always wears a big red hat when she walks?"

Lillian nodded and slurped her coffee. "She found a homeless man asleep in her kitchen last week. He'd walked in through her garage. She screamed and he ran out, but still, right there in her kitchen."

"We have homeless people in our neighborhood?"

"They're everywhere, don't you know."

Some of my neighbors had bought their homes with burglar bars attached and many had security systems installed, the Goldbergs included, after a rash of burglaries a decade earlier. I had neither, in spite of the running lectures from my son, Daniel, who lived with his family forty-five minutes away in Converse.

My neighborhood was an older suburb on what used to be the far north side of San Antonio until the city expanded even farther north, and the 1604 loop was constructed. Property values had dropped since Scott and I had bought the house nineteen years ago, and the once neat ranch-styles were showing their age. Beyond the 1604, "big hair" houses with multiple roof gables, soaring arched windows, and two-story entryways sprung up. I stayed put after the divorce, resisting Christine's lobbying to move back to Austin. The mortgage was paid off, and an annuity from Scott's military years, the cupcake shop profits, and my book sales put me on the low side of comfortable financially.

This area had always been a safe place to walk until well after twilight, even for an older woman alone, and a place to sleep without worry, provided your deceased best friend wasn't haunting you in nightmares.

"I'll tell you what," Lillian said, "I'm sleeping with a loaded gun on my nightstand from now on. You're a woman living alone, too. I suggest you do the same."

"Do you really think that's the wise thing to do?"

"That could be you or me carried out of that house. Shoot somebody, save somebody, that's what I say."

"I've never owned a gun."

"Time you got on board, honey."

———

Behind the wheel of Mellow Yellow, I spied the sign for Pflugerville that I had passed dozens of times between Austin and Round Rock. The road there was a diversion to the east off I-35. I had never visited the funniest-named place in Texas.

My GPS led me easily to Mr. Asher's address near the town's historic district. His house was a well-kept, white one-story with a gray roof that stood well away from the street, half-hidden by a huge live oak. A slate walkway curved up to a pillared porch. I rang the bell, the door swung open, and I faced the man I had spoken to in the church after Roanne's funeral.

He stood tall and square-shouldered, his longish silver hair swept back off his high forehead. His brown eyes sparkled. He wore a green cardigan over a checked shirt buttoned at the throat, khakis, and gray Nikes. I imagined that was how David

Cassidy would look if he had lived to seventy-five and morphed slightly into Mr. Rogers. I stood there dumbstruck like he had called on me in class after I had failed to read the history chapter assigned the day before.

"Connie? Well, this is a surprise. What are you doing here?"

"Mr. Asher, I'm sorry. I should have tried to call first."

"No, no. I'm being rude. Come in, come in."

The house smelled like day lilies. A vase of them stood on a credenza under a wedding photo of a younger Mr. Asher and a petite brunette with a dimpled smile and a bouquet of the same type of flowers. Sunshine streamed through the multi-paned, wavy-glass windows. The living room was small and furnished simply with wing-backed chairs and a curved couch offset with lamps with beaded shades. A thick Persian rug lay over the hardwood floor. A large, amber-colored dog bounded toward me from another room.

"Whoa, fella," Mr. Asher said. The retriever skidded to a stop inches from my feet and looked up at me, panting expectantly.

I patted the dog's head while I apologized again. "I shouldn't have barged in like this. I was hoping I could talk with you. I'll only take a few minutes. I don't want to interrupt your family time."

"It's fine. It's just me and Crockett here." The retriever trotted to Mr. Asher and bumped his head against his leg. Mr. Asher vigorously rubbed the dog's head and throat. "My wife died eight years ago. Breast cancer."

"I'm so sorry. I promise I won't take up much of your time."

"Take as long as you need, if you don't mind talking and walking. Crockett and I were about to go for our morning jaunt."

He grabbed a leash off a hook behind the door, and the tethered Crockett leapt in little circles until we were out on the sidewalk.

"You have a nice home," I said, unsure as to how you begin a personal conversation with a former teacher you haven't seen since high school graduation.

"Well, a bit big for me, as my three sons keep reminding me every time they visit, but all my memories of Jeanine live with me, and I have an excellent housekeeper."

The early spring air had already warmed to non-outerwear level for me although we walked at a slow pace. I tied my hoodie around my waist while Mr. Asher stayed covered up in his cardigan. Mexican plum trees had started to burst forth with their fragrant white flowers. I breathed in the perfume and prepared to get to the point of my visit.

Mr. Asher jumped in first. "What have you done with your life, Connie?"

I was off the spot, much like being second to give your speech in front of the class, a reprieve for only the moment while anxiety built as you waited for your turn.

"My life. Well, I graduated from UT, BA in journalism, married an army guy, divorced said guy. I have a wonderful son, lovely daughter-in-law, two cute-as-bugs grandchildren."

"Excellent."

"And I'm a published mystery writer. Thirteen books so far."

"Awesome. I'll have to look you up on Amazon. I've dabbled in a bit of writing myself since I retired from teaching, not quite as prolific as you though. For the past seven years, I've been working on a history of the German immigrants who settled in Texas in the 1800s. I suppose it'll be finished one of these days."

We turned a corner. Crockett tugged at the leash. "There's a little lake up here we stroll around," Mr. Asher said. "It's Crockett's favorite part of the walk."

"Sounds nice."

Mr. Asher slowed a step, and Crockett let out a little whine.

"You and Roanne stayed friends all these years?"

"Yes, through thick and thin and everything in between."

"I'm guessing she is what you want to talk about."

He was giving me the perfect starting point, but the words I had come to say about Roanne were piling up in my throat and wouldn't easily come out. "Mr. Asher, thank you for coming to the funeral."

"Please, call me Judd."

I giggled. If he only knew the occasions when Roanne and I did just that.

"It is kind of a funny name, I guess."

"Sorry. I wasn't laughing at—about Roanne, I'm assuming you know how she died."

"Yes, it was on the news. So very tragic."

"I talked to her on the phone just a few minutes before. She mentioned you."

Mr. Asher stopped in his tracks, and Crockett whined again. "Me?"

"She said when you were our teacher, you had the answers, but you wanted us to figure them out for ourselves. Then she said some things... It was all very cryptic. You used to push us to figure things out, and I'm hoping you can help me make sense of it. She said she was angry and that it was too late for her. But she told me to speak up, and don't let them have the final say."

We had reached the edge of the lake, and Crockett tugged forward, making Mr. Asher dig in his heels to keep control. "Hmm. Who did she mean by 'them?'"

"I'm not sure, but she was talking about men in her life who had wronged her, like Johnny, her ex. He really did her dirty."

"And she wants those people not to have the final say?"

"Yeah. I keep thinking of the scenarios you would give us from history. What happened, why did it happen, and what if something could have changed that?"

"Roanne killed herself and her ex-husband. Why?"

"Because, she said, she was trapped in anger, and that was her only way out."

"Are you wondering what if, what if you could have done something to change that horrible event? Blame is a useless exercise, Connie. I did it with my wife. Blaming yourself won't bring Roanne back."

"Nothing will."

"But what if the situation came up again? That's what I tried to teach you kids. What if you could do something different the next time?"

"There isn't a next time. Roanne is dead."

"Yes, it's too late for Roanne. So, maybe the 'what if' in the same situation applies to someone else. Like you."

"Me? I might reach a point where I'm trapped in anger, where I could do what she did? But I couldn't. Kill myself? Kill another human being? I couldn't."

"Did you think Roanne could?"

I was silent. Roanne had bought a gun fifteen years ago and never used it until the day she died.

"What should I do?"

"What did Roanne say?"

"Speak up. Don't let them have the final say."

"Do you know who 'them' is for you?"

I froze. "The paper targets."

Mr. Asher turned around from where he had gone two steps ahead with Crockett tugging away at the leash. "Targets?"

"It was years ago when Roanne and I talked about that, and I'd have to add a couple, but, yes, that's them.' "

We rounded the far end of the lake and passed a group of floating ducks. They erupted in loud, nervous quacks as Crockett sniffed the air, then barked, sending the waterfowl exploding into the air to a safer landing spot in the middle of the lake.

"Have I helped any?" Mr. Asher asked.

"More than you can ever know. Thank you so much, Ju—sorry, you're Mr. Asher to me. I hope I didn't take up too much of your morning."

"Not at all. I wouldn't mind a visit now and then. Do you still live in Austin?"

"No. I've been in San Antonio for almost twenty years."

"Oh, not so convenient then." His face sagged with apparent disappointment.

"I still come up this way sometimes to visit my sister in Austin or Roanne's sister in Round Rock."

"It would be lovely to see you again."

———

When I returned home, I learned from the TV news that two suspects had been arrested in the invasion of the Goldbergs' home, but Rachel Goldberg had died from injuries suffered in the attack.

I woke up multiple times during the night to scratching noises at the bedroom window and the creak of a door opening. When I got up to check, wielding a discarded, bent curtain rod, I found only phantom invaders, but those somehow seemed scarier than the real thing. In the blink of an eye, death by violence had come to the Goldbergs and to Roanne. A cold sweat drenched my skin and soaked through my pajamas.

In the morning, I drove to the nearest Academy Sports and Outdoors and bought a Glock 19. I said its name over and over, trying to get used to being a gun owner.

– 1989 –

"He is so-o-o adorable," Roanne cooed.

She took Daniel out of my arms with a bit of resistance from me. At one week old and four days after being placed with Scott and me by the adoption agency, I was still unsure the whole event wasn't a dream. Roanne snuggled my baby boy to her breast and bent close to his face.

Daniel's dark blue eyes fluttered open, and his rosebud mouth twitched in a sucking motion. Silky wisps of dark hair peeked out from under his white knit cap. The blotchy redness of his newborn skin had begun to fade to a creamy, light tan.

"I'm your Auntie Roanne," she said in a high-pitched prattle. "Yes, I am, precious."

Scott's and my one-bedroom apartment in San Antonio near Scott's job at Fort Sam Houston was barely big enough for three, let alone ten women at a baby shower, but Roanne had organized the event to a T. She and Darla had come from Round Rock earlier in the day and decorated the compact living room with blue streamers and cutouts of strollers and rattles and booties. Christine had brought two-dozen blueberry-lemon-cheesecake cupcakes, and Roanne had made a list of silly games to play.

"One of these days," Scott had said that morning, before making himself scarce, "when I retire from the army, I'd like to buy a house here." I liked the city, too, and Scott was only a year away from twenty years of military service. He was still on the fence about retiring at the twenty-year mark or staying in the army a few extra years, chasing the possibility of achieving one more rank.

Daniel squirmed in Roanne's arms, screwed up his tiny mouth, puffed out a little gas, and yawned, shaking off a short nap. The guests oohed and aahed over every sound and movement.

"Do you want to hold him, Darla?" Roanne asked. She handed off the baby, not giving her sister a chance to answer, because who doesn't want to hold a newborn?

Darla awkwardly cuddled Daniel for a second, shoved him back into Roanne's arms, and ran to the kitchen.

The female chattering that had filled the room went silent like the sudden shutoff of a dripping faucet. Roanne and I looked at each other. She bit her lip. Her eyes teared.

"How stupid of me," she said. "It's been two years since Andy died, but that baby smell must have triggered it. I'm such an idiot."

"Anyone for more champagne?" Christine offered the quieted guests. She raised a heavy green bottle, and several of the ladies held out their flutes.

I stroked Roanne's upper arm. "You didn't mean it, sweetie. Give her a minute, then check on her."

I took Daniel, nestled him to my shoulder, and gently patted his back. He mewed into my ear. One of the guests reached for him, and I passed him into her waiting arms.

Darla and Phil's second son had died at two and a half of pneumonia. They had had a hard time conceiving Matt, and when they lost Andy, Darla was convinced that God had taken him because she wasn't grateful enough for her first child. Guilt and grief tangled up in religious fervor was a powerful one-two punch. Periodically, Darla would have a meltdown.

Daniel, tired of being passed around and gushed over, started to fuss, wrinkling up his face like Mr. Magoo, signaling a round of squalling. I took him back to his crib and placed him atop the sailboat-print sheet. A mobile with yellow and blue stars and moons dangled above him. I patted and rubbed his back. As he breathed, his ribs moved against my hand like butterfly wings, and he fell asleep, his fist curled into his cheek.

A half hour later, I found Roanne and Darla seated on the

floor inside my pantry, their arms wrapped around each other. A half-empty tray of cupcakes lay near Darla. Apparently she had gobbled up six of them. Her mouth was smeared with blue frosting and pressed against Roanne's shoulder. Some of the cupcakes hadn't stayed down. A swatch of dried, blue-tinged vomit stained the sleeve of Roanne's new cashmere sweater. Another patch of puke, like a crusty amoeba, stuck to Roanne's neck just below her ear lobe. Darla sobbed softly. Roanne stroked her hair.

As long as I had known them, Roanne and Darla had rubbed each other the wrong way like a big toe inside a too-small sneaker. They couldn't avoid bumping against each other, and the friction often caused a painful blister that took time to heal.

According to Darla, any problems Roanne had were caused by her lack of faith, and she never tired of letting her big sister know. Roanne attended church on Easter and Christmas and didn't want to be preached to in between. This battle over Roanne's soul made for many an uncomfortable social gathering.

I suspected Darla blamed me as a bad influence when it came to Roanne's lack of religion, but the fundamental thing between those two was more primitive. Jealousy. Darla, the younger, chubby sister, had grown up in the shadow of her prettier sibling. Darla had a way of making Roanne feel guilty for being tall and thin, as if she had chosen her body type to purposely hurt her sister.

"Oh, go ahead and have that second dish of ice cream," Darla had told Roanne earlier at the party. "It won't make a flip of difference on you. Unfortunately, the good Lord didn't see fit to bless me with physical perfection."

No one could say mean words in the sweetest of tones quite like Darla. Roanne's response was to smile while seething and to make sure Darla saw her put an extra scoop in her ice cream dish.

But now, Roanne was down on the floor with Darla, soiled with her barf, holding her, until her little sister was ready to let go.

My foot scraped the floor and Darla looked up, tears standing in her eyes. "Oh, Connie, I'm so sorry for ruining your baby shower."

"No, Darla," I said. "You didn't ruin anything. Daniel is asleep. I told the ladies that you aren't feeling well. A couple of them had to leave early, and the rest won't care two shakes about it. Take as long as you need."

I shut the door of the pantry so that they could have their privacy and walked back into the living room. Christine knelt at the coffee table, setting up a game that involved stacking wooden baby blocks. I grabbed her arm, pulled her to her feet, and the blocks went skittering. Her eyes widened in surprise. The remaining guests glanced our way, then went back to their chatting.

Thrown off balance, Christine listed to the side. I put my arms around her shoulders and rocked her.

"We'll never let anything come between us, will we?" I said. "We're sisters, stuck with each other forever."

She pressed her cheek against mine. "Forever and a day."

– 2019 –

Daniel was at my door before I had a chance to finish my first cup of coffee. A six-foot, toned marathon runner, he was dressed in shorts, T-shirt, and athletic shoes. Occasionally, he slowed down for his mom and came by unannounced to share a walk. I was about to tell him I'd need ten minutes to get ready, but he brushed past me and into the house before I had a chance to say "Good morning" and invite him in.

"No arguments, Mom, it's done. I've made the appointment for this afternoon," he said as casually as if he was telling me he'd brought me a bagel for breakfast.

I followed as he headed for the kitchen and grabbed a bottle of water from the fridge door.

"Appointment for what?"

"Top Flight will be here at three to install your security system."

"But, I—"

"But, nothing." He guzzled the water. "Mrs. Goldberg was killed two days ago, right across the street."

I was about to tell him I had taken my own security measures, that I was now armed and dangerous, but that didn't seem like a reassuring thing to say at the moment. My mindset had been that security systems and burglar bars were the relinquishment of freedom, admission of fear, surrender to the bad people. I wasn't going to be a little old lady hiding in a fortress. Now, that seemed silly and indulgent in light of my neighbor's death.

I plopped down in a kitchen chair, shut my eyes, and breathed out a long sigh.

"Mom? Are you okay?" Daniel put his arm around my shoulders. "I realize you've been through a lot lately, and this is another change to process."

"We've both been through a lot lately. You lost Roanne, too." He averted his eyes, but not before I noticed the discomfort there. Daniel's way of easing the pain of my loss was to avoid speaking about his Auntie Roanne, who had been a fixture in his life although without the closeness he had with Zoe. But, perhaps, that avoidance was his way of managing his grief.

"I'm sorry I wasn't with you at the funeral," he said. "I should've tried to reschedule my job interview."

"You had to make the best decision for your family. I was fine. I'm fine now. A security system is an unnecessary expense."

"I'll pay for it if that's a problem. This is not giving up your independence, this is taking control of your safety."

I patted his hand. "You're such a good son. You're not paying. You don't have that job in Dallas yet."

He kissed my cheek. "How could I not be a good son with a mom like you?"

I never brushed off that compliment, I embraced it. Raising Daniel had not been easy, but he was my one sure accomplishment. When strangers remarked that they could see the obvious resemblance between us, that my son had my eyes, I would sometimes forget that he had not come from my body. The resemblance was not genetic and was not even obvious. Our eyes were not the same, his more silver than blue. It was the love between us that made others see likenesses that weren't there.

Daniel was white and Native American, like Scott whose mother was Cherokee. My son's Chickasaw ethnicity had meant extra red tape to navigate when we adopted him. Tribal rights had to be considered, but we also received strong support from the adoption agency to place him with a couple who shared his mix of ancestry.

Scott and I had tried to get pregnant for seven years. Our hopes had seesawed up when my period was late and down with my eventual flow of blood. In vitro was not much beyond experimental back then, and only rich people could afford extraordinary fertility measures. For many of those unsuccessful years, we had gone back and forth about adoption. When I had been ready to adopt, he was uncertain. When he had been on board, I was hesitant.

Finally, our ages had become the tipping point. We had learned that the adoption process could take a year or more. I was approaching my mid-thirties and Scott was already closing in on forty. He had begun, to my irritation, to refer to himself as "an old man." We had applied as adoptive parents, and a year later, Daniel, all six precious squirming pounds of him ready to take on the world, had come to us at three days old. His dark blue eyes turned silver-blue within a month, his skin took on a tawny shade like Scott's that bronzed easily in the sun, and his feathery tufts of hair grew into thick, dark curls.

My now thirty-year-old son squeezed me to his chest. "Hopefully, Braden and Charlotte will look out for me when I'm sixty-five."

"I'm not sixty-five for three more months. And, don't worry. You and Amy are raising good kids."

"Right, but they won't appreciate us until they have their own, just like me." He drained the rest of the bottled water and lifted me to my feet. "Grab your shoes, Foxy Lady. Let's get outside. You're looking a little tired. The fresh air will help you sleep better tonight."

I turned my head to avoid looking at the Goldbergs' house as Daniel and I walked briskly to the corner and along the street parallel to mine. It was one of my favorite streets, overhung with large, spreading pecan trees like the ones in my teenage stomping grounds in Austin. We talked about the Dallas schools that the kids would attend if Daniel was offered the job with Texas Instruments and how supportive Amy was about the possible move, even though she would have to give up her cellist position with the San Antonio Symphony.

"Have you seen your dad lately?" I asked, knowing the question would hit Daniel out of the blue. I hadn't seen or asked about Scott in years.

"Yeah, last month, at Johnny's burial service." I assumed he had gone to the service for Zoe more than for Johnny or his dad.

"How was he?"

"A little drunk. Understandable, you know, his best friend and all. His hip's bothering him a lot. He uses a cane now."

Scott carried a piece of shrapnel in his hip from his combat days in Vietnam. The pain had progressively worsened as he aged. The drinking had, too.

"He drove all the way back to Marble Falls drunk?"

"No, Jan took his keys. There was a little drama, but she didn't back down."

"I was thinking I might go visit him sometime next month."

Daniel stopped in his tracks and stared at me. "Really?"

"Maybe." I switched subjects. "How is Zoe?" Roanne's youngest daughter and my son had been best buddies since they were kids. I rarely saw her since she moved to Arlington, in the Dallas metro area, and she had stopped visiting or talking to Roanne years ago. But even though Zoe hadn't responded to my phone calls since Roanne's death, and I hadn't seen her in months, Daniel was sure to have some idea of how she was coping.

"She was like a zombie at the service, pulled into herself. I haven't talked to her since. I'm keeping my distance, giving her space."

"You know Zoe best."

"See you on Sunday," Daniel said as we hugged goodbye and exchanged "I love you's." The promise of another visit from my son in a few days was an unexpected bonus.

Christine called as Daniel's car pulled away.

"When are you moving back to Austin?" she said without so much as a "Hi, sis."

"You must have heard about the Goldbergs," I said.

"Right. So when—"

"I'm staying in my home. Don't worry. Daniel is on top of this. My security system will be installed today."

"Thank goodness. You're lucky to have him. They say daughters are the ones who stay close, but mine? Not so much."

"How are your girls?"

"Lexie has no plans to come back from Oregon. I can't believe it's been three years. Barry and I are going to hook up with her in LA in May to meet her significant other, some hot-shot videographer."

"And Xena?"

"She's off to hike the Appalachian Trail in three months, right after graduation. Then backpacking South America. Was a 'gap year' even a thing when we were eighteen?"

"Not for us, apparently. She's hiking alone?"

"With Buster," Christine said, referring to my niece's sweetheart-intimidator Rottweiler. "But, still, really? Maybe we shouldn't have named her after the Warrior Princess."

"Sounds like you have plenty to worry about besides me."

"I do worry about you with all that's happened in your life lately. You're not sleeping, you're dealing with grief. Have you considered seeing a grief counselor?"

I paused to frame my answer just short of a lie. "I've been talking to someone about Roanne."

"I don't want to add to your anxiety."

"Wait. Are we talking about something else now?"

Christine went quiet, like she had something to say but was unsure if this was too sensitive a moment. I waited.

"Are you coming to the Mass on Sunday?" she asked.

I had forgotten about the service. The significant date in the approaching week was March 6, the one-month mark for

Roanne's death. But, months ago, my older brother, Frank, had arranged a memorial Mass at St. Ignatius in Austin on March 3, the first Sunday of the month to observe the first anniversary of our mother's death. She had been a parishioner for fifty-two years, since the time we moved into the house on Pecan Street when I was twelve. All my siblings would be there. Frank and his wife would drive in from Oklahoma.

"I don't know," I said. "I'm not comfortable about it."

"This is about Joey being there?"

A knot in my stomach tightened at the sound of his name. If there was anyone on Earth I actually hated, it was my twin brother.

"Of course it's about Joey being there."

Christine heaved out a long sigh. "I wish you two could find a way to bury the hatchet."

"It's not my hatchet. It's his. He's the one who did those awful things before Mom died."

"I know. I'm totally in your corner. Couldn't you come because you have a right to be there as much as he does?"

Christine knew how to get to me. "You're right. I do. But I don't feel safe under the same roof with him."

"You wouldn't have to talk to him or even be near him. I'll be your buffer, on your hip every second. And Daniel will be there, right?"

"Yes." It suddenly occurred to me what Daniel had meant by "See you on Sunday."

"Barry will come if you want him to," Christine continued. "He's not flying until next Tuesday. Extra muscle just in case."

Christine also knew how to make me laugh. I pictured Barry, Christine's genuinely nice-guy husband in bouncer stance. Barry had always had my vote for brother-in-law of the century. On the other hand, I couldn't stand the way Joey's wife played the perpetual victim, always feeling slighted by everyone. And Frank's wife couldn't contribute anything to a conversation unless it was about *Dancing With the Stars*.

"So you're coming?" Christine asked.

"Yes."

"Don't forget to turn the alarm on before you drive up."

"Alarm? Oh, the security system. Goodness gracious, one more thing to remember."

"It'll become routine. You'll feel safer, sleep better."

I hesitated, wondering if I should even ask my next question. "Do you think I should maybe get a gun?"

"You? Ms. 'Never a gun owner' Canelli?' "

"I'm rethinking some things," I said, hoping she wouldn't press me for details.

"I think you should only have a gun if you could actually use it. Otherwise, you're bringing something deadly into the mix that can be used against you."

"I'm not going to let Joey push me around anymore."

"Wait. Are we still talking about a gun for home security?"

"I've gotta go."

"Connie?"

"See you on Sunday."

– 1970 –

I held up the back cover of my brand new *McCartney* album six inches from my mother's face. "Mo-om, look what Joey did."

Mom was in the bathroom in the middle of changing out of her baggy Bermuda shorts into a gingham-check pantsuit.

I had left the still-sealed album on my bed while I talked to Roanne on the kitchen phone just ten minutes before. Now the cellophane had been torn away and on the back cover photo, oversized glasses had been drawn on Paul and three of his teeth blacked out with ballpoint pen. "Faggot" was written on a patch of sky behind him with an arrow pointing to his head.

Mom stepped back from the photo. "Well, hmm, that wasn't a very nice thing to do."

I stomped my foot. "Roanne's coming over to listen. You have to make Joey buy me a new one."

"Well, aren't you making a mountain out of a molehill?" Mom propelled a fresh coat of aerosol spray onto her red hair, which was pulled back in a French twist.

I coughed and backed away as the sticky mist descended on me.

She twisted a lilac-colored lipstick from its tube and applied it to her half-open mouth, "freshening up," as she called it. Still, her outer eyelids looked dragged-down, tired from staying up late, getting up early. All so that she could cook and scrub and fold and polish and straighten, and endlessly pick up things that were in the wrong places.

"The record is fine, isn't it?" she asked.

"That's not the point. Why does he always get to come in my room and ruin my stuff? And you never do anything to him."

The doorbell rang.

"I'll ask your dad to give him a good talking-to." She walked past me toward the kitchen, already disinterested in my distraught state.

"You always say that, and nothing ever happens." I stomped my foot again and turned to answer the door. "That's Roanne."

"Just a minute. You still have to do the dishes before you and Roanne listen to records."

"Why do I always have to do the dishes?"

The Sunday dishes were my one big job at home. Mom cooked a huge dinner after Mass, and we ate in the early afternoon, not at our regular weekday dinner hour. On Sundays, the dirty dishes were massive: roasting pans, casserole pans, cake pans, mixing bowls, salad bowls, serving bowls, serving utensils, and not a single paper plate. The only time I got a break was when Dad was in the mood to grill, but then there was always that Pyrex pan with the stuck-on baked beans.

"You all have chores, Connie," Mom scolded. "Christine dusts the living room furniture. Frank cuts the grass. Joey takes out the garbage. And you do the Sunday dishes."

"Why can't we switch? Why don't you make Joey do the dishes, and I'll take out the garbage?"

Mom smiled and shook her head. "Now wouldn't your dad have a fit about that. Washing dishes is a girl's job."

"Mr. Lopez washes the dishes at our cafeteria. There are no girl jobs and boy jobs."

"Well, according to the law of God, there are."

"God? Has he heard of women's liberation?"

"Don't talk that nonsense in this house."

"Rose!" Dad called to Mom from the den. "Are you ready?"

The doorbell rang again.

"You better let Roanne in," Mom said. "Dad and I are going next door to visit with the Baileys. Go ahead and listen to your records, but don't put off doing those dishes for too long."

She turned her back and walked out through the den. I opened the door for Roanne with a scowl still on my face.

"What's wrong?" Roanne asked. She wore white bellbottoms that matched mine except she had sewn a border of lace to the hems to make them long enough to cover her ankles. Her straw-colored hair was straight as a stick, her bangs brushed her eyelids. I had ironed my hair that morning to flatten out the waves, but in the humid air, it was already reverting to its natural state.

I showed her the vandalized album cover. "Joey, that's what."

"What a jerk."

"Hey, Rodan," Joey greeted Roanne as we walked down the hall to the bedroom I shared with six-year-old Christine.

Roanne despised Joey from the first time they met even before he nicknamed her after the monster in the Japanese horror movies.

"Speak of the devil," she muttered. "Hey, Fart Face," she responded to him. "Get a life."

We locked ourselves in my room. I slid the shiny black LP out of its sleeve, set it on the rotating turntable, and lowered the arm. The needle touched down, and after the brief opening track, Roanne and I joined Paul singing, "That would be something, really would be something..."

We swayed with the music, our heads side to side, as we sat on the end of my bed. An acrid odor tickled the insides of my nose.

"Meet you in the fallin' rain, mama," we sang.

"What's that smell?" I asked in mid-refrain.

"There!" Roanne pointed at the door.

A burning kitchen match appeared through the crack between the bottom of the door and the floor. "Heh, heh, heh," came Joey's laugh from the other side.

Roanne grabbed a tattered tennis shoe from a corner and snuffed out the match. A second one followed, then another and another.

"Cut it out, Joey!" Roanne yelled.

"Stop it!" I screamed. "Or I'll tell Mom."

"O-o-o, 'I'll tell Mom,' " Joey mimicked. "So what."

I grabbed the old tennis shoe's mate, and Roanne and I smacked out the flames as Joey passed more lit matches under the door.

"Childish jerk!" I yelled. I landed my shoe on another miniature flare.

After ten minutes of snuffing out matches, finally, Joey's footsteps receded down the hallway. He was off to find other mischief.

"Which of you is older anyway?" Roanne asked.

"Me, by four minutes. Not that he didn't try to stop me."

"What?"

I pulled up the hem of my flared pants to expose a row of tiny, red, crescent-shaped marks. "You see this?"

"Yeah, I've seen it before, a birthmark."

"Do you know how I got it?"

Roanne shook her head. "Un-uh."

"When I was coming out of my mom, Joey grabbed my ankle and held on to keep me from being born first. He was digging in so hard, it made a permanent mark."

"Wow, how did you get out?" she asked in awe.

"I had to kick myself free. That kid was a little bully even before he was out of the womb."

She sat back on her heels. "Is that really true?"

"Well, it could be."

Side One of the album had finished, and the needle was stuck, making a "shuch, shuch" sound as it bumped against the edge of the LP's label.

"Your mom and dad should seriously do something about that kid," Roanne said. She pulled a bag of M&Ms out of her macramé purse, tore open the top, and tossed a couple of the button-shaped candies into her mouth. "He'll be one of those mass murderers someday."

I pulled a bag of Oreos from under my bed, twisted one of the cookies apart, and licked the creamy white filling before biting into the chocolate disks. "For some reason, it's always guys who do that, right?"

"Exactly. Well, there was Lizzie Borden."

"Oh, yeah."

"And I heard Jack the Ripper might have been a woman."

I lifted the turntable arm and set it back in its holding bracket. "I gotta wash the dishes. Ugh."

"I'll help."

"Did Lizzie Borden have a brother?"

– 2019 –

Joey stood, in a dapper gray suit, at the top of the steps to the church's side entrance as I drove up. I had meant to arrive well before Joey did for our mother's memorial service, but he had beat me to it. He held the door open for his wife, who wore a shapeless beige dress.

By the time I parked, they were inside and out of sight. I gripped the handle of the car door, but I couldn't make my hand open it. My heart hammered, my palms were clammy. How was it possible that dealing with Joey in my sixties could get me as worked up as it did when we were kids?

"Thanks a lot, Mom, Dad," I said to no one who cared, least of all my dead parents.

They hadn't believed in hands-on parenting. We kids more or less knew right from wrong, but there were no consequences or rewards for our actions. No lessons were passed down. We were not punished or encouraged. Those things would have required engagement, monitoring, follow-up; and Mom and Dad, hard workers both, had always been too exhausted for that.

I sat frozen. Christine and Barry would arrive soon. I could walk into the church with them.

A rap on the driver's side window startled me. Daniel's face appeared on the other side of the glass. A few feet away, Amy and the kids walked toward the church. I motioned for Daniel to get into the passenger side. He waved at Amy to go ahead.

"What's going on, Mom?" he asked as he shut the door.

"I'm having a hard time getting out." I breathed rapidly. The sound seemed to fill the car.

"Is it serious? Do you need to go to the hospital?"

"No." I forced some shallow breaths. "I saw Joey go in, and

you know I have an issue with your uncle."

Daniel took my hand and stroked it. "I'll sit with you until you calm down. I never understood what the deal is with you and Uncle Joey. He gave you a hard time when you were kids, but I don't get this paralyzing effect he still has on you."

Joey had always been a mean kid. He'd shove Christine and me or throw a rock at Frank's head when his back was turned, just because. He'd sneak into Christine's and my room and destroy whatever possession might be important to us, a book, a stuffed bunny, a poster, an album cover. Christine would cry, and I would complain to Mom. She'd wag her finger at him and say, "Wait till your dad comes home, Mister." Dad would shake his head and yell at Joey, "Go clean your room!" and collapse into his recliner, and that was that.

"It's not just about when we were kids," I told Daniel.

"Why don't you ever talk about it?"

"Because it's just too—too painful. And I don't want to burden you with my issues."

"It's painful for me to see you like this. Not talking about it has you trapped in your car. And I have broad shoulders."

I exhaled long and slow. "It's about your grandma."

"Grandma Rose was cool. She was independent, living on her own until the day she died. She went out the way she wanted."

"She tried to anyway."

Dad had died of congenital heart failure at the age of eighty-two. Mom continued to live in the house on Pecan Street alone, self-sufficient and free at last at seventy-six from taking care of anyone else.

During that time she had told me, with a giggle, "I feel kind of guilty, but it's nice to have the house all to myself. Sometimes I eat a sandwich in the middle of the night, and I leave the crumbs on the counter until the next day."

I gave Daniel's hand a weak squeeze. "She never knew anything else but cooking and cleaning and picking up after everyone," I said. "But, when your grandpa died, she discovered all these new ways to keep herself busy. 'I get to do the outside things now,' she told me. She was excited like a little kid. She said, 'I can mow the grass and trim the hedges. I like that better than sweeping the floor or scrubbing the toilet.'"

"She was one tough lady," Daniel said, smiling with an apparent memory. "When she would ask me to help in the yard, I could barely keep up. And her rose garden was awesome."

"Yeah, the rose garden, that's where Joey started getting into her head, like a worm into an apple."

Christine and I had often visited Mom together on the weekends, making a big meal and staying to do the dishes. Joey had flown in a couple of times a year from one of his two homes on opposite sides of the country. I was sketchy on exactly how Joey made his money, but it involved investment analytics, and Mom thought he was a big wheel. Frank had come to see Mom every few months when he took a break from his alpaca farm in Oklahoma.

Daniel stayed silent as I explained. "I visited her just after her eighty-first birthday. It was around this time of year. I found her sitting on her bed crying. I asked her what was wrong. 'I can't take care of my roses and my yard anymore,' she said. I asked her if she was sick, if she'd hurt herself. She said she was fine, but Joey had told her it wasn't safe for someone her age to work in the yard. 'He has someone watching me,' she said. 'If I try to mow the grass, they'll call him, and I'll have to go into assisted living.' She cried her heart out, saying over and over, 'I don't want to be put in an old folks' home.' She was so scared."

"That must have about killed Grandma not to be able to work in her garden. I thought she was just not feeling up to it when she got older. You set Uncle Joey straight, right?"

"I tried to. But, he had your grandma so terrified, she

became her own worst enemy."

I had called Joey and told him to stop threatening our mother. He told me he was doing what was best for her and that the rest of us would be happy if she fell in the yard and died. Christine and Frank had tried to persuade Mom to stand up to Joey, that we wouldn't let her be taken to a facility unless that was what she wanted. But Joey had put the fear in her, and his message was the one that stuck.

"She did whatever Joey told her to do to appease him." Daniel's hand closed into a fist against my hand. "She listened less and less to the rest of us. Whatever Joey said was her reality. And more and more what he said was some lie about me, and, like a parrot, she repeated it. 'Joey said he gave you financial advice and you didn't even tell him thank you.' 'Joey said you're wasteful and extravagant with your money.' 'Joey said you took some furniture from the garage.' 'Joey said you're too busy to come for my birthday.' 'Joey says you don't love me.' "

"Didn't you tell Grandma those things weren't true?"

"If I pushed back, she accused me of attacking him, 'Your own brother!' she would say."

"If I were you, I think I would have stopped talking to Grandma."

"I nearly did. The almost last straw was about the election: 'Joey said if that woman had smiled more, she might have gotten more votes. Nobody likes an angry woman.' And I said... I said, 'Eff what Joey said,' only I said the actual word."

Daniel grabbed my arm and gave it a little jerk. "My mom said the 'F' word?"

"Yeah, I did, and then I said, 'And eff Joey,' and I hung up on her. Of course, I called her back the next day and apologized, and we both cried, and she kept blubbering, 'I don't know why you kids can't get along.' "

"But, damn, Mom. You're his sister, his twin sister. Why is Uncle Joey so hateful to you?"

"I honestly don't know. Things have been the way they are between us for as long as I can remember. I used to joke with Roanne that he never forgave me for being born four minutes earlier than him."

It had seemed the more influence Joey had over my mom, the worse her health had become. At eighty-seven she had developed pulmonary hypertension and had to pull an oxygen tank behind her with tubing connected to her nose. Her general condition had deteriorated from there. She would spend the majority of the day in Dad's old recliner.

By that time, Joey's lies and the arguments over the lies had cut my visits to every few months, my phone conversations with my mom reduced to ten minutes a week.

"I'm sorry, Mom," Daniel said, patting my hand. "Did you have a chance to mend your relationship before she died?'

"No. Things actually got much worse. Remember when your grandma was real sick last year?"

"Right after the New Year. She had pneumonia. I visited her in the hospital a couple of times. I should have gone more."

"When she came home, I tried to see her. Joey called the cops on me."

Daniel's jaw dropped. "No way!"

In late February, Mom had been released from a rehab center to her home, but she couldn't manage much more activity than sitting up in a wheelchair to eat with the help of a live-in caregiver. The rest of the time she was confined to bed. I had tried to enter the front door with my key as I had done so many times before, but Joey had arrived ahead of me and blocked the door with something heavy.

I had paced on the porch, unsure of what I should do next, then called Christine on my cell.

Minutes later, two Austin Police cars had pulled up. I thought at first that Christine had called them, but it had been Joey. What had he told them? That I was breaking in? That I was violent?

"Sad but true, Daniel. They referred to me as the 'suspect' and within a few minutes Joey was outside telling the officers in the careful voice of a reasonable man that I was a physical threat to our mother and that I was trespassing. Christine arrived a few minutes later, and after a lot of shouting between her and Joey, the officers finally determined that Joey didn't have the right to bar me from my mother's house."

"Good," Daniel said. "So Uncle Joey had to back off."

"Not quite. After the police and Christine left, the caregiver and I gave your grandma a shower, her first bath since being home. Joey stood inside the bathroom doorway and filmed us with his cell phone. "

"That's disgusting!"

"I told him to stop as I washed Mom's privates, and he said, 'No. If you do something wrong, I'm going to make sure it's on video, and I'll make you pay.' Thankfully, your grandma couldn't hear so well and was too ill to be aware of what was going on."

"But the caregiver must have known."

"She was doing her job. We both had hold of your grandma. We had to concentrate on her."

Joey had kept his cell phone trained on me as I sat by Mom's bed after she was showered and dressed. She had lifted her head, and said, "My Connie, you're here." The caregiver said she had been asking about me, wanting to see me. All the while Joey had kept recording with his phone.

"I couldn't believe what was happening. Joey followed at my heels from room to room, taking video the whole time I was there and talking to me in a nasty tone."

"What did he say?"

"'You don't care about her. You don't have a relationship with her. Get out of here. No one wants you here. Don't come back.' He kept coming closer to me, intimidating me. When he yelled, 'Get out!' he spit in my face."

"What a total piece of sh—But you didn't let him stop you,

did you? You went back, right?"

I hung my head and sighed. "No."

I had stayed overnight at Christine's and had texted the caregiver the next day to ask when Mom might be awake so that I could visit. A response had dinged on my phone, but it wasn't from the caregiver.

The text from Joey had read, "Mom was very upset after your last visit. It's not a good idea for you to come here. You're a threat to her safety. If you try to see her again, I will watch you very closely and record you to make sure you don't do anything to harm her. It's too bad you act like a daughter for show but don't care about our mother."

I looked out at the St. Ignatius parking lot that was filling up. Car doors slammed, and people called greetings to one another. I turned back to Daniel.

"I didn't go back. I could see what Joey was doing, trying to fabricate some harm to catch on video. He could easily do something to hurt your grandma and make it look like I did it. He could turn the charm on and off with the police, with anyone. I wasn't going to fall into his trap. It wasn't just dangerous for me, it was dangerous for your grandma."

Daniel's fist came down on his knee. "But you had a right to see your mother."

"I planned to see her once Joey went home, but—" My voice choked, and tears pooled in my eyes. "Three days later, she died. Any chance we had to reconcile died with her."

"Oh, Mom." Daniel wrapped his arms around me. "I'm so sorry he did that to you. That bastard's going to hear from me before he leaves the church today. He'll see what intimidation really is."

"No." I gently pushed Daniel back. "Don't run interference for me. I'm the one who has to stand up to him, when I'm ready."

"But, Mom—"

"The point of standing up for myself is standing up for

myself."

The driver's door swung open. "Are you ready?" Christine asked, leaning into the car.

I bit my lower lip almost hard enough to make it bleed. Ready? Was I? "As I'll ever be." I stepped out and caught Christine's hand.

Barry came around to the passenger side and held the door open for Daniel.

"You can handle this," Christine said, with a gentle squeeze of my fingers. "You can keep calm and handle being in that church with Joey."

"Yeah, but how I'd like to handle Joey is way on the other side of keeping calm."

"Then, it's a good thing you're not packing, right?" Christine said, managing to look stern and joking at the same time.

I shrugged and walked around the rear of my Bug to join the men.

Christine raised her forefinger like a parent whose child had walked off in the midst of a scolding. "We talked about this."

"Right. No gun," I said and held my hand over my heart. "Promise." The Glock had lain in a closed drawer in my nightstand since I had bought it. I had avoided pulling the drawer open to even peek at it. What had Christine said about not owning a gun unless you could use it?

"Mom, what is she talking about?" Daniel cut in. "What gun?"

"It's nothing," I said. "Christine, you can frisk me if you want."

"Now, you're just being silly," she said with an eye roll.

"Yes, I am. How about you get me across the parking lot without me passing out?"

"Okay. Breathe. Here we go," Christine said.

Christine and Daniel each took one of my arms, putting

me between them while Barry walked ahead, my security detail guiding me into the church, where the monster awaited in a dapper gray suit.

70

– 1970 –

Roanne squeezed my hand as we stood for the beginning of the service in St. John's Lutheran Church. We had permission to skip the whole day of school. I had never been in a Protestant church before. Basically, it wasn't that much different from a Catholic one, just plainer, no icons and statues and chalices and candelabras.

"It's not fair," Roanne whispered between sniffles. "Why him?"

She kept her eyes straight ahead, like me, trying to avoid looking at the center aisle. Mrs. Slater's wet sobs carried from the end of the pew.

Roanne's older brother had left for Vietnam less than a year ago. It didn't seem possible that Chip was now something in a wood-and-brass box covered by an American flag.

"I know," I answered, sure that she was thinking the same thought as me. If God needed to take somebody's brother, why didn't He take Joey instead of Chip? It was a horrible thought, and in church, too, but I didn't care. I was not yet sixteen, but, if God could let this happen, I was never going to set foot in a church for the rest of my life. At least once I moved away from home.

When the final hymn trembled out of the organ and the mouths of the congregation, six pallbearers came forward. Two of them—my dad and Roanne's uncle—were in black suits while my older brother, Frank, wore his Junior ROTC uniform. The others were in army dress blues. The men grabbed the brass handles of the casket and lifted it. As they walked past, my dad stared ahead, stone-faced. Behind him, Frank glanced at me, then Roanne, his eyes filled with tears, and he stumbled. The other men caught the shifting weight of the casket. Frank regained his balance, and the procession continued.

Frank had talked to Dad and Mom a few weeks ago about joining the marines when he graduated from high school in thirteen months. Dad thought it was a great idea; "No better way to make a man out of him," he had said to Mom, but she had teared up and run out of the room. I listened to them arguing in their bedroom later that night.

Before Mom and Dad married, he had served in the air force in Kansas, far from any combat zone even if the US had not been between wars. Two years was the extent of his military tolerance before he went back to college to earn a master's degree, then to begin a career as a civilian government employee.

I suspected Dad supported Frank enlisting because he wanted the same bragging rights as Mr. Slater. Roanne's dad had never missed an opportunity to bring up that Chip was defending the United States of America by jumping out of aircraft into raging battles in Southeast Asia.

I remembered a night last summer, sitting with Mom and Dad, our eyes glued to the TV news reports about a place called Hamburger Hill on the other side of the world. Seventy-two Americans dead, almost four hundred wounded, to take a hill covered with thick jungle, then abandon it two weeks later. The report had mentioned an Airborne division. Mr. Slater had told Dad that Chip was in training with the 101st in Kentucky. I had wondered if Roanne was in her living room at the same time watching the same news, scared for her brother.

A few weeks later, Roanne had read me a letter from Chip after he had landed "in country," anxious for his first taste of combat. He was "raring to go," he said. "Don't worry about me. Charlie can't kill me. I'm Superman. Keep smiling, Annie." Chip was the only one who called her that.

I barely knew Chip. But, I had heard enough about him from Roanne to know that he was her hero, while her parents constantly disappointed her in that role. He was three years older than Roanne and me, a tall, muscular guy with a surfer look, blond hair sweeping over one eye, a golden tan, and a brilliant smile. He was almost eighteen, a high school senior, when the Slaters moved into the house on Pecan Street. Then, a few months later, when the Slaters and Canellis had become regular visitors in each other's dens and dining rooms and back yards, Chip enlisted in the army and was gone.

To Roanne, he was the Man of Steel. It seemed every sentence Roanne spoke lately began with "when Chip gets home." He had been due to complete his tour in Vietnam in three months. She couldn't wait for him to see how grown-up she had become, and she had been nearly almost certain that once her brother was safe stateside, her mom would stop drinking so much.

Outside the church, I put my arm around Roanne's waist as she waited for her family before we piled into cars to head to the cemetery. Mrs. Slater, propped up by a grim-faced Mr. Slater, shuffled out, squeezing hands offered in condolence and nodding to each person with a teary, empty stare like a sad bobble head. Eleven-year-old Darla, her blonde hair pulled back with two barrettes, wore a brave face, her chin jutted forward. She seemed more like a grownup than her parents, bucking up under the day's weight bearing down on her small shoulders.

We let the three of them pass, Darla trailing behind Mr. and Mrs. Slater, and Roanne and I followed toward the parking lot.

When we were almost to the Slaters' blue Chevy station wagon, Roanne called to her sister. "Darla, do you want to ride with me and Connie?" The Slaters had agreed to let Roanne ride with me in my dad's car.

Darla whirled around and walked over to Roanne. Her eyes were shining with tears.

"What is it, honey?" Roanne asked.

"Chip is in heaven like the reverend said, isn't he?

Watching over us?"

Roanne placed her palm on Darla's head. "Yes. That's right."

Through the open window of the blue Chevy, Mr. Slater called for Darla.

Roanne took her little sister's hand, walked her to the station wagon, and shut the back door once Darla was inside. Darla gave a small wave through the murky window.

On our way across the lot to Dad's old Mercedes sedan, Roanne stared into space. Dad, Mom, and Frank were already in the car, and Dad had started the engine.

"Do you suppose Darla's right?" Roanne asked.

"About heaven? She's a kid, Ro."

"Watching over us."

She slid into the back seat next to Frank, and I followed, the leather seat a cool shock against the back of my bare legs. As I slammed the door shut, Roanne mumbled under her breath, so low I barely made out the words:

"Keep smiling, Annie."

– 2019 –

When Christine, Barry, Daniel, and I entered St. Ignatius through the vestibule, the pews in the front half of the church were already filled with mostly older women, my mother's longtime fellow parishioners. Many, like Mom, had outlived their husbands. The strains of organ music drifted above the shuffling of hymnals and murmuring voices in prayer or gossip. Out of long-ago ingrained habit, I dipped two fingers in a font of holy water near the door and made the sign of the cross.

My eyes searched with dread for the outline of Joey's head, the cut of his shoulders. The nave, I remembered from catechism class, was the area where the congregation sat. The altar section was the sanctuary. Another word for safe place. But, walking down the center aisle past the empty rear pews and under the vaulting space above, I was exposed like a frightened animal in a forest clearing with no place to hide if a predator appeared.

The first time I went to Mass at St. Ignatius, at twelve, I was awed by the soaring ceiling with gold rafters, the stained-glass windows depicting the stations of the cross, the giant crucifix suspended over a marble altar. The terrazzo floor, like multicolored stones spread under a glossy, frozen stream, impressed me most. Before we moved to Pecan Street, our family had attended Mass in plain chapels on bases in Tennessee, Kansas, and North Texas, where Dad worked as a government civilian.

By the time of Mom's funeral, fifty-two years later, the luster of St. Ignatius had faded. It had the look of a dull, outdated suburban building surpassed by more contemporary facilities.

I gripped Daniel's hand when I spied the back of Joey's

head in the front pew on the right side, next to his wife and beside Frank and his spouse. Panic fluttered in my chest. My eyes darted from row to row.

"Safe zone, left, front," Daniel whispered in my ear and led the way to where Amy and my two grandchildren, Braden and Charlotte, sat across the aisle from Joey and Frank.

Christine and Barry slid into the pew behind Amy and the kids, joining their teenage daughter, a lone representative of my nieces and nephews.

"Hey, by the way," Daniel whispered again. "I got the job in Dallas."

"Oh." I was happy and sad at the same time. "Congratulations. You'll be moving to Dallas soon?"

"Six weeks. We'll talk later, okay?"

Daniel steered me to his left, positioning himself between me and Joey in the pew across the aisle, a protective barrier should my twin give me so much as a dirty look.

"Look, Grandma," six-year-old Braden piped up in an above-church-level voice. He pointed in front of us between the lectern and the altar. "It's Great-Granny when she was pretty."

"Pretty, pretty," his three-year-old sister parroted.

A photo of my mom was displayed in a gilded frame set on a tripod. The picture was from her teased-and-sprayed, big hair days, when she was in her late fifties. I had not been reminded in some time that she had been a beautiful woman with a lovely smile and sparkling, deep blue eyes. In her last years, I had come to think of her as a sour-faced, mean, old lady who never had anything kind to say to me. But, once, we had taken walks together and shopped for sundresses and done each other's makeup, and she had made me a birthday cake decorated with daisies when I was down in the dumps about turning forty.

The trappings inside the church were so abundant—the statues, the candles, the banners, and cloths—it took a moment for me to appreciate the special flowers behind the photo and also on the other side of the altar. A dozen arrangements of pink roses, Mom's favorite flower and her namesake, decorated the front of the church. Their sweet perfume filled my nostrils. I remembered the rose bushes in her backyard when they were in full bloom, velvety red, creamy pink, and a pale salmon.

The ritual of the Mass kept me calm. I fell seamlessly into the up-and-down of standing, kneeling, sitting, standing and the memorized recitations, declarations, and responses: "Lord have mercy..." "Glory be to the..." "I believe in the Father..." "Lamb of God who takes away the sins of the world..."

Kneelers banged up and down as the faithful exited pews and paraded to the front of the church to receive Communion, then returned to their seats. "Body of Christ" was a chant that lulled my thoughts to a standstill.

"The Mass is ended. Go in peace," the priest declared, and my anxiety returned with a vengeance, in my sweaty palms and pounding heart. I thought about Roanne to focus myself. Her last words had been about anger and about speaking up, having the final say.

I almost wished I did have a gun. A shot would have been a quicker and easier action, like an efficient turn of a scalpel to excise the cancer of hatred and anger that had been eating at my insides for years. I had told Christine I was as ready as I'd ever be but not just ready to enter the church. I had to act. It was now or never.

I scooted in front of Daniel and leaned into Christine's ear over the back of the front pew. "I need to go."

"Wait," Christine said, "I'll come with—"

"No." I pushed past her as she raised up, pushing off Barry's knee. The other attendees began to fill the center aisle.

My shaky knees protested, freezing my feet to the floor as I trained my eyes on the side door. "Damn it, you have to do this," I lectured myself.

I hadn't actually meant to speak my self-motivation out loud and only realized that I had when I heard Braden's voice. "Grandma said a bad word."

My daughter-in-law Amy responded, "Shhh. That's not a bad word when grandmas say it."

The priest shook hands and chatted with my siblings and with Daniel and his family at the front of the church. That gave me time to get into position. When my brothers and sister, with Joey in the lead, started down the aisle toward me, most of the general congregation was already flowing toward the vestibule at the rear of the church.

I stood with my back to the glass door, blocking the side exit. Joey bore down on me, a solid six feet, three inches of him, barreling toward my five-two frame.

"Get out of my way," he said.

"It's not *your* way, and no, I won't move until I've had my say." I took a deep breath. "What you did to me and to our mom was despicable. You destroyed my relationship with my mother, and you prevented us from seeing each other to have any chance to mend fences before she was gone. You stole that from me, and you stole that from her. And, for what? For pure meanness."

Christine and Barry had separated from a crowd of stragglers and were nearing the intersection where the main aisle met the side passageways. Daniel was caught up with Amy and the kids, still in the front pew, probably tying Braden's constantly loose shoelaces or coaxing Charlotte, who by this time would be fussing that she was too tired to walk and begging to be carried. I refocused on Joey and what I had to say, and I pushed forward.

"You're still the little bully you were when you were a kid, sneaking into my room to destroy what I prized most," I said to my twin. "How miserable it must be to live within the empty shell of your body. One day, the weight of your evil will crack you open like a hollow bone. I'm done carrying what you did to me. It's all on you now. You'll no longer affect me. I dismiss you from my life."

Christine and Barry had almost reached us, a few paces behind Joey, Barry's arm lifting, ready to reach out and jerk Joey back. I fixed a steady stare at my would-be rescuers, lifted my palm in a firm "stop" gesture, and they froze, leaning slightly forward, prepared to pounce at a second's notice.

Joey took a step closer, a hateful sneer on his face. "Get out of my way," he spat.

I shut my eyes. I thought of Jesus on the precipice in the desert with Satan. I trembled from head to toe, but I forced my eyes open, drilled them into his, and kept my voice steady. "Be gone. I dismiss you." I could feel the closeness of his body hovering over me, inches away, his breath blowing hot against my forehead. "I dismiss you," I said louder.

I held my breath, anticipating that he would strike me or shove me aside or heave me through the glass door.

The air around me pulled back. Joey turned on his heel and retreated, his footsteps clipping on the terrazzo tile. His shoulders flexed and his arms pumped as he almost bowled over Christine and Barry, and quick-stepped toward the exit at the opposite side of the church. He blew past his wife and through the door, slamming it in her face. My legs turned to noodles. My head was a balloon ready to float away.

Christine and Barry swooped to my side. Daniel raced toward me with a quick glance back at the door where Joey had exited and with his eyes wide in alarm.

"Hey, Mom," Daniel said, "What just happened with you and Uncle Joey? Did he hurt you?" He offered an arm to steady me.

"No," I said, latching onto his forearm. "And he won't ever again."

Voices buzzed around me as we walked out of the church and down the steps to the parking lot. My face felt cold and clammy. Cars, lined up to turn onto the street, blurred into each other. Pinpoints of yellow light danced in front of my eyes. My legs wobbled, and my feet searched for the ground each time I took a step.

"Are you all right, Mom?" Daniel asked.

"I didn't think I could do it," I said, unable to make my voice rise above a loud whisper.

My knees buckled and scraped the asphalt before Daniel caught me under the arms, and everything went black.

– 1980 –

"I'm between a rock and a hard place. No matter what I do, I'll be wrong." Roanne dabbed at her reddened eyes with a soggy Kleenex. "Johnny says I'm being selfish. 'A job is more important to you than me and Stella?' That's what he said to me last night."

She pulled up to the speaker in the Whataburger drive-through lane. Stella, who was almost two, was asleep in her car seat behind me while I rode shotgun.

It had been four years since Roanne received her teaching degree from UT. She was married and pregnant with Stella less than two years later and then had thrown herself full force into stay-at-home-mom mode. She hadn't applied for a full-time teaching job until recently but worked as a substitute from time to time.

After each day subbing, she had called me in Panama to give me a play-by-play of what "her kids" did that day, their moments of enlightenment or disappointment. "I feel like I'm making a difference," she would say. She had told me of another substitute teacher running out of her classroom in tears after the students started chanting, "We want Ms. Kirkland," Roanne's married name. Now Roanne had been offered a position at a junior high near her Round Rock neighborhood.

"Whataburger with mustard, no mayo, bacon, cheese, onion rings, small fries, and a large chocolate shake," Roanne said into the metal box. She turned to me. "What do you want?"

"You didn't just order for both of us?"

"Very funny. Don't go health nut on me right now. I need comfort food. And you have to get something. For solidarity."

"Okay, I'll have a lemonade, a small lemonade."

"Solidarity?"

"And a Whataburger Junior?"

Roanne repeated my request through the speaker, added bacon and cheese, and pulled up in line.

"And all of a sudden," Roanne went on, "he thinks we should start going to church, says it would be good for the family."

"I never thought of Johnny as a churchy person."

"I think he's been talking to Darla. She called me the other day and out of the blue she invited me to a Bible study. She told me I needed to stop listening to false prophets like Barbara Walters telling me I could have it all. She said juggling wasn't the same as parenting."

"How did that go?"

"Like usual. I told her she was an idiot, made her cry, probably caused her to eat a bag of Snickers. I wallowed in guilt the rest of the day, made Johnny's favorite homemade mac 'n' cheese for dinner, had good sex. All problems solved."

"Yeah, which is why we're here getting comfort food."

"Exactly."

Roanne rummaged through her purse for her wallet while she drove up to the pickup window. I pressed a ten into her hand. She grabbed the bags of food, passed them to me, and parked in the near-empty burger joint lot. I fished out the burger and the onion rings for Roanne and set the drinks in the console. Stella stirred in the backseat and made a mewing sound but didn't wake up. Roanne glanced back at her daughter.

"Do you think leaving Stella in day care five days a week would make me a bad mom?"

"You're a wonderful mom. Who says that staying home with your kids is all that great for them anyway?"

Roanne took a big bite of burger and nodded. Grease oozed down the corner of her mouth, and she caught it with her tongue. She chomped off half of an onion ring.

"The day care in our housing area is super nice and only two blocks from the school," she said. "We took Stella for a visit, and they absolutely loved her. Johnny was even impressed with the place."

"But not impressed enough to agree that you should take the job?"

"He said I should wait until Stella is in kindergarten, three more years. Full-time positions don't come open that often, and teaching junior high is what I always wanted to do. If I don't take this chance, I might never be anything but a sub. Besides, until Johnny gets a permanent job, we could really use the money, with the new house and all."

Johnny had gotten fed up with military life and separated from the army a year before. He and Roanne had bought a house in Pigeon Creek, a new development in Round Rock, only months before he put in his separation paperwork.

Scott had broken the news to me about Johnny's "stupid" decision. Johnny had his code, Scott had said, that made it an ordinary task for him to drag a wounded buddy three miles through a Vietnam swamp of water and human waste when there was no chance that the soldier would survive. But that unwavering loyalty went hand in hand with Johnny's fierce sense of pride.

Johnny had been passed over for a long-awaited promotion. There had been some incident, a report, disparaging remarks from a commanding officer to whom Johnny had shown unflagging allegiance. According to Johnny, his CO had stabbed him in the back, and that's why he was done with the army.

"Looks like Johnny got fed up all right, fed up with getting a regular paycheck," Scott had said. "He failed to realize that the civilian world doesn't give you a housing allowance to pay your mortgage."

Roanne's unfinished burger rested in her lap. "You don't think he would leave me, do you?" she asked.

"If you took the job? Not in a million years. Johnny loves you and Stella, and he doesn't want to lose either of you."

Stella began to fuss. I peeked around the seat at her. I was still getting used to how adorable she was, with huge brown eyes and wisps of blonde hair drawn up in two small pigtails. She had a bubbling laugh and a comical frown that made her look like a Munchkin. I had met her for the first time only a month before, when Scott and I returned stateside. Johnny and Roanne had stayed in Killeen the whole two years we were in Panama, except for Johnny's nine month unaccompanied tour in Turkey, and Roanne had sent me a hundred photos of the baby.

Stella rubbed her eyes with chubby fists and squirted out a couple of tears. As she came fully awake, she let out a wail, strained against the straps of the car seat, and kicked her feet. One of her pink tennis shoes flew off and bounced off the back of my seat.

Roanne broke a fry in half, blew on it until it stopped steaming, and handed it to Stella. "Here you go, sweetie." Stella sucked on the fry and was quiet again, contentedly surveying the parking lot through the back windows, swiveling her head back and forth to catch every person, bird, or car that came into her view, not missing a thing.

"What if I tried out the job for a year, and, if it caused too much trouble at home, then I could quit? It wouldn't be like I was choosing a job over Johnny and Stella."

"Yeah, but..."

"But, what?"

"Wouldn't that look bad on your work history the next time you applied? You have to consider what's right for you as well as everyone else."

"That's just it. I know what's right for me, but that isn't what's right for Johnny and Stella, so, my right doesn't count, does it?"

"You could talk to Johnny about it some more. Tell him

how important it is to you, how good it will be for Stella to be around other kids."

"I want to be a good mother, I want to be a good teacher, but I want to be a good wife, too." She put the remains of her burger and onion rings back in the bag and rolled it up. "Three more years is not such a long time."

Roanne handed Stella another fry, grabbed the untouched shake out of the console, and opened her door, clutching her bag of food.

I washed down the last bite of my down-sized burger with the last of my lemonade. "You're not tossing that, are you?" I asked.

"Yep, I didn't want it as much as I thought I did."

She slid out the door and shoved the food into a nearby trashcan.

– 2019 –

I counted the wildflower paintings on the walls of Chief Docent Supervisor Elizabeth Burnett's office while I fidgeted in a chair waiting for her to return for our "chat." Thirty-four, from massive works in gilded frames to groupings of miniatures, explosions of bluebonnets and Indian blanket and primroses, surrounded me.

"You hit Mr. Schertz?" Ms. Liz, as all the docents at the Witte Museum called her, said at almost a screech level. She slammed the door behind her, strode over to me, and hovered like a towering shadow, shooting sparks from her eyes, her silver beehive poised to spontaneously combust.

"'Hit' is a little exaggerated," I said, weakly defensive. "A slap, more like a tap, on the hand." Ms. Liz's whole face drew into a frown. "I had warned him very politely, twice actually when he touched the toe, but when he went for the tail, he crossed the line."

"*He* crossed the line?" She moved behind her desk and sat down, a tall woman who loomed, even from her chair. The gold chain on her red, cat-eye glasses quivered as she spoke. "Mr. Schertz's company is one of the Witte's most generous donors. Your behavior was extremely inappropriate. We're lucky he isn't filing an assault charge."

"*My* behavior? I was defending *our* dinosaur from *his* assault. And he cursed at me." George W. L. Schertz had leaned all of his beer-bellied, gas-and-oil-executive stature into my personal space and threatened to get me "fucking fired." I had raised my chin defiantly to his chest level and countered that I was not an employee, but a volunteer.

"Connie, we've had shining reports about you over the years," Ms. Liz said. "How many has it been?"

"Five." I enjoyed my volunteer time at the Witte,

answering questions about the Texas history and Wild West exhibits. The dinosaurs were my favorite because they brought in all the wide-eyed, ooh-ing and ah-ing kids.

Ms. Liz's violet-red lips became thinner, and she made a little throat-clearing sound. "Five years. But with today's outburst and rude comments you made to guests during your prior shift, I must say, I'm a bit concerned about your continued presence here."

"I'm sorry," I said, hoping to head off a chat on my feelings and boundaries or a suggested time off so that I might reevaluate my core values. Ms. Liz liked to play the stern mother hen. "I admit I haven't been myself lately. I'm not sleeping well."

My fuse had been getting shorter. Even before I threw a classmate in the pool and quit water aerobics, I had smashed up a birthday cake I made for my neighbor because it came out lopsided when my normal fix would have been to add extra frosting on one side to even up the cake. This morning a nightmare had jerked me out of my sleep again. In my dream, I had been throwing rocks, not at a tree but at Roanne. She pulled out her gun and pointed it at me. My eyes had flown open, my heart had raced. I had almost called Christine at 3 a.m. for the second day in a row. Thankfully, I had managed to pull myself together before disturbing my sister and Barry.

"Be that as it may," Ms. Liz continued with a sterner than usual tone, "we have our reputation to think of. Such aggression simply can't be tolerated from a docent. I'm afraid I have no choice but to terminate your services, effective immediately. Of course, you'll still be welcomed as a visitor at the regular admission price." Ms. Liz put out her hand, palm up. "Name tag, please." Her lips were a straight line.

I gulped down my shock at her rash decision and handed over the three inches of black-and-white plastic. It was just as well. My busy schedule left little time for volunteering. I was finishing my latest book, and soon Christine and I would have to plan the spring menus for our cupcake shops. I also had plenty of work to do on my new project, months of research and meetings to arrange. I had confronted Joey, but he was just the beginning. I had made a list.

———

With my afternoon free to dive into another Maxie Dallas chapter, I spent an hour writing and rewriting a single line of dialogue before calling Christine and telling her about the ugly end to my museum docent career. She asked if I was still seeing a counselor. I told her I'd rather talk to her. Then I dropped the news that I was going to Houston to confront Benny Bing, and after him there would be more.

"Big Benny Bing the RV King? That's insane," Christine's shocked voice rattled through the phone. "When you stood up to Joey, it took so much out of you, you passed out after," she reminded me.

"Oh, that. It was nothing."

"In spite of almost falling flat on your face, I was a hundred percent behind you even though confronting Joey was risky. But now, you have a what, hit list? Why?" she demanded.

"Because," I explained, "every time I stand up to one of those bastards and call them out for what they did, I have one less reason to end up as desperate as Roanne."

"You'd never do what she did."

"Do any of us know what we would do? I don't want to be caught in the same trap as her even if the end is not the same."

"A call-the-bastards-out crusade. But where's the resolution? Do you really expect any of these jerks to admit responsibility?" Christine asked.

"No, but this is not about them," I said. "It's about me."

"Do I get to know who these assholes are and where you plan to meet them? This is not just insane, it's unsafe," she said. "I'm going with you."

"No. You have a life, a husband, a child. I'll be fine. They're the ones who should be worried. Hell hath no fury like a woman wronged, etcetera."

"This is nothing to joke about. You could get hurt."

"I should get a gun?"

"You're prepared to shoot someone?"

"Of course not."

"So..."

"No gun."

"And I want to be in the loop at all times."

"How about, before each meetup, I let you know who and where and when, and I'll text you that I'm okay or not," I told her, intending to do at least some of those things, when necessary. After all, the plan was still in flux. "And you can't tell anybody, I mean anybody."

That had earned me one of her exasperated sighs, but she agreed and backed off after a final salvo. "Whoever comes after Benny, I wish you the worst of luck finding them," she said.

Christine had a point. After hours of research on social media over the past few weeks, I still wasn't sure where the rest of the "bastards" were or how I would have control over where I would meet them.

Trying to keep my word, at least this time, to inform Christine, I told her as much as I thought she needed to hear about me and Benny.

Big Benny Bing the RV King owned a string of RV sales lots across Texas. To hear him tell it in late-night TV ads, if you couldn't find the perfect RV on one of his lots, that RV could not be found. For many years, wearing a crown and fur-trimmed red robe, and shaking a scepter, he repeated that message on the airwaves at maximum volume.

He had to be around eighty by now, and his son had taken over the cheesy royal impersonation, but the commercials remained consistently obnoxious. If not the classiest RV hawker in the state, Benny was the most well-known.

"Before he was the RV King," I told Christine, "Benny was the manager at Wet Winky's hands-on car wash on Fifty-Second."

Back then, when Benny was a young man, the only thing Big about him had been the huge belly that hung over his horseshoe belt buckle.

"He hired me as a cashier the summer I was seventeen. Ten to six on weekends, a dollar-sixty an hour." Frank would give me a ride to work in his burnt-orange Datsun those few months before he left for boot camp in California. I'd take the bus home.

"I remember you working there," Christine said. "Dad took me through the car wash one time. He got me a slushy after and gave me the money to give to you. I thought you were big stuff, my sister had a job."

I had been proud to punch a time clock, greet each customer as they handed me their cash, and thank them with a smile and a claim ticket. Benny never had reason to find fault with my work. He had been pleasant but curt. Until that busy Saturday morning when my cash register had failed. I laid out the scene for Christine.

The store had only one cash register, and I had been the sole weekend operator positioned in a corner behind a counter that displayed racks of mini-tree-shaped air fresheners, gum, and novelty key chains. Without a functional machine to register sales, I had been keeping track on a notepad, taking cash, giving back change, and writing out receipts by hand. The line had backed up to the door, about a dozen customers, all men and one young woman with a fussy toddler. The shuffling feet and heavy sighs of impatience from the crowd had made me increasingly anxious with each laborious transaction.

"That's when Benny walked in." As I talked to Christine, my heart began to race as it had that day. "I was relieved that he was going to help me out. 'Why is there a line?' was the first thing he said, or rather shouted. It wasn't a question, it was more like an accusation that I had somehow caused a backup, and he wanted everyone to hear. 'It's not working,' I said. I pointed to the dead machine."

He had stepped over to my station and craned his neck over my shoulder.

"He said, 'It's not working or you're not working?' Again, he announced this to the whole room."

"And that's supposed to make things better?" Christine said. "What a jerk." The clink of metal against metal and the slow whirring of something being stirred came through the phone.

"What're you cooking?" I asked.

"Spaghetti sauce. What did you say to Benny?"

"I said, 'The cash register's not working.' My hands had started to shake."

I remembered my fingers had stuck to the bills as I tried to count out change to an older man.

"Benny said in a nasty tone, 'What did you do? Is it plugged in?' I started stuttering, trying to explain I hadn't done anything, of course the thing was plugged in. He was treating me like I was an idiot."

The older man had looked over the money I had handed him, said I shortchanged him. I had apologized and tried to fix it, but Benny grabbed the money out of my hand and recounted the correct change to the man.

"I have a feeling that wasn't the worst of it," Christine said.

"No. Benny looked at the people in line and said, 'Big boobs, tiny brain, am I right?' "

Christine blew out a puff of breath. "Son of a—did anyone in the store speak up for you?"

"Not a chance. A few of the men looked uncomfortable, but, still, they smiled and nodded, like, yeah, the things men have to put up with. I'm sure my face was red as a radish. The one woman in the store just stared at a row of candy bars. She must have wanted to go through the floor, humiliated for me. Benny apologized to the crowd, with his big-man-in-charge voice, for my tiny brain or big boobs, I'm not sure which, but for whatever I had done to purposely cause the situation, and he promised he would 'get this girl's mess straightened out as soon as possible.' "

"What an ass!" Christine said. She stirred again, then slurped and smacked. "Mmm, needs more basil. Sorry, go ahead."

"I don't remember what exactly happened then. I think Benny brought a calculator in from the office, and the register was fixed at some point."

"You quit, right?"

"No, I was getting a paycheck. There weren't a lot of jobs open to girls, pretty much babysitting and delivering newspapers, that was it. I hated coming to work after that. I would throw up every Saturday and Sunday morning."

"That really sucks," Christine said. "But, that was way back when you were seventeen. I don't mean to be insensitive, but why is this such a big deal now?"

"That was my first job, and I learned a lot from Benny. He taught me that day that no matter what job I held, no matter how competent I was or how hard I worked, I could always be crushed by a man in charge."

It dawned on me that Mr. Schertz had played the Benny card, too. I had struck him with an ineffectual slap, but the big, bad donor man had me thrown out the door. I'd get a second shot at Benny, though, and this time I'd have nothing to lose.

The doorbell sounded. I walked to the door with Christine's voice in my ear, supportive but irritated. "Don't forget to text me from Hou—"

The rest of Christine's words evaporated when I opened the door. A slender young woman with almond-shaped eyes and long, straight, black hair stood on the porch. A red Honda hatchback with a gray fender was parked in the driveway.

She bit her trembling lower lip and twisted the fingers of one hand inside the other. "Auntie Connie, I didn't know where else to go," she said, shifting her shoulder under the weight of a bulging backpack.

"Christine," I said into the phone, "I have to go. Zoe is here."

– 1996 –

When I pulled up in her driveway, Roanne was standing on the top step of a four-foot, aluminum ladder, spreading swaths of white paint over the double garage door with a roller.

Although fainter under the coat of white, the word spray-painted in neon orange showed through. "Pervert."

She looked at me with weary, dark-ringed eyes, her face streaked with paint drips as I walked up. A crack in the closed blinds appeared in the front window of the house across the street. A neighbor picked up a rolled-up newspaper at the end of the driveway next to Roanne's yard and stared in our direction as she walked back to her front door. In the distance a lawn edger whined and a service vehicle beeped its backup warning. No sign of a vicious vandal with a spray-can stood out among the brown and beige brick facades, the silent manicured lawns, or the trees with leaves stilled in the warm morning air.

I grabbed the side of the ladder to hold it steady while Roanne climbed down.

"Let's go in the house," I said.

She set the roller in the paint pan on the top of the ladder. Her shoulders hunched as she held back sobs. I wrapped an arm around her.

"Are the girls all right?" I asked.

She nodded. We sat down side by side on the couch in the dark living room. The blinds were lowered, and the lights were off. The air smelled of toast and nail polish. Two glasses with the remains of strawberry milkshakes crusted around the sides were set on the coffee table beside a bowl containing a handful of popcorn. Fleece blankets, one in neon leopard print and the other decorated with Jasmine from *Aladdin*, lay wadded up next to the table. Leftovers of movie night with

Stella and Zoe.

"I had Johnny come and pick them up early," Roanne said. "Stella wasn't thrilled. We were going to the mall today, but Zoe was out of here in a flash."

"Did they see it?"

"Probably."

"Who would do such a hateful thing?" The blinds peeker? The newspaper retriever? "Have you called the police?"

"What for? So they can treat me like a criminal, too?"

I grabbed her hand and shook her arm. "Roanne, you have to fight this. Make the school district conduct a thorough investigation instead of leaving things at 'inconclusive.' The accusations are false. People need to know the truth. You didn't do anything wrong."

She pulled her hand away and shrugged. "It doesn't matter. No one cares about the truth. They all want to believe a seventh-grade teacher had sexual contact with a thirteen-year-old boy. I don't even know what the contact is or who the kid is."

"Whoever he is, there is no proof. There is no evidence. No charges have been filed."

"How long do you think an investigation would take? Meanwhile, how long am I going to be getting those side eyes and whispers at the grocery store? The nasty phone messages and the hang-ups? All the newspaper and the TV have to do is mention that an investigation is going on and that keeps the tongues wagging."

"People are always going to gossip," I said.

In Round Rock it had only taken two paragraphs in the local section of the paper to kick things off, just an inkling, no parties identified, no facts substantiated:

> Round Rock Independent School District is conducting an investigation of sexual abuse of a minor involving a male student and a full-

time teacher at Pigeon Creek Junior High School, according to school officials. Authorities could not discuss the date or nature of the incident or if the incident was a one-time occurrence.

The district was advised of the alleged incident through an anonymous source with close ties to the family of the seventh-grade student who reported that the alleged incident took place on school grounds within the last six months. The teacher involved in the alleged incident is a longtime member of the Pigeon Creek faculty, according to a source close to the investigation, and remains on administrative leave since the beginning of May. No criminal charges have been filed.

Just enough information was out there to feed the speculation in a small town, and the smaller community of Pigeon Creek. Roanne's neighbors knew she was a junior high teacher and that she had not been going to work. From there, talk spread like wildfire.

Roanne arced out her arms around something huge and invisible. "This is bigger news around here than that hornet's nest Oprah stirred up about burgers and mad cow disease," she said and reached for a nearby box of Kleenex. "You were a journalist, you know how the public memory works." She blew her nose. "If an investigation clears me after weeks, months, who knows how long, most people are still going to think of me as the pervert teacher. There won't be any follow-up story saying nothing happened. I want it all behind me."

"It will be at some point, but—"

"I'm turning in my resignation tomorrow, effective immediately."

"You can't mean that. You love teaching. Talk to your

lawyer. Fight back."

"No, I'm done." She slumped into the sofa. "The divorce has about tapped me out, and I can't afford to keep fighting Johnny for custody of Stella and Zoe. He swore he'd make me pay for cheating on him, and he's made good on his promise."

"And that's what this is all about?"

"Exactly. There's no way he's not behind all this."

"That sounds crazy even for Johnny, to want revenge for something that happened ten years ago."

She shook her head. "You don't know how crazy Johnny can get. I should have never told him."

"Why would Johnny be in such an uproar over it now?"

She dropped her head. "I chickened out. I never told him back then when I said I would. Remember when we ran into each other last year at the No Drama Lounge?"

"You and Johnny had had a big fight. Johnny made some cracks about maybe you were stepping out on him."

"Well, it didn't get any better after that. He was at me for weeks, same old broken record. I was so sick of him accusing me, I just blurted it out. 'Okay, okay, I cheated on you ten years ago. Is that what you want to hear? Does that make you feel better?' It was so long ago, it was like it happened to someone else. I told him how sorry I was, I never wanted to hurt him, I never stopped loving him."

"That must have hit him right between the eyes. To him it's like it just happened. After he's had some time—"

"Not a chance. For goodness' sake, he filed for divorce the next day. He said even after a hundred years, he'd never forgive me. He said Scott was right, if you're suspicious, there's usually a reason you feel that way."

"Scott should have kept his big mouth shut." Scott had asked me if Roanne had cheated on Johnny. I had lied. I'd happily do it again to save her this pain. Maybe I could still do it, tell Johnny that Roanne made it all up in the heat of the moment because he kept accusing her. I'd swear to Johnny that she never went out on him, never—no, it was too late for that.

Roanne held her face in her hands. "He said he'd fix it so I'd lose my job, make me look like an unfit mother, take my girls, and now he's done it."

"But you're not giving up? The custody case isn't over," I protested, almost shouting.

"Yes, it is. I told Johnny today I'm dropping it. I can't keep putting Stella and Zoe through this. If I let them live with their dad permanently, maybe they won't hate me forever."

"They don't hate you."

She glanced at a side wall where a collection of photos hung. A stray bit of sunlight winked through a gap in the closed blinds and illuminated the faces in the frames from years ago. Stella, a lanky grade-schooler, with blonde pigtails, a freckled nose, and a snaggle-toothed grin. Zoe, a chubby-cheeked baby in a frilly polka-dot dress with a red bow holding up a stalk of black hair in the center of her head.

"Stella's her own person," Roanne said. "She'll be off to college next year to begin a life apart from me and Johnny. No need to pick sides. But, Zoe, she blames me for everything that's messed up in her life, and her dad can do no wrong. I suppose it's her way to deal with her world being turned upside down."

"She's ten. When she's older, when she has the facts, she'll understand."

"If Johnny doesn't poison her against me. She barely says two words to me when she and Stella come over."

I calmed my voice. "After the divorce is final, and he moves on, he'll be more reasonable."

She stared at me with a crooked smile. "Johnny can't be reasonable about betrayal. Getting even is how he moves on."

"And what about you?"

"I'll get another job, not as a teacher, obviously. I'll sell the house, move into an apartment, maybe on the other side of town where the neighbors won't know me."

I wanted to weep for her. Hadn't she given up enough already? The split level in the Pigeon Creek subdivision had been her dream home when she and Johnny moved in seventeen years before. She had put off starting her full-time teaching career until Stella had started school, but it had paid off. She had the job she had always wanted, in a junior high classroom, for the last twelve years.

"I'll dye my hair and wear some big Jackie O glasses," she wisecracked with a crooked smile. "I'll be fine."

I stood up, my fists clenched, and shouted at her. "How can you throw in the towel like this? How can you be such a coward?"

She looked up at me, unflinching. "What should I be?"

My fists clenched harder, and I stamped my foot. "You should be fighting mad."

She gently took hold of my wrist and smoothed out the fist with her other hand. "Oh, Con, what good would that do? I've already lost."

"What's going on, Zoe?" I asked.

The chubby infant Roanne and Johnny had brought to Texas was now a thirty-four-year-old woman who wore a face on the verge of collapsing into tears. She slipped her backpack off her shoulders and plopped down on my couch.

Zoe had come into the world in 1985 with two strikes against her. She was born in China in the midst of that country's one-child policy, and she was female in a culture that preferred male children. Zoe was cast out into an orphanage, a statistic in the upswing of abandonment of baby girls by parents who didn't have a boy on the first try.

Roanne had dangerously high blood pressure during her pregnancy with Stella, and her and Johnny's desire to have a second child wove a silver lining for the orphaned infant. At the age of fourteen months, Zoe was flying across the globe with her new parents to a new home in Round Rock, and a new eight-year-old sister.

"I had to get out of Arlington," Zoe said. "I just couldn't deal with regular stuff, everyone going on with their lives at work and shopping and going out when my mom and dad are dead and my world's upside down. How can everything still be the same for everyone else?"

She wept into her hands. I sat down next to her and snuggled her to my shoulder. "I know, sweetie. You can stay as long as you need to. Daniel's old room is the guest room now. Get situated, and I'll make us some dinner."

She threw her arms around my neck and hugged me tight. "Thank you, Auntie Connie. Thank you so much."

I lifted a strand of her hair caught at the corner of an eyelash and smoothed it away from her face. "It'll be good to have you here. We have so much to catch up on." She pulled back. I was rushing things. I went to more neutral ground. "I hope you like spaghetti squash."

She managed a smile and leaned her head toward the back of the house. "I'll go wash up."

An hour later, at the dining room table, I poured merlot and served a squash casserole.

"I know your favorite is lasagna, but this is my pasta-free alternative," I said. "I'm trying to eat low carb."

"It's fine. It's good." Zoe turned up her glass, held it out for a refill. I poured her another. She drank half the glass, then twirled a forkful of squash and stuffed it into her mouth.

As a child, Zoe was constantly in the kitchen with Roanne, starting out on a stool in an apron that fell to her ankles, developing into a mini chef. Italian dishes were her specialty, everything except veal, in defiance of the cruel way in which it was produced. Judging by her thinner face and bonier shoulders since the months when I had last seen her, it had been a while since she had eaten a hearty meal, home-cooked or otherwise.

"Are you still working as a nursing assistant at Baylor Scott and White?" I asked.

She talked around her mouthful of food. "Yep."

"The long-term care center, right?"

"Yep."

"I heard you were taking classes, working toward a BS in nursing."

She looked down at her plate and didn't answer.

"I heard that from Stella. She calls now and then."

She avoided making eye contact and took another bite.

"Is your new condo working out okay? Stella said it was really nice and close to your work."

She looked up with a twisted smile. "Everything's good. Except, of course, my mom killed my dad, then killed herself, so..."

I laid my silverware down and placed my palms on either

side of my plate, unsure if this was a good time to reach out for her hand. "Oh, sweetie, I can't imagine what you must be going through. I'm still trying to understand. But one thing I know for sure is that your mom never stopped loving you. She wanted things to be better between you."

"Like how exactly? I had to go through all of school since I was ten having kids ask me, 'What's it like to have a pedophile for a mom?' "

"It wasn't true, Zoe. You know it wasn't true. She was a good person."

"If you don't count that she cheated on my dad with that guy from the furniture store. That's why Daddy left her."

"You were a kid. How do you know that? Johnny told you?"

"No, he wouldn't do that. Stella—our family database—told me like five years ago. That filled in some of the blanks for me."

"There were a lot of reasons why your mom and dad didn't work out. Neither one of them was totally at fault. You should cut your mom a break."

"Don't tell me what I should do." She dropped her fork, and it clattered on her plate. "Them being dead is totally her fault. And you didn't do anything to stop her."

The accusation cut through me like a knife. "I'm so sorry, hon. I didn't wish any harm on your dad. I never wanted to see you hurting like this." A lump was rising in my throat. I choked it back down. "I wish I had seen it coming. I wish with all my heart and soul I had been able to stop it.

"Do you want to talk about it?" I asked. I reached out to put a hand atop one of hers.

She pulled her hand into her lap. "I can't right now. Can we just leave it?"

"Sure. Whenever you're ready."

Zoe kept her gaze cast down on her plate. For a few minutes, the only sound in the room was the soft scrape of her fork as she pushed the last bits of her food into a little mound.

"Do you want more squash?" I asked.

She nodded. I refilled her dish.

"I'm sorry," she said. "It wasn't your fault. And I'm sorry I haven't been to see you in forever. I wasn't mad at you. I—" She gulped down a sob.

"I know, sweetie, forget about all that. You're totally welcome to stay with me whether a day or a year goes by in between, but I have to go out of town tomorrow for a business meeting."

"Is it about your books?"

I shook my head. "Something else."

"I read one. Uh, something about angel food cake?"

"*The Angel Food Assassin*. That was a fun one. Did you like it?"

She nodded. "Yep. I think so, I don't remember it much, it was like a year ago."

"I have shelves full of Maxie Dallas mysteries you can entertain yourself with while I'm gone, other books, too. Make yourself at home. There's plenty of food in the fridge. You'll be okay, right? I can ask Daniel to come by and check on you if you want. "

"Don't worry. I'm not going to go whacko. If my mom had some crazy gene, it didn't get passed on to me, that's the good thing about being the adopted kid."

"I only meant you might want some company, and you and Daniel have always been close."

"Yeah, sorry. I would like to see him, but not right away." She reached out her glass.

I poured her the remainder of the merlot.

"Do you have more wine?" she asked. "Or something else?"

"No, but I'll go shopping later this week. Red or white?"

"Whatever." She shrugged and downed the rest of her drink.

I swirled the shallow pool of wine in the bottom of my glass. "Are you sure you'll be okay tomorrow?"

"Where are you going?" For a second, Zoe looked like a scared little kid.

"Houston."

She fidgeted with the corner of a napkin. "Maybe I could come?" A little kid's pleading voice.

I tapped my glass nervously with my fingernails. "Not a good idea. I want to get in and out as quickly as possible." Truth was I didn't want Zoe to see me if I was in tears or had steam coming out of my ears after seeing Benny, and I didn't want to drop her off, as vulnerable as she seemed, to wander Houston alone while I carried out my plan. "I'd reschedule if I could." But I couldn't. I had had to conjure and connive to make the meeting happen on that particular day.

Zoe's heavy sigh was pure disappointment.

"I'll be home early evening, we could order a pizza, watch a movie?"

"Whatever."

"You'll be okay?" I asked again, aware of the hollowness in the question. Even if it was for only part of a day, we both knew I was abandoning her.

– 1975 –

A gust of wind billowed Roanne's skirt and lifted it to the top of her thighs.

"Hey, Blondie! Want to wrap those long legs around this?" A man in a hard hat, T-shirt, and grimy jeans growled and grabbed his crotch as we walked past construction scaffolding in front of a drugstore in downtown San Antonio.

Roanne's cheeks glowed red. She caught the skirt hem and held it down. We were headed for a restaurant-bar on the riverwalk, a getaway from Austin, the first day after finals our junior year at UT.

"You're disgusting!" I shot back.

Male sniggering followed along with a shout from another male worker, apparently directed at me. "How about you, Little Red? Want to su—"

We hurried to beat the "Don't Walk" sign to cross St. Mary's Street and scooted around the corner of Commerce in our platform heels to the nearest steps that would take us down to the river. We had already trekked four blocks from our parking spot in our cute summer footwear, and the non-cute blisters on my toes were on fire.

"Why do they do that?" Roanne said, still flustered and stumbling on the seams and rises of the rock path along the river. "Women see guys with their shirts off on the street, and we don't scream out stuff at them."

"It's about men being able to get away with it. Like my mom says, 'Boys will be boys.' "

We walked over a stone bridge to the other side of the river. The late afternoon and evening crowds of revelers who would fill the shops and eateries and bars along the curving waterway were still hours away. Our destination was just ahead, past a bend in the walkway, where a towering cypress tree rivaled the height of the high-rise hotels and reached its canopy over the water.

"Do you think Johnny and Scott do that to women when we're not with them?" Roanne asked.

"No, they're nice guys. Otherwise, we wouldn't be going out with them, right?"

We had met Johnny and Scott through one of Roanne's matchmaker friends, who got it right for once, and we'd been dating them for the past three months. Scott was the first guy who had ever pulled a chair out for me at a restaurant, even if we had been at Billy Joe's Bar 'N' Grill. He brought me daisies from the grocery store. He apologized when he let a curse word slip in the presence of a woman.

Our emotions were oil and water on the Fall of Saigon—his anger, mine sadness and relief. He was into the Eagles while I was into Elton John. But whenever he left Austin to go back to Fort Hood, I couldn't wait to see his smile again, the way it crinkled up the corners of his hazel eyes, and to have his strong arms around me lifting me off the ground for a kiss. Sometimes I thought I might be in love.

"Do you think they've never done that, ever?" Roanne asked.

"Maybe when they're out drinking." Scott had told me about some of the wild times he and his army buddies had had at the bars in Southeast Asia. "Nice guys but not saints."

"Maybe men can't help it, like a primal thing."

"We're not living in caves anymore," I said. "Their brains that control their mouths are supposed to be more advanced than a Neanderthal's. They can choose to be nice guys."

A hostess at a Mexican restaurant welcomed us to an outside table shaded by a yellow umbrella. The green-gray river lapped at the edges of the historic paseo, the wake from a passing flat-bottom boat filled with tourists and locals acting like tourists. Some of them waved, and we waved back.

"They don't think about how it makes us feel, that's for

sure," I said, inching my chair closer to the table. "What those guys said makes me feel so gross, I want to scrub all over with a bar of Lava."

"Ugh. How about margaritas instead?"

The server set a basket of chips and two bowls of salsa, green and red, in the middle of the table. We ordered strawberry margaritas.

"You know what's gross?" Roanne said. "I was with my mom at H-E-B a couple of days ago, 8 a.m., she's still sober, so...we were pushing the cart along, minding our own business, and right there in the produce section this dude walks by and says to her, 'Baby, you got some nice melons.' "

"No!"

"Yeah. And she's over forty, for goodness' sake."

"What did your mom do?"

"She smiled and did this little upper-body shimmy thing."

"That is gross."

"That's not all. I said, 'Mom, what're you doing? Aren't you upset about what he said?' She said, 'Honey, when they stop saying it, that's when I'll get upset.' "

"You're sure she was still sober?"

"Pretty sure." Roanne dipped a chip into the milder red salsa. "You don't think that's how we'll feel when we get old, do you? That we'll be thrilled at some construction guys yelling disgusting things at us?"

"Are you kidding? No way." I scooped up the spicier green salsa on a chip and shoved it in my mouth.

Playful voices drifted down from a balcony of a riverside hotel. A string quartet spun its sweet, trembling sounds from across the water. Raucous male laughter exploded from a foursome in business suits at a table nearby. Two of them were kind of cute. The traffic and construction and gross construction workers on the street above seemed a world away from this retreat under a yellow umbrella that rippled in a soft breeze.

Our server walked toward us holding a tray with two icy, pink drinks garnished with spears of fruit. As she passed the table with the four men, one reached out with a grin to his buddies and tapped her butt. The other three sniggered. The server flinched, bit her bottom lip, and continued to our table, steadying a shaky smile.

"Did you see that?" I whispered to Roanne.

Roanne looked up from twirling a chip in the red salsa. "What?" She rubbed her palms together. "Here come the margarita-a-s."

"Nice."

– 2019 –

Twenty-foot-high lighted red letters flashed "Big Benny's RV World" atop a glass palace surrounded by three acres of parked recreational vehicles. The letters could be seen for half a mile from Houston's southbound Katy Freeway. A garrison-size American flag rippled on a pole above the building's roof. I wondered if veterans and self-proclaimed patriots really steered their business toward the places with the biggest flags.

The showroom's double glass doors parted. I walked into a soundless space. The artificially chilled air enveloped me. A gold statue of the king himself stood in the middle of the roomful of gleaming, giant-wheeled beasts. The king reached a scepter, which resembled a huge chicken leg, toward the rafters of the distant ceiling.

"Welcome to Big Benny Bing's," sang out a tall slender blonde in a blue skirt-suit and six-inch heels who approached with an outstretched hand and a Vanna White smile. "How can we help you today?" she drawled.

I shook her smooth, cool hand. "Connie Canelli. I have an appointment with Mr. Bing."

"Of course. Please, have a seat." She motioned to a softly curved, dove-colored couch. "Mr. Bing's assistant, Ms. Harcourt, will be right with you. Can I get you anything? Coffee? Soda? Herbal tea? Sparkling water?"

"No thanks." I sank into the cushions. On a side table, beside a stack of RV magazines, sat an apothecary jar filled with M&Ms. Roanne's favorite. Maybe it was a good omen. I lifted the top from the jar, about to nibble on a candy or two, but changed my mind and closed the container. It was best not to have chocolate smeared on my teeth when I met Benny, a man important enough to have two employees to screen his visitors.

I watched my greeter click away in her slim skirt and heels. I wore pressed jeans, a black blazer, and flats. My hair was loose and pushed behind my ears to expose pearl earrings. My black tote was an understated faux suede. I was going for professional yet casual. After all, this was an RV sales lot, but now I felt underdressed. My throat was dry, and I regretted that I hadn't asked for sparkling water. I stood as another tall slender blonde, in heels and suit, but slightly older than the welcome woman, walked up.

"Felicity Harcourt," she said. "So good to meet you, Ms. Canelli. We were so excited to receive your letter on this momentous occasion. Mr. Bing was truly touched."

The "momentous occasion" was tomorrow night's big to-do at the Westin Galleria to honor Benny with a lifetime businessman achievement award. I had read about it in the *Houston Chronicle* almost a month ago. Counting on Benny's sense of self-importance having only grown with time, I figured he couldn't resist the chance to meet a woman who started her employment career as an impressionable girl under his wing and who wanted to offer her gratitude. Or so I led his people to believe in my letter. I wasn't looking for anything from Mr. Bing, I had written, just a chance to shake his hand and tell him I had never forgotten my first job.

Felicity walked me to the perimeter of the showroom and to a glass-walled office. Its interior was concealed by closed ceiling-to-floor blinds. She rapped gently on the door. "Mr. Bing?"

"Come," answered a creaky male voice, nothing like the arrogant twang that had made my younger self shrivel.

The assistant swung the door open to reveal an oversized desk that came up to chest height on the sour-faced gnome sitting behind it.

Without Felicity's introduction, I wouldn't have known who he was. "Mr. Bing, Ms. Canelli."

I stepped toward the desk and extended my hand. The

gnome made no attempt to rise or return the gesture. He stared at me with watery gray eyes underscored with puffy bags of flesh, and he motioned to a red leather couch. I awkwardly withdrew my hand and sat. Felicity had noiselessly backed out and shut the door.

"My, my, so you worked for me at Winky's, eh?" His thin lips pulled back to expose yellowed teeth.

It took me a moment to recognize that he was smiling. I uncomfortably smiled back, letting my gaze drift behind his bald, freckled head. I realized that I had never seen the top of his head before. In his younger days he always wore a baseball cap, perhaps hiding premature hair loss. On the back wall were a dozen photos of a younger Benny cutting ribbons at his various business locations and shaking hands with various dignitaries with large stomachs and long ties.

"You were a cashier, I understand." The crackly voice brought my focus back to his face.

"Yes, I was."

"Ah, Winky's, that was a long time ago. You were a kid, first time you had a job."

"Yes, I was."

"You were a good girl? Didn't give me any trouble, did you?"

My skin crawled at his condescending tone, shades of the Benny of bygone days. "No, sir," I managed as sweetly as I could.

His yellow teeth jutted out again. "Heh, heh. Well, this is some reunion, ain't it? You coming in here after all these years to personally thank me for helping train you up right for the professional world."

I smiled and folded my hands in my lap. "You didn't exactly help me, Benny. I can call you Benny, right? That's how I knew you then. I'm assuming people don't actually call you 'King.' "

"Uh, yeah, uh Benny's fine." He seemed a little thrown off,

like he realized something had shifted in the room.

"No, you didn't help me, Benny." I said his name like an insult. "You certainly didn't help me when the register broke down with a store full of customers. What you did is humiliate me, treat me like a bug you could squash under your boot. It took me a long time, years, to realize I had the right to be treated with respect in the workplace."

"What is this? Some kind of shakedown?" His face reddened, and his narrow lips twitched. "You won't get anything from me, sister. I don't even remember you. Who are you? A pathetic old woman holding a grudge for forty years worming your way in here under false pretenses starting some shit. "

"I don't want anything from you, like I said in my letter. And what I am is a survivor. Not because of you, but in spite of you and men like you."

He sniffed and raised his chin, a clumsy attempt for a haughty look from under hooded eyes. "I'm a respected businessman, lifetime achievement award honoree, I'm—"

"When I was seventeen, you were a small-time boss with a big belly who liked to throw his weight around. I'm guessing that's all you've ever been, maybe with some nicer clothes and accessories you picked up along the way, but still just a dressed-up bully."

He huffed and snorted and tapped his gnarled fingers on the desk.

"I was the professional that day the register went down," I said. "I was the one who didn't lose my cool. I did my job to the best of my ability. And I found my way in the working world without treating people like you do. So, you can have your award for all the achievements you think you should get credit for, but what I'm giving you is what you really deserve, the shame you should have been wearing all these years, not me. You can have it."

"I'm not ashamed of anything I've ever done." He leaned

forward and a series of raspy coughs rattled out of his throat.

I paused until the coughs quieted. "That's sad then, because you've never learned anything."

Benny cleared his throat and shook his head as if he was trying to shake off the next round of coughs. He clutched at his chest. His chin moved up and down and his mouth worked like a fish out of water. His face took on a lavender tint.

Was he having a stroke? For goodness' sake, I didn't come here to kill the guy. What had I been thinking? He was old. He was in poor health. They only give out those lifetime achievement awards when they know you have one foot in the grave and the other on a banana peel.

I rushed to his side, put a hand on his shoulder. "Benny, Benny, what is it? Should I call Felicity?"

He gasped.

"Should I call 911?" I pulled out my phone.

He gasped again, deeper this time.

"Try to take a breath. Let me help you." I worked my fingers between his top collar button and his jowly neck, trying to work the button loose. "Benny, I'm so sorry. I didn't mean—"

He clamped onto my wrist with his wrinkled claw and looked up at me, his eyes as cold and flat as a shark's. His top lip curled up in a sneer. His skin color was returning to its more normal yellowish-gray hue. "Is that it?" he said. "Are you done pitching your hissy fit?"

I shook my wrist loose and backed up. "I'll be out of here soon. I wanted to give you something, a token of my regard on this momentous occasion." I drew a shoebox out of my bag and set it on his desk. My hand hovered over it while I considered taking it back. Perhaps the token was too much. What if he really did have a stroke?

He stared suspiciously at the box for a moment. "Get out of here, you crazy old bat!" he croaked. A speck of spittle shuddered at the side of his mouth as he spoke. He struggled to his feet and stood, propping his bent frame on a cane. "Get out before I throw you out!" A coughing spasm overtook him, and he fell back into his chair.

Clicking heels approached with urgency. I smiled and looked back at Benny before I turned to open the door. He was incapable of throwing me or anyone out. In his crippled state, he couldn't even match my modest height. When I was seventeen, I had cringed before Benny Bing. Now he was just a small, sputtering curmudgeon.

I walked through the door into the showroom as the blondes dashed toward me, their mouths hanging and eyes wide, a couple of spooked deer tipping along on high heels. I sidestepped them, slalomed around the giant vehicles, and walked casually and professionally to the front exit.

"Mr. Bing, Mr. Bing, are you all right?" His minions called out in high, thin voices.

A barrage of curse words exploded behind me as, I imagined, Benny opened the box to reveal a gold-lacquered, plastic trophy. It was made in the image of a naked man with a huge belly that almost obliterated a puny worm of an appendage at the crotch. Engraved on the plate of the trophy's platform were the words: "Benny Bing, the Tiny King."

The automatic doors swished open. I strode, my head held high, into the dazzling sunshine.

Roanne and I stood in a zigzagging line with hundreds of others at The Summit, waiting for the entrance to open. Bodies jostled against each other and pitched conversation and singing broke out. The anticipation of seeing Queen perform live at the band's first concert in Houston vibrated through the crowd like the loose lid on a boiling pot.

"Hey, whaddya think?" A muscular black dude standing in front of us put the question to Roanne. He wore dreadlocks and a leather vest over a bare chest. His eyes were a pale green.

"About?" Roanne said.

"Does ya name rule ya destiny?" said the black dude's buddy, a frizzy-haired blond guy with "Edge" tattooed on the side of his neck. Both guys spoke with some kind of northeastern accent.

"If Freddie Mercury hadn't changed his name, would he be a superstar? Like ya name is ya destiny and ya destiny is ya name, right?" the blond guy said.

"Exactly," Roanne said. "David Bowie, Elton John. If only I hadn't been stuck with Roanne Slater, who knows the heights I could have reached?"

"Row-a-uhn," the black guy said with a fake drawl, laughed, and pointed to me. "Whozya friend? Daisy Mae?"

"Is everyone from Baww-ston rude?" I said, trying to sound insulted, but my tone was softened by the attraction to his green eyes. Still, he had insulted Roanne first, and I was used to defending Roanne from people who teased her when we were kids. We were twenty-three now with bigger battles to fight, but old habits died hard.

Roanne had told me the story long ago about the origin of her name. Mr. Slater wanted to name his first child Roland, after himself. But Mrs. Slater insisted on Charles after her dad. It didn't matter anyway. Everyone called Roanne's older brother Chip. When kid number two turned out to be a girl, Roland was out of the question again. Mr. and Mrs. Slater could have gone with Annette after Mrs. Slater, but this time Mr. Slater insisted on a compromise, "Roanne."

"Brooklyn, not Boston," the black guy said.

"Connie, not Daisy. And you are?" I asked.

"Elvis."

"Sucks for you, dude, that destiny has already been taken."

When we finally got inside, we found ourselves fifty feet from the stage. Freddie Mercury pranced out in a harlequin jumpsuit. Roanne squealed and waved her arms above her head. If Johnny could see her now.

She and Johnny had argued the night before in front of Scott and me over our last wild girls' night before Roanne would become a married woman in ten days. Johnny wanted to spend every weekend with her until the wedding and was all hurt feelings to discover that Roanne wasn't a hundred percent in agreement. Roanne had eye-batted and smooched her way out of trouble, with a promise not to get too wild and an assurance that we weren't exactly going to Mardi Gras to flash our breasts for beads or anything else.

And I had reminded Johnny that we weren't going to allow ourselves to be kidnapped by underground militants, because I had an interview for a reporter job at the *Austin American-Statesman* the next afternoon.

Scott and I had nearly gotten into our own fight after I had made a crack about Johnny in particular and men in general and maybe even Scott being control freaks, when it was only one night, for goodness' sake. Scott had mellowed out after a couple of beers, Johnny had called Freddie Mercury a "fag" and made some other nasty comments, but, in the end, everyone had kissed and made up, and the guys had told us to have a good time before they headed back to the barracks at Fort

Hood.

The Summit crowd stomped and clapped like one huge beast, pounding out a rhythm. Freddie raised his microphone stick, and the crowd erupted with him in one voice. "We will, we will rock you!"

Everyone was on their feet, making a human wall in front of me. I jumped up and down. "I can't see!"

I was grabbed around the waist from behind. Elvis lifted me up on his shoulders and held me there as he swayed to the music. I wore a black bohemian dress, and for about ten seconds I was uncomfortably aware of my crotch veiled in thin fabric rocking against the back of the neck of a guy from New York whom I had known for less than an hour.

Roanne was dancing like she had been charged by a lightning bolt, her hair sweeping in wide arcs like a golden flag as she swung her head side to side. She reached up and grasped my hand, her electric energy zapped into me, and we melted into the vocal sea.

A joint was passed my way, I took a hit, passed it to Roanne, and she inhaled and handed it off to Elvis's buddy. Another smoke followed and a few more after that. We sang and sang and sang until my throat ached. I can't remember how many hits I had, but by the second encore and Freddie's hip-shaking rendition of "Jailhouse Rock," I was flying, and Roanne looked like she had seen the rapture. We ended up in the back of a black van with crushed velvet curtains with the two guys from Brooklyn.

Sometime before dawn, Roanne's sobbing woke me up. The clammy air smelled of sweat and weed. My mouth was dry, and my skin was sticky. I peeled my naked body away from Elvis's. He mumbled something that sounded like, "Hey, baby," or "Hey, Daisy." I couldn't remember the sex with him, only that we had done it. The memory was like watching it happen to me but with no memory of the sensation.

In the dark, my fingers pushed through the nap of shag

carpet until I found Roanne's and my wadded-up clothes. I crawled over a set of legs toward the sound of Roanne's whimpers and bumped into her bare shoulder. She was leaning against the back door of the van pulling her arm free from under the crooked elbow of Edge's pale, prone body.

"Here's your stuff," I said, tossing her duds at her. "Let's go."

I found the door handle above her head and pushed it. The passed-out guys didn't stir as we climbed out. The dimly lit parking lot was deserted except for the van and my orange Datsun, a hand-me-down from my brother Frank, which waited a few yards away.

I wasn't sure about Roanne's mental state, but my brain was still dancing in and out of a moving fog. The cool air raised gooseflesh on my bare skin. We pulled on our clothes on the way to the car. Roanne continued sniffling on the drive to Truckers Paradise off Interstate 10 West.

When we walked into the all-night diner, blinking against the harsh light, several cigarette-smoking, loud-talking, scruffy-looking dudes gave us the once-over. The place was long on truckers but short on paradise. In the grungy, smelly bathroom, we peed and washed our faces, and I noticed I was wearing only a sock on my left foot. After we slid into a booth, we ordered black coffee and a whole apple pie that we began eating with spoons straight from the disposable aluminum pan. Our waitress walked off chuckling and shaking her head.

Roanne sniffled and blew her nose with a napkin between bites. "I'm a terrible, horrible, rotten person," she said.

"You're not."

"I cheated on Johnny with some dude called Edge."

"You were stoned. I was stoned." I scraped a chunk of crust and gooey filling from the bottom of the pie pan with my spoon. "People make questionable decisions when they're high." I shoved the spoonful of pie in my mouth. The generous cinnamon prickled my tongue. "I cheated on Scott." Somehow it seemed that sharing the guilt would be helpful.

"You feel as rotten as I do?"

"Scott and I aren't getting married." That seemed less helpful. It was weird to be aware that my thoughts were jerky and slow to come together, not fully gelling until after I spoke.

"But, eventually, right?" Roanne asked.

I shrugged. "Probably."

She squinted hard at me. "Are you still high?"

"Possibly. You?"

"I'm straight." She frowned and tapped the back of her spoon against her bottom lip. "We have to tell them, right?"

"Whoa." We were still thrashing around in the realm of bad decision-making as far as I could tell. "Will that undo what we did?"

"But we should be totally honest, right?"

"Okay, right. Let's be totally honest. If Johnny and Scott ask if we got high and balled a couple of guys from New York in the back of a van, we'll say 'Yes! Right on!' "

Roanne squinched up her face like she was in math class trying to solve a complicated equation. "But, husbands and wives shouldn't have secrets from each other, right?"

"Okay, let's say, when you and Johnny are married for like twenty years and you have four babies, you tell him about your big, bad, secret night in the last days of being wild and single." I was possibly talking more rapidly than usual. "And y'all can have a good laugh. Or, let's say, you tell him now, and have a huge, gigantic fight and possibly get the wedding called off."

Roanne pursed her lips, tapped the side of her coffee cup, and met my eyes with an uncertain gaze. "So we keep last night a secret?"

I did the closing zipper motion across my mouth.

"Okay, but I'm never going to lie to Johnny again, ever."

We had finished all but three bites of the pie. I dropped my spoon into the pan and waved to the waitress for our check.

"Are you okay?" Roanne asked. "For your interview?"

"I will be. It's not for five hours." My thoughts were already more anchored than when we had walked into the diner. My left foot had awakened to the cold and wetness under its soggy sock. We were only a hundred and sixty-five miles away from home. We'd never see those two guys from across the country again. In two hours we'd be back in our normal lives. Waking up in our apartment, having Cheerios for breakfast, watching some silly rom-com on TV before we went to bed, for the next week anyway, before the wedding.

My eyes let go a flood of tears.

Roanne laid her hand on my wrist. "Con, what's wrong?"

"I'm going to miss you. I'm going to miss us."

"What're you talking about? Johnny and I will be in Killeen, only seventy miles away. We'll see each other all the time. You and me, just like always." She stood up. "Every time you have a little weed, you go all sad and weepy when you come down. You'll feel better once we're back home. You'll do great at your interview. We'll forget all about last night, okay?"

I wiped my eyes with the backs of my hands and shoved a last bite of pie in my mouth to keep the words from spilling out. Three houses down on Pecan Street, dorm rooms next door as freshmen at UT, the apartment on Fifty-First for the last four years. I was glad we had been so reckless on our last wild night together. It wouldn't be easy to forget. And, once Roanne moved out, I wanted to remember when it was just us for a long, long time.

- 2019 -

I fidgeted in the dark to connect my key with the lock on my front door. I hadn't thought of turning on the porch light when I left for Houston in the morning, expecting I'd be home before the last of the sunset's waning light.

The knots in my stomach had melted away after leaving Benny's. I had spent the afternoon leisurely lunching in downtown Houston, mentally rerunning my triumphant visit to the RV lot. Then, in mid-spoonful of the last of my leek-and-potato soup, a twinge of shame had hit me over that petty, little trophy I had given to Benny. On a long, post-lunch walk along Buffalo Bayou, I had rebuked myself that it was usually better to take the high road, and had vowed that's what I would do from then on.

Back on the actual road, I had been quickly reminded that leaving Houston so late in the day had landed me smack in the middle of rush-hour traffic coming into San Antonio. My penance for basking in my successful meeting while leaving Zoe alone for longer than I had planned.

While I walked from my car to the front porch, my phone went off—Christine, most likely wondering why I hadn't texted her after the meeting. I'd catch up to her later. The key turned too easily. The door was unlocked. I nudged it open, holding my keys pointed between my fingers like makeshift brass knuckles.

A groan from the middle of the dimly lit living room made my scalp tingle and my breath catch. I tripped over an object by the door. A shape shifted on the couch. Of course, it had to be Zoe. I exhaled with relief. The urgency in my bladder after the long drive pulled my focus to the hallway, toward the bathroom.

I was two feet from the bathroom door when a figure

emerged and crashed into me. I stumbled back, reached for the hall switch, and flipped on the light.

The naked man jumped back with a shriek, like a stepped-on cat. "Who the fuck are you?" he said with a bewildered squint, shielding his privates with fumbling hands. He was young, close to six feet. His face and arms from the biceps down were bronzed and the rest of him fish-belly pale. I had never seen him before, full frontal or otherwise. He reeked of booze.

"Who are you?" I shot back.

He blinked. "I, uh, I'm a friend of Zoe's."

"What are you doing in my house?"

"Uh, we ran out of vodka. So, uh, I was about to go to the store?"

"Find your pants, and get out of my house!"

"Yeah, uh, my uh, sorry."

He nodded like a big, dumb puppy, shuffled off to the living room, and picked a crumpled pair of jeans off the floor.

"Keep going!" I yelled. "Before I call the police."

He hopped on one foot while pulling up each leg of his pants.

"Go!" I yelled, stretching out my arm and pointing at the door. He stumbled away and gathered up what I must have tripped over when I came in, his shoes. Shirtless, with his hand on the knob and a white piece of clothing bunched under his arm, he twisted his head around to look back at me, his stubbled jaw hanging. Then he was out, the door slamming behind him.

I rushed into the bathroom and barely got my pants down before I peed into the toilet. Then in a panicky afterthought, I ran to the door and turned the deadbolt. It dawned on me that this was exactly the kind of situation in which I was supposed to race into my bedroom and grab my loaded gun. But, I had forgotten to be afraid—or brave—like a gun-toting home defender is supposed to be.

A dozen crushed beer cans littered the living room floor, and an empty fifth of vodka lay next to the couch, where Zoe was sprawled, conked out and naked. A strand of hair was stuck to the side of her gaping mouth, and her tongue poked out like a lizard's, trying to push it away. Her hand trailed onto the carpet. Purple panties and bra dangled off the arm of the sofa. No injuries were visible.

"Zoe." I turned on a lamp and shook her shoulders. "Are you all right?"

Her eyelids fluttered. She craned her neck to look up at me, struggled to open both her eyes, and pushed herself up on her hip. A goofy smile slashed her face. "Hi, Auntie Cahh-nee. What's up?"

"That's what I want to know. I came home to you passed out and a naked man walking out of my bathroom."

Zoe's eyes tracked in front of her, then rolled back, and she propped the side of her face with her hand to regain focus. Her face wobbled into another smile. She tapped a forefinger against her mouth. "Oh, that was... What's his name? Sigh... Sigh-mun, yeah that's it, Simon." Zoe smacked her lips like her tongue was too big for her mouth.

"You and Simon are friends?" I asked. I pulled a quilt off the back of the sofa and draped it across her.

"Yep," she said. The quilt slid down to expose a breast as she inched into a sitting position. "We met today at Spec's."

I sat down next to Zoe. "What were you thinking?" I said, managing to keep most of the anger out of my voice. "You picked up some guy at the liquor store and brought him here. He could have—anything could have happened. What did happen?"

Zoe shifted her shoulders up and down and moved her head from side to side. "We had a pa-a-r-t-a-ay!"

I grabbed her shoulders and shook her. "If you try anything stupid like this again, I swear, you're out of here." I shook her again. She gave me a vacant stare. "Do you hear me?"

She shrugged off my grasp. "Yeah, yeah. Whatever. What's the big deal anyway? You got a cigarette?"

"I don't smoke, and I didn't think you did either."

"You just don't have a clue."

"Oh? Is this your lifestyle now? Is this what you do?"

She drew her knees up to her chest under the quilt. "What if it is? You're not my mom. Oh, yeah, neither is she. You can't tell me what to do."

"In my house, I can, young lady."

"Fine. I'm getting the hell out of here." She snatched her phone, in a teal, cheetah-print case, off the coffee table, sprang to her feet, then held the sides of her head. "O-o-o." She fell back on the couch. "I'm going to be si— si—" She folded forward and threw up. The clear, foamy puke stank of vodka and spread onto the coffee table and dripped over the edge. She began to cry, big, ugly, gulping sobs.

I pulled her to me and stroked her tangled hair. "It's all right, sweetie. It's all right. We'll figure this out."

"Where's Daniel?" she wailed. "I need Daniel! Oh, shit, I need Daniel!"

"I'll call him, sweetie. I'll call him right now."

The inconsolable cries faded to whimpers.

– 1995 –

Daniel came out of his bedroom in his red Power Rangers pajamas, his chin on his chest.

"Hey, buddy, what's up?" I asked my six-year-old.

He pressed his face into my shoulder and sniffled.

I was sitting with Roanne at my dining room table. We'd been talking and shedding a few tears over coffee and cinnamon rolls. Roanne had driven down to Austin with Zoe after organizing a day camp visit in Round Rock for Stella. Johnny was at his job.

She'd timed her arrival for after Scott had left for work. Roanne and Johnny were in the middle of a divorce and living separately, the girls stayed with Johnny most of the time. With Scott's fierce loyalty to his comrade in arms from their Vietnam days, he had proclaimed Roanne unwelcome in our home, at least when he was there.

"Maybe we could have patched things up if Johnny had stayed in the army for at least twenty, like Scott," Roanne said, continuing with the conversation we were having before Daniel interrupted. "We wouldn't be fighting over the bills stacking up as well as everything else."

Daniel buried his face between my shoulder and chest and sobbed. I threaded my hand through his dark curls.

"Money problems make everything else worse, that's for sure," I said, "but it's not like things are so rosy with us. The retirement check helps, but Scott's not happy as a civilian. I guess you can take the man out of the army, but you can't take the army out of the man."

Daniel sniffled louder. I lifted his chin and brushed the tears off his cheeks. "What's going on, honey? Did you and Zoe have a fight?"

The sound of Zoe humming and singing drifted from the

bedroom. Daniel and Zoe had bonded from the first time Zoe held him as a newborn when she was four. Naturally, as the older of the two, Zoe could be bossy. Toddler Daniel didn't mind, but first-grade Daniel wasn't always the willing underling to his ten-year-old buddy.

Daniel shook his head in response to my question.

"Zoe, come here, please!" Roanne called.

Zoe, in purple leggings and sweatshirt, bounded in. Her large feet, disproportionate to her slender body, slapped the wood floor. "Are you taking me back home to Daddy?" she asked as she stood in front of Roanne, an expectant look on her face.

Roanne sighed a ragged breath and recovered with a smile. The time Roanne had with her daughters had become short and bittersweet. "Not yet. Daddy's at work." She put an arm around Zoe's waist and pulled her near. "You're having fun here, aren't you? I think Auntie Connie is going to make those lemon cupcakes you and Daniel like."

Zoe's face brightened, and she turned to me. "The ones with the little pieces in them?" she asked.

"Those are the ones," I said.

"Yay." Zoe clapped her hands.

I gazed at my son's still sullen face. "No smile, even for lemon cupcakes with the little pieces in them? Tell me what's going on."

He looked up at me, at Zoe, then back at me. "Zoe says I can't marry her."

Roanne and I had indulged Daniel's fantasy from the time he was three, when he announced that he and Zoe were going to marry when they were grownups. We thought it was cute. We had laughed, called it "precious."

"You don't have to worry about deciding who you're going to marry for a long time," I said, managing not to laugh at my little boy's serious frown.

"But she said never!" Daniel yelled. "She said I can't marry her because I'm her brother. She said brothers and sisters can't get married."

"Zoe's right. Brothers and sisters can't get married."

"But I'm not her brother."

Zoe, who had been standing calmly by, walked over to Daniel and put her hand on his shoulder. "You're like a brother to me, like the best brother in the whole world. You can't be my husband. That would be disgusting."

Tears pooled in Daniel's eyes, and his lower lip stuck out.

Zoe put her arms around Daniel, pulled him away from me, and smooshed him against her. "It's okay, Daniel. People who are married get divorced and then they're never together again, but if you're my brother, we can be together forever, okay?"

Daniel wiggled out of the hug. A smile spread across his face. "Okay. Let's play Mario Brothers." They walked back to the bedroom hand in hand.

Roanne blinked back tears and forced a smile. "Those two."

"Yeah," I said, "they're kind of amazing. Whatever else went wrong with you and Johnny, it was a brilliant decision to adopt Zoe."

Roanne shook her head. "More of an act of desperation by Johnny than a decision. We were slipping apart. He was in and out of work. My job was carrying us. He wasn't providing for me and Stella the way he had always done. You know how Johnny is."

"His male pride was on life support, having to live off a woman's paycheck."

"Exactly. He didn't know I had been with someone else, I had already broken it off, but Johnny had a sense that he was losing me. I could see it in his eyes every time he touched me, and every time I pulled away."

Joyful shouts and laughter spilled out of the bedroom, along with the beeps and buzzes of the video game, as Daniel opened the door and headed to the bathroom.

"Y'all thought the baby would mend your marriage," I said.

Roanne nodded. "He didn't necessarily want a second baby, but he knew I did, and he knew a pregnancy might kill me. We would have spent years on the adoption waiting list for a white infant. He did the research, found out China had baby girls to spare. He did all that before he even talked to me about it. It couldn't have been easy for him to make that choice. He definitely wanted a son instead of another daughter. And he had spent years seeing Asian faces as his enemies in war."

"Wow," I said. "Don't take this the wrong way, I know Johnny was crazy about you. I just never thought Johnny could deal with all that so that you could have a baby. That's incredible."

"I know everyone else doesn't see it, but Johnny's had his flashes of knight in shining armor. It was really hard for him to let his feelings come out, but when he did..."

Roanne lifted her coffee cup to her mouth, hiding her trembling lower lip.

"Zoe was the little miracle that brought us back together," she said. "When we came off that plane in Texas, our family was complete, Johnny, me, Stella, and Zoe."

She swiped at her eyes and stared over my shoulder. "On the drive home from the airport, we were crossing the bridge over the Colorado River. Stella always looks for kayaks down below when we make that trip."

"Christine would do that, too, when she was a kid."

"This time she wasn't even looking out the window. She was frozen in the back seat, staring at her new sister, like she was under a spell. A shower had just passed over. The sky was dark behind us, but ahead it was all bright blue and sunny. Johnny reached over and took my hand."

She spread her fingers and looked at her hand. "I can

almost feel it, even now," she said. "In that moment, I loved him so much, no matter what we had to face from then on, I was so sure nothing was ever going to break the four of us apart."

Tears stood in her eyes.

From behind the bedroom door, Zoe's giggles cascaded like piano scales. The corners of Roanne's mouth lifted, and she rested her chin in her hand as if to prop up her quivering smile.

I reached over and tapped her elbow. "She's still a miracle."

– 2019 –

Daniel set a cup of herbal tea in front of me on his kitchen bar. Most of the other rooms in his and Amy's house were packed up, ready for their move to Dallas. Four empty coconut-water bottles were lined up on the nearby counter next to a stack of dirty dishes. The smell of eggs and cheese and spinach lingered in the air, mixing with the aroma of a fresh pot of coffee, and the still-warm apple crumble cake I had brought over.

"It was rough, but she's made it through the last seventy-two hours," Daniel said. "The alcohol is out of her system."

Zoe's detox had left its toll on Daniel, too. His jaw was unshaven, his eyes puffy and bloodshot. He smelled stale, like wet clothes left in the washer too long.

"For now. We don't even know how deep she is in this," I said. "I didn't even leave her for a full day, and she... She could have been raped or kidnapped or killed. Not likely she's practicing safe sex. And she has so much to lose—school, her job."

The hiss and swoosh of a running shower sounded from the bathroom down the hall. Daniel poured himself a mug of coffee, pulled a chunk off the cake, and sat down on the bar stool next to mine.

"The good news is she's not taking drugs along with the alcohol," he said.

"She's telling the truth about that? She lied about everything else."

"My radar works pretty well. Remember, I was there once?" He finished off the piece of cake in one bite and rubbed his belly. "I did not need that. But it was so good."

"I know you were there, baby." I patted his arm. "Thank God, you put your life together, and you have Amy and the kids."

Remembering Daniel at eighteen was like rerunning a horror movie. An addiction to oxycodone after a basketball injury had turned him into a monster who stole, lied, threatened, hurt the people who loved him. At times, I thought I'd rather be dead than see him that way for another day. If not for his coach convincing him to go into rehab, he would have been lost forever.

He returned the arm pat. "And I have a new job in Dallas." My eyes misted. Even though my son had not lived with me for a decade, my house had begun to feel more empty in recent days, with the realization that he would soon be too far away to pop over in the middle of the week. Daniel rose to top off his coffee, and, while his back was turned, I dried my eyes on my shirtsleeve.

"While Amy and the kids are getting settled in the new house, I've asked Zoe to stay with me, so I can help her get things together," he said.

"Are you sure you can handle this? With moving and everything?" To give Daniel a hand looking after Zoe, I could put off my trip to El Paso to meet the man who was next up on my crusade list. I'd leave out the details about him, but I would have to tell Christine something soon—"someone I knew in college"—since I planned to ask my brother-in-law Barry to arrange a discount plane ticket. Otherwise, I'd have to drive the long, flat, mind-numbing stretch from San Antonio to the border city at the far west end of Texas. But the dread of the trip was nothing compared to my anxiety about confronting Brent Kincaid.

Benny Bing was a frail, old man who couldn't harm me. But, Brent, although he was in his sixties, was another story. He had been an athlete at UT when we dated, and eventually went on to a coaching career at UTEP. I had seen a photo of him on the sidelines of the football field in the *El Paso Times* from five years ago. He was a big man, still in good shape.

Daniel's coffee cup clinked as he set it on the bar. "I can handle it. Zoe has always listened to me."

Zoe had had a stubborn streak from the time she was a little kid. She ignored everyone else who talked until they were blue in the face trying to change her mind, but she listened to Daniel. When she was twenty-six, she'd reversed course on marrying a pro football player after a heart-to-heart with Daniel. Later, she had learned that the amorous athlete had been implicated in burning down the house of an ex-girlfriend.

"But, it's going to take more than rehydration, a home-cooked breakfast, and some hugs," Daniel said. "We've been talking about rehab programs."

"Are you getting through to her?"

"I think so, but I know how manipulative substance abusers can be. I could confiscate her money and her phone to keep her here, but that doesn't do much for trust, and, without that, she'll shut me down." Daniel cocked his head. "Is that the front door?"

I had also heard the click of a turning knob and the swish of air followed by a soft thud coming from the direction of the living room. I stood. "Maybe I didn't shut it all the way when I came in."

In the living room my purse lay on its side on the sofa with the contents spilled onto the cushion. A car engine started just outside, and, through the open blinds, I saw Mellow Yellow rolling backward down the driveway toward the street.

"Daniel!" I yelled. "Someone's taking my car!"

A cloud of steam poured into the hallway as Daniel threw the bathroom door open and shut off the water. I ran after him toward his garage, hopped into his SUV, and the tires squealed as we took off after Zoe, who was already a block and a half away.

"Trust, huh?" I said as I clicked on my seat belt in mid-car chase. "Add to your confiscation list any nearby car keys."

Daniel sat rigid, focused ahead, and put his foot into the

accelerator until we had closed the gap on my Bug on a frontage road that led to the expressway. Pieces of ragged rubber from a shattered eighteen-wheeler tire littered the pavement. Zoe sped up and swerved around the debris, then zigzagged, apparently losing control of the car. It careened off the road onto the grassy shoulder and came to a stop.

The VW door swung open, Zoe stepped out, and Daniel pulled his vehicle behind the Bug. Zoe took off in a jerky trot toward a line of trees, like a cornered fugitive in a true crime show, running with no place to go.

"Zoe, stop!" Daniel shouted. "We only want to help!"

He raced after her, caught up within several seconds, and corralled her arms. They fell forward in a clump of Indian paintbrush and dandelions. Daniel rolled Zoe onto her back and straddled her, pinning her upper arms while she flailed her fists. The image of Daniel above Zoe, holding her down, blurred and became Brent and me in our twenties in the same position in another place. My heart thumped wildly. The image reshaped itself into Daniel pulling Zoe up and into an embrace, stroking her back, murmuring into her ear, her cheek nodding against his shoulder.

When Daniel and Zoe returned to the SUV, Zoe let go a stream of apologies and shame, blubbering from the back seat, "I know you think I'm a total loser, Auntie Connie, a total freaking loser."

All I could manage to respond was, "Why?" I was asking about more than my car.

"I wasn't going to buy booze," she protested. "I swear." Daniel's eyes shot a hard, skeptical stare into the rearview mirror. "I was only trying to go to your house and get my car," she said to me. "So I could go back to Arlington, to work and school." She blubbered some more.

"But, why didn't you tell us?" I asked. "We would have—"

Daniel cut me off. "That's total bullshit, Zoe."

"No, Daniel, I swear. I don't want to screw things up for

you."

"The only way you can screw things up for me is if you keep lying." He swung around to face her. "Haven't we always trusted each other, been honest with each other?"

She sniffled, rubbed snot from her nose with the back of her hand, and nodded.

"I don't have your life," Zoe said. "I don't have a family and a nice house and all my shit together like you. You want honest? I dropped out of school, my job fired me, I got evicted from my apartment."

Daniel leaned farther into the back seat. "You've still got me. You've always got me. And a place to stay until we figure this out."

"Shit, Daniel. I can't hold it together for more than a couple of days. I can't do it. Just let me go. Please. Let me go."

"No, not a chance." He grabbed her arm and pulled her closer to the back of his seat. "I'll make a deal with you. I leave for Dallas in two and a half weeks. You stay with me and stay sober until then, and, after that, I'll back off or I'll help you with whatever you want to do, get into rehab, live in your car, go back to Arlington, whatever."

"Daniel," I butted in, "are you sure that's a good idea?"

He ignored me and focused on Zoe. "From this second on, the slate's clean. I trust you. You trust me. Do we have a deal?"

Zoe pulled loose from Daniel, rocked forward and back, her arms wrapped around her rib cage, her face squinched up like Roanne's had when she was thinking about something serious.

"Zoe," I said, "there's no way you're going to live in your car."

She ignored me and locked eyes with Daniel. "You trust me. I trust you. We have a deal."

Daniel swiveled to face the windshield, started the engine, and turned to me. "Mom, are you okay to drive your car back?"

I looked at Zoe, then Daniel. I was an extra person in the

scene. "Sure."

After Daniel drove off with Zoe, I lay back against the headrest in my car, shut my eyes, breathed deeply, and tried to push worries about Zoe out of my head. My limbs were drained and limp from the last exhausting hour. The midday sun glared off the windshield and soon warmed the small pocket of air that surrounded me. My fingers, wrapped around the keys in the ignition, loosened their grip and fell into my lap. I began to drift off. Thoughts of what awaited in El Paso bounced inside my head, like a bunch of balloons tapping at a closed window, noiseless but insistent.

Strong hands gripped my upper arms. I tried to lift myself, but a force pushed me down. A weight pressed against my chest.

"Stop it! Get off me, Brent! No!"

My screams woke me to the familiar interior of Mellow Yellow. The tightness around my arms disappeared. Breath filled my lungs. My sweat-soaked clothes clung to me. My thighs were clenched so hard, my muscles cramped. I took deep breaths, and slowly the tension flowed out.

I could take my gun to El Paso. I had meant to practice loading it. The guy at the shooting range had done it for me during a safety lesson. Stowed in my nightstand drawer next to the Glock was a box of fifty 9mm shells, the smallest count I could find, resisting the pitch of the gun salesman to stock up. Fifty rounds of any kind of ammo seemed excessive for anyone not named Rambo. I didn't plan to use the gun, but Brent had overpowered me before. I wouldn't let it happen again.

– 1970 –

My feet cleared the last level of the green, wooden bleachers, and I scanned the grassy area between the football field and the parking lot, looking for Roanne. A stream of fans, whooping and high-fiving, flowed around me, emptying the stands on the visitor side of the field. Our high school team had annihilated South High fifty-six to seven on the other team's turf.

Folks in our neighborhood, even families who didn't have high school kids, scheduled their Friday nights around the Bonham High games, and Roanne and I would be among the cheering crowd in our blue-and-white sweatshirts. We were juniors, underclassmen no more. I had my learner's permit, and sometimes Dad let me drive with him to the home games. Roanne was dating Mitch McCormick, the senior quarterback, and the Bonham Bobcats were rolling toward the state championship. Things were going well, even on the days when we didn't check our horoscopes in the newspaper for guidance.

Roanne had walked to the parking area after the game to personally congratulate Mitch on his six touchdown passes before the team boarded the bus back to the school. She and Mitch had been going out for three weeks, after he bumped into her in the cafeteria, sending her opened carton of chocolate milk flying. He had apologized, bought her another chocolate milk, and asked her out that afternoon.

"It was destiny," Roanne had told me. Her horoscope that day had forecast "an unexpected encounter will have a strong effect." Plus, Mitch was a Scorpio, the most compatible match for Cancer, Roanne's sign. I was, apparently, supposed to be on the lookout for an Aries, the ideal fit for Gemini.

I spied Roanne walking across the grass, but, as I moved

toward her, she picked up her pace and headed the opposite direction. I ran to catch up.

"Hey, Ro, where're you going?" I grabbed her arm. When she turned toward me, I gasped.

Her bottom lip was split. A trickle of blood had dried on her chin. One side of her face blazed red, and her eyes were puffy from crying.

"Ro, what happened?"

She looked around to where the crowd was dispersing well behind us, but she kept her voice low. "M-Mitch," she sobbed.

"Mitch did that to you?"

"When I found him in the parking lot, he was with that cheerleader, Peggy, the one with the pigtails and the big bows. He had his arms around her waist. We got into an argument."

"We have to find your dad, maybe we should call the police—"

"No!" She grabbed my upper arms. "He said he was sorry. I don't want to get him in trouble."

"You can't let him get away with this."

"He's not a bad guy. If I report it, he could lose his chance for a scholarship from Notre Dame. I can't mess up his life because he lost his temper one time." She put her hand to her swollen cheek. "It's nothing, just a bruise."

"But, Ro—"

"I'm not going to tell anyone, and you can't either."

"Here comes your dad and sister." Mr. Slater walked toward us in his slow, rocking gait with Darla beside him sucking on a bullet-shaped, red popsicle. "What're you going to tell them?"

"I fell coming down the bleachers, okay?"

I bit my lip, looked at her brutalized face, then at her dad and Darla closing the gap between us, and back at Roanne.

"Okay?" she repeated, her tone frantic.

"On one condition. You don't go out with him again, no matter how sorry he says he is. Promise me."

"I shouldn't have said anything about Peggy. I overreacted. He's not going to do it again."

"Are you sure?" I dug in my purse, pulled out my compact, and held up the small, round mirror to Roanne's face. "Are you sure he's not going to do that again?"

Roanne flinched at her reflection, wet her finger, and rubbed the blood off her chin. She shoved the compact toward me. "All right, I'm done with him."

"Promise?"

"I promise."

Mr. Slater and Darla walked up. Roanne turned to the side but not quickly enough to hide her face from her little sister.

"Holy moly! Did you get in a fight?" Darla said.

Mr. Slater grabbed Roanne's arm and spun her around in front of him. When he saw her face, he pulled his chin in and frowned.

Before he had a chance to say anything, Roanne spoke up, "I fell on the bleachers. I was running down, and I slipped. Someone spilled a drink."

Mr. Slater leaned in closer to Roanne's face, inspected it, and frowned again. "You need to slow down. You got yourself good. Did you see what happened, Connie?"

I wanted to shake my head and run home, but Roanne was giving me the side-eye. "It was so fast. She stepped in a puddle of Dr Pepper, and her legs went out from under her. There was nothing I could do. Or anyone could do, really." Parts of that were kind of the truth. I did see a little kid spill a Dr Pepper right after halftime. His mom sat in it and started hollering at him.

Mr. Slater wagged a finger at Roanne. "You gotta watch yourself, girl. The emergency room ain't free. And I ain't made of money."

"You don't have to take me to the emergency room," Roanne said. "It's just a bruise."

"Good thing, too, your mother costs me plenty." He

pinched her chin between his thumb and forefinger and inspected her face again while she winced. "Better get some ice on that lip when we get home." He let go of her face and turned to me. "Connie, I didn't see Joey out on the field tonight. Is he hurt?"

I shrugged. "I don't know." Joey had gotten in a fight with a teammate at practice and was benched for the next two games.

I moved closer to Roanne and tuned out Mr. Slater. He was droning on about the Bobcats' win-loss record from last season.

"Does it hurt much?" Darla asked her big sister.

"Some."

"Here." Darla handed her popsicle to Roanne. "Ice for your lip."

She took one of Roanne's hands, I took the other elbow, and we quickened our steps across the grass, leaving Mr. Slater behind.

– 2019 –

I arrived at The Crossing, a neighborhood bar near the El Paso airport, an hour and a half before the meeting. In a corner booth, I sipped a martini to relax my anxiety. The extra time would allow the buzz to wear off enough to keep me alert.

I had contacted Brent via Facebook with a believable enough story, that I was a novelist researching El Paso as a locale for my next book. I said I had found his page online and thought it might be fun to pick the brain of a longtime local resident whom I had also known during our college days.

His response was an enthusiastic "Come on down," and he even referred to me as "Connie with the flaming red hair," a clue that he had at least some memory of me from when we were at UT.

My cell buzzed. The caller ID showed the call was from my editor, Claire. I let it go to voicemail. My April 1 rewrite deadline had passed two weeks ago, while I focused on my "call-the-bastards-out crusade," as Christine had dubbed it.

A tall man with ruddy cheeks and silver hair, wearing a UTEP sweatshirt, walked in, cast his eyes around the bar, and squinted at me. I waved him over.

He slid into the booth across from me with a wide grin. "Connie, Connie, Connie. You're not a redhead anymore, but I've undergone a few transformations over the years myself." He ran a hand through his thinning hair.

I remembered how blue his eyes were, and those hadn't changed.

"You look good," he said and motioned to a server. "What're you drinking?"

I tilted the empty martini glass and smiled. "I'm afraid one is my limit. Water's fine."

"Water it is," he told the server, "and an IPA." He leaned

toward me as the server left to retrieve the drinks. I tried not to be obvious about drawing back a couple of inches. "So, you're a mystery writer. I looked you up online. I was impressed."

My fingers tapped nervously on the table. "Not exactly Nora Roberts, but I do all right."

"Any way I can help, I'm happy to do it." The server delivered the drinks. Brent upended his glass and took a generous swallow. "How does this work? Do you have a list of questions for me? I can talk forever on El Paso. There's hardly a place I haven't been to or an odd fact I don't know."

"If you don't mind, I wanted to chat for a bit, kind of reminisce."

"Sure thing."

My throat turned dry and scratchy. I took a gulp of water. "Do you remember the first time we were together?"

He cocked his head from side to side like he was trying to remember. "We went to the 'Dillo. That unknown guitar player, that skinny kid from New Jersey got everyone hyped up. What was his name again?" He grinned like he was telling himself a joke. "Oh, yeah, Springsteen."

That was one of many times as a college kid that I hung out at the Armadillo World Headquarters, an abandoned National Guard Armory that became a music mecca in Austin. But I wasn't here to talk about great memories of the famed but now defunct 'Dillo.

"I mean the first time we were to-*geth*-er," I said.

He stared at me. His eyes widened as what I was saying apparently clicked. "You mean intimately?"

"Yes."

"I remember you were really into it." His voice had a swagger.

I shook my head. "You must be remembering the wrong girl. I was anything but 'into it.' In fact, I said I wasn't ready. I said 'no,' I said 'stop,' but you did it anyway."

Again, I felt his large hands pulling at my clothes, peeling them away, his knee pushing my legs apart, his breath hot against my throat, the smell of Polo cologne, his tongue in my ear, the pain rammed up into me with a succession of grunts. My will holding my body rigid, my eyes squeezed shut, hot tears leaking from the outside corners and wetting my hair at my temples, the mantra in my head, "Let it be over, let it be over, let it be over..."

The clink of glasses at the bar pulled me back, and I was aware of his casual voice.

"I admit, I did come on strong in those days," he said. "And you girls said 'no' all the time when you really meant 'yes.'" He smiled as though we were shooting the breeze over some long-ago breach of etiquette. He took another pull on his beer.

"I meant 'no.' There was no confusion about that. You held me down on your couch. You raped me."

He choked on the beer and slammed the bottle down on the table. "What? I ra— No way. If I did, you would have called the cops."

"I was too humiliated, ashamed to tell anyone. Nobody talked about date rape in 1974. I blamed myself for putting myself in a bad situation."

"Then flash forward to the 2000s, Me Too, and, all of sudden, you and all these other women decided they were raped three, four decades ago. Well, here's my take on that. These women, for one reason or another, are unhappy with how their lives turned out. They can't lose those fifteen extra pounds, they didn't get their dream man, their kids are acting up in school, they have an opioid problem. They ask themselves, 'When did it all start to go wrong?' and they pick out some dude from the past and put it all on him."

"You think this is about extra belly fat?" Both my fists came down on the table, rattling my water glass. "This is about sexual assault. You tell me how many times a week when you're out and about, cruising down a bike path, walking across a parking lot, playing basketball on the corner after dark, you have to think about someone knocking you down and forcing himself inside of you? Women have to think about that all the time."

"Well, well," he stammered, "that's how things are. That's anatomy and animal instinct. Men are more powerful physically than women. That doesn't make us all monsters."

"And yet, I'm sitting here with a loaded gun in my purse, just in case." I had managed to slip one round in the Glock. I had left the other forty-nine in the box in my nightstand.

Brent's head snapped back, and his eyes cut to my purse on the seat beside me. He leaned over the table again and narrowed his eyes. "You're threatening me? I'm warning you, I don't scare easy. What do you want?"

"I want you to do the right thing. Tell me you know what you did, you raped me, and it was wrong."

"I won't, because I didn't. And I'm not going to say that I did just to buy into your self-pity, so you can record my confession on your phone, invent some criminal charges or sue me. Remember, we started dating again in the fall semester. We even had sex a few times during those months. I guess I must have done you better, and you decided that was consensual."

"It's taken decades for me to come to terms with that. I wasn't with you to absolve you. I was trying to absolve myself by reinventing my memory of you."

"Victim psychology bullshit. I'll countersue your ass off if you try anything. I won't take this lying down."

"An ironic choice of words. I'm not interested in publicly accusing you. I only wanted to say to your face what you did, whether you want to go on lying to yourself or not."

"I'm lying?" He pushed his beer to the side and leaned across the table.

Without taking my eyes off him, I reached for my purse on the seat and fingered the catch open. My thumb slid along the grip of the gun. We were locked in a stare down for half a minute before he pushed back with his palms pressed against the edge of the table.

I pulled my hand up from under the table, his shoulders tensed, then relaxed when my hand came up with a ten-dollar bill and my cell. I tapped on the phone screen.

"What are you doing?" he said, eyeing me warily.

I continued to tap. "I'm not recording. I'm calling an Uber." I tossed the bill on the table and stood up.

Brent twisted around in his seat to keep me in his sight. "If I need a lawyer, I have one."

"Do you have a conscience?" I walked out.

I stood on the dark sidewalk outside the bar to wait for my ride share. The area seemed seedier than it had in the daylight. The nearest streetlight wasn't working. The pavement was cracked, uneven, and smelled of urine. Traffic was sparse. A group of men in hoodies gathered on the corner, cursing and laughing loudly. A man in a dirty parka and knit hat ran down the sidewalk, careening toward me. The blast of a car horn from the opposite direction startled me and jerked my head toward the sound.

A forearm closed around my throat from behind. I grabbed his arm, dug in my nails, tried to pull out of my attacker's grasp. "Stop it, Brent!"

I planted my feet and managed to turn into his body, spinning halfway out of his hold. He shoved me down on the sidewalk. When he bent forward and grabbed my purse, I was staring at a man with a knit hat and a dirty parka, in his twenties, with a face tattoo. I gripped my purse as hard as I could, but it was slipping out of my grasp as he tugged at it. I had to bring that stupid gun, and now he was going to take it and kill me.

"Hey, punk, get away from her!" Brent's voice boomed from the door of the bar. He rushed at the attacker who let go of my purse and stood to defend himself. Brent punched him in the jaw, and the man staggered. He had almost regained his balance when Brent drew his fist back for a second punch, but the guy scrambled away, picking up speed as he rounded the corner.

I pulled myself to my feet. My legs were jelly.

"Are you all right?" Brent asked, reaching his arm toward me but not touching me.

"Y-yeah." My throat was sore, the side of my neck was tender. For a second, I lost my bearings. Then I remembered I was in front of the bar, waiting for an Uber. My eyes refocused on the street. A white Nissan slowed and pulled up to the curb.

"Is that your ride?" Brent asked. "Check the license plate."

I glanced at my phone, matching the numbers to the car, and nodded. "It's okay."

Brent opened the car door, and I scooted onto the back seat. I looked up at him. "Thank you," I said with a pang of guilt overlaid with confusion that turned my stomach.

He backed away with a disgusted scowl. "Don't mention it. I'm the bad guy, remember?"

I shrank down in my seat and turned away from the window as the car glided up the street headed to the El Paso airport. I had been prepared for the men on my list to be arrogant, nasty, threatening, even dangerous. What I had not prepared for was for any of them to be heroic. What was I really confronting but ghosts of men who no longer existed? Where was the righteousness in that?

– 2007 –

"How did I let this happen, Ro?" My voice was hoarse from fatigue and crying.

I sat in the hospital waiting room, my pajama top haphazardly tucked into my jeans, sockless feet shoved into tennis shoes, bare toes curled. Roanne had just arrived and held tightly to my hand.

My eighteen-year-old son was lying somewhere in the inner reaches of an unfamiliar medical building where healthcare personnel I had never met were trying to drag him out of a drug overdose and back to life.

"I watched him walk across the stage in his cap and gown three weeks ago. He was set to go off to Baylor in September. Why didn't I see this coming?"

"All you need to have on your mind right now is that he'll be all right," Roanne said. "It doesn't help Daniel to beat yourself up. You got him to the hospital. You did the right thing."

The waiting room air was cold and scrubbed clean of smell. My toe tapped uncontrollably against the red and lavender swirls of the thin carpet.

Roanne walked over to the window and pulled back the thick, cream-colored drapes. The silvery-blue glow of dawn leaked in, showing small fingerprint smudges, where fidgety children had pressed against the glass at some time in the past. The light made the two unoccupied rows of purple-cushioned chairs seem emptier and revealed that the colorless walls were actually pale green.

Daniel had first been prescribed oxycodone in December after shattering his ankle during a high school basketball game. Why hadn't I seen the signs earlier? Pinpoint pupils, the lie to cover up. "Just tired, Mom. I stayed up all night studying for my chemistry test." The mood flashes from happy-go-lucky to belligerent and threatening.

He had waved me off after he slipped in late at night, seemingly intoxicated but not smelling of alcohol, and escaped to his room, slamming the door in my face. When I had found the extra pill bottle, the one with no label, he'd said he had misplaced it weeks ago after picking it up from the pharmacy and then found it under his bed. It wasn't a new bottle, he had said, but an old one that had been missing.

We had argued almost daily, about where he'd been, who he'd been with, why he was late. I ranted, pleaded. He hurled vile names. Once, he had shoved me against the kitchen island and bruised my hip. He had then stormed out and was gone for two days.

Cash had gone missing from my purse, but I couldn't remember spending it. A pair of diamond earrings had been misplaced, although I couldn't recall the last time I had worn them. The TV in Daniel's room had suddenly disappeared. "Best Buy had a trade-in deal," he had told me. He had ordered an upgraded model for his dorm room, but the store was temporarily out of stock. "Should be here in four to six weeks," he had said. The new TV never appeared, and a voice nagging at the back of my brain had told me I should have known better.

Several hours before agonizing within the anemic green walls of the hospital waiting room, I had been sleeping fitfully, excited about Roanne arriving in San Antonio in the morning. We had planned an early hike to Comanche Lookout. Around 3 a.m. a crash in Daniel's room had awakened me. I had found him on the floor, the pieces of a broken lamp scattered beside him, his body twitching, a leg raised with the foot tangled in the sheet, damp spikes of hair pasted to his corpse-white face, his lips blue. I had screamed into the phone to the dispatcher. Minutes had stalled like an eternity while I waited for the ambulance.

Roanne pulled her backpack from under a waiting room chair, fished around in the pack, pulled out a bag of M&Ms, and offered them to me. I waved her off. She was dressed in khaki shorts, a plaid shirt tied at the waist, and hiking boots with pink laces, all ready for our outing. When I had called her, she had detoured to the hospital.

"You have to eat something," she said. "Do you want me to see what I can find in the vending machines? Something warm?"

"Daniel's coach is here. He went for coffee."

I had called Steve Landry, the basketball coach, after five tries and five frantic voicemails to Scott and to his new wife. Neither had called back. I hadn't been able to think of who else to call, besides Steve, after the ER personnel took my unconscious son away on a gurney, and I was alone and trapped by a whirlwind of panic in the waiting room.

The double doors down the hall swished, and Steve walked in with two twelve-ounce Starbucks cups, steam escaping from the vents.

"Here you go," he said, handing me one.

I introduced Roanne, and Steve handed his drink to her, insisting he really didn't need it. I took a sip of coffee and struggled to keep it down.

"Have they told you anything?" Steve asked, folding his long frame into a chair across from mine, then leaning forward, the muscles around his eyes squeezed with concern. He was a six-and-a-half-foot, former college athlete with a short Afro, huge hands, and feet that seemed inhumanly large in red and black Jordans.

I shook my head. "Not yet. It's been more than three hours."

"I think that's a good sign," he said.

I was going to ask him why, but I let it go. People said random stuff to make you feel better when they didn't know what else to say.

"Thanks for coming," I said.

He nodded.

The doors swished again and Scott bulled in, bleary-eyed, hair sticking every which way, in a T-shirt and sweatpants that bagged at the butt. He would have just driven a hundred and forty miles from Marble Falls to San Antonio.

"What the hell's going on?" he bellowed. He came toward me.

Steve stood and took a protective stance between Scott and me with his palms outward. "Let's calm down, man."

"Who the hell is this?" Scott said, jerking his thumb toward Steve but looking at me.

"Coach Landry, Daniel's dad," I said.

Scott huffed and glared at me. "Where's Daniel? Somebody better start talking."

"The doctors are working on him," I said as calmly as I could manage, although my voice trembled. "We're waiting for information."

Scott leaned in past Steve. Six inches from my face, his angry mouth flapped. "What the hell happened?" he demanded.

My hands shook. "He took an overdose of oxy."

"Oxy? What's Daniel doing with oxy?"

"He's been taking it since December," I said, "when he hurt his ankle. And, then..." I choked down a sob. "It got out of hand."

"And you didn't notice?" His words felt like slaps across my face. "My son has a drug problem, and you don't have a clue?"

Roanne moved behind my chair and put a hand on my shoulder. "This is not helping, Scott."

Scott leaned toward Roanne, his torso hovering over my body. "I see the gang's all here." He growled out the words, then dropped into a seat, leaving a vacant chair in between him and me.

Steve walked to the window, pretended to look out while

keeping a sideways glance focused on Scott. Roanne stayed on guard behind me. I shut my eyes and took deep breaths, trying to block out Scott's huffing and throat clearing. Roanne's fingers tapped gently against the back of my chair. Steve muffled a cough. Female voices and an elevator bell sounded in the distance.

Scott shifted in his chair and barked, "You really fucked it up this time, Connie."

A wail of anguish built in my chest. Yes, I had. And now my precious boy—

Sharp footsteps approached, my eyes snapped open. Everyone in the room turned toward the hallway opposite the exit. A fiftyish man wearing horn-rimmed glasses and a white coat, and holding a clipboard, walked to the center of the room.

"Mr. and Mrs. McHenry?" he called out.

It was odd to hear my former married name but, at that moment, inconsequential. I stood. Scott was on his feet beside me. Our hands reached between us and intertwined in an anxious grip. We leaned toward the doctor.

"Daniel will be all right," the doctor said. "The nurse will be out shortly to take you back to see him."

"Thank God!" Scott and I blurted out in one voice. We fell into each other's arms and sobbed.

– 2019 –

My editor called repeatedly the morning after I returned home from El Paso, and I continued to avoid her. I had dealt with Christine with a quick text, "I'm OK." But, when my ringtone erupted for the sixth time, I decided to face the music and my missed deadline like a grownup. I snatched up the phone, but it wasn't Claire. Daniel was calling from Dallas, knocking the air out of me with his news.

"What do you mean, Zoe's missing?" I asked. "Aren't those rehab places strict about clients leaving the premises?"

Daniel and Zoe had stuck to their contract. She had stayed sober for the two and half weeks she stayed with Daniel, then decided rehab was her best alternative. Daniel and Stella had coordinated her admission to a substance abuse center in Virginia since the waiting lists for the ones in Texas were so long. I hadn't had a chance to say goodbye to her. Her flight to Richmond, where Stella would meet her, had left San Antonio just hours before I left for El Paso.

"Apparently, she didn't get that far," Daniel said. "I took her to the airport and walked with her as far as the TSA line. That's the last time I saw her. I had to take off for Dallas. It wouldn't look good to be late my first day on the new job. Stella called last night, said Zoe never showed up."

"Didn't she have a connection in Atlanta?"

"Even if she missed her connection, there were two later flights. She should be there by now. And her cell goes straight to voicemail."

"Goodness gracious, Daniel. What do you think happened?" I looked out my front window at Zoe's red Honda that had been parked in my driveway since she had left to stay at Daniel's house.

"She got cold feet about the rehab, ducked out of the

airport in San Antonio or in Atlanta, maybe went back to Arlington. I don't know."

"Have you reported her missing to the police?" For a split second, I was relieved that Roanne would not know about this, would not worry herself sick.

"Yes, but it's not a high priority. She wasn't impaired the last time I saw her. I couldn't offer any information that would raise suspicion of foul play. Just the opposite, she's an adult with no history of mental illness or harm to herself or by others who is not in the habit of letting family know her whereabouts."

I tried to remember any person or place Zoe had mentioned when she was staying with me that might give a clue as to where she would go. That naked guy in my house. What was his name? It was one of the lesser Chipmunks. Simon. Simon with no last name, a drinking buddy she'd met at a liquor store. At Spec's, a chain outfit. They were all over town.

"Do you have a recent photo of Zoe on your phone?" I asked Daniel. "You young people are always taking photos."

"Yes. I took some this week. I gave those to the police."

"Send those to me."

"What're you going to do?"

"Hit the bars and liquor stores, see if anyone recognizes her."

"Wait, Mom, there are hundreds of bars and liquor stores in San Antonio, and we don't even know if she's still in town. And it's not safe for you to do that."

"A needle in a haystack. Do you have a better idea?"

"I've talked to Uncle Barry. He's going to use his connections with security at the airport. At least we might be able to find out if she got on the plane in San Antonio."

"How long is that going to take?"

"We should hear from him by tonight. Sit tight and try not to worry. That won't help."

I gave sitting tight and not worrying a try for about three minutes. My head pounded. Sleep had eluded me for months since Roanne's funeral. I still woke up in the wee hours angry and shaking, thinking about her. The confrontations with Joey, Benny, and Brent hadn't kept that panic at bay. I searched through the medicine cabinet for ibuprofen and instead found a bottle that looked empty but rattled with a single, tiny pill when I shook it. Christine had given me the Xanax long ago to help me sleep on the plane during a book tour, but I hadn't taken it.

Diving back into my writing would take my mind into another space, away from Roanne and Zoe, for at least a while. The medicine I needed was Claire's gentle, persistent nagging, telling me to get my butt in gear, but a lone orange tablet was all I had at the moment, and I swallowed it.

I opened the most recent Maxie Dallas file on my computer. At what chapter had I left things? I did a word search for "pineapple." That's where I had taken a wrong turn, according to Claire, taking Maxie out of cozy mode and putting her into attack attitude, about to sling a pineapple at the head of a chauvinist cop. If I wrote at least one sentence, I could truthfully tell Claire, the next time she called, that I had been working on the book.

Yes, I was working, and the mad swirl of agitation in my head was calming to a slower, manageable rotation. I rewound the scene with Maxie and the jerk detective and the pineapple on the table in front of Maxie. How could I make this work as a cozy mystery scene?

Another actor entered the scene, taking shape on the screen with the tapping of my fingers on the keyboard: a millennial woman with short spiky hair, a "Lemonade" tattoo on her arm and another of a bee on her neck. Maxie's niece, an apprentice detective, wouldn't make anyone a pineapple upside-down cake, least of all the jerk detective. She could hurl a large piece of fruit at that guy's head on behalf of Maxie and all women who had been the object of male condescension. Or she could tell him off, let him know how much of an ass he was, making the throwing of a pineapple unnecessary. I'd introduce her as a minor character who could show up later in a subsequent Maxie Dallas mystery or in a series of her own.

If only I could get Claire to buy in. I'd present my idea to Claire ahead of time, or should I rewrite the scene, send it off, and surprise her? I couldn't decide. I was so relaxed. My wrists were heavy.

That kick-ass gal needed a name, a millennial name. Jessica, Amanda, Amber, Danielle. Zoe. Zo-o-o-o...

The discomfort of my cheek smooshed into the keyboard eventually woke me. The last sentence of the new scene in my novel was "tttttccchhhhyyyykkkkkk."

I had been asleep for almost three hours. I checked my phone for calls from Barry or Claire, but neither had reached out to me. I had to do something other than wait. I called Zoe's number. Maybe she would pick up if she saw the call was from me.

"Bueno?" a tentative female voice on the other end said.

"Bueno? Is Zoe there?"

"No entiendo."

"Who is this? *Quien es?"*

"Maribel. I am cleaning at the airport. I take the phone."

"You took Zoe's phone?"

"I find. I take the phone now. I take to lost and found."

"Lost and found? You found the phone at the airport? At the San Antonio Airport?"

"Si. I am cleaning *en el bano.* I take the phone to lost and found." She hung up.

I called the number again, and it went to voicemail. I Googled San Antonio International Airport and found a number for the lost and found. The recording told me it was open until 6 p.m. and that a description and identification was required to retrieve a lost item.

I rushed to the airport and to a gray counter tucked in a corner near the baggage claim area. I had never noticed it before, but I had never had to check on any lost items. Three people waited in line in front of me, but a half hour later I was face to face with a smiling, young, Hispanic woman.

"Can I help you, ma'am?" she asked, not unpleasantly, but with a voice that revealed she had said the phrase a hundred times that day.

"Yes. I talked to someone earlier, a cell phone, an iPhone with a teal, cheetah-print case was turned in today."

The counter woman disappeared into a back room and returned with what looked like Zoe's phone. I pulled out my ID.

"Ms. Canelli," the representative said, "do you have something that will show this is your phone?"

"Well, it's actually not my phone. It belongs to Zoe Kirkland, my friend's daughter. She's missing. Her phone might have some clue about where she is."

"Is she a minor under your care which would give you the authority to claim her property?"

"No. She's thirty-four. I've known her since she was a baby. Her mom was my best friend for fifty years. She died." The woman at the counter was staring at me like I was speaking space alien. "Zoe was staying at my house. She was upset about her mom. She had been drinking, and—" I stopped my runaway mouth to mentally regroup. "I have the number." I punched in Zoe's number, and the phone on the counter buzzed.

"Yes, ma'am, but without proof—"

"Look." I scrolled through my phone. "Here, she's in my contacts. Here's a text from her from last week. Here's a photo of us together. Why would I have all this if I wasn't telling you the truth? I need her phone. Give it to me." I reached for the phone.

The representative slid the phone back and under the

counter. Her face had turned into a wall. "Ma'am, I can't allow you to take the phone. Can you step aside please?"

"That's it? Step aside?"

"Step aside, ma'am." Her eyes cut to the left toward the terminal exit.

I was conscious of a large man in uniform between the counter and the glass double doors, about sixty feet away. This was an airport. These people didn't play around. Still, Zoe's phone was the only clue that she had been in the terminal.

"Just one more thing, please," I said, relaxing my shoulders into a less threatening posture. "Can you check for another lost item?"

The woman cut off a sigh with a pained smile, something else she had likely done a hundred times in one day. "Describe the item, ma'am."

"A North Face backpack, gray with aqua piping. It may have ID inside for Zoe Kirkland."

"But you're not Ms. Kirkland, ma'am. That's not your property."

"No, but can't you still check? Please?"

"Any suspicious or abandoned bags are handled by security, ma'am."

Of course. I had heard the announcement dozens of times in airport terminals. "Report any suspicious or abandoned bags to security."

The man in uniform was headed my way. Had the rep pressed a panic button hidden below the counter?

I couldn't help Zoe by being hauled into the bowels of the airport and interrogated by security forces. I nodded a quick "thank-you" and made a wide, moseying circle around the nearest baggage carousel, taking a long, casual stroll to the exit to look like the opposite of a suspicious person running away.

By the time I wound my way home through an hour's worth of traffic, I had become a reasonable person again. I would call Daniel about the phone so that he could pass the information on to the police. And I'd call Stella. Next of kin probably had some authority when it came to lost and found phones, and Stella could throw around her status in the FBI. She was a budget analyst, but she could leave that part out.

Barry called just before midnight. He had managed to convince an airport security officer to allow him to view videotape of the TSA queue and of the Southwest gates where Zoe would likely have ended up before her flight.

"I would have liked to send you a copy of that tape, but that was not going to happen," Barry said. "I was pushing my luck as it was, even though my guy at the airport is a longtime buddy."

"Did you see her on the video?"

"Yes. I took notes." The rattle of paper came through the phone. "She definitely goes through TSA, and she makes it to her gate. The tape is grainy and has no audio, but judging by her posture and movements, she's very antsy, pacing back and forth, standing up, sitting down, unable to keep still. About forty-five minutes from the first sighting, she goes off-camera for a good while, and the next time she's seen, she's shouting something, flipping someone off, and staggering a bit. Apparently, there's a bar in that area out of camera shot. She may be impaired at that point and is told to leave, which she takes exception to. She stumbles off toward the gate, stretches out on a row of chairs, and falls asleep for the next couple of hours."

"She must have missed her flight while she was passed out."

"Right. When she gets up, she looks around like she's trying to get her bearings, walks to the window, and stares out at the tarmac for a while. Then she heads for the exit back out of the secure area."

"She left the terminal."

"Most likely. That was the last sighting, about one a.m. yesterday."

"Did she have her backpack when she left?"

"Hmm, yeah, I saw it, she did."

So, Zoe didn't leave town, she probably had at least some money and her ID. And she had been missing for nearly forty-eight hours. I had witnessed some of her risky behavior. That was plenty of time to be hurt or worse.

– 1969 –

Roanne and I huddled on the edges of the "Fall Frolic" dance in the Bonham High gym. The room was semi-dark, and circles of colored light played off the ceiling and walls. Most of the kids at the event were sophomores, like us, and juniors. Seniors were too cool to come, and freshmen were too timid.

We watched a dancing dude in a wide-collared tan shirt and lime green bellbottoms. His elbows and knees jerked like muscle spasms, but the girl gyrating across from him was all smiles like he was cool.

"I think kids should at least try to match up their dance moves," Roanne said. "She's hula hooping, and he's all herky-jerky. Doesn't look right together."

"Well, who wants to do whatever he's doing?"

"Exactly."

The last beats of "Build Me Up Buttercup" faded.

"Oh, my goodness, he's coming over to us," Roanne said and took a step back.

"Actually, he's coming over to you."

The dude had long black hair with bangs that hung in his eyes. "Hi," he said to Roanne with a fake deep voice. He wore a gold choker with an arrowhead in the middle. In his platform shoes, he was still shorter than Roanne. "Wanna dance?"

"Sugar, Sugar" started up. Roanne inched forward.

There was something familiar about the guy. I sniffed. He smelled of too much Hai Karate, the way the bathroom at my house smelled sometimes. I leaned my face into his. We were almost nose to nose.

"Frank?" I reached toward the hair of my year-older brother. "Are you wearing a wig?"

He caught my hand and put his other hand over my mouth. "Keep it down, will you? None of the girls will dance

159

with a guy with a buzz cut."

Frank, because he had reddish hair like mine, looked practically bald with his hair shaved close to his scalp.

"You're the one who wanted to be in ROTC," I said.

"Yeah, well, I like ROTC. I like to dance with girls, too. Why do y'all have to be so stuck up? What do you say, Roanne? Wanna dance, or not?"

Roanne giggled and took a step forward.

"You're really going to?" I said.

"Yes," she said, then almost apologetically, "you know how I love this song."

"Then you should just dance by yourself."

"No way. That would be dorky. Come on, Frank."

She bopped out to the dance floor with my older brother behind her.

"Hey, don't flip your wig!" I called after him. He turned around and glared.

Frank and Roanne didn't put on too bad of a show until he started that broken-wing chicken move. Roanne turned sideways and tried to look like she was dancing with another guy. Frank didn't seem to mind. He just kept jerking away in his lime bellbottoms.

I looked around to see if anyone was coming over to ask me to dance. Nobody glanced my way. I walked around the perimeter of the room and waited for the next song. Mom said boys thought girls who asked them to dance were "easy." If I wanted them to think I was "nice," I was supposed to wait to be asked. It had something to do with boys needing to be in the driver's seat.

Dad always drove our car if he and Mom were together. It wasn't a big deal, just the way things worked. The few times I had seen Mom plop down in the driver's seat ahead of Dad, he had said, "Scoot over, sweetheart. I'll drive." And that was that.

I spotted the cute guy who had tried out for the part of

Curly in *Oklahoma!*, the Bonham winter drama production. I had auditioned for Ado Annie but was cast as one of the nameless dancers. I caught potential Curly's eye but couldn't remember his name. No matter. All I had to say, if he didn't say it first, was, "Do you want to dance?"

He was walking toward me. And then, an "easy" girl in a pink mini skirt and white boots intercepted him.

I wondered if "easy" and "nice" were the only labels assigned to girls, and were boys slapped into categories that defined if they were good or not so good, too, or were they all just jocks or nerds? And who thought of this stupid system of waiting or asking anyway? I could dance by myself, but I didn't want to look like a dork.

– 2019 –

"Connie! You are a goddess!" Claire's exuberance blasted through the phone. My temple was already throbbing from my night of choppy sleep, but at least my editor wasn't going to chew me out for missing my deadline by almost three weeks.

"You like it?"

"I love it. You found a way to keep our solid audience and bring in a whole new generation of readers. A millennial sleuth, a whole new brand."

"Only with your expert guidance that put me back on the right track. I'm glad you're pleased."

"Eh, sweetums, not totally pleased. The name Zoe's just not doing it for me. Too hippie-chick for me."

She was right. Zoe's disappearance was weighing heavily on my mind. I didn't need to think it and type it over and over as part of my work to remind myself that she was missing or to keep hope alive that she would soon turn up.

"What are your thoughts, Claire?"

"I'm feelin' Nicole. Nicole Castillo. Let's make her half Hispanic."

"Perfect, as usual."

"Maxie could call her Nicky," Claire said.

"How about 'Nicks?' But only at particularly endearing moments."

"Yes. I was thinkin' we could take this a step further, honeybee. If Nicole, Nicks, develops a following, we could launch a whole new series with a millennial female detective."

"That's why you're the genius editor."

"Like you didn't already think of it, girlfriend. I see a little swag in these new chapters, a step out of the box. Beyoncé tattoos, really? Like you've tapped into some new level of empowerment. Am I right?"

"Well, yeah, I guess so."

"You keep doing you, girl. I can't wait for the next round."

As soon as the call ended, I settled at the computer with a second cup of coffee. I would knock out that next round without delay. Was my call-the-bastards-out crusade really having positive effects that I hadn't seen? Strengthening me in ways I hadn't expected? Or had I hit a good patch of creativity because I needed a mental defense mechanism to offset my recent worry and months of grief?

If I plunged ahead on my crusade, the next person on my list was Pete Daly. It was unlikely that in three years he would have become as worthy of redemption as Brent Kincaid.

I detoured from the Maxie Dallas file and searched the Internet for Pete's website and his latest Jake Lovelle mystery, *Palmania*. My computer screen showed the crime novel's cover, bordered with turquoise-tinged palm trees, the background red with a fading sun, the black silhouette of a body sprawled at the foot of one of the palms. The authors' names were, in super-large font "Pete Daly," and in much smaller lettering a second name. So, he had found another female co-writer. "Mai Miller," I said it out loud, and it rolled across my tongue like the bitterness of a spurned lover catching a first glimpse at her replacement.

Mai and I had crossed paths at a writers conference several years ago. She had been struggling to interest an agent in her Chicago-based mystery with a female Amer-Asian detective.

At the bottom edge of the cover even tinier letters read, "With Greta Grant." Greta was Pete's girlfriend, at least that was her status two years ago. What did "With" even mean? She gave him a hand? Job?

If the book was a huge hit, was picked up as a movie or TV show, Mai and "With" Greta, would share with Pete in the big bucks that could have been mine. A twinge of jealously passed through me.

Pete and my ex-husband had become buddies while Scott

was in Vietnam as a soldier and Pete was a freelance combat reporter. The friendship lasted after the war, after Scott and I married, and while Pete had begun a new career as a best-selling mystery writer. Jake Lovelle was his hard-boiled, military-veteran detective.

Scott had invited Pete to dinner soon after we moved to San Antonio. The cracks in our marriage had started to spread, but we were still a couple of years away from full implosion. That night, I had burnt the roast duck that was meant to impress the great writer. Scott ridiculed my cooking skills in front of Pete, who graciously ordered Chinese takeout.

Through the years, Pete and I had stayed in touch through e-mail and phone and, after Scott and I divorced, he'd occasionally visited me, had taken me out to dinner. He picked the place and picked up the check. We had become pals. It had been the kind of friendship between a man and woman that depends on not having even an atom of sexual chemistry. With no possibility of sparks, we could talk without boundaries about sex, love, and even politics. He was my guy-girlfriend, and I was his girl-buddy.

Three years ago, Pete had come to me with a proposition. "I want you to collaborate with me on my next book," he'd said. "It'll be a hybrid, Jake Lovelle and Maxie Dallas working a case together."

He had encouraged my writing, bought and read all my books. He had never thrown around his big-time-writer weight, but I was well aware that he orbited in a different galaxy of successful writers than I did. Pete Daly wanted to write a book with Connie Who? It had to be a joke.

"You mean I'd be your co-author?" I had sounded like a rock star groupie.

"Co-authors, partners," Pete said. "Fifty-fifty on the work and the credit."

"Both our names on the front cover?"

He had chuckled. "Well, maybe mine would be a little

bigger to draw in the fans."

We had talked frequently after I said "yes" to his proposal, mapping out the characters and plot of *Palmania,* and the setting, which would be California's Coachella Valley. I joined Pete in Palm Springs, and together we researched the surrounding area, absorbed the ambiance of the off-the-grid communities of Slab City and Bombay Beach.

For a year we had traded detailed notes on plot outlines and character sketches and photos of places where we would set scenes. Jake and Maxie's sleuthing would begin with a body dumped at the foot of Salvation Mountain, a fifty-foot-high artwork of clay, straw, and paint, ribboned with biblical passages, hearts, and flowers rising in the Imperial County desert.

I had had to schmooze Claire and Diamondback to assure them that my work with Pete would not derail my work for my regular publisher. According to Claire, I had come narrowly close to being sued by Diamondback for the use of the Maxie character in a book to be picked up by another publisher.

I had no idea there would be so many ins and outs, ups and downs to saying "yes" to Pete. Finally, in mid-2017 he and I had been poised to dive into the writing, probably just another day at the office for him, but, for me, the big break of my career. But, first, we had to take care of another item we had previously discussed in vague terms: the contract. We would knock out the dry but necessary details of Pete's and my equal partnership in a half-hour phone call.

On that call, out of the blue, Pete had let me know that a third party had become involved. Greta Grant, Pete had informed me, would be considered a writer although she wouldn't actually be writing but reviewing and editing and revising. I didn't know Greta from Eve. I had no idea if we would click in a working relationship, but Pete had already made a deal with her as to her percentage of the royalties.

Surprises number two and number three had been that Pete expected to retain sole copyright and absolute final say whenever he and I had any creative differences on the new novel.

"Standard industry practices," he had called it.

"Not negotiable," he had said when I pushed back. "It was my idea, so we do it my way. If you're not in, you're out."

I had whined something like, "How could you do this to me?" and had made some pitiful plea like "I thought we were friends."

"No need to get emotional," he had said. "It's not personal, it's business."

I closed the computer window with the *Palmania* cover, pulled up my email, searched for "Killer Pete," and resurrected the old personal address that I hadn't used since our bumpy breakup. I drafted a message asking if we could get together while I was "passing through Southern California to see an old friend," without saying the old friend was him.

I would save the draft to think about it, send it later, or not at all, depending on if my crusade was even worth it anymore. If I did meet with Pete in Palm Springs, I could conveniently meet the next guy on my list in Los Angeles, only a half hour away by plane, but, for that one, I would need to cross a million-mile-wide emotional gulf.

My finger tapped nervously against the computer screen. Too late, I realized I had hit "send."

Pete's responding message arrived that evening. "Hey, Connie! Fantastic to hear from you, kiddo!! In PS until the end of May. Hit me up when you get to town!"

Like we were still buddies. He'd see how buddy-buddy we weren't—if, a big "if," I decided to confront him.

Claire had seen some crazy infusion of empowerment in me. A real turnaround. Most Improved Player. Yay, me!

An accomplishment reached pathetically late in the game.

It was one thing to be put in my place by Benny when I

was a seventeen-year-old cashier or by Brent when I was a sexually inexperienced college student, but the other men on my list had run their game on me when I was a mature woman, one, apparently, who had been a slow learner. I had still been the nice girl when Pete had told me the equivalent of what my dad used to say to my mom: "Scoot over, sweetheart. I'll drive."

– 1976 –

Roanne was wandering around the azalea bushes in the front of our Austin apartment building with a flashlight when I returned from my three-hour statistics—ugh!—night class at UT.

"What're you doing out here?" I asked. I guzzled a bottle of Yoo-hoo, my only dinner so far. I was craving a pepperoni, mushroom, black olive pizza and regretted that I hadn't stopped to pick one up at the Pizza Hut down the street.

"I'm looking for Brandy," Roanne said.

Brandy had almost gotten Roanne and I kicked out of our apartment several times. But we forgave her, because she was so cute. The honey-colored cocker spaniel with soulful brown eyes looked like she was smiling when she panted, her little tongue like a ribbon of pink velvet. Johnny had delivered the six-month-old pup to Roanne before he left for ten weeks of cold weather training in Fort Lewis, Washington. To keep Roanne company, he had said, someone she could cuddle through the lonely nights without him.

His romantic gesture hadn't taken into account our apartment complex's "no pets" policy, so we had to keep Brandy quiet and out of sight.

"I didn't realize I'd left the door open when I checked the mail," Roanne said, her voice pitched with anxiety. "Help me look?"

We tiptoed down the meandering sidewalks that were lit by carriage lanterns on black wrought iron posts with Roanne passing the flashlight beam over the dark spots in the bushes and under the redbuds and crepe myrtles.

"Brandy." We called her name in strained whispers, in case some nosy neighbor or a late-working manager became suspicious of two women calling an unauthorized pet.

A biting wind raked my face. The temperature had dropped significantly since midday. The weather forecast had warned of the second in a series of severe winter storms that would roll through central Texas over the next few days. I shivered in my light denim jacket. Roanne pulled her ratty brown sweater tighter around her PJs.

Something clattered around us on the walkway like spilled marbles.

"Ouch!" Roanne cried.

"What's—" I didn't have to wait for an answer. The hail had started stinging my face, too.

"Oh, the poor little puppy, she must be terrified," Roanne wailed.

We threw caution aside and called Brandy's name more loudly, widening our search perimeter to the parking lot and the trash enclosures while the ice pellets dinged our bare heads. Something scratched and skittered next to the garbage bins.

"Is that her?" Roanne cried.

I pulled open the wooden gate of the enclosure.

"Eek!" I jumped back as a portly raccoon ambled out and disappeared into the nearby bushes.

We circled the complex again, wet and chilled to the bone, although the hail had dissipated to needles of sleet. Roanne's flashlight beam died to a weak flicker.

"This is no good. We're going in circles," I said. "How about we go back to the apartment and wait to see if she comes home?"

"No, let's keep looking. She could be lost. She's just a puppy. "

"We'll find her."

"What if we don't?" Roanne's voice rose again. "She's out there freezing and scared. She was depending on me to keep her safe. How am I going to tell Johnny? He'll think I'm an irresponsible airhead."

"This is not a love test. Don't overreact."

"You don't understand. You've never been responsible for anyone except yourself."

I was annoyed and tired and hungry and cold and wet, and Roanne wasn't completely right about my responsibility experience. I was the one who had taken care of Christine when my parents weren't home, even when she was a baby, and I was only ten. My brothers couldn't be trusted to take care of a child any more than they could be trusted to separate the laundry into whites and colors. But, I couldn't say a cross word to Roanne. She looked like a lost puppy herself.

"Okay," I said, patting her shoulder, "we'll make another pass around the complex."

"What if she ran into the street?" Roanne put her palms to her wet, red cheeks. "Oh, my goodness, what if she got hit by a car?"

"Or, she could be waiting by the front door, trying to get in. You should go back to the apartment and stay by the door, and I'll drive up the street and look for her. If she ran outside the complex, she couldn't have gone far."

"What if a big dog attacked her?"

"There aren't any big dogs out here. No pets, remember? Go home, and I'll look for her on the street. Go." I gently pushed her forward.

I cruised down Fifty-First Street, my wipers squeaking against the mist on the windshield, the headlights picking up a beam of tiny droplets. I realized how futile it was to try to locate a small dog through the darkness, rain, and blinding headlights from cars passing on the other side of the street. At least I hadn't spotted any lumps of road kill. I drove two blocks in one direction, turned at the nearest light, and drove two blocks the opposite way before returning to the apartment.

Roanne was sitting on the porch when I returned, her clothing soaked, her wet hair stuck like tendrils of seaweed to her face, her shoulders convulsing with the cold. She looked up hopefully, and, when I shook my head, she buried her face in her hands.

I took her inside, convinced her to strip off her wet clothes, wrapped her in a quilt, and led her to the couch. I heaped my wet jacket and shoes in a pile by the door.

"I'm going to make some tea," I said. Roanne stared like a zombie. "She'll probably come scratching at the door any minute."

"I'll leave the door open for her," Roanne said through sobs. She pulled the quilt around her shoulders and headed for the door. The cold air whooshed in as I went to the kitchen to put on the kettle.

I rummaged through a cupboard, found the tin of cinnamon tea and a jar of honey, and set two mugs on the counter. The storm had picked up momentum, and sleet rattled against the kitchen window.

Roanne had become attached so quickly to Brandy and to Johnny. She dove into relationships, while I waded into the shallow end and inched forward, stopping short of the deep water. Scott and I had been together for a year, but I was still unsure if it was true love, not like Roanne with Johnny.

The kettle whistled. The clatter of ice against the window abruptly stopped. When I took the kettle off the burner, another sound, a whimper, came from the corner pantry. I pulled open the door. Brandy peeked from behind a fallen ironing board that blocked the bottom of the door so that she couldn't strike her paws against it to push it open.

I lifted the puppy out and carried her into the living room where Roanne huddled on the floor, staring toward the front door.

"Guess who I found trapped in the pantry."

Roanne leapt up, took Brandy, and snuggled her against her cheek. Brandy's tiny tongue flitted in and out across Roanne's nose. "Oh, that tickles," she protested. Then she leaned in. "I promise I'll never let anything happen to you.

Gimme that puppy love."

She was like a kid with that dog.

That's the way Roanne loved. The puppy, Johnny, everyone. Childlike, arms wide open. Disarmed. Defenseless. I didn't want to surrender like that, but at the same time, I envied her because she could.

Icy air blasted in and slammed the front door against the wall. I shut the door against the storm.

"Ms. Canelli? This is Elena Cardenas." The voice on the phone confused me.

I didn't recognize the name. The only connection I could make was the Hispanic customer service representative at the airport lost and found to whom I had talked two days before.

"From the airport?" I asked.

"I'm a Realtor, Ms. Canelli. I'm selling your son's home. We have kind of a situation here."

"A situation? Is something wrong with the house?"

"Not the house exactly. I came over this morning to get things ready for the showing this afternoon." She paused, and agitation poked through her pleasant professional tone. "I found a woman on the bedroom floor. Her clothes are dirty, she reeks of alcohol, and her face is bruised. I thought she was a homeless person. Apparently she had broken the window to get in. But, she said she lives here with Daniel. I called Daniel in Dallas, and he said you would handle it."

"A young Asian woman?"

"Yes. Do you know her?"

I breathed out a long sigh of relief. "Yes, yes. Tell her I'm on my way."

En route to Daniel's house, I called him in Dallas. "She's back! Zoe's come back!" My words and tears bubbled over.

"She's okay?" he asked.

"Yes," I said, although I didn't know if that was true. She wasn't missing anymore, and that was good enough for right now.

"I'll be off work in an hour, then I'll drive down," he said, and hung up before I had a chance to say anything else.

When I arrived at Daniel's house, Zoe was sitting in the bare bedroom with her knees pulled to her chest. Her snarled hair hid her face. I knelt beside her, cupped her dirt-streaked face in my hands, and raised her chin. Her lower lip was split, her left eye swollen above a discolored cheek. The knuckles of her right hand were bruised. One leg of her jeans was smudged with mud; her shirt collar was stained with dried blood. She stank of liquor and faintly of urine. Tears carved grimy tracks down her cheeks.

"I'm sorry," she sobbed. "When I'm with Daniel, I know I'm going to be all right. But, when I had to walk through that airport alone, I freaked out. I couldn't do it without him."

"I understand, sweetie. It's a setback, that's all. We'll get you back on track." I cradled her face against my shoulder. "First, let's get you to the hospital."

Her body tensed. "No, please. I don't want any strangers poking at me. Just take me home with you."

I pulled her hair strand by strand from her face. "You need to have your injuries checked out."

"I've done medical evaluations before. Nothing's broken. I was roughed up a little by a couple of guys, that's all."

"Roughed up?"

"They hit me, took my backpack, my liquor. I got off one good punch. They weren't fighters."

"Sexual assault?"

"No. Once they got the booze, that's all they cared about, and it wasn't even a full bottle."

"But they got your money and ID and everything you had."

"Not everything. When I bought the liquor, I stuffed the change and my driver's license in my pocket. I lost my phone somewhere, but I had enough cash to get the bus to here."

"Daniel's on his way from Dallas."

"He'll be so disappointed in me."

"He won't give up on you, and I won't either. Let's go home."

When Daniel called back, Zoe was in the shower, and I was baking cupcakes, trying to harness my nervous energy. He insisted I book him and Zoe on a flight to Richmond late that evening. He had already talked to Stella about going forward with the rehab plan in Virginia. I filled Zoe in, expecting some pushback, but she silently agreed, once she was convinced that Daniel would make the trip with her.

Still, I was relieved when she fell asleep on the couch in one of my oversized T-shirts while I washed her clothes. As long as she was napping, I wouldn't have to keep an eagle eye out to make sure she didn't run off in another panic.

When Daniel arrived, four hours later, he quietly put his arms around Zoe. He didn't mention that we had been worried sick about her, or how reckless she had behaved, or how ungrateful she had seemed. For him, the last four days had evaporated.

"I'm a jerk," Zoe said, molding her face into his shoulder.

"Yes, I know," he said, "but even jerks shouldn't have to face adversity alone."

"I broke your bedroom window."

"I can get that fixed. You're safe. That's all I care about. Are you ready to go?"

She shouldered a backpack I had given her and positioned my spare sunglasses on top of her head.

"Yep. I have Margaret Atwood's latest, you have Drake on your phone. All the travel essentials."

"Not quite," Daniel said. "Mom, where are the Uno cards?"

"Uno!" Zoe clapped like a hyper little kid.

"In the desk in your old room, maybe?"

Daniel jogged to the bedroom to look for the cards.

"It'll take a good half hour to get to the airport!" I yelled after Daniel. "I'll print out your boarding passes. Then we better get going."

I sat down at the computer. The most recent flight information page came up on the screen, with flights to Palm Springs that I had been checking out after I booked the flight to Virginia. None of the flights to California were reasonably priced. If I passed on meeting with Pete, I could save a chunk of money.

"No, you're not driving us!" Daniel shouted from the bedroom. "I've already called an Uber! And I sent the boarding passes to my phone!" He emerged with a box of cards. "Got 'em. All ready to go."

"Take some cupcakes," I said.

"Lemon?" Daniel asked.

"With the little pieces of grated lemon peel mixed in?" Zoe asked.

"Yep," I said.

"Yums!" Zoe cried and trotted to the kitchen.

I sat at the computer, staring at the words "Palm Springs" and imagining Pete's smug face.

"Mom? Mom?" Daniel shook my shoulder.

"What?"

"You were lost in space there for a minute," Daniel said. "Hey, don't worry. Stella will be waiting for us in Richmond. Zoe's been pre-checked into the facility for tomorrow. Seamless. I'll be back in Dallas tomorrow night. I told the job I've had a complication on the house sale. They said no prob. Look, we got this."

"I know, baby. It's not that."

"Then what?" He leaned over my shoulder to look at the computer screen. "Palm Springs? Are you planning to meet one of those guys?"

I turned my head to look up at him, about to say, "How do you know about that?" before the obvious answer clicked. This was my sister's way of letting me know she wasn't going to stop getting in my business just because I hadn't been sharing my plans with her.

"What has your Aunt Christine told you?"

"She said Uncle Joey was just the beginning, that you're meeting up with men from your past, that you're on a revenge campaign. I figured she had gotten it wrong. My mom? Doing some *Mad Max: Fury Road* thing? No way. But now you're making travel plans, and you're acting worried, so was Aunt Christine not exaggerating?"

"My little sis loves a good embellishment, like a triple extra twirl of frosting on her cupcakes." I sighed, smiled, and patted his hand, mimicking calm and reassurance. "Yes, I am on a journey, but it's not about revenge. It's about resolution. And, as it turns out, I'm having second thoughts. I may call it quits."

"Aunt Christine said you were determined to go ahead, that quitting wasn't an option, even when she tried to stop you. She was concerned about your safety." He squatted down to bring himself eye level with me. "Was she right? Did someone hurt you?" He turned a fist inside his other hand. "If they did, you just tell me who and I'll—"

I put up my palm. "I promise, I'm safe. We meet in public places, like Joey in the church. I confronted him, and I was fine, better than fine. Anyway, most of these guys are old, broke-down, with bad knees. I can easily outrun them, if I need to. Nobody's hurt me, just the opposite." I casually pulled up the collar of my shirt on the side of my neck where the El Paso mugger had left a still fading bruise. "Someone gave me a helping hand, and it's thrown me for a loop."

"You want to quit because some dude was nice to you?"

"Like I said, this is not about revenge. So, do all these guys deserve to be called out? Doesn't the good they may have done balance out with the pain they caused me in the past? Am I just holding onto grudges and carrying that with me forever?"

Daniel stroked his chin. "I see what you mean. Someone commits a bad act, like he sets fire to a building and accidentally kills someone, but then years later he saves some kids from a burning house. But one doesn't erase the other. They're like two accounts you keep throughout your life. Take me, for example. I was a drug abuser, I caused you an incredible amount of pain. I lied to you repeatedly. I stole from you. I said horrible things to you. I physically hurt you. I—"

I took his face in my hands. "In your heart, I knew you weren't a bad person, that my good Daniel was in there somewhere fighting his way back out. You're my blessing. I don't know what I'd do without you."

He put his hands over mine. "Mom, I appreciate you every day for always being in my corner. There's nothing I wouldn't do for you. But I don't get to own that now and not also own the addict and thief and liar and bully that I was. You're not holding grudges. You're holding people accountable."

I dropped my hands into my lap and relaxed my shoulders. "You're right. But, still, maybe it's not such a good idea, disrupting those men's lives, stressing them out for the sake of my self-esteem."

Zoe walked out of the kitchen and glanced at Daniel's phone perched on the arm of the couch. "Uber's here," she said.

Daniel tossed her the pack of cards. She muffed the catch, and the box landed on her feet.

"My bad," Daniel said.

Zoe shrugged, rearranged a plastic container filled with cupcakes in her backpack, and dropped the cards in. Daniel pulled me out of my chair and hugged me. I looked over his shoulder at Zoe.

The headlights of a car pulling up in front of the house shone behind her through the blinds, blurring her for a moment to a dark silhouette, only the side of her face illuminated. Her cheek glistened wet, her uninjured eye stared wide, the toes of one shoe fidgeted atop the other. She looked like a little girl hesitant to get on the bus for her first day of school.

I went to her, and she leaned into me. Her chin hooked my shoulder, reminding me that she was taller than me by a couple of inches. Her chest quivered against mine.

"Hey, no time for tears," I said. "Things will get better. You'll get better. We'll see each other again soon."

Zoe nodded her jaw into my neck. I brushed back her hair, kissed her temple. She let go of me and rushed out through the front door, leaving it open for Daniel.

In the doorway, Daniel turned to face me. "Mom, do what you set out to do, as long as you're careful. Your self-esteem is important. So what if you shake up a few jerks and make them think about what they did? It's not like you're out there in camo face paint, ready to pull out your mega weapon and even the score."

Christine couldn't have told him about the gun. She didn't know about it. After El Paso, the Glock had become an overwhelming presence lying in my nightstand drawer. Twelve inches from where I slept, it nagged at me: "Will I protect you? Or will I get you killed?" Like mental Russian roulette. I had unloaded it, moved it, locked it in the glove compartment of my car.

"Me? With a weapon?"

"Right. I'm a hundred and ten percent sure you're the last person on Earth who would ever touch a gun."

"You know me like a book."

I hadn't planned to start bawling, but as soon as I heard Roanne's voice on the other end of the phone, the dam burst.

"Con, what's wrong?"

"Scott got orders. We're going to Fort Clayton, Panama." I twisted a corner of the quilt in my hand, fidgeting while I sat on the edge of my bed.

"Florida? That's great."

"Not Panama the city. Panama, the country, the one with the canal. He has to report in thirty days."

"I'll be stuck all summer sweltering in Killeen, huge and miserable. I'm so jealous. Why are you crying?"

I had been an army wife for four months and would be an honorary auntie in another four. A month after their December wedding, Roanne and Johnny's first baby had been conceived, even if they hadn't known until late March.

"I don't want to leave! Not now." I dug my heels into the carpet as though I expected to be dragged off at any moment. The apartment on Fifty-First in Austin already seemed like someone else's. After Roanne and Johnny had moved to Killeen, I had stayed, coming home each day to what seemed like an abandoned space, Roanne's homey clutter swept away, the brightness gone out of each room, the walls turned dingy.

Then Scott moved in, and the apartment filled up again with new sounds and smells and things to be done. He brought his stereo system and his records, Willie and Stevie Ray and Jimi. His jeans and cowboy boots occupied a third of the bedroom closet. A pile of his pocket stuff—keys, wallet, change—appeared on the corner of the dresser. His battered chili pot and bags of spices took over the top shelf of the pantry, the one I couldn't reach without a step stool.

The scent of Irish Spring pervaded the shower. A can of

shaving cream, flanked by razors and stick deodorant, tattooed a rusty ring on the lone metal shelf of the medicine cabinet. The second bedroom became a storage area for spare motorcycle parts. With Scott's name added to the lease, Roanne's and my former apartment became the official first residence of Staff Sergeant and Mrs. McHenry.

My orange Datsun had given up part of its designated parking space to Scott's Honda Gold Wing. He commuted the seventy miles to Fort Hood while I worked as a reporter at the *Austin American-Statesman,* my first career job out of college. Gathering news in the field, writing a story on deadline, and seeing "By Connie Canelli, Staff Writer" the next morning on the newsstands was a rush I had quickly gotten used to. I had settled in at my half desk in the newsroom. I had my own phone extension.

"I have to give my notice at the *Statesman* after only seven months," I whined to Roanne. "Who's going to hire me at a newspaper in a foreign country?" I sniffled and blew my nose. "My future employers will want to know why I quit, why there's a gap in my employment. 'Moved because husband is in army' doesn't sound good on an application. It'll be like a single woman saying 'I'm engaged' in the job interview, or a married woman saying 'of course, I want to have a baby.' Kiss of death. Another woman who isn't serious about her career, who should stay home and bake cakes."

The meaning of "military spouse" had sunk in and wrapped itself around my brain. I had signed on to push aside any career plans of my own, indefinitely, in deference to Scott's.

"C'mon, it won't be as bad as all that," Roanne said.

"You'll see, if the time comes when you're out there knocking on doors."

"When, not if. Meanwhile, you have a chance to see the world. And you're sure to find a job on base," Roanne said in an overly enthusiastic tone.

"Four years of college and maybe the PX will hire me as a cashier? I was doing that in high school."

"You'll be back in the States in two years. So, your career as a serious, award-winning writer is delayed a little. You still have your whole life to win the Pulitzer."

"Hopefully. When does Johnny get orders?"

"In September. His wish list is Fort Sill, Oklahoma; Fort Polk, Louisiana; and Fort Stewart, Georgia. He's a true country boy, just wants to stay close to home. But, he says the first thing the army does before it assigns a duty station is toss your wish list into the circular file. I try to count our blessings, focus on the military benefits. Steady income, so we can save for a house. Free medical care."

The tears started again. "I won't be there when the baby's born."

"I wish I could pop him out within the next thirty days. Some things just can't be rushed. You can call me for weekly updates."

Roanne's doctor had put her on semi-bed rest for her last fourteen weeks. Toxemia had made her blood pressure shoot up and her hands and feet swell. She downplayed the condition, and she hated for me to ask if she was feeling okay. I swallowed down the question. Apparently, Johnny asked her fifty times a day and drove her crazy.

"How do you know it's not a her instead of a him?" I asked.

"Fifty-fifty odds, but Johnny is a hundred percent invested in a son. I told him I hope he did it right because the male chromosome determines the sex of the baby."

"What did he say to that?"

She laughed. "He said I didn't know what I was talking about, that I was making that up."

I sighed. "Men have such a heavy burden to bear."

"What's that?"

"Always being right."

"Exactly. Luckily, stroking the male ego is an easy job. And you have to admit, we have a couple of the decent ones. They've never really asked us to do anything we absolutely don't want to do."

"So, I really want to go to Panama, let my journalism credentials gather dust, and leave my best friend when she's about to have a baby?"

"Palm trees, beaches, two oceans. Two years in a bikini. From someone who's about to transform into a stranded whale and spend the next few months in a hot, cracker-box apartment, that sounds like paradise."

"Okay, I'll count my blessings and stop blubbering."

"Don't say 'blubber' to an orca woman."

"Sorry."

– 2019 –

Pete's directions left me puzzled. My rental car wasn't headed up a rocky hillside to his luxury villa that I had read about online. The one with a magnificent waterfall pool perched high above the valley and the city of Palm Springs. Instead, I was driving into a community on the west side of town, the name "Rancho Cielo" carved into the wooden archway at the entrance.

The one-lane, one-way road meandered through a trailer park unlike any I'd ever visited. No rusting units on blocks, no trash or car tires or busted patio chairs leaning against the outside walls. These were upscale residences, with spacious wooden decks attached, gazebos lush with hanging baskets of flowers, elaborate cactus and succulent gardens, luxurious awnings. I passed a couple in pastel shorts and straw hats walking a pair of miniature dogs.

The road curved in a loop, eventually coming back to the entrance, I assumed. Before I completed the circle, I reached my destination, a brown mobile home with a roofed patio that backed up to a wooded area. The next unit down was pink from the walls to the deck to the planters on the deck. The only non-pink embellishment was a gray-white, five-foot replica of the "Discus Thrower," although he was wearing a pink scarf around his neck. The home of one of Palm Springs' many gay retirees, no doubt.

I parked and rang the brass ship's bell hanging on the porch of the brown unit, unsure, until Pete's slight frame and grizzled face appeared in the doorway, that I had the right place. He wore baggy shorts, a faded blue T-shirt, and flip-flops.

"Connie, come on in, buddy. You went back to red. I like it."

It took me a minute to realize he was referring to my hair. Three years ago, when I last saw Pete, I had already let my hair go silver. Last week, I had had it colored back to the flame hue it had been when I was younger, but I hadn't done it for Pete. Telling him that, of course, would assure him that I had.

"My condolences on the loss of your friend, very tragic," he said with a kind of sad puppy look.

My head jerked back as his words caught me off guard. "How did you know?"

"Scott and I still talk now and again."

"Oh." I nodded and slipped past him to avoid the hug he was about to offer. "Nice neighborhood, but not what I was expecting."

"This is where I hang out when I'm working," he said. "The big house is full of distractions, women, dogs, one posse or another, eating, drinking, partying. I don't even know who half of them are. The price of being rich and famous and having an entourage, I suppose."

"I read that your house has thirty rooms. Couldn't you find a nook or cranny of solitude in there somewhere?"

"Just the thought of other people moving around in the place takes me out of the zone. I prefer it here where my creative juices can flow, viscous and unchecked."

I was reminded that Pete had a way of making a benign phrase sound disgusting. He led me to a room at the back of the house where the sun poured in through a wide skylight.

"How about a drink?" he asked, walking to a sleek, brushed-metal mini bar. "This is the time of day when I usually make myself a Manhattan. White wine is your drink, right? I have an unoaked chardonnay, a South African chenin blanc, a New Zealand sauvignon — "

"Sure. Half a glass is good." I settled into a blue-and-white striped lounge chair.

He poured me a full glass of pale lemon-colored wine, took the chair across from me, sipped his Manhattan, and let out a sigh of satisfaction.

"What have you been up to, kiddo?" he asked.

"Working on the next Maxie Dallas book."

"Right. Maxie still sleuthing on her off time from baking coconut cream pies and banana muffins?"

"Maxie's in stellar form, and sales are holding steady. How about you?"

"Can't complain. Jake Lovelle is back in action, following a trail to Pakistan. I'm about to drop him into some hot water, a hostage situation, an elaborate escape. Fun stuff, but Jake is kind of a sideline at this point in my career. The big bucks are in the conference circuit, TV appearances. And the movie rights, of course. I'm on Netflix now."

"Congrats." I raised my glass to him. "Are you and Mai still partnering?"

"That was a one-off."

"Quick honeymoon."

He crossed his ankle at the opposite knee, and I unwillingly noticed he wasn't wearing underwear.

"The parting was mutual. Mai is working on a memoir about growing up as a child of an American GI and a Vietnamese local. I'm acting as her consultant. Kind of a mentor-father figure."

"You? A father figure?"

"I did have a lot of honeys when I was in Vietnam. Mai actually could be my daughter."

I cringed and willed my eyes to stay above his chin, even though I felt that thing pointing my way. "Consultant, hmm, a little work for a lot of credit on the back flap."

"Absolutely."

"Credit is important."

He smiled, took a substantial swallow of his drink, and smacked his lips, clueless about where I was steering the conversation.

"What would you call taking credit for someone else's

work?" I asked and sipped my wine.

He set down his glass and hinted at a frown. "A bit of misappropriation, perhaps, or an alternative interpretation of who did what. It happens."

"I'd call it stealing."

One corner of his mouth turned up. "Ah, you're still pissed about that copyright thing. I explained that to you. It was all about simplifying the process if the book was picked up by Hollywood. It's standard procedure for the big-boy writers. Have your agent explain it to you."

"Elvis's manager had a standard procedure he would pitch to songwriters. If Elvis recorded the song, the deal was the songwriter had to turn over ownership of half of the publishing rights."

"Interesting. Contracts are seldom, strictly speaking, fifty-fifty. If you're Elvis, naturally, you get a bigger piece of cake than the little guy."

"And you're always Elvis, strictly speaking."

"Well..." He shrugged and slurped his drink.

"And I, the little lady, pay the cost of playing with the big boys. You wanted to take my creative product and call it yours. Yep, sounds like stealing to me."

Pete threw me a deadpan look.

"I trusted your word that we had an equal partnership, and you stabbed me in the back." Hurt crept into my voice. "How could you do that to me? We were friends. We shared how we felt about things."

"There you go again, making a purely business issue about feelings," he said. "I won't pretend. It pains me that you ended our friendship over this."

I downed my wine and stood up. I couldn't sit there and listen to his nonsense and let him rile me up. I wasn't going to play the part of the hysterical female for his entertainment. I paced around the edge of a round glass table with a bowl of fruit in the center.

"Pains you? I doubt that you gave our friendship a hiccup of thought." I picked up a grapefruit from the bowl and rolled it between my palms.

Pete shook his head and smiled, obviously not in pain. "Is that a girl thing? You got your feelings hurt, so we can't ever be friends again? Guys just blow that shit off. How could you have a football team if players refused to play every time they got pissed at each other?"

I put the grapefruit down and tossed a papaya back and forth between my hands. "It isn't about hurt feelings. It's about betrayal."

"O-o-o-o. Betrayal. That's dramatic."

I set down the papaya and lifted the largest piece of fruit from the bowl. "Ah, a pineapple."

"Yep. The old bird in that pink trailer next door has the hots for me. She brings me those every week, says the pineapple is a symbol of hospitality, her weird way of trying to worm her way into my heart, I suppose."

"How thoughtful of her." So, his neighbor was a woman with the hots for Pete, not a gay dude. I had miscalled that one. "It's a refreshing fruit, healthy, good for your heart and digestion, makes a nice centerpiece, too."

I studied the haughty set of his mouth, his eyes looking through me as if he had already shooed me out to go on with his important day. My pulse quickened. My cheeks flushed. I gritted my teeth.

The pineapple's spiny heft was satisfyingly solid in my hand. I glared at him. "A pineapple can also be dangerous. As a projectile, its weight and texture could cause some ugly damage on impact."

I lifted the pineapple and lined it up with Pete's head, curled my fingers into the prickly surface, tightened my grip. It wasn't a particularly precise weapon, like a gun.

Earlier in the day, I had parked my car in the San Antonio airport's long-term garage, weighed the chance that Pete might act dangerously, and transferred my gun from the glove compartment to its hard-plastic case. I had popped the cased gun, sans bullets, into my suitcase before I pulled my luggage out of the trunk. But, during the drive to his house, I had realized that Pete was the kind of guy who might call my bluff if I pointed a gun at him. To save myself the humiliation of facing him like a fool with no ammunition to back up my threat, I had left the impotent Glock in the suitcase. Pete wore all the bravado of a cowboy, but words were his weapon, and, when used against him, the only bullets that hit their mark.

The pineapple's spiky skin dug into my palm. Pete crossed his arms and raised a crooked eyebrow. His posture said, "Your move." He kind of looked like a pineapple—his rough, leathery face, a tuft of white hair standing up in the middle of his elongated head. I smiled at the thought of two pineapples colliding.

My elbow quivered as I prepared to cock my arm. I studied his eyes and the set of his mouth for the slightest crack in his steely stare-off. Five seconds in, there it was, a flicker of anxiety, a twitch of uncertainty: Will she or won't she? Do I duck or wait it out, call her bluff? His head flinched a fly's width to the side.

My elbow quivered again before I lowered it. Me going off on him would be his victory. I wasn't going to play his game. He was the classless jerk in this story, not me. I set the pineapple back on the table.

"I'm done here," I said.

He slowly let out a breath. "What was all that?"

"Just working through a scene for my latest Maxie mystery. My detective comes up against a condescending ass and... I like to get a feel for the mechanics."

"Huh." He stood up, wobbling as he pushed off from the arm of his chair. I sensed that the Manhattan wasn't his first of the day. "I'll walk you out. Believe it or not, I'd still like to work with you on another book."

"I think I'll pass."

"Don't you want to hear about it?"

Before I could say, "I couldn't care less," he continued, "I was looking forward to seeing you today, kiddo, not just for old-time's sake. I have a project in the works that I wanted you to be part of. In fact, there is no one better than you. You have the personal insight on this story that no one else possesses."

"How's that?" I asked, kicking myself mentally for letting him know I was intrigued.

"I'm working on a nonfiction book, murder-suicide cases with a focus on the opposite-gender dynamic, how it's unusual for the woman to be the killer of the man in that situation."

Warmth crept up my neck to my face. My jaw clenched. "You want me to help you write about my friend killing her ex, then putting a gun to her head?"

He gave me a smile like a pat on the head for figuring that out. "Right. I wanted to tap into the whole female rage thing. You have a unique perspective. Your input would be invaluable."

I pushed down the urge to grab the pineapple and hurl it after all. Female rage wasn't something a man could tap into like cutting a bite of steak, sawing it between his teeth for a while, then spitting it out and pushing the plate away.

"You want me to be the vulture that helps you pick away at the bones of my friend to make a few bucks."

"Come on, kiddo. I have more sensitivity than that. It's a shitload of bucks. I'm already spinning a deal with your name tentatively in the mix. I know how these things work. This story has bestseller and Netflix series written all over it."

Nineteen years ago, I was over the moon when Claire broke the news that Diamondback had agreed to publish my first book. When she called, I was in the kitchen of Scott's and my new place in San Antonio, lifting a pair of temple jar lamps I'd ordered out of their shipping box. The lamps had been well-packed with a couple of pounds of packing peanuts.

When I got off the phone, I screamed at the top of my lungs and flung handfuls of foam bits into the air, and from there I went nuts launching the puffy pellets like confetti all over the room.

Scott came home in the middle of my celebration. I grabbed him and danced him around, our feet crunching on the packing peanuts.

"What's going on? Are you crazy?" He kept asking while trying to push me away, like he was two minutes from calling the men in white coats.

When I pulled myself together enough to tell him about the book deal and the $1,000 advance, he was immediately on board, spinning my future where I was a best-selling author launching a world tour. We had an Olympic swimming pool, I had a half-acre kitchen with an industrial-size oven, and he had a gray Porsche with burgundy interior. For the next few years I lusted after that dream scenario like a kid hoping for a new bike every Christmas but always falling short of the wish coming true.

The reality was that once the Maxie Dallas series got going, I earned enough in book sales to make one extra mortgage payment each year. As years passed, I made peace with not hitting the top of the bestseller list or sitting on the stage with Oprah, and I was grateful for my moderate success. Being paid for doing what I enjoyed was a blessing. I had a following, not Oprah-level fans, but nice, mostly Texas women from the suburbs, book-clubbers. Still, I wondered, even if I didn't care about fame and fortune, did I have what it took to be a big-time writer whose name on the book cover was double the size of the title?

Pete was dangling the chance for me to find out.

"Look at it this way," he said. "Some hack way below my skill level is going to tell that story his way at some point. If you're on this project with me, at least you'd have some influence over how the story is told."

All I had to do was say "yes" to working with Pete, act like we were buddies again—ugh. And, after I spilled out Roanne's agonies and ecstasies and laid bare all the threads in the bond between us, Pete would have the copyright certifying it was all his work and the final creative word about how it would all be used, how it would be flayed open for the world to gorge on. He was the famous writer. He was the one who knew how the business worked. He was Elvis.

"No, thanks," I said. "I reject your offer."

He chuckled. "I almost had you, didn't I? I could see the wheels turning."

My face burned. I shuddered like he had brushed up against some private part of my body accidentally on purpose.

"Right," he said. "Your game is fluffy detectives who make fluffy cakes. Pity, because you have the talent, but you don't have the guts to take on something hard to progress to the next level. To be a serious writer. To play with the big boys."

Is that who the big boys were? Serious writers? Why were they the measure of what was "serious?" Had I been writing to someday—swoon!—be like Pete? A tumbler clicked into place in my brain. "Playing with the big boys gets you off," I said, "but it doesn't float my boat."

"Rowboat," he muttered just loud enough for me to catch it.

"Thanks, Pete."

"For?"

"Giving me back my perspective. As a writer, I like what I do. I really like what I do. I like the view from the rowboat. For the last three years, I've been grieving over a stolen opportunity, but actually I dodged a bullet. Work with the great Pete Daly? I wouldn't do it for a million bucks."

He shook his head, cast his eyes down like he felt sorry for me. "You can take the pineapple. A parting gift."

"No, I'll leave it for you. It'll go down a lot easier than that massive ego you can't manage to swallow."

I turned on my heel and walked out, smiling like a chocolate lover who's discovered a Belgian truffle in the bottom of a seemingly empty bag.

On the plane between Palm Springs and LAX, I pulled out my laptop and researched the characteristics of millennials and created a profile for Nicole "Nicks" Castillo. I added a silver stud to her left nostril. I changed her hair to wavy and dark, which she wore pulled up in a twist on the top of her head. She had earned a degree in communications, but five years later she was unemployed with a hefty student loan debt.

She was hopeful to the point of being annoying to her Aunt Maxie, tech-savvy, and environmentally responsible. She carried a collapsible metal straw in her backpack to use when she dined out. She collected recyclables from Maxie's trash and kindly lectured her aunt on how hamburgers and plastic are destroying the planet. She lived with two roommates: Bryson, who was funded by his rich daddy and pursuing a tennis career, and Ocean, a performance artist who was sexually fluid.

Maxie Dallas was going to be impressed with her new sidekick, enough to exit the stage when Nicole launched as the heroine of her own series, with some guest visits every now and then from her mentor aunt.

A thrill rushed through me like hot blood, that sensation I got when I knew my writing had hit the nail dead on the head. Bang! It was great to not be Pete.

I pumped my fist. "Yes! My book, my way," I said, loud enough to make the passenger next to me lean back from his laptop and stare at me.

The "final descent to Los Angeles" announcement came over the speaker. Christine had arrived in LA a day ahead of meeting Barry and their West Coast daughter. She would pick me up and take us to a hotel, but she would also stick around an extra day and rescue me if I started to fall apart during the next confrontation on my list. She would even understand if I got cold feet and backed out altogether.

The drop in altitude was smooth, but my stomach drew up in a knot. The next one would be different from the others. What he said, or didn't say, would cut deeper than the others had. Because I was in love with Theo Harris.

– 1993 –

"Why?" I yelled at the TV mounted on a pedestal across from the foot of my hospital bed and dropped my hand with the remote to my side.

I sat, propped against two pillows, my legs outstretched, my bare toes exposed, with a sheet tucked tightly around me from chest to ankles, looking like a burrito. Under the wrapping, I wore a loose sundress, ready to be discharged from Brooke Army Medical Center as soon as the doctor arrived to sign my paperwork. Roanne had driven from Round Rock to San Antonio to take me home.

"Why what?" Roanne asked.

"Why the fuck is Samantha with Darrin?" I said, muting the syndicated episode of *Bewitched*, the sitcom about a witch married to a mortal man.

"Con! You cursed!"

"So?"

"You don't curse."

"What can I say, having my female parts cut out brings up the worst in me."

Roanne scooted up her turquoise plastic chair so that her knees were pressed against the side of the bed. "Oh, sweetie, don't think of it like that. You don't even need that equipment anymore. You already have Daniel."

"I've had those parts for thirty-nine years, so, excuse me if I—" Tears gushed down my face, taking me by surprise. "You know, if I was man, this would be called castration."

"Hey, I didn't mean a hysterectomy isn't a big deal." Roanne patted my leg.

I swiped a dribble of snot from under my nose with the back of my hand. Roanne handed me a stack of tissues from a box on the nightstand.

"Have you talked to Scott to let him know the operation went okay?" Roanne asked.

"No. It's the middle of the night in Korea."

She shook her head. "Why couldn't the army wait an extra week to send him over there? He'll be there for a year. What's the rush?"

"If he had retired three years ago at twenty, that wouldn't be an issue." I blew my nose hard, dabbed my eyes, and choked off the tears.

"You would think they would make an exception if your wife is in the hospital having major surgery," Roanne said.

"Have you forgotten now that Johnny's been a civilian for a while? The army has its own agenda that comes before all else."

"Exactly. The mission's always first and if the army wanted you to have a wife, it would have issued you one."

"I'm glad Scott's not here. I feel ugly." I lowered my chin to my chest and sniffed. "I don't smell right."

"As soon as we get you home, you'll feel better."

The incision on my lower abdomen pinched. My feet were hot. I wiggled my toes and glanced back up at the TV. "What is it with her?"

"Who?"

"Sam. She's gorgeous. She's smart. She has supernatural powers. Yet she's with Darrin. All he does is complain and fuss at her, and he won't let her be herself. And he's not even good-looking."

"Switching Dick York to that other Dick wasn't any improvement. I like the first one better."

"They're both dicks." I reached for the water pitcher on the nightstand. Pain grabbed my midsection and stopped me short.

"Take it easy, girl," Roanne said. She adjusted a pillow behind me, and I rocked back against it, one butt cheek at a time, while she handed me a paper cup of water.

"Do you think the surgery was the right thing to do?" I asked.

"You've been bleeding and in pain for years. It's over with now."

I pressed my fists into my temples. "It's over with, all right. I'm going to be on hormone replacement and gain twenty pounds and my sex drive will be kaput."

"Says who?"

"Guadalupe."

"That nice lady who's watching Daniel?"

"Yes. My neighbor's mom. My Spanish is not great, but I can understand '*horrible*,' and '*gorda*' and 'sex *no mas*.'" I made a distressed face like Guadalupe had when she said those things. "But..." I smiled wide like Guadalupe had a second later. "'*No mas regla.*' I can skip a whole aisle at the grocery store."

Roanne stroked my leg. "And no more passing out and trips to the emergency room. I'm sure Guadalupe's wrong about the sex thing."

"What if Scott leaves me for some young chick? It's so unfair. I didn't ask to be defective."

"You're not defective, and Scott's not going anywhere."

"I have to..." I inched sideways toward the edge of the bed. "...pee."

Roanne pulled the sheet away and braced my arm. I swung my legs over the side of the bed, slid my feet into my fuzzy slippers, and shuffled to the toilet. A pulling sensation rippled through my lower abdomen as I urinated. I sat for a moment, unsure if I was done peeing, then signaled for Roanne to help me upright.

I leaned against her and walked, hunched over like an old lady, back to the bed.

"I don't feel very sexy right now," I sighed, winded from the short walk. I lowered myself onto the bed's edge, my legs hanging over, dangling my slippers off my toes and letting them drop to the floor with soft plops.

Roanne rested a hand on my knee. "Give it time."

I had had my first D and C at the hospital at Fort Hood just before my twenty-ninth birthday, after a half-day of passing fist-size blood clots. At that point, Scott and I had been trying to get pregnant for two years, starting soon after we returned stateside from Panama. We had failed. I had failed. On that day, when I came home from the army hospital, I heard a radio report about a newborn abandoned in a Dumpster. Other women were throwing babies away while I was unable to have one. I had clawed at my belly trying to get out of my traitorous body. Scott had found me on the floor, my hands covered with blood from the scratches.

We tried for five more years, even after the doctors said our chances of success were under two percent. A fertility "workup" showed Scott's swimmers were amassing and training for the Olympics, but I had only one healthy ovary and both Fallopian tubes were twisted and encased in scar tissue, a useless pipeline for an egg. By the time we adopted Daniel, eleven years into our marriage, a chronic pain in my left lower abdomen had become nearly unbearable.

With Roanne's hands behind my knees, I slowly lifted one leg at a time back into the hospital bed. I stared at the lumps and bumps of my sheet-covered body. "Why did this happen to me?"

Roanne pulled the turquoise chair up to the bedside and sat. "You said the doctors could never tell you for sure," she said. "Maybe low-grade infection? PID? Gynecology is pretty much guesswork, isn't it?"

"I think the GYNs have a dart board for possible causes whenever a woman comes in with a problem. A fourth of the dart board is pH imbalance, another fourth is failure to pee immediately after you have sex, and the other half is 'I don't know.'"

"Sometimes things just mysteriously happen to women."

"Demons visited me in the middle of the night?"

"Or visited Scott."

"No." I gingerly swung my legs back into the bed and inched back against the pillows. "There are other causes of PID."

"Guesswork, yeah, but isn't it the most—did the subject ever come up?"

"No." Not with Scott. One of those GYNs, during an appointment for one of my problems, had asked about my "sexual partners." I had dismissed his offensive suggestion. "I'm married," I had said. "My husband is my only sexual partner, and I'm his." I had been so sure.

Roanne fiddled with the cups stacked next to the water pitcher on the nightstand. Something metal clattered on the floor down the hallway, followed by the rise of voices at the nearby nurse's station. "Do you want me to check at the desk to see if the doctor is on his way?" she asked, already standing to go.

"Sure." I fished around in the tangled sheet for the remote and unmuted the TV.

Roanne had taken a step toward the door but turned her head toward the screen at the tinkle of a xylophone, the sound that accompanied Samantha's nose twitch whenever she worked her witchy magic.

"When we were in high school we thought that show was so cute," I said. "Remember how we would practice twitching our noses in the mirror?"

Roanne smiled. "You could never get it right, and you'd get frustrated and stomp your foot."

"Now, all I can think is when is that chick going to wake the fuck up, excuse my French, and lose that loser?"

"Don't be so hard on Samantha. She puts up with Darrin because she wants a home and a marriage and a baby, like most women. She wants to be normal."

"She's way too good for him."

"No couple is totally even. I think sometimes it's easier for us to tolerate their shortcomings than the other way around. We're more understanding by nature."

"Like me and Scott?"

"No. I didn't mean that. You're both fine."

"He should at least be here with me, after all I've had to go through. Dick."

"What?"

"York." I waved the remote at the TV. "I like him better than the other one, too."

– 2019 –

Christine and I stared down eight floors to the parking lot from the balcony of the LA hotel. "That's him," I said, my knees quaking. "Is that him? Oh, my goodness, that's him. He's early."

A tall, dark-skinned black man with a graying beard leaned against a black Mercedes SUV. He wore a billed leather hat pulled low on his forehead, but his profile was clearly visible. He lifted his chin and blew a stream of smoke into the pink-streaked evening sky. That stray cigarette he couldn't stop himself from having, but he wouldn't smoke around me.

"Whoa!" Christine said. "You had an affair with Idris Elba's dad?"

"Slightly older brother at the most, and when you're with someone for ten years, it's not an affair, it's a relationship."

"Come inside. Calm down."

I followed my sister into the room. "I can't calm down."

Christine dug into her purse. "Here. I have one Xanax left over from the flight."

I waved off the pill. "No thanks. I'll take some deep breaths."

"Sit," Christine said. "I'll make you a cup of tea. Let's talk while you pull yourself together. He can wait."

I nodded and perched on the corner of the queen-size bed, inhaled deeply and exhaled slowly.

"Do I look okay?" I asked while Christine filled a cup with water from the bathroom sink, dropped in a tea bag, and set the cup in the mini microwave.

I wore a form-fitting, sleeveless black jumpsuit, dressed for a date even though I hadn't been on one for years.

"It depends on what message you want to send," she said.

"The message I don't want to send is, 'I'm a pitiful mess

without you.'"

Christine handed me the tea and pulled up an armchair across from me.

"You look great. I can't believe you never told me about him."

"I never even told Roanne."

"I imagined you and Roanne told each other everything."

"If we did, she wouldn't be—" She wouldn't be dead. "He was married. He is married. She would've told me to end it, to protect me. I didn't want to be protected. Not from having him."

"I never would have thought you could be with a married man," Christine said. "I thought you'd be more careful."

I blew across the surface of my tea, watched it ripple, and took a sip. "It's lonely out there when you're fifty, divorced, and you haven't dated since college. You think *it* will never happen again. Then you think you'll lose the desire for *it* to ever happen again. And you don't know if not having that desire would be better or worse. I'm happy for you and Barry, but you have no idea."

"I have my own anxieties. Married to a pilot who's away from home a lot, with all those flight attendants throwing themselves at him. Didn't you feel guilty? About what you were doing to the wife?"

"I couldn't let myself think about that. He was the one cheating, not me. And I deserved to be loved, too. I was not going to listen to any voice, inside or outside my head, telling me 'no.' "

"If I'd known," Christine said, "I would've given you lots of unasked-for advice, to at least save you from being hurt."

"I gave myself all that advice, over and over. But I was grabbing hold of what I thought I would never have another chance at. That just blew all those red flags to kingdom come." I slipped my foot into a metallic-colored wedge and bent to fasten the strap. "Plus, he's one irresistible guy."

Christine drummed her fingers on her knee. "I'm curious...is it true black men have a rule they won't..."

"Won't what?"

"Go down on a woman."

I rolled my eyes. "I'm sure not all black men are the same about sex any more than only the gay guys in Palm Springs have statues outside their homes of nude Greek men wearing pink scarves."

"Not sure what you're talking about, but the answer is no?"

My face involuntarily unfolded a smile.

"Look at you, grinning like a Cheshire cat. It was pretty damn good, huh?"

"He had cracked the code."

"Come on, spill the tea."

I looked down at my cup. "What?"

"Tell it. I might have to give Barry some hints. Help your little sis out."

"Okay." I took a deep breath. Christine leaned in. "It doesn't matter what a man does in bed as long as he always makes the woman feel like it's all about her. He would actually ask me what I wanted."

"Barry used to ask me. I'd say, 'exhaust me.' Is that how you felt after? Exhausted?"

"I felt invincible."

"So, it was mainly about the sex?"

I tightened the strap on the second shoe. "It wouldn't have lasted on just the sex. He was a true friend. He listened to me. I could be myself around him. In twenty-four years married to Scott, I was always trying to be what I thought he wanted me to be, and to say what I thought he wanted to hear."

"You should have gotten out sooner. Maybe you would have met this guy when he was still single."

"Who knows? It's strange how things happen."

I had met Thelonius "Theo" Harris, named by his father, a

big fan of Thelonius Monk, at the bar in Houston's downtown Hilton. I had been attending a book fair at the hotel, and he was meeting a client as a tax attorney for Shell Oil. We had sat down next to each other on the only two vacant bar stools. He made a comment about the basketball game on the TV behind the bar. Was I a Lakers fan? I said "no," but the chemistry was instant. Everything else was "yes."

I explained to Christine the logistics of the liaison. Theo would see me about twice a month, sometimes more often, in San Antonio. It had been a perfect setup. His wife worked in LA and commuted to Houston once a month, and any acquaintances who might bump into him were in Houston.

"I remember those years. You had this glow about you," Christine said. "I thought it was your power yoga class. Little did I know..."

"All those years weren't glowy. One of those years I was in hell with Daniel and his drug addiction. Thank goodness, I had Theo as my oasis, or I might have lost my mind. And, thank goodness, neither you nor Roanne guessed about him, nor, goodness gracious, Daniel."

"After all that, he ghosted you? The wife must have found out and put his balls in a vise."

I cringed, although I didn't think that had happened, metaphorically or otherwise. But, after ten years of a little sign here, a little sign there, putting two and two together, the wife usually knows. Still, she could have made herself not know. I had done that with Scott for years with what might have been dozens of women.

Scott had come home late or stayed out until the next morning so many times I had lost count, and I had stopped asking for explanations. The asking led to fights, slammed doors, screeching tires, and more staying out. I had found the receipts with drink charges for two, the cigarette butt that wasn't his brand in his truck's ashtray. An itch, a burn, a pain, more pain, worse pain had sent me to the gynecologist, and ultimately to a surgeon. Scott had apparently started using protection in the last years of our marriage, but even a torn condom wrapper under the passenger seat didn't shock me awake. I could always tell myself, no, he wouldn't do that to me. There had been no reason. Up until reasons hadn't mattered.

I set my half-empty cup of tea on the nearby windowsill. I hadn't heard from Theo in five years. We had an agreement. I would never contact him unless he contacted me first. It was our number one safety rule. Sometimes, his contact came just before our arranged rendezvous, to call things off as I sat anxiously in a motel room. That was the way things were, gut-wrenching disappointment and waiting weeks longer to be together because the original plan didn't work at the last minute. When Theo's phone calls, texts, and emails stopped abruptly, I never broke the contact rule. I waited. And waited. Until three days ago.

I had sent a message to his secondary email address, the one he had used last, hoping it was still active. I had given him the name of the hotel, the day and time to meet, and thirty hours to answer, just enough time to think this might be the only chance he would ever have to see me again. He had responded with his standard "HOIC." Our code. The Sam and Dave song, "Hold On, I'm Coming." I had a laughing fit the first time he had used it and explained the letters. His second email had said he was taking me to a Lakers game.

"So, where to now in this Lifetime movie?" Christine asked.

I shook my head. "There's no 'happily ever after' waiting for me with Theo. That's why I need you around. I need to stay on track. I can't fall back into those deep, not-so-old feelings. I won't be able to get back out."

"A basketball game should be safe enough, hard for you to talk to him, but safe. And I've got all night and then some to keep you out of trouble. Barry won't get in until tomorrow afternoon, and we don't meet Lexie until evening. If you call, I'll come rushing to the rescue in my Prius rental Batmobile, wherever you are."

"What'll you do while I'm on my rendezvous?"

"I need to update the cupcake website with the spring menu and review the contract for the expansion and new party room at the San Marcos store. You're all set for us to meet the remodeling crew next week, right?"

"That's next week?"

She pursed her lips and sighed. "Should I plan to do that on my own?"

"I'll be there, I'll try to be there."

"Right. It's all on me."

I threw her a sheepish smile. "Thank you for coming out here a day early."

"Finally, when your heart is at risk, that's when I get called in." Another sigh. "But, whatever. You need me, I'm here."

"You're the best. "

I hugged her, took a last sip of tea, and went into the bathroom to fluff my hair—red again for Theo—brush my teeth, and reapply my lipstick.

A text dinged on my phone. Theo was in the lobby. I had come to the edge of that million-mile emotional gulf. Showtime.

– 1985 –

"I've ended it, I know it was a mistake, so you don't have to lecture me," Roanne said.

The phone connection crackled so that I could just make out her words. There was no chance to drive over to her house in Round Rock from four thousand miles away for a heart-to-heart chat. We talked every week on the phone, but we hadn't seen each other in a year, since Scott had been stationed at Fort Greely near Delta Junction, Alaska.

"I haven't lectured, I wouldn't," I said. "I didn't say anything."

"Except for saying as the 'other woman,' I'm, at best, number two, his wife is the priority, and I'm the option. That really hurt."

"I was trying to save you from getting hurt. You don't want to give up on your marriage for some temporary excitement."

"I wasn't giving up on Johnny. I only wanted to feel good again. What if Scott was—Scott's not there, is he? He doesn't know, does he?"

"No, I wouldn't tell him. He's at some meet-and-greet or having a few with the guys after work. Half the time, he forgets to call. You know Scott, Mr. Social, the life of the party."

"I wish you were here, Con. You might as well be on the moon."

"The moon, yeah, walking through the ice fog in my winter gear." I laughed. "You should see me in my puffy moon boots and down parka and quilted mittens. I look like the Marshmallow Man from *Ghostbusters*."

My first winter in Delta Junction I had stayed inside and cried for days. The temperature had plummeted to forty below and the darkness seemed endless. Scott had gone on cold-weather training maneuvers, and I was stuck in our rented two-room cabin afraid to venture out on the icy roads.

I still missed Roanne so much, it physically hurt. I feared that we were adrift without each other. Roanne's affair had lasted only three weeks, but I couldn't help but think that I could have talked her out of the bad decision at the start if I had been there.

"When did you call it off?" I asked.

"Yesterday. Omar and I had lunch at La Quinta. I was feeling rushed. I had a class to teach in the afternoon."

Roanne had first told me about the affair after the first full sexual encounter at a motel on the edge of town. She was breathless when she spoke about her and Omar, like they were playing in the big, movie love scene in *Doctor Zhivago*. I had had an urge to hum "Lara's Theme" as she talked.

Omar was Jordanian, an American immigrant success story, the patriarch of a family that owned and operated an upscale furniture store in Round Rock. Roanne had met him at the store while eyeing a trestle table with upholstered chairs. She had been teaching math part-time at a private school for almost two school years, but her salary and Johnny's unemployment checks wouldn't support a nine-hundred-dollar dining set, especially not with their hefty mortgage payment.

Roanne hadn't been looking for an affair, especially not with a married man, but it was obvious from our talks that she had been starved for attention, for the romance of her and Johnny's early days. According to Roanne, they were fighting a lot. About not enough money—her. About not enough sex—him.

"I try to be supportive," Roanne had told me. "He's having a hard time finding a job. He feels useless. I get it. But I teach four days a week, I cook when I get home, I pick up the house, I do the laundry, I help Stella with her homework. After she's in bed, I do my lesson plans."

Johnny, apparently, would sit on the couch like a lump of self-pity, staring at the TV, oblivious to what Roanne needed, a little help and some human contact apart from sex.

"When we're in bed," Roanne had said, "he can't be bothered with foreplay before he jumps me. It doesn't feel like making love. It feels like he's taking all his frustrations out on me."

And along came Omar, a handsome, well-off older man, who took Roanne out to lunch, sent flowers to her classroom, lavished her with attention, and bothered with foreplay, lots of it, apparently.

The phone crackled over Roanne's words. "I..." *crkkkk* "...Omar I didn't have time for sex" *crkkkk* "...lunch."

No time for sex, the defining moment; they were becoming like a routine married couple, life was getting in the way of romance. "He was upset about that?"

"No, not at all. Omar doesn't get upset. He's always pleasant. We had a nice meal, Caesar salad. He even talked me into sharing dessert. He was feeding me a spoonful of crème brûlée, and he said, 'You are so beautiful.' "

That didn't sound like a breakup story. Did he get too serious, say he'd leave his wife for her, and that's when she ran for it?

Roanne continued, "'But,' he said, 'you would be gorgeous if you had breast....' " Crkkkk.

"He said what?"

"Breast implants. I laughed. I took it for a joke. I said, 'How would I pay for a boob job on a teacher's salary?' He said, 'I can pay for it.' I laughed harder. I said, 'And how would I explain my new breasts and how they were financed to my husband?' He laughed. I didn't."

"Ro, he was saying your body—" Crkkkk.

"I know. Right in the middle of a mouthful of crème brûlée, I saw him. I really saw him. I was with a man I was willing to risk my marriage for, and he was cheating on his wife, a man who was good-looking, but fifteen years older than me, with a little paunch and a thin spot at the top of his head and a bit of sag at the jaw. And he was telling me I wasn't perfect enough for him."

"What did you say?"

"I told him my husband liked me the way I was. He said, 'So you're with me because why?' And then I said, 'Exactly. Why?' I told him I didn't want to see him again, and I walked out."

"Good for you, girl. Do you think he'll stay away? He could make trouble for you and Johnny."

"He can't make trouble if I come clean with Johnny."

"Yeah, but do you think that's a good idea?"

"I swore before we were married that I would never keep another secret from him. I love him. He loves me. He'll forgive me. It may take him a while, but he will."

"You and Omar, how many times?"

"Six. That sounds bad. Once sounds bad. I'm an idiot. Johnny's the only man I've ever loved. How could I have just completely forgotten that?" Chimes sounded in the background, followed by the croaky howl of Roanne's aging cocker spaniel. "Oh, the doorbell. Now who—can you hang on for a minute?"

While I waited for Roanne to return, I traced a heart on the frosted kitchen window. I hoped Roanne knew what she was doing. She really did believe that love conquered all.

A female moose stood twenty feet away from the window, her lower legs sunk in the deep snow behind the cabin. She was heavy through the abdomen. She'd be dropping her calf soon. The moose raised her bulbous head to munch at the branch of a birch tree, making a rustling sound. A raven squawked above a stand of black spruce. The sky was fading to gray with the first peach-colored streaks of sunset, the light lasting a few minutes more than the day before.

Spring would arrive on the wings of Canada geese in two more months. It comforted me to think of those same geese wintering in Texas near Roanne before they made their journey up north.

Roanne came back on the phone, breathing hard, and the pitch of her voice rose. "What is he thinking? A dozen, no ten, white roses? Is this some kind of apology? Does he think I'm going to pick things up again with him? No way, Jose, and to send them to my house? If Johnny weren't out on a job interview, I'd be in deep kimchi, as he would say." Paper rustled. She gasped. "Oh, my goodness, they're from Johnny. Why would he, out of the blue, send me roses?"

"An early surprise? Tomorrow is Valentine's Day?"

"Oh, that's right, I have to make cupcakes for Stella's class. Oh, the bus will be here any minute. I need to meet her at the corner. I'm so flustered right now. White roses, ten years since Johnny and I met, on Valentine's Day. He's still a hopeless romantic." She sniffed. "Ah, they smell so beautiful." She sniffed again. "Mmm. I must have been out of my mind to go looking for greener grass outside my backyard."

"You're the hopeless romantic. Are you going to tell him the day before Valentine's Day?"

"That would be bad. I'll wait until he has a job. I don't want to kick him while he's down. I'm sure it will only be a couple of weeks more. You don't think it'll be too late for me to make it right with him, do you?"

What could I say? The first time she walked into a hotel room with Dr. Zhivago might have been too late. But the roses. Johnny did love her. They had ten years invested in each other. They had Stella.

"It's never too late for a new beginning." The inspirational saying I had seen on a poster at the dentist's office popped into my mind and out of my mouth. I could see the curvy, gold lettering across a scene of spring flowers blossoming, bunnies peeking out of the grass, and birds winging across a bright blue sky. I hoped, for her sake, that, at least this time, I had found the right words.

– 2019 –

I walked across the lobby toward Theo, a mirage that sharpened into focus as I came closer. The square of his shoulders, the slight tilt of his head, a smile spread across his face. He opened his arms wide, and I eased into his embrace, felt the flex of his forearms around my shoulders, inhaled his smell of faint cigarette smoke and expensive cologne, curled my fingers into his back. We both broke the hug a minute in, before either of us could get lost in it.

I had plenty to say, but my throat squeezed shut.

"I wasn't sure about the game," he said. The rich rumble of his voice was instantly familiar. "If that's a good choice."

"It's fine."

We walked to his car, and he opened the passenger door for me. The interior smelled of new leather.

"How's Daniel?" he asked.

"Doing well. He just landed a good job in Dallas. I have a second grandbaby, Charlotte."

"That's great."

"Your daughter?"

"Good. She has a 'life partner.' I'm still getting used to these new labels." He took the ramp onto the freeway. "Are you still writing?"

"I'm working on the fourteenth in my mystery series. You haven't been tracking my books?"

"I should have. I will."

"You don't have to."

"I will. Promise."

His shoulder leaned toward me, then retracted, like he was about to let go of the wheel, touch me, but pulled back. Our clipped banter continued as we glanced sideways at each other, intermittently, then pulled our eyes straight ahead.

"How are you?" he asked.

"Good. Staying healthy."

"And happy?"

"Mostly."

"Are you with someone?"

I hesitated, wanting to be less than direct, but game-playing is not what I did with Theo. "No."

"Why not?"

"You're a tough act to follow."

" Aww, you're trying to be nice," he said.

"No, not really."

He was silent for a couple of beats. "You look fantastic." His gaze lingered on me.

"You, too." I had to turn my face to the window to hide a surge of longing and the instinct to reach out and touch him, stroke him.

I took a breath and made my voice light. "How do you like LA?"

"Lovin' it. House in the hills. The firm's doing great. You have the city, the country, the beach, the mountains, the woods, everything here. And the people are beautiful."

"I'm happy for you." I didn't mean it, not totally, I also meant I was sad for me.

He parked, and we walked hand in hand to the Staples Center. I memorized the way his fingers curled and readjusted and tapped against mine, so that I could call up the feeling later.

Inside, the arena was rocking. Our seats were eight rows behind the Lakers bench. Great seats, but not for a serious conversation. For two quarters I pushed what was on my mind aside, and we were just a couple spending time together, enjoying a basketball game. We turned to each other now and then and smiled. He touched my leg. I brushed his shoulder. We jumped out of our seats and cheered when LeBron dunked. We put our hands to our heads and dropped our jaws when the refs called fouls against the Lakers or didn't call fouls against the other team.

I waited until halftime. I wanted to say my piece in a calm, firm tone, but I had to raise my voice to be heard over the performance of the Laker Girls and the crowd noise.

"You cut me off without a word!" It came out like a shriek.

"I moved to LA, started my own firm. You knew that was what I was working toward." I had no trouble hearing his deep, reverberating, level voice.

"You didn't give me any warning!"

"I thought it would be easier on you. I didn't know if we would ever have the opportunity to be together again. For sure, it would never be like it had been. Instead of building your hopes up and then disappointing you, I thought it would be better to just leave."

"But not a word? All this time?"

He hung his head for a moment, searching for an acceptable answer, I supposed. "I have my own law practice, but I'm not on my own at work. Jennifer—"

"No, please." Another one of our rules was that he would never say his wife's name to me.

"I'm sorry. She's the office manager. She monitors all my phone calls, messages, in and out. I can't take the risk. Even that old email or my text in the hotel lobby could have blown everything up if I didn't remember to immediately delete."

"I didn't know what else to do."

"It's okay. I kept it under the radar." He leaned into me, his brown eyes wet. "I never wanted to hurt you."

My bottom lip trembled. I was going to flat-out start bawling. I gritted my teeth, then made myself speak. "Would you get me some nachos, please?" I quavered.

He leapt up and stepped over me to exit our row, thrilled that I had given him an escape from the charged moment.

I barely finished half the nachos and surrendered the rest to Theo. We watched the rest of the game without talking. I don't know what I had expected as his explanation for exiling me to limbo for five years. A coma? Lost in Bora Bora? Certainly not "I did it for your own good." I was deflated. Empty.

I had never been to LA before, but, after the game, it was obvious that we were headed away from the Staples Center a different way than we had come. We had left the freeway and were winding up into the hills with the city lights sprawled below us. I didn't say anything. I wasn't sure if I wanted the night to end or if I wanted it to last. I closed my eyes and let my body sway with the movement of the car until the motion jerked to a stop.

I looked up at a huge ship with soaring decks and wings. It took a moment for me to realize I was staring at a magnificent house. Behind the glass front a waterfall cascaded from the third to the first floor.

Theo turned off the engine. I could almost hear the faint sound of the falling water in the still night.

"I want to show you my home," he said.

"Your and your wife's home."

"She's out of town." He turned to me, touched my thigh. A spark jumped through me.

I threw my door open, walked to the front of the car, and leaned against the hood, my arms crossed. A slice of moon reflected in the glass wall. He exited the car and stood at the opposite side.

"I was hoping you'd spend the night," he said, then sidestepped closer. "I had a plan, I didn't know if I would set it in motion. At the game I kept running it through my mind, should I, shouldn't I?"

"A plan?"

"To whisk you away, before you could say no." He brushed my bare arm. "I can see behind those eyes. Right now, you don't know whether you want to fuck me or kill me."

I wanted to do both. Repeatedly. "I can't go in the back

door anymore."

"I'll take you in the front door tonight, all night."

The liquid heat that rushed through my body was so intense, I was sure I would burn him if he touched me again. The smell of him filled my head, and I could taste him on my tongue. I didn't need to go in the house. He could throw me onto the hood of the car, and enter me, and I would scream a feral yowl that would shatter the glass around that waterfall.

In my dreams. Later. Multiple, multiple times.

I backed away from him.

His eyes tracked mine. "So, it's kill me."

That lopsided, dimpled grin released a swarm of butterflies in my stomach, but also made my blood boil with a fleeting violent thought. Luckily for both of us, I had not opted to try to sneak a gun into the Staples Center, even if I could have sneaked it past Christine.

I bit my lip to stop the tremble and got back in the car. He slid into his seat. A cool breeze swept across us through our two opened doors.

"I can't blame you," he said.

"It was exhausting, the sneaking around, the elaborate plans, the backup plans. The backup to the backup plans."

"It was gloriously worth it all. Do you regret it?"

"The anxiety over getting caught, the—" Who was I kidding? "Not a second."

"We're a rare match. The best of lovers who can talk like the best of friends."

"I've missed that the most," I said. "The way you comforted me when my dad died, when Daniel was on drugs."

"All that drama at my job, the cops shooting my cousin, my daughter coming out."

"Who's the best, Dennis Edwards or David Ruffin?" I laughed, remembering our in-depth discussion over the vocal range of the lead singers for The Temptations.

"Jiffy cornbread or scratch?" He laughed.

"We could always talk."

"We were there for each other, for sure."

"I thought when the other part ended we could still be friends, stay in touch, all above aboard," I said. "Better than lovers, a lasting thing, someone in my life to share a laugh, a tear, or to call me once in a while to say, 'How are you?' Is that too much to ask after all the time we spent together?"

He drew in his lower lip, fidgeted with the edge of his jacket sleeve. "Explanations would be required. A close female friend suddenly shows up? I don't see how we could make that work, all above board, like you said."

A memory I had long ago pushed to a remote crevice of my mind rushed forward. When I was eleven, my family lived in Kansas, where every fall for two years, I traipsed through the slush in my red rubber boots, selling candy bars door-to-door to raise money for my school's Christmas pageant. On one of those trips, a scowling old man opened the door to my smiling, hopeful face as I held up a candy bar wrapped in gold foil. I was explaining the almond and no-almond varieties when he slammed the door in my face. I stood on his porch, unable to lift my red rubber boots, and busted out in tears. Theo's words hit me like the same kind of rejection.

"It was a fantasy at best," I said, trying to shrug it off while a lump built in my throat. "But, I can't even say how much that disappoints me."

"I'm sorry that disappointment is all I have to give you," he said, his words pushed out as if he was overcoming a lump in his throat.

We shut our doors at the same time with a final, single bang.

As the Mercedes headed back to the hotel, we had an hour to say or not say whatever else had to be said or left unsaid. The frustrated glances we exchanged shouted, "Say something!" "Do something!" But neither of us knew how to break the silence.

He pulled up in front of the hotel, parked, and stared straight ahead, his hands massaging the steering wheel. Neither of us made a move to open a door. Silent, excruciating minutes ticked by.

I nudged his arm with a knuckle and said in a jokey tone, "Hey, I'm tired of carrying the conversation here."

He swiveled his head toward me. "You're the writer. Never at a loss for words. What's on your mind?"

"I'm not so good at speaking what's on my mind." I pulled at the leg of my jumpsuit, let it pop back against my knee, smoothed the fabric with my palm. "What I've been doing the past few months... what I've been saying... I'm speaking up to certain men who at one time in my life made me feel worthless."

"Me? You felt worthless when you were with me?"

"I felt incredible when I was with you and worthless when you disappeared with no explanation after ten freaking years."

"But, I told you—"

"You told me shit. It doesn't matter with any of the rest of them who couldn't look me in the face and own up to what they did. I had no expectations for them. But you, I didn't see you in that crowd. I saw you standing out, head and shoulders above the rest. Up was the direction I wanted to look to see you. I wish I hadn't come all the way out here to find out I was wrong."

I opened the door, hopped out of the car, and walked toward the main door of the hotel. A car door slammed, and footsteps scuffed on the asphalt, running up behind me.

"You weren't wrong." Theo grabbed my shoulders and whirled me around. "I cut you off. I did want to save you from being hurt. But, more than that, I wanted to save myself from having to watch the hurt I put you through. I wasn't making it easier for you. I was making it easier for me." His chest heaved. "It was cruel, it was cowardly, and it's the lowest thing I've ever done. You did nothing but make me feel good. You didn't deserve to be treated that way." He ran his hand softly along my jaw. "I know I can't make it up to you, but I'm so, so sorry, baby."

I blinked hard to stop the tears clouding my vision. "I'm looking up and—"

"Do you see me, baby?" He rubbed the tears from under my eyes with his thumbs.

"I'm getting a definite glimpse."

"I do love you."

"I know."

"It was always up to you to end it," he said.

"So, I've had all the responsibility."

"You've had all the power."

He guided me into his chest and held me carefully, like he would a child.

He released his hug and spread his arms wide. "It's all on you, baby. What now?"

I took his hands in mine and reeled myself into him. "Theo, you have a beautiful life. Go live it." Standing on tiptoes, I kissed his cheek.

I walked away, not looking back. When the lobby doors slid closed behind me, I could sense him standing there, watching me go.

Inside the hotel room Christine was stationed on the edge of the bed facing the door, like she had been there all night waiting for me to walk in. She tapped her foot on the carpet, dying to ask me how things had gone.

"I'm changing my flight to the red-eye tonight," I said. "I'm done here."

"Are you over him?"

"No, but I'm past him."

"You loved him?"

"Still do."

"Do you want me to take you to the airport?"

"Yes. The sooner the better. Just give me a few minutes in

the bathroom."

I sat down on the edge of the tub, turned the shower on to block the noise, and cried until my ribs hurt.

– 2008 –

I spotted Roanne and her date at a table in the middle of the C'mon Inn, while Christine and I wandered around the bar's perimeter, looking for a vacant booth. The dive on Austin's east side was known for its awesome and cheap happy hour appetizers.

"Here," I said, pointing to seats that would put us near the hall that led to the restroom, directly across from the end of the bar. We would have a diagonal line of sight about twenty-five feet from Roanne's table with three tables staggered in between.

"Perfect," Christine said as we slipped into the booth. "Not too close to raise suspicion but a good side view of both of them."

The place was crowded and buzzing with loud talk and laughter. A young woman in tight jeans and a sequined sports bra was singing "I Will Survive" with the karaoke machine. Servers in tight black pants and white belly shirts weaved among the tables.

We ordered white wines and a sampler platter and settled in to play wingmen for Roanne and her first online date, a handsome man, late fifties-ish, with abundant silver hair and a neatly trimmed beard of the same shade. We had our signals worked out. Roanne would smooth the back of her hair with one hand for "Meet me in the bathroom for an update." Smoothing with two hands would mean "Get me out of here, now!" And switching her purse, where it hung on the corner of her chair, to the opposite corner would mean "Going great! Leave!"

I had discovered Roanne's online dating project two weeks before when she, Christine, and I were at C is for Cupcakes in Austin, testing new flavors to celebrate the shop's tenth anniversary. We had narrowed the winning candidates down to Pink Paradise with lychee fruit, Confetti Storm filled with candy flakes, and Blue Velvet, which was Red Velvet with blue frosting.

Roanne had seemed unusually focused on her phone, scrolling and tapping. When I had asked her about it, she showed me the dating app. I had rolled my eyes.

"Don't knock it till you've tried it," she had said.

She then had shown me a dozen photos of men in their fifties, or so they said in their dating profiles.

"Look at this one," she had said, expanding the view of a silver-bearded guy with a black Lab. She clicked on his profile and read aloud as I followed along on her screen. "'Educated, fun-loving, affectionate silver fox looking for my vixin.'"

"'Vixin?' With two *i*'s?" I had clicked my tongue. "And who refers to a woman like that, anyway?"

"You don't think I could be a vixen?" had been her feelings-hurt reply.

Two women dressed in all black, including motorcycle boots, took the karaoke stage and belted out "Love Shack."

Roanne and the Silver Fox, aka Larry, who looked north of five years older than his online photo, were smiling and sipping their drinks.

"You don't think he could be a serial killer?" I asked Christine. Our appetizers arrived, and I dug into the shrimp-and-cheese stuffed mushrooms.

"The guy who lets you go in front of him in line at the H-E-B could be a serial killer," Christine said.

"I just want her to be careful. With her body and her heart."

"Have you tried Internet dating?" Christine asked, sawing her teeth into a triangle of flat bread spread with feta cheese and basil.

"No. I think I'm more the meeting-someone-in-real-time type. Organic, isn't that what the young folks say?"

"Organic is not necessarily healthier." She raised her wine glass to her lips.

Christine and I talked about the best and the worst qualities in men, finished half of our snacks, and ordered two more wines. Every few seconds, we glanced over at Roanne and Larry. He seemed to be leaning closer to her over the table, probably to hear her above the noise, but nothing looked out of order, so far.

I took a gulp of water to wash down a potato skin and peeked over my glass at Roanne. "There's the signal," I said. "One hand on the back of the head."

"Are you sure?"

"Yes. Keep an eye on him. I'll be back soon." I scooted out of the booth and made a beeline for the bathroom. Out of the corner of my eye, I saw Roanne walking away from her table, headed in my direction.

Roanne and I exchanged glances when we were both inside the crowded and tiny bathroom, waited five minutes to use the stalls, then another few minutes for four chatty women to leave. I leaned against the sink counter.

"You're looking hot," I said. She was dressed in black pencil pants, a leopard print top, and black heels.

She smiled crookedly, a bit embarrassed. "Too much?"

I shook my head. "How does he rate so far?"

Roanne stared into the mirror and fluffed her hair. "Two stars. Two and a half, if he wasn't a stereotyping, borderline homophobe."

"How did that even come up twenty-five minutes into a first date?"

"He spotted you and Christine when you walked in and immediately had your number."

"What? He thinks Christine and I are lesbians?"

"He says it's easy to pick out 'lezzies.' He calls it 'the dynamic.' Old woman with a young woman—"

"Wait. Old?" I twisted around to look over my shoulder at

my reflection. I leaned into the mirror and rubbed away a mascara smudge under my right eye.

"The feminine one in a dress with long hair, the butch one in pants with a shaved head, he said."

"So, I like dresses." I straightened the bodice of my white maxi and adjusted my cleavage. "Christine likes jeans with holes in them. And she doesn't have a shaved head. She has a modern pixie."

"Holding hands across the table, he said."

"Well, that there is a dead giveaway. Hell—lo. We are sisters. So, he's probably uncomplicated sexually, not bi, traditional, middle-class guy. What else has he said?"

"He's already told me six times how attractive I am."

"That's good, right?"

"I don't know." Roanne pulled a black-and-gold tube of lipstick out of her leopard print bag. "He keeps scanning me. You know what I mean." She stared at me and ran her eyes slowly up and down my body without moving her head. "And when I talk, I don't think he's listening. It's like he's looking past me. Is there something more interesting than me at the bar?"

"There's a lot going on out there." I had noticed several unpaired, young women hanging around the bar. "Is he telling you much about himself?"

"A lot about his ex, how horrid she was." She neatly applied a paprika color to the peaks of her upper lip, pressed her lips together, and moved them side to side.

"I don't know much about online dating, but isn't that a turnoff? 'My ex was a jerk, I suspect you could be a jerk, are you a jerk, I'm trying to find out if you're a jerk.' "

"That's not all he talked about." One of her gold hoop earrings was caught in a strand of hair, and she flipped it free. "He's traveled to Greece and New Zealand and Iceland. That's kind of fascinating. And he owns his own business. Something to do with security, remote cameras, tracking devices, something techie I don't really understand."

"A real James Bond," I said with an eye roll.

"He's good-looking," she said, halfway like a question, and I nodded. "He has a personal trainer. He swims a lot. He owns a house with a pool."

"So he says. Does he have children?"

"A son, in his thirties, still in school, going for his PhD. And a three-year-old daughter."

"Ah, the younger woman must have dumped him not too long ago."

"He was Plan C for that one, he said."

"C as in child support."

"He's now focused on..." Roanne did air quotes. "'...a more mature partner.'"

"Hmm. That's promising. What qualities is he looking for in a woman?" I asked.

"Tall, blonde, pretty, he said."

"But what qualities?" I repeated.

"Affectionate, attractive, loyal. I think he mentioned loyal twice."

"It sounds like he's looking for another dog with prettier hair."

She shrugged. "You're not impressed."

"Are you?"

"I don't see a second date. Do you think they're all like this?" she asked.

"Probably not. You know what they say about kissing frogs."

"It would be helpful if they all came with labels: 'Frog.' 'Prince.'"

She tossed her lipstick into her bag. "Better get back," she said. "On the bright side, the food is good. The beer-battered onion rings are heavenly. And he's picking up the check, haven't had a man do that for me in a while."

"It is happy hour."

Roanne was about to push the bathroom door open when Christine popped in. She pushed her palms out and backed us up to the sink.

"Okay, Roanne," she said, "are you becoming invested in this guy?"

"Invested?" She pulled her cell phone out of her purse. "It's been a half hour. "

"I just wanted to let you know that—" Christine began.

"Oh, goodness," Roanne cut her off. "It's Friday. I have to call Zoe." She ducked into a stall and shut the door. Her murmuring voice rose and fell.

"Zoe and her are talking?" Christine said. "That's great."

"Not really. She's been calling Zoe every Friday night for the past six months, but Zoe doesn't answer. Roanne leaves a message, but she never gets a call back. She says she's not going to give up, that someday they'll reconnect."

"Oh, that's sad."

"Call me soon. Love you," came Roanne's cheerful voice from behind the stall door.

I put my finger to my lips to shush Christine as Roanne emerged with a forced smile and damp eyes.

"So, Christine, what's up?" Roanne asked.

"As soon as you were out of sight, he was on that gal in the purple romper at the bar like white on rice."

"The one with the butt cheeks hanging out?" I said.

Christine flicked a forefinger in my direction. "Bingo."

"Should I ask him about it?" Roanne said. "Or continue with the date as if nothing happened?"

"Ditch the guy," Christine said. "There's a little club around the corner with a jazz trio and half-price drinks for another hour. I looked it up online. Let's check it out."

Roanne marched out and up to the Silver Fox with Christine and me several paces behind. He was out of breath and adjusting back into his seat. He smiled up at Roanne like the puppy who had eaten the new cell phone.

Roanne remained standing while Christine and I caught up to her. "Thanks for a nice evening, Larry," she said. "I'm leaving now with these lesbian vixens."

His jaw dropped, and his face reddened. We busted out in giggles as we scampered toward the door.

– 2019 –

The morning sun glared off wet patches on the highway from an overnight shower. The harsh light bore like a drill bit into my forehead. I fought the urge to turn around and head back south to San Antonio, where I could crawl into my bed and pull the covers over my head for the next week. I had slept for only a couple of hours on the red-eye from LA.

Settled in a window seat somewhere over the Rockies, with a pair of Christine's calming, de-puffing gel pads over my eyes, I had drifted into a steamy dream. Theo and I lay entwined on the beach, the surf teasing our bodies with cool fingers as it came ashore and depositing a residue of sand and salt on our skin as it receded. Until Scott, in a tailpipe-smoking dune buggy, came roaring toward us. I jumped to my feet, clutching a large seashell. Scott bore down, leaning forward with a mean grimace under mirrored shades, his ponytail blowing out behind him from under a blue bandanna. I raised the seashell, the gun, and aimed it at his grinning face. My trigger finger twitched. Boom!

I had woken up in the dark. What have I done? My heart raced. I was surrounded by slumped human shapes, the plane banked to the left, and the lights of San Antonio came into view. Once I was home, I had decided to hit the next entry on my crusade list without delay, the one I dreaded most, to jump in before I had a chance to back out or to let Christine talk me out of it, to banish Scott from turning any more of my dreams into nightmares.

I had never been to Marble Falls, but it was two hours away, according to my phone navigation system. If the meeting with my ex-husband didn't go too badly, if I got away safe and sound, I would be home by the end of the day. I would be coming up on him unannounced, at his home, his territory, out in the country, out of the view of anyone except, possibly, his doormat of a wife. I didn't want to limp into the lion's den like vulnerable prey nursing my emotional wounds from LA with no backup. My gun rested in my glove compartment as it had for a month, but for this trip, it was loaded.

An hour into the drive, a tightening knot in my stomach joined the throbbing in my head. I squinted to block out the glare off the road. In my pain-fogged state, it took a while for my brain to decipher the directions from the electronic voice on my phone. "...toward Highway 71 north."

I had missed my exit, but when I tried to take the next one to backtrack, my hands froze on the steering wheel. I continued on I-35 toward Austin.

The GPS voice spit out conflicting directions, interspersed with an insistent "Proceed to the route."

"Pull yourself together," I scolded myself. I couldn't face Scott in this condition. I needed to be more cool steel than fragile flower. But, I didn't want to turn tail and go back home. If I could talk to Christine, she'd drag me off the edge. But my sister and lifeline was still in LA, and, after all she had done for me, I wasn't going to take away any of her time with Barry and their oldest daughter.

I was nearly clear of the Austin city limits. The most direct route to Marble Falls after missing the 71 was the 45 toll road that would take me west. Ahead, sunlight winked off reflective white letters on a green sign, the exit to state road 1825 East to Pflugerville, the opposite direction from Marble Falls. I took the exit.

———

"Well, what an unexpected pleasure," Mr. Asher said as he opened the front door. Crockett nudged against his leg, trying to reach me. I patted the retriever's nose, and he jerked his head up to lick my fingers.

"Unexpected, again," I said. "Here's my peace offering." I handed Mr. Asher a cake that I had picked up at a nearby bakery. Under the clear plastic cover, its whipped cream frosting was garnished with sliced bananas and drizzled with chocolate syrup. "I didn't know what you like. It's banana and coconut. I hope it's okay."

"Thank you. It looks delicious. Very tropical." He took the cake and carried it into the kitchen and retrieved a knife from a wood block. "I'm going to have some right now." He set out two saucers.

"None for me, thanks. I won't stay long, Mr. Asher."

"Gosh, Connie, I really wish you would call me Judd." He smiled with a twinkle in his eye. "I know about the girls at school calling me by my first name when they thought I wasn't listening. But that was when I was a teacher, and you were a student. Now we're more like friends, I hope." He winked at me. "'Mr. Asher' makes me feel so old. Only six years is not such a big difference for two adults, huh?"

I smiled and nodded politely. What would Roanne say? Mr. Asher was flirting with me.

He took two tall glasses from a cupboard. "Tea?"

"Sure. Thanks, Mr., uh, Judd." My face warmed as I said the name.

"Crockett and I are enjoying the sun in the backyard while it lasts. I heard we might get some rain later this week." With Crockett in the lead, he carried the saucer with his slice of cake to the patio, while I followed with the glasses of tea.

I settled in a plastic Adirondack chair, and Mr. Asher sat in its twin beside me. Crockett chased an elusive cardinal around the yard. The grass was shaggy, a week or two overdue for cutting. Bushy oleanders bordered a weathered back fence. Yellow-orange marigolds and pink petunias added an explosion of color to flower beds that circled two towering red oaks.

"I've been enjoying your Maxie Dallas mysteries," he said.

He scooted toward the edge of his chair, about to stand up. "I'll be right back."

He returned a few minutes later holding copies of *Sugar Shocked* and *Three Thousand Calorie Murder* and a pen. He held them out to me. "Do you mind?"

"I'd be happy to," I said. I turned to the title pages and in the sweeping, rounded hand I had practiced since my first book signing, I left my autograph. "To Judd. Enjoy this and all the mysteries of life. Best, Connie. 5-23-19."

He looked over the inscription with a pleased smile that traveled from his mouth to his eyes, and I caught a glimpse of that heartthrob handsomeness from high school days.

"Thank you very much," he said. He set the books down and took up his cake, balancing the saucer on his knees. "Maxie is quite a character. Betty Crocker and Emma Peel rolled into one."

"She's a bit feisty."

"Well, in a ladylike kind of way. She reminds me of my wife, although Jeanine could be very un-ladylike when she was fighting for a cause. She used to say that it was okay to be the nail ninety-five percent of the time, because nails held things together. 'But at least five percent of the time,' she said, 'you have to be the hammer.' "

"She was a smart woman."

"That she was." Mr. Asher munched his cake and licked his lips. "I always thought you were one of my brightest students. Of course, Roanne was pretty sharp, too. But, you, well, I thought you really got it. Teaching kids facts doesn't matter, teaching them how to figure things out is what's important." He leaned toward me. "Was there something in particular you came to tell me?"

"Yes." I paused and took a deep breath. "I'm standing up to them."

"Them? Oh, the targets you told me about."

"My sister's named it the call-the-bastards-out crusade."

He chuckled.

"I'm a bit beat up after the last round," I said. "I suppose I'm here to regather my purpose. After I talked to you before, I felt so much more focused. I needed to take another little breather."

"You'll soon be ready to come out swinging again. Jeanine would have liked the hammer in you. And I like it, too."

He finished off the cake and set the empty saucer down under his chair. Crockett came bounding over as if on cue. The dog poked his head between Mr. Asher's shins, and his tongue made fast work of the cake crumbs and smears of icing left on the dish. Then he spied a squirrel and took off after it.

"Jeanine would have liked the cake, too, the bananas. I used to take her out for a banana split every Friday."

"It's so sweet the way you remember her in ordinary things."

"Our memories of those who are gone are their legacies. A beautiful or a painful legacy depends on the love shared while the person was alive, not the manner in which that person died."

"Since Roanne has been gone, I can't keep the memories away." His kind gaze put me at ease, and my words flowed out. "I'm bombarded with the memories. They've been stacked up in the back of my mind all those years since the time we were fifteen. Now that I'm almost sixty-five, I see that those scenes we played out together explain her. And they explain me."

"It's a great feeling when any part of life starts to make sense, isn't it?"

Crockett ran up with a long, crooked stick clamped between his teeth and deposited it at Mr. Asher's feet. He threw it into the yard, and the dog ran to retrieve it.

"I was going to grill some steaks. Would you like to stay for a late lunch?" he asked.

"Thanks, but I can't. I'm driving to Marble Falls."

"Marble Falls? Pflugerville is a good distance out of the way."

"Like I said, I needed a breather. The next stop is going to be a real doozy."

Crockett returned with the stick and let Mr. Asher tug it out of his mouth before he threw it again.

He reached over and touched my arm. "Well, you'll be fine. I'm glad I could be here for you, Connie."

"Could I ask you, uh..."

"Yes?"

"Why did you come to Roanne's funeral? It was nice of you to do that, but you hadn't stayed in touch, so, I was curious."

He rocked forward and looked out over the yard. "You're right. I hadn't seen Roanne since graduation, at least as far as I can recall. Pflugerville is only six miles from Round Rock, so, who knows, we might have passed at some point. Two days before she died, I happened to be in Round Rock. I stopped at a Hallmark shop to get a Valentine's card for my middle son, a kind of peace offering. We had had some harsh words, we hadn't spoken in almost a year, and I'd been sad about that."

Crockett had found a bird or some other small moving object to harass in a corner of the yard and had abandoned the game of fetch.

"Roanne rang up the sale, although I didn't know it was her at the time," Mr. Asher said. "She gave no sign that she knew me, and I didn't recognize her. She sent me off with one of those parting phrases that store people say, 'You have a lovely day, now,' but there was something in the way she said it that made it personal, like she sincerely wished I would have a lovely day. Not a 'nice' day, a 'lovely' day."

He paused and smiled, apparently remembering Roanne's sendoff. "I know that sounds silly, but it just gave me a little lift, and I kept thinking afterward how there was something familiar about her. When I read about the shooting, saw her photo and the funeral notice in the paper, that she lived in

Round Rock, I wanted to show my respects. She seemed like a kind person. I wished I had said, 'You have a lovely day, too,' instead of just giving a nod."

"Did you and your son reconnect?"

"We did."

"Good for you."

I reached for his hand. He took mine and pressed it against his cheek. The action was unexpected yet natural. We leaned toward each other. At close range, his eyes were deeper brown than I had realized, with tiny gold flecks.

Our lips touched, I tasted the banana cake. The kiss ended before either of us seemed to realize that it had happened.

He spoke first. "Well, that was—"

"Nice," I said.

He smiled. "I really enjoy your company." He lowered his eyes, looking a bit embarrassed. "Maybe now that you're not a schoolgirl, you think I'm more frog than prince?"

"Actually, I really enjoy your company, too." We sat in silence for a few minutes before I rose to leave. "Next time, I'll stay longer."

He stood. "If we had each other's cell numbers, we could make a plan."

I handed him my phone, and we exchanged information.

At the front door, he took one of my hands in both of his. "Good luck, and be careful." Crockett pushed past him and licked my hand.

My head pain had disappeared, and the lonely ache that had settled into a hollow inside my chest when I left California had eased. I gazed into Judd's dancing brown eyes. Next time would come after this crusade thing was over, when I was back to seeing my grandkids, and hanging out with Christine, and writing about Maxie and Nicole, and when I had figured out if a gun was friend or foe. Next time, yes, it would be a lovely day.

– 1976 –

Roanne, Darla, and I went back to their house on Pecan Street after Mrs. Slater's funeral. It was just us and Mr. Slater. No one had planned a get-together with family and friends, but I had brought a chocolate cake. It seemed like a pitiful expression of sympathy, but it was the best I could come up with. When the Canellis and Slaters had gathered several times a year for backyard barbecues, Mr. Slater had always gone back for seconds of chocolate cake.

After the church service, Roanne's dad didn't look much in the mood for cake or anything else. "Maybe later," he said with a vacant stare.

His dark suit was rumpled, one pants leg crawled up his ankle and stuck at the top of a thin brown sock. His eyes were rimmed with red, and the capillaries on either side of his nose stood out. He shuffled to the bedroom he had shared with Mrs. Slater at the back of the house. From the kitchen, Roanne, Darla, and I heard the creak of the bed as he deposited his stout body. Then came the sound of sobbing.

"He looks so old," Roanne said.

"I'm going to my room," Darla said. She raced off, and seconds later a door slammed.

Darla had found Mrs. Slater dead in her bed two weeks ago when she came home from school. "She looked like she was disappearing into the covers," Darla had told us. "She was as tiny as a child. Her face was like paper, like see-through." Darla sat with the body for four hours until Mr. Slater came home.

Roanne said her mother drank more after Chip died. She had rarely ventured out of her bedroom. It had been almost a year since I had seen her, last summer when Roanne and I had come by to take Darla to the DMV to get her first driver's license.

Mrs. Slater, in the kitchen turning drumsticks in a frying pan, had looked like a worn-out copy of a once tall and shapely woman. She stooped in a flowered housecoat, her braless breasts loose and sloppy. Her washed-out blonde hair was pulled back in a stringy ponytail. Her ratty pink slippers were on the wrong feet. When she had turned to face me, her eyes were lightless. She had looked like a ghost, already gone from her family. She had died at forty-four.

I set the cake on the kitchen counter next to a plate of dried scrambled eggs, someone's untouched breakfast, left to ruin.

"I'm going to check on Daddy," Roanne said.

I followed her down the hall. When Roanne and I were girls, her parents' bedroom had been the off-limits sanctuary where Mrs. Slater stayed out of sight when she was intoxicated.

Mr. Slater had shed his suit coat and sat on the edge of the bed on a faded blue bedspread, his hands folded between his legs, his head drooping. He looked up when we entered as if he were expecting us.

"All her stuff," he said. "What do I do?"

Two pairs of Mrs. Slater's shoes were lined up next to a bulky dresser. The top of the dresser was strewn with costume jewelry and dusty perfume bottles. Pink pajama bottoms hung over the footboard. In the half-open closet, dresses and pantsuits were lined up, outfits that Mrs. Slater probably hadn't worn in a decade.

"We'll come over after graduation and help you box it up and take it to Goodwill," Roanne said. "If that's want you want."

Mr. Slater looked confused. He may have forgotten that Roanne and I were graduating in two weeks from UT, or he couldn't picture his wife's belongings mingled with those of strangers at a thrift store.

He picked up a gold-framed photo from the dresser, the

Slaters' wedding picture, one of those old portraits that was partially colorized with the bride's and groom's cheeks unnaturally rosy. "Ah, she was a beauty," he said. "Like Grace Kelly."

I tried to connect the movie-star face in the photo, the wavy, shoulder-length blonde hair and red-lipsticked smile, with the haggard figure bent over, frying chicken in the Slaters' kitchen when I last saw her.

Roanne took the photo from her father and set it back on the dresser. "What was Mommy like when you were first together?" she asked.

A gleam came into Mr. Slater's eyes, and the corners of his mouth turned up.

"She was kind of wild. She loved to dance."

"Was she a good dancer?" Roanne asked. She sat down on the bed next to Mr. Slater.

"Oh, yeah, she could do that swing. We'd go to a joint in east Austin and she'd have the whole place jumping. No one called her Annette back then. Everyone called her Nettie."

"What songs did she like?" Roanne asked.

"The boogie-woogie stuff but the slow stuff, too. You kids know who Nat King Cole is?"

"Yes, Daddy," Roanne said. "He's Natalie Cole's dad. Did you and Mommy have a song?"

Mr. Slater grinned and stood up. "Come here." He pulled Roanne to her feet, took her hand, put the other on his shoulder, and his arm around her waist.

"Daddy, what're you doing?"

Mr. Slater swayed and sidestepped as Roanne moved stiffly with him. Then he began to sing, hoarse and off-key. "Unforgettable, that's what you are. Unforgettable though near or far..."

Roanne laughed and struggled to follow his lead.

"Unforgettable in every way..." His voice cracked. He collapsed, weeping, onto the bed.

Darla came running in. "You're upsetting him," she fussed at Roanne. "Let him rest." She turned down the covers. "Here, Daddy, lie down. You'll feel better after a little while." She guided his head down on the pillow and pulled off his shoes.

Roanne and I slunk off to the patio. We sank down into the watermelon-pink cushions of a double-seated gliding rocker.

"She was a dancer," Roanne said. "They called her Nettie." She grinned, but within a second the smile faded. "She had stories to tell me, and I never gave her a chance. If I could just talk to her…"

A light rain began to patter on the patio's tin roof, masking Roanne's words and soft sobs. I put my arm around her shoulder, and we moved in the chair, forward and back.

- 2019 -

I was heading out of Pflugerville the back way to hook up with the toll road going west to Marble Falls when Darla's number showed up on my phone screen. After Roanne's funeral, her younger sister and I had gone back to the distance between us. I had left it to Stella to fill her aunt in on the turmoil surrounding Zoe and her admission into a rehab center in Virginia.

Darla was one of the last people I wanted to talk to. In spite of my interlude with Mr. Ash— Judd, I was still tired, a bit cranky, and on my way to see someone I despised. I could do without a barrage of Bible quotes. But, my conscience needled me about not showing Darla more kindness over the past two months. I picked up the phone.

"Hey, Darla. How are you?"

"I am comforted in the Lord. He shall not let even a sparrow fall."

I didn't have a comeback for that. "I'm driving. Can we do this another—"

"This won't take but a second. Phil and I packed up Roanne's things from her apartment. Well, mostly Phil, but you know how he is. Always stepping in to make things easier on me."

I pictured Darla's lanky, sandy-haired, bespectacled, accountant husband, patting a shoulder, reassuring with a kind word. He was a sweetheart. Without Phil, Darla would have long ago slipped over the edge into a coma from comfort fudge and cheesecake.

"We found Roanne's memory box," Darla said. "Did you know about it?"

"Memory box? No."

"It's full of a bunch of mementos. You know what they say,

240

one person's trash... I thought you might want to go through it to decide if you want to keep anything. No rush, the next time you're up this way?"

Guilt pinched me again. That was Darla, more thoughtful and considerate than she was annoying.

"I'm actually on my way to Marble Falls right now," I said. "I'm on this twisty Ranch Road and—oh, bad omen—Jonestown is coming up. I'll come through Round Rock and stop by on the way back to San Antonio."

"Marble Falls? You're seeing Scott?"

"Yes, to talk."

"Good for you. Forgiveness will set you free, dear."

I didn't want to hear a sermon, so I didn't tell her that I wasn't at the let-bygones-be-bygones level yet. Maybe one day I would be, but forgiveness would be on my timetable, and it wouldn't be anytime soon.

"I should be at your house well before dark," I said. "Gotta go. My turn is coming up. I'll text you when I leave Marble Falls."

"Keep an eye on the weather. We have storms moving in."

I took the curves carefully while I peeled the paper liner away from a blueberry muffin and bit into it, my on-the-run breakfast I'd swiped off my kitchen counter before leaving home. Ahead of me, the sky was clear, but muggy air blew in through the half-open windows. When I passed the sign for Rusty Allen Airport, the sky was roiling toward me from the north, heavy and dark. Minutes later, the rain came down in sheets. I slowed to a crawl, straining to make out the yellow center line. I swerved as a truck blasted past going the opposite direction, swamping Mellow Yellow with a wall of water that obliterated my visibility for a good three seconds.

In the rearview mirror, the faint glow of headlights drew closer. No doubt, my taillights were invisible in the water kicked up by my tires. I looked for a place to pull over before the vehicle rammed the rear of my car. The headlights were almost on top of me. I eased my Bug onto the shoulder, its right tire caught on the change in surface, and it came to a stop, the right side listing toward a low spot off the road.

The car behind me cruised past, trailing a wave of water and shaking my Bug so that I thought it might topple over. I flipped on my emergency flashers and gripped the steering wheel, with no choice but to wait out the storm. I was afraid of being hit and injured by a passing car if I stayed on the driver's side, but I was afraid that if I moved to the passenger side, my weight might be enough to roll the vehicle onto its side.

Thunder rumbled in the distance, and lightning slashed bright zigzags above the treetops. Darkness swallowed up the remaining daylight. I called Darla, but the call didn't go through. The winding road away from the interstate and state highways was in a dead spot for cell service.

My stomach growled. I dug a baggie of cashews from the console and retrieved a half-empty water bottle from the floor. The only thing I had packed for an emergency was my gun, not much use against a big, bad storm.

Two hours passed. The sound of rushing water outside the door grew louder, and a weird sensation ran through me, that floating stomach feeling in an elevator just before it comes to a stop. The car was lifting ever so slightly and settling back down. The road was flooding.

I was going to die in my vehicle alone on a winding road between Marble Falls and Round Rock. Daniel and Christine would be sorting through boxes of my belongings, separating the precious keepsakes from the disposable clutter.

I tried to think of a backup plan if the water rose higher. The best I could come up with was to crawl onto Mellow Yellow's roof. But, if I opened the door, I feared a deluge would rush in and drown me.

I said the "Hail Mary," the only prayer I could remember, and held my heartbeat and breathing to a reasonable level for the next few hours by playing mental games. I counted to one thousand, then backward to zero. I recited the capitals of all fifty states, likely mixing up New Hampshire and Vermont. I sang old commercial jingles, "See the USA..." "Mr. Clean, Mr. Clean..." "Is it true blondes have more fun?" "VD is for everybody..." I listed all the characters in all of the Maxie Dallas mysteries, by book, in chronological order by publishing date.

I lifted my feet up and down, testing for puddles from leaks through the bottom of the door. The water gurgled as it bumped against the car, but, so far, my feet stayed dry.

During my second round of "Hail Mary's," the rain began to slow, but the darkness and the rivulets running down the windows made it hard for me to see what was outside.

Bright, white orbs blinded me through the windshield. Was I going into the light already?

The driver's door swung open. Phil pulled me out into knee-deep water and pushed, pulled, and carried me to his F-350, where Darla held open the truck door. Darla and Phil had apparently put two and two together, my failure to show up at their house when I said I would and my last known location on Ranch Road. Ten miles later, down the road toward Round Rock, the rain stopped as abruptly as it had started.

———

I awoke the next morning to wet, feathery tickles on my nose and cheek. When I peeled my eyes open, come-hither brown eyes stared back at me from the square, white face of a Cairn terrier. I found myself in a nest of abundant pink quilts, dressed in unfamiliar, bunny-print PJs in Darla's spare bedroom.

Twenty or so cardboard boxes were stacked against the wall, the contents of Roanne's apartment and the last few years of her life. A banker's box covered in turquoise-and-lime paisley fabric was set on the floor near the foot of the bed—the memory box.

I scooped up the puppy, dug myself out of the proliferation of puffy covers, and peeked out between the curtains. With blue skies and sunshine as far as I could see, I was thankful for the gully washer that had given me a day's reprieve from a confrontation with Scott. As soon as I could pick up my car from the mechanic's shop, where Phil had had it towed for a safety check and dryout, I would be on my way to Marble Falls.

"Bitsy!" Darla called from the half-open door. I wondered how early she rose to shape her hair into that perfect coiffure of blonde cotton candy. Perhaps she slept sitting up to preserve her 'do. "There you are," she said and lifted the terrier from my arms and snuggled it to her chest. "Our new little girl. They keep me hopping, but I couldn't do without my kids."

As if on cue, Baxter and Bailey, "the boys," scurried in, yipping and nipping at Darla's ankles.

I was suddenly ashamed. Darla had been the one on the front lines for her family since Roanne's death. Three yappy balls of fluff showed her more support than I had.

"Thank you, Darla," I said.

She looked puzzled. "For last night? We couldn't leave you out in the storm. It was not any trouble to come after you."

"I don't have words to thank you and Phil for saving me."

"It was the Lord who reached out his hand."

"I'm sorry."

"For what?"

"For not telling you how grateful I am that you took care of all the things that the rest of us didn't have the stamina or the grace to manage. Arranging the funeral and the burial and the friends and family. Going through Roanne's things, cleaning out her apartment, disposing of her property, handling all the loose ends that she left dangling. And, goodness gracious, identifying her body." Tears stood in my eyes. "How you had the strength, I can't imagine."

She patted my arm. "I wasn't on my own." She craned her head back and shut her eyes. "He's always with me. My rock."

"Thank goodness for Phil."

"I meant Jesus Christ. But, yes, Phil, too." She set Bitsy down.

The front door creaked open, bringing outside noises in— the squeal of brakes on a sanitation truck and the roar of a lawnmower. Phil called out that he was home and ready to take me to pick up my car. The dogs scurried out to welcome him. I kicked myself into gear, washing up and changing into my clothes from the day before. The jeans and T-shirt smelled of fresh dryer sheets. Of course, Darla had gotten up early enough to wash and dry my clothes and leave them neatly folded on the bed.

Within an hour I was driving a slightly musty Mellow Yellow toward Marble Falls. I kept a lookout for debris on the highway, dodging branches ripped from trees, an abandoned tire, a mailbox knocked off its perch. The blue-and-green memory box sat beside me, a persistent passenger nagging for my attention, pulling my eyes away from the road.

After nearly thumping over a roadkilled possum before swerving at the last second, I pulled over at a wide spot on the shoulder and lifted the lid of the box. I didn't know what to expect. A curling stream of vapor like from Aladdin's lamp? The smoky essence of a spirit rushing out at me while issuing a loud moan?

I reached in and touched the first object. Since Roanne's death, I had been snatched into scenes of our past and had felt the ache of her absence deep in my bones. But the things inside the box weren't dreams or feelings. They were solid with weight and dimension and texture. She had held them, folded them, stacked them, placed them carefully in a treasure box, remembered the event they symbolized with a smile or a tear or a flare of shame or defiance.

A bundle of letters tied up with a faded blue ribbon. The envelopes edged with red and blue hash marks crinkled when I drew them closer to read the return address: "Spc4 Charles Slater," followed by his Social Security number, a box number, and another series of digits preceded by "FPO." Her brother Chip's letters from Vietnam.

I left the bundle intact and dug out the rest of the items one by one.

Roanne's corsage from the night of our senior prom. The flowers had shriveled to papery stumps protruding from a wire wrapped with green tape with a tail of yellow and white ribbons attached.

A fridge magnet in the shape of a seashell on a turquoise background, with a gold label at the bottom that read "Padre Island." That fateful day with Scott and Johnny when I had too much to drink and Roanne was too caught up in the moment to talk some sense into me.

Ticket stubs from the Houston Queen concert. What were the names of those New York guys we had hooked up with? Freddie Mercury had worn a skin-tight harlequin jumpsuit. That I didn't forget.

A twelve-by-two–inch nameplate made of woodgrain with a chipped corner and letters engraved in white. The letters spelled out "Mrs. Kirkland," identifying Roanne's classroom at Pigeon Creek Junior High School.

A creased, yellow newspaper clipping, dated June 16, 1963. The headline read, "Soviet Orbits First Cosmonette." Had Roanne fantasized about a bolder career than teaching, aspiring to be the US version of Valentina Tereshkova?

A sleeve of waxed paper, the contents dried and dusty. Pressed flowers—ten white roses, with a card, "Love, Johnny."

I lifted out another stack of mail bound with a wide rubber band, the large, colorful envelopes of greeting cards, fourteen of them, addressed to Zoe Kirkland in Arlington, Texas. They were all unopened and returned to Roanne. Zoe might have refused them or Roanne might have not known her correct address. All the postmarks were from the month of Zoe's birthday, the dates from 2019 back to 2006, the year after she had moved out of her dad's house in Round Rock to begin her adult life.

I peeled the last item off the bottom of the box, a sheet of pink construction paper folded in half, a hand-made card. On the front, a flower's petals were colored in red crayon with the flower center a wallet-size, school photo of Zoe with her two front teeth missing. Inside, a profusion of yellow butterflies with blue spots were drawn in a child's hand alongside the sweetest of messages: "Happy Mother's Day to the best Mom in the hole wid world!! Love, Zoe."

On the back was a blob of rolled-up Scotch tape, still sticky around its dirty edges. Had the card been fixed to Roanne's fridge? I couldn't remember seeing it there. When I pressed the card against the front of the dash, it stuck, lopsided.

I placed my hand over my heart. "I'll bring her back to you, Ro. I swear."

I turned the key in the ignition and pulled out onto the road. Maybe the universe was trying to warn me by redirecting me to Judd's house and then stranding me in a storm on my way to meet my ex-husband. I had been twenty years old when I first met Scott McHenry on a blind date. My eyes were wide open now. Nothing was going to stop me from our last encounter, universe be damned.

– 1978 –

Scott and I sat on a worn, striped blanket on the beach at Padre Island. His arms and shoulders had turned a deep bronze from only a day in the coastal sunshine. I, in my burn-and-peel skin, nestled in the Y of his spread legs and leaned back into his bare chest. His fuzzy body hair tickled my sun-tender shoulders. His hands rested on my thighs at the edges of my bikini. I reveled in the smell of the salty air and Coppertone. A seagull shrilled overhead, and the surf slapped and swooshed against the shore.

Scott gurgled from a bottle of tequila that had been on ice during the entire three-hour trip from Austin, then passed the booze to me to take a swig. The late March sun danced in and out of the clouds, alternately heating and chilling us.

Johnny reclined next to us, his skinny legs stretched out like matchsticks from his baggy shorts. He wore a faded red T-shirt with the sleeves torn off. I had never seen Johnny shirtless. According to Scott, Johnny was embarrassed by his bird chest. Scott had the opposite issue. He could go half-naked every day, but I didn't like girls drooling over his pecs, so, for me, he made an effort to cover up.

Johnny propped on one elbow, took a drag on a cigarette, and flashed his million-dollar smile. Johnny had the whitest teeth I had ever seen on a guy. A lock of jet-black hair fell across the bridge of his biker shades as he looked out toward the green-gray surf.

At the water's edge Roanne played tag with the waves. Brandy, her cocker spaniel, chased at her heels and flinched whenever the surf sprayed its honey-colored coat. The breeze fluttered the skirt of Roanne's white bathing suit above her long, tanned legs. She was four months pregnant but barely showing.

"Isn't my wife gorgeous?" Johnny said, taking another puff and not waiting for an answer. "I'm the luckiest man in the world."

The four of us hadn't gotten together in almost a month. Johnny and Roanne had been busy in their new community in Killeen, making new friends. Pinochle with Joe and Becky, watching the game at so-and-so's, going over to whatever their names were to see the new baby. Married couples.

Johnny stabbed his cigarette toward us. "Y'all should take the plunge."

"No thanks, buddy," Scott said, taking the bottle back from me. "I'm fine living the single life. No one to explain to every time I go out. And I hear as soon as you're married, they start having a lot of headaches."

I turned and popped Scott in the chest with a weak punch. The booze had relaxed me to the point that I could barely make a fist. I did have a headache the last time he wanted to have sex, but that was a side effect of my new birth control pills. Usually I was the one who was more raring to go.

"Just the opposite, how do you think we put that bun in the oven?" Johnny said. "Twice on weekdays and four times on Saturday and Sunday."

"You're kidding," Scott said, passing him the bottle.

Johnny took a drink. "Swear to God. Since I put that ring on Roanne's finger, she's turned into a regular nympho. But that's not even the best part. I'm telling you, man, there's nothing better than coming home to someone every day who is waiting for you. That's the best, man."

"You don't say."

"I do say. Look, man, what are you waiting for? You love Connie. She loves you. Y'all been together three goddamn years. How long are you going to keep spinning your wheels? Don't you want to marry her?"

Scott looked at me with eyes like a rabbit caught in a trap. "Of course, I want to."

"Well?" Johnny locked eyes with Scott in a "dare you" staredown. They did this all the time, but usually it was over who could drink the most shots or eat the most jalapenos. "Isn't she the one?"

I laughed nervously. Scott had told me he loved me, and I had told him the same, but this was turning into something more than lighthearted fun. "You're full of it, Johnny," I said. "Let's go for a swim," I said to Scott, trying to pull out of his arms and rising unsteadily to my feet.

A series of yips from Brandy and a peal of laughter from Roanne traveled across the sand as a seagull dipped low over them.

Scott pulled me back down between his legs. "Of course she's the one. I'd marry her today if there was a place that'd do it right quick."

I whirled around and stared at Scott, my jaw hanging, then at Johnny who was laughing under his breath. "Stop kidding around, guys."

"Are you serious, Scottie Mac?" Johnny said.

"As a heart attack. Today. Right now," Scott said.

Johnny had a glint in his eye. "In Vegas they got these wedding chapels you drive up to just like ordering a cheeseburger."

"We don't have to be back on base for four days," Scott said. His hazel eyes, watery from the booze, grew a bit brighter, and his golden caterpillar of a mustache twitched. "We'd have to drive for what? Twenty hours straight?"

"That's about right." Johnny's eyes gleamed again. "We'll switch off."

"Whoa, don't I have anything to say about this?" I protested. "And, anyway, I don't have any makeup or a toothbrush or a pair of clean underwear. And what about the dog?"

Scott pulled himself up on one knee, swayed back and

forth a few times, and finally held himself steady. He took my face in his hands, and I strained to focus while he smooshed my cheeks into my nose. "C'mon, babe. What do you say? I love you, Connie Canelli." He planted a sloppy kiss between my mouth and my jaw.

"I—I don't know what to say," I stammered. "This isn't how I pictured—"

Johnny chuckled. "Better say 'yes,' Connie. He may never have the balls to ask you again." Then Johnny started chanting, "Say yes, say yes, say yes, say yes..."

Roanne ran up with Brandy scampering behind her. The seawater dripped off her body onto Johnny's legs as she scooped the spaniel up in her arms and knelt down next to him. "What's going on?" she asked.

"Just go with the flow, babe. Say yes, say yes, say yes, say yes..."

Roanne looked around to each of us, puzzled, then giggled and joined in, "Say yes, say yes, say yes..."

The dog wriggled out of Roanne's grasp and added its high-pitched bark for punctuation.

The frenzied chant in my ears and the tequila in my brain put me in a trance. "Yes!" I shouted. "Yes!"

"Whoo-hoo!" Johnny yelled, like he had just seen the Dallas Cowboys score a touchdown. "Let's hit the road, amigos!"

Brandy let out a loud yelp.

Scott threw his arms around me, and we fell down on the blanket beside each other.

"Where're we going?" Roanne asked. The dog panted and turned its wide, brown eyes toward Roanne, then to Johnny, as if it was expecting an answer, too.

Johnny bent her back in a dance dip and kissed her hard. "To Vegas, baby! Scott and Connie are getting married!"

Roanne screamed and jumped up and down, clapping her

hands. The spaniel sprung up on its hind legs, pawing at the air, mimicking her. She motioned for me to get up and join her, but I was half-wasted and wobbly. I didn't want to do anything stupid like fall on my face.

– 2019 –

Scott's rust-red ranch house stood on a double lot of dirt and patchy grass. I parked in the gravel driveway behind a blue Dodge pickup with a "Freedom Isn't Free" bumper sticker. My fingers tapped against the latch of the glove compartment. Should I or shouldn't I? Beads of sweat tickled my upper lip. I pulled out the gun, opened my purse, and strained to wiggle it in. It was a tight fit, too tight. I'd probably shoot myself in the foot trying to jerk it out if I needed it in a hurry. I returned the weapon to the glove compartment. I'd take the purse with me anyway. It would give me something to hold onto.

I walked past a vintage Harley leaning against the side of the house under the wide-spreading branches of a pecan tree. Next to the bike, old, blackened nuts littered the ground and collected on the top of a mottled fifty-gallon barrel.

The carcass of a June bug, caught in the screen door, fluttered with the vibrations of my vigorous pounding against the aluminum frame. The door opened to a foot-wide gap. A thin blonde woman in jeans and a black cami peered out. Smoke curled from the cigarette she held between two fingers that gripped the door edge. The bare toes of her one visible foot curled on the clay tile floor.

"Hi, Jan," I said, staring at the signs of smoking-induced aging in the roadmap of wrinkles around her mouth and eyes. "I came to see Scott. I see his truck out front, so I assume he's home."

She shot me a wary look and made no move to swing the door open.

"I'm not here to cause any drama," I said. "I just want to talk. It won't take long."

Scott had hit the jackpot in Marble Falls, a boating, fishing, water sports center. His dream, like that of many men over fifty, was to own a motorcycle or a boat. I knew from Daniel that Scott had both, although his bum hip kept him off the bike. As a bonus, he managed a boat repair shop owned by his second wife's family.

Jan was the younger model who caught Scott's eye when his second puberty kicked in around the big five-oh. We had started sliding toward a divorce about a year before, spurred on by his drinking, but the thirty-five-year-old blonde on the side sent us careening to the end of our marriage. At this point, I held no ill will against her. She could have the miserable asshole.

She shrugged. "Sure. Come on." She led me to the kitchen, motioned for me to take a chair, and walked to the adjoining living room. A court TV show played in the background. I placed my purse on the table in front of me, a barrier of sorts to keep Scott's hands on his side of the table.

A male voice muttered and minutes later Scott walked in with a lean-step, lean-step to his left side on a cane, swinging his free arm, taking up as much space as possible. He wore a black T-shirt with a stretched-out neck and faded jeans that hung below his protruding gut. He propped his cane against the nearby counter, pulled out the chair across from me, screeching it against the floor, and dropped his bulk into the seat.

His face was damp. The smell of sour sweat laced with liquor wafted across the table. He had put on at least thirty pounds in the years since Daniel and Amy's wedding, the last time I had seen him. The extra poundage folded in loose, soft rolls around his middle, under the arms, and in the jowls and neck. A wiry, gray ponytail hung down his broad back.

He spoke through tobacco-yellowed teeth before I had a chance to greet him even with feigned politeness. "If you've come to offer condolences for that bitch killing Johnny, you can shove them where the sun don't shine."

"I lost a good friend, too. That's not why I'm here."

"What then?" He took a pack of cigarettes and a lighter out of his T-shirt pocket and lit up.

"I came to drop off some baggage."

"You got something in that purse?" He jerked to the side, lowering his right shoulder, reaching an arm under the table.

The smoke irritated the inside of my nose, but I did my best to ignore it.

"No. I'm trying to resolve things between us in a better way than what happened to Roanne and Johnny."

"We resolved things between us seventeen years ago. It's called a divorce decree."

"That piece of paper didn't do justice to the damage that I suffered at your hands."

Scott scoffed. "Okay, let me have it. Give it your best shot." He remained tilted to the side, like he was scratching his ankle.

"You cheated on me, not once, not twice, constantly, every time you left the house for all I know. That was bad enough, that you had to stick your dick into everything that moved and lie to me about where you were. But what is unforgiveable is the physical abuse."

Scott sat up straight. "What the fuck? I never hit you."

"No, you didn't. What you did was pass on about every STD known to the human race, with the exception, thankfully, of HIV."

He squirmed and took a drag on his cigarette.

"Now, just so you understand, no matter what you might want to tell yourself to ease your guilt," I said, "I was never with anyone but you while we were married. So, whatever I contracted, and you know I had something almost all the time, that was you."

"You're telling me I gave you the clap, and that's physical abuse?"

"Oh, it goes beyond that. When I was twelve a friend at school told me I was going to get something called a period and that if I had sex, I might get pregnant and ruin my life, and if I took the pill I would likely not. That was the extent of my reproductive health education."

Scott tapped his fingers on the table and poked the inside of his cheek with his tongue, simulating boredom, but I was determined to say all I had to say. He was going to hear me, like it or not.

"I thought infections, abdominal pain, passing clumps of blood at all times of the month, were things that happened for no particular reason other than Eve biting an apple."

He smirked. "It sucks to be female. So, what?" The ash on the tip of his cigarette fell onto the table.

"I didn't know then that what you were passing on to me from the skanks you were with destroyed my reproductive organs. I was in pain because of you. I couldn't get pregnant because of you. I had a hysterectomy when I was thirty-nine because of you."

"That's bullshit. You can't prove that."

"Regardless, I know it's true. I am literally the body of evidence."

"What do you want now? Compensation? Revenge?" He leaned to his right side again, his arm dangled down.

"No, Scott. I've been more than compensated. God or whoever is in charge knew what he was doing. Because I couldn't be a mom the traditional way, I was blessed with the most amazing, loving son any mother could wish for."

"We both adopted Daniel."

"But I raised him while you were sitting on a bar stool or, more likely, banging someone you picked up off a bar stool. So, thanks, I'll take the credit for Daniel becoming a wonderful young man."

He smirked again. "Mother of the year. You raised a drug addict."

"I raised a son who overcame being a drug addict. I'm lucky to have Daniel and Amy and my beautiful grandchildren. Did you know Braden will finish first grade in two weeks? And

Charlotte, she's not a baby anymore, she's already three."

"Yippy, Skippy, your cup runneth over. And I don't see the grandkids a lot. What's the point here?" He took two more puffs on his smoke, then tossed the butt into the sink behind him.

I clutched the purse in front of me, dug in my nails. "For a lot of years after the divorce, I hated you. The point is, I'm no longer going to clutter my life with the horrible things you did to me. I'm leaving them here, you own them. My heart and my conscience are clean. This will be the last time I see you, talk to you, think about you, or have a speck of feeling, including disgust, for you."

I pushed back my chair, stood, and gathered my purse. Scott reached down under the table, then leapt up, overturning his chair, and pointed a pistol. I jumped back and clutched my purse to my chest. My heart hammered.

"Put that purse on the table!" he yelled. He leaned on the table with his free hand to steady himself on his good side. His right pants leg was pulled up, caught at the top of his ankle holster.

My breath had been knocked out of me. I couldn't speak. I set the purse down.

"Slide it toward me!" he shouted. "Slowly."

I leaned over the table and pushed the bag with my fingertips. Out of the corner of my eye, I saw Jan hovering in the doorway.

"Honey?" she said. "What's going on?"

Scott didn't take his eyes off me or lower the gun as he spoke to her. "Go back in the other room. I have this under control."

"Under control? What the fu—"

"Get back in the other room," he snarled, still glaring at me.

Jan shuffled away out of sight. A few seconds later, the volume of the court TV show amplified to blast level.

Scott waved the gun at me. "Back away from the table." He grabbed the bag with his free hand. "You're not going to go all Roanne on me."

He flicked the purse's catch open and spilled the contents onto the table: a loose credit card and driver's license, my phone, a stick of gum, a wad of tissues. A gold tube of lipstick rolled over the edge of the table and plinked on the floor. Scott's jaw hung open. He stared at the scattered items and fell back into his chair. He lowered the gun to the table and laid it down. His chest heaved with ragged breaths. Sweat poured down his temples.

"Are you okay?" I asked. "Should I call Jan? Do you need medication?"

He shook his head.

"Can I get my stuff?"

"Go ahead."

I scooped my items into the purse, picked up the lipstick, and reclaimed my spot standing on the other side of the table.

"You thought I was packing? You thought I came here to shoot you?" I said. "I admit there were times I fantasized about doing that. But, I have the power over how I respond, and I'm not going to waste any bullets on you." And my purse was too small for the dang gun.

I tucked the purse under my arm and stepped toward the door.

"Hey," he said, struggling to his feet again. "You wanna make it all about the bad stuff." He reached for his cane and leaned on it. "We had some good times." That grasping-for-straws tone was the one he had used during the morning-after remorse when he had stumbled in drunk as a skunk the night before. "Remember the first time we met?"

It had been Valentine's Day, 1975, a Willie Nelson concert in Zilker Park in Austin, a fix-up for Roanne and me by Roanne's friend, Mandy, Candy. Bambi. She hung out with military dudes. I didn't want to meet a military dude. I had been fighting through the last stages of the flu and was spacey from a dose of Nyquil that hadn't quite worn off. Roanne had dragged me out. I had complained all the way. I had wanted to cuddle up on the couch with a nice, big, sexy bowl of chicken soup. I was still griping when we saw them, Johnny and Scott.

Roanne had said, "Don't be such a drag. You can even have the tall, good-looking one if you want." I thought she had been the one high on Nyquil, not me. The other guy was short and skinny with slicked-back hair and with a smirk that was between endearing and annoying.

"It wasn't exactly love at first sight," I said to the overweight, crippled, nicotine-dependent alcoholic standing in his kitchen.

"You weren't feeling well that night," Scott said, still stuck in the haze of the past. "Do you remember what you said when you saw me?"

I involuntarily smiled at the memory. "Hello, chicken soup." Scott McHenry had been a good-looking, charm-dripping son of a gun. I sidestepped toward the kitchen door and toward the entryway. "But, in all fairness, I think it was the Nyquil talking."

"We danced a lot that night. Remember 'Whiskey River?' "

"Whiskey River, take my mind..." Scott sang in my ear, as Willie sang on stage. "Yeah. That was a long time ago."

"We made some good memories."

"And you played me for a fool. Our whole marriage was a lie."

"C'mon, Connie. You don't think we had love at one time?"

"No. We got married because Roanne and Johnny did. They had to go and fall head over heels. The two people we cared about most in the world were leaving us behind. The love we had for them tied us together. And then, we were stuck.

"We were doomed for failure," I said, "the second we said 'I do.' "

Scott blinked rapidly. He appeared too dazed, at least for the moment, to hit back with more sharp words.

I walked out the front door and crossed the patchy lawn to where I had parked. Scott followed me, rocking forward on his cane. His huffs grew louder and faster, an angry bull pawing at the ground, getting ready to charge. I had left him in the worst place possible: facing his own shortcomings. His rage was building. I was afraid.

"All that stuff you said is bullshit!" he yelled. "You were the failure! You were the one who couldn't get pregnant! You were the one who walked out of the marriage!"

I quickened my pace to my car.

"You were the one who didn't stop her!" Scott's words almost knocked me to the ground.

I jerked open the driver's side door, slid in, and leaned toward the glove compartment. I eased my hand over to the latch, popped open the compartment door, and felt the grip in my palm. I lowered the gun to the seat beside me and pulled the door shut.

Scott approached within three feet of my rolled-down window. His face was red and screwed up like a mad dog's. My heart thumped like a wild rabbit's foot. He stretched his arm toward the holster at his ankle. I cringed and slid my gun to my right hip. He pulled his hand up, empty. He had left his gun on the kitchen table.

He stepped closer and stopped within a foot of the open window, leaned heavily on his cane, and lowered his face to meet mine with a mean scowl.

"I'm glad she offed herself," he said.

Stop talking, Scott. I inched the gun toward my lap.

"Johnny should have blown her away long ago," he snarled.

Don't say another word, Scott, or so help me...

"That twisted bitch deserved to die."

I threw the door open, hitting his legs full force. The cane flew out of his reach, and he landed like a large sack of potatoes, on his back with an agonized groan. In a second I was standing over him, holding the gun with both hands, the muzzle shakily aimed at his head. "Shut the fuck up, Scott!" I yelled. "Or I swear I'll kill your sorry ass!"

He half slid, half crab-walked back from under me and pulled himself to his knees with his hands out in a defensive posture. "Okay, okay," he stuttered. "Take it easy."

I followed the movement of his head with the gun.

He pulled one knee up. "C'mon now, Connie. Put that thing down. Someone could get hurt."

I stepped closer and shoved the gun at him. "Get back."

He pulled himself shakily to his feet. "I need my cane."

I stooped to pick up the cane while keeping my eyes and the gun trained on him and tossed the cane to the far side of the driveway.

"Hey," he yelled. "I can't walk without that."

"Then you better start crawling."

"Connie, please."

I motioned toward the house with the gun. Scott took a few steps, then half crouched and moved forward, dragging one leg behind him, balancing himself with one hand on the ground. I followed as far as the side of the house as he huffed and puffed and shuffled like Quasimodo to the edge of the porch where he plopped down in a heap, breathing hard. His head tilted upward in my direction. The look of a frightened animal bounced across his eyes.

I kept the gun pointed at him, still clutching it in both hands, my arms extended stiff and straight.

"What're you gonna do?" Scott wailed.

"Stop talking!" Rivulets of sweat ran down the sides of my face and into my eyes. I squinted to keep his crumpled form in focus. In the five feet between us, the air pulsed like rising heat waves. My heart pounded. My head was about to explode. The house, the sky, the ground, everything around me turned red for a second, like I was looking through a reflector. My trigger finger quivered. I pointed the gun directly at Scott's head.

"Noooo!" he cried, folding his chin into his chest and raising his hands in front of his face.

I studied his twitching fingers, then swung my arms to the left and fired into the fifty-gallon barrel. The loose pecans on top bounced like marbles shaken in a jar. Two more shots boomed out and spouts of water erupted from the barrel's side. My ears were ringing. I blasted three more shots into the metal drum. Vibrations thrilled through my arms. Ten more shots. A puddle spread below the riddled target. The gun had no more to give, and the air turned silent except for a low, steady hum.

My arms drained of energy and dropped to my sides. I waited for my shoulders to lift with relief, but my right arm was dragged down with the weight of dead metal.

– 2001 –

"Mom?" Daniel's jerky voice came through the phone from our house in San Antonio. His words had been cracking and squeaking as, at the age of twelve, he was edging into puberty. But his present tone was tinged with more than adolescent awkwardness. "I'm scared," he said.

The clock on the nightstand in Roanne's and my Dallas hotel room read 1:12 a.m. Roanne and I had had a full day of massages, facials, steam baths, and other pampering at the Stonebridge hotel and spa during our girls' weekend. We had been taking the road trips around the date of our birthdays, mine in June, hers in July, for the past nine years, except for the year of Roanne's divorce. We would leave early on a Saturday for a fun destination somewhere in the state, spend the night, then return home on Sunday.

Now, my heartbeat was taking off at a gallop. "What's going on, sweetie?" I asked my son. "Isn't Dad there?"

"He's drunk again," Daniel said. "Someone came in the house with him."

"Someone like who?"

"A woman. I heard her voice. They were arguing. I think she's gone now."

A woman? Had this happened before? When I was out for a book signing? At a basketball game with Daniel? "What's your dad doing now?"

"Yelling. Throwing things."

"At you?"

"No. I'm in my room. I sneaked out to get the phone. I locked my door. I don't know what to do."

"Okay, sweetie, I'm going to call Sean's parents to make sure they're home. I'll call you back in five minutes, and then I want you to go out the window, very carefully, and go to

Sean's." Daniel's bedroom window was only a couple of feet above ground at the back of the house, where he could exit easily and unnoticed by Scott. "I'll leave for home right away."

"How long will it take for you to get here?"

"Five hours to San Antonio. I'll pick you up at Sean's in the morning."

"Are you going to tell them Dad's drunk? I don't want them to know."

"Don't worry about that." I was fairly sure that Dave and Sandy, Sean's parents, and most of our other neighbors knew Scott sometimes came home smashed. I had seen their stares when they came out of their houses on the way to work or school the morning after Scott rammed the garage with his truck. His handiwork was hard to miss, the punched-in metal door folded around the pickup's front. Another time, he had taken out our mailbox at the curb.

I shook Roanne awake and explained that Scott was drunk, Daniel was scared, and we had to cut our weekend short. She looked dazed more at my news than because of the sudden interruption of her sleep.

"Daniel needs you. Let's go," was all she said before gathering up her belongings.

At a 7-Eleven, we grabbed coffees, and Roanne snagged a bag of M&Ms before we hopped onto I-35 South.

"Do you want me to drive?" she asked.

"Maybe later. I have to have something to focus on right now or else I'll just go to pieces."

"How bad is it?"

"Scott's always liked to go out and get plastered once in a while. You know that."

"Exactly. Him and Johnny letting off steam, tons of times over the years." She popped M&Ms into her mouth one at a time in a steady stream.

"It seems like it's almost every week now. Sometimes he goes out at night, and he doesn't come home until the next day. I don't know who he stays with." That woman Daniel said he heard in the house? "I used to go crazy worrying about him bleeding in a ditch. But, now, God help me, Ro, there are nights when I wish he wouldn't come home."

"He's not hurt you, or hurt Daniel, has he?"

Scott had never hit me or our son. He had shoved me when I got in his face about the destroyed mailbox. And there were times he had forced himself inside me, rough and sloppy, like I was just a hole to use for his release.

"No," I said. "Most times he stumbles in and passes out on the bed, and the next day he doesn't remember much of anything. He tells me I'm making a big deal over nothing. I think this is it. I think I've reached the end."

Roanne looked out the window, silent for a few minutes. My coffee had cooled to the point that I could gulp it down, a third of the cup at a time.

"Not divorce?" she said.

Divorce. The bitter thought of it twisted in my gut. Even though I had given up on religion long ago, the residue of my Catholic-girl conscience had never stopped telling me that divorce was the ultimate shame. I had rationalized myself into knots over the past few months. Scott was a beer drinker. It wasn't like he was getting wasted on hard liquor. I had witnessed a real alcoholic, Roanne's mother, skid into darkness.

Scott wasn't like that. He drank himself blind on weekends. Yet, when Monday rolled around, he was back at work, functioning like an adult. And he was a regular guy around the house most of the time, mowing the lawn, sneaking a kiss on my neck when I was washing dishes, not doing anything more annoying than turning the TV up too loud. Still, the excuses seemed flimsier each time I ran them through my mind.

"What else is there?" I said. "I can't keep doing this."

"Do you really want to break up your family? If there was

a way that Johnny and I could have worked it out, I wish we could have. Maybe Scott needs more time to adjust. You've only been in San Antonio for a year. He was laid off for a few months. He's still getting back on his feet. You don't want to jump the gun if there's any chance."

What about my adjustment to living with a drunk? What about Daniel having to sneak out a window in the middle of the night? What about Scott bringing a woman into our house with our son in the next room? I wasn't jumping any gun. Whose side was Roanne on anyway?

I stopped short of going off on her. She spoke from a tortured heart. Her and Johnny's divorce had rippled out into seemingly endless pain. Their split turned her teaching colleagues against her. It shut off communication between her and Zoe. It pitted Stella and Zoe against each other. It tore a rift between Roanne and her dad. It strained the volatile tie between Roanne and Darla. It had even fueled fights between me and Scott.

Roanne and I didn't speak for several minutes. I focused on the yellow line on the highway as it spooled toward me out of the dark, absorbed the bumps as the tires hit the seams in the pavement, until she broke the silence.

"What about marriage counseling?"

My body tensed, and I clenched the steering wheel. "Pfff. Scott will go to a marriage counselor right after he confesses his sins at an AA meeting, which will be right after hell freezes over."

Roanne tapped on the dashboard, apparently thinking something over. "Do you want me to ask Johnny to talk to Scott?"

I jerked my head to stare at her. "You'd do that? I thought you and Johnny didn't talk."

"We don't. But, he's still best buddies with Scott. Johnny will do anything for him, he'll turn him around."

"Okay." I agreed more to ease Roanne's mind than mine.

How had Scott and I come to this place? I had told myself that the drinking had turned him mean. But, had it been the other way around? The meanness always there under the charm had turned him to drink. The snarl in my gut began to untangle. Whatever magic Johnny might work on Scott, I didn't care. There was nothing left worth saving. I was done.

"Do you want me to drive when we get to Waco?" Roanne asked.

"No, I'm wide awake now."

– 2019 –

"You are stunning, little sis," I said as Christine stepped out of her bedroom and into her living room, looking like she had been costumed and plunked onto the wrong movie set. She wore a narrow, royal blue sheath ruched at the right hip. The asymmetrical neckline dove to just above her left breast. Her red-carpet outfit contrasted with her south Austin home's bohemian décor: oversized fringed shawls draped over furniture, ropes of temple bells and carved elephants, odd-shaped mirrors with mosaic frames.

She struck a pose with one foot thrust forward, showing off her silver and blue pumps. "You don't think the shoes are too much?"

"Four-inch heels? Impressive. I can't go past three and a half." I mimicked Christine's pose with my lower red heels while I balanced a cheesecake on a plastic tray on my palm. "Those shoes are totally appropriate. Your last child's graduation? Go for it, girl."

"This is definitely a milestone moment. Xena walking across the stage. Me coming home to an empty nest."

"Not quite empty, but I guess Barry is gone a lot."

"We should get going." She grabbed a clutch purse and keys off a side table and spurted off toward the kitchen, to the side door that opened into the garage.

I hurried to catch up to her. "This cheesecake needs to go in the fridge. It's amaretto-chocolate chip with almonds in the crust. I hope Xena likes it."

"She'll love it, if she comes home tonight." Christine was almost out the door.

"Are we running late?" I asked. "I thought I was early." I pushed a carton of eggs and a half-gallon of soy milk to the side of a shelf in the fridge and popped in the dessert.

"No, yes," Christine stammered. "You never know about the traffic."

Christine dropped her keys on the threshold and stopped to swipe them up. Her hands were shaking. Something was bugging her, but at least whatever the distraction was it had kept her from asking how things had gone with Scott. She seemed to have enough on her mind without me spilling the beans about lying to her for months about my gun-owner status and then shooting off a Glock at the home of my ex-husband.

I didn't know if I would ever tell Christine how I had lost control with Scott, or how close I had come to being harmed. A certainty had landed with a solid thud in my conscience on my way back to San Antonio that day. When Scott had had the upper hand, I had held the line, and when I had had the upper hand I had pulled back before I crossed a line of no return. When I could have done the worst, I didn't, and that victory would not be diminished even if no one else knew.

I grabbed a box of Kleenex off the bar and waved it at her. "You forgot your most important accessory." I glanced behind us toward the front of the house. "Are we waiting for Barry, or is he in the car?"

"He's meeting us there," she said.

I barely had a chance to toss the Kleenex box on the dash and pull my right leg into Christine's RAV4 before she started backing out. I jerked my seat belt across my chest and clicked it. "Why are you so antsy? Is there something wrong?"

"It's a big moment. Xena's leaving for the Appalachian Trail tomorrow. I'm feeling a bit out of control, not totally behind that gap year thing. Hopefully, she can still get into MIT next year. I'm trying to wrap my head around not having a say about her life path."

I patted her leg. "Don't worry about it. It's a year out of a whole lifetime. She'll still be a NASA star one day. Our dad would be proud."

"Yeah, after I let him down," Christine said. "He couldn't understand that my dream was to own a neighborhood business and know all my customers' first names instead of going for an aerospace engineering degree."

"Did we have the same dad? The highest expectation he had for me was to marry a guy with a good job."

"He had another ten years to evolve by the time I graduated from high school. It was a different time."

"Your career dream worked out for me," I said. "Thanks to your business smarts, we are cupcake moguls, if owning two shops qualifies for mogulship. But overachiever that you are, you also married a pilot. Dad was over the moon."

I slid off balance on my seat as she sped out of her riverside neighborhood and took the corner onto Barton Springs Road too sharply. Then, she swerved our conversation to a different topic.

"So, Lexie and the big-time LA videographer, Georgio, are getting married," she said.

Christine and I had not had a chance to catch up since she and Barry returned from their visit with their older daughter in California.

"Georgio? Was that totally unexpected? Is that good?"

"Yes. He's quite a character, very artistic, very talented, very gorgeous. And, also totally unexpected, in seven months, I'm going to be a grandma."

I squeezed her arm in place of a full-on hug. "Congratulations. That's amazing."

"I wish Lexie could have come to Xena's graduation, but she has some big exhibit to curate in San Francisco."

"Lucky in career and romance, just like her mom," I said.

"Yep." She gnawed her bottom lip.

"Is something bothering you?" I asked.

Her voice quickly, and not quite genuinely, brightened. "How's Daniel and the new life in Dallas?"

"I'll soon find out. He's invited me up next weekend. It'll

be my first look at the new house."

"It'll be nice for you to get away to see someone you want to see for a change after what you've been through the last four months."

I tapped my fingers on the dash. "Know what? You and Barry and I should go up sometime, and we could have a little family get-to-together."

"Yep, so how's your love life going?"

"My love life? Where's this coming from?"

"I met the project manager for the remodel at the San Marcos shop. He seems like a really nice guy, nice-looking, too," she said, that brightness forced into her tone again. "The two of you might hit it off. I sometimes worry about you being alone for so long. You're an attractive, amazing woman, you should be out there, having fun. By the way, I'm liking the resurrection of you as a redhead."

I fluffed my hair. "Thanks, my sister the matchmaker."

"A possible friend, that's all, but I talked you up. He seemed interested," Christine said. "I have his card."

"I think I might have already found a possible someone who's interested. He's a really nice guy. Actually, he was Roanne's and my social studies teacher senior year at Bonham. He came to Roanne's funeral, and we've met a couple of times since then."

"An old teacher?"

"Only six years older. Judd Asher."

Christine's jaw dropped. "You're going out with Dashing Asher? He was my senior social studies teacher, too."

"Dashing Asher?"

"That's what all the girls called him. We had the biggest crush on him. He had this Indiana Jones vibe going on."

"David Cassidy plus ten years becomes Harrison Ford?"

"David who?"

"Never mind. Anyway, Judd and I haven't gone out yet."

"But you plan to."

"Definitely."

A light rain pattered against the windshield. Christine turned into the high school parking lot.

"Oh, great. Rain," she said. "We'll be dodging puddles in our heels."

"Yeah. Too bad Barry isn't driving. We'd get curbside valet service. Is he coming straight from the airport?"

Christine pulled into the first available space, two rows from the school entrance. The rain spattered harder. "About Barry."

"Yeah?"

She turned off the engine. "We've decided to separate."

"Wh-what? You and Barry? Not the flight attendant thing?"

"Nothing like that. The short version is our last kid has left the nest, and we've forgotten how to be together, just the two of us. Our stay in LA brought that into excruciating focus. We're putting up a united front for the graduation, not ruining Xena's night. When she gets back from her hike in December, that'll be soon enough to break the news to her and Lexie."

"But, you're not going to get a divorce?"

My heart thumped as I waited for her answer. If Barry and Christine couldn't make their marriage last, the world of men and women and relationships was hopeless.

Finally, she said, "We don't know yet. We need some time to evaluate."

A lump rose in my throat. I couldn't hold back a gasp that was about to gush forth into sobs.

"Hey, I don't need your tears," Christine said.

I sniffed hard and steadied my voice. "I'm here for you. Whatever you need."

"I might need a shoulder to cry on every now and then and some big sisterly advice."

"You got it."

"Look, sis, I'm going to be okay no matter how this plays

out. Barry's not going to disappear from my life. The love is still there even if we're not living together. He's always going to be around for Lexie and Xena. We're redesigning the bridge, not burning it."

The rain was coming down harder. "I have an umbrella way in the back," she said.

I pulled a Kleenex from the box, turned my head, dabbed at my eyes, and blew my nose. "Sorry. What you must have been going through these last few weeks, and I didn't have a clue. I should have been there for you."

"You had a lot going on emotionally yourself, with your crusade and all." She pressed the power liftgate button to the left of the steering wheel to pop the rear door open. "So, did you shoot Scott down?"

A pulse of dizziness rushed through me. "What? Shoot him?"

"It's a metaphor. Goodness, honey, you look like you've seen a ghost. Did you tell him what's what?"

"Yes." I took a deep breath to clear my head. I wasn't worried that Scott would file a report with the police saying I'd pulled a gun on him. He would never want to admit to anyone that I had him cowering like a scared, little kitten. "Some bridges are meant to be burned, and I took that one down to the ashes."

"Details?"

I shook my head. "Tonight's not the night for that."

Christine patted my shoulder. "Okay, have it your way, it's not like you've shared a whole lot up until now. But you did what you said you were going to do, took your power back from all of them. I'm proud of you."

"Thanks, but—"

"You are done with all that, right?"

Something tugged my right shoulder down, that weight I had felt as I walked away from Scott's house. "That's the thing. Yes, I have no unfinished business with Scott. But I feel like I walked out of a movie while the credits were rolling, and I really need to go back and stay until the screen turns black. I think there's one more I have to deal with."

"Now I'm getting worried about you. Have you been doing this so long that you are always going to find one more person to confront? Can't you let this go?"

"I'm at the finish line, I swear. I just have to cross over it. It won't be a confrontation, at least not like the others."

"Who is this guy? Remember when you promised you'd keep me in the loop?"

"I think I suggested more than promised?"

She did the exasperation exhalation. "Is this the one who's going to feel some remorse?" she asked.

"He's pretty much beyond feeling anything. That's all I'm saying. You'd think I'm crazy if I told you more."

"Have I ever thought you were crazy?"

I rolled my eyes. "We have a graduation to attend. Let's go."

Christine opened her door. The rain pounded against the asphalt like the hooves of stampeding horses.

"No guts, no glory!" she shouted and dashed to the back of the vehicle for the umbrella.

I lurched after her. We were two women, unafraid to get our feet wet.

– 1972 –

"Daddy! Mommy! Connie and the guys are here!" Roanne shouted toward the back of the house as she opened the door to let in Keith, her prom date, my date Denny, and me.

Keith stepped in first and stared Roanne up and down. "Wow, babe, you look super fine."

Roanne shrugged and giggled. Her floor-length dress was a pale yellow embossed fabric with sheer long sleeves that ended in satiny cuffs. Her hair was swept up to the crown of her head and fell in a soft, curled ponytail to the nape of her neck. She sidled up to Keith. His six-four frame filled out his wide-lapeled, white suit. The bangs of his shoulder-length, blond hair grazed the top of his eyes. He and Roanne looked like models on a magazine cover.

"You look great, too, Connie," Denny chimed in, squeezing my waist.

I rolled my eyes. "Yeah, thanks." I had gone for a more psychedelic look, a bell-sleeved short dress with orange and pink swirls. His burgundy suit clashed with my outfit, and his wild, curly hair had been newly mowed, like a trimmed chia pet, but I didn't mind.

Denny and I had dated for most of senior year. He had a cool car, a white Pontiac Firebird with blue racing stripes, but he wasn't like some of the rich boys at school who only went out with super-thin girls with stick-straight hair. Denny was sweet, a little shy, and he laughed at my lame jokes.

"This is for you," Keith said to Roanne. He drew a wrist corsage of white roses from a clear plastic box he held behind his back and slid it over her hand.

"And here's yours," Denny echoed, handing me my wrist corsage of daisies and baby's breath.

"Daddy! Mommy!" Roanne called again.

A round man with a buzz cut and a ruddy, jowly face walked into the entryway.

"Hello, Mr. Slater," I said. The guys mumbled something that sounded similar to my greeting. I hadn't seen much of Roanne's dad since Chip's funeral two years before. He looked heavier and shorter, compacted.

"Connie," he said, nodding to me, but he didn't acknowledge Denny and Keith. Denny stuck out his hand, and Mr. Slater stepped forward awkwardly and shook it.

"Your mother's not feeling well," Mr. Slater said to Roanne. "She's lying down." He leaned his head toward Keith. "Who's this?"

"You remember Keith Allen, Daddy. He used to live around the block, on Hackberry."

"That little, skinny kid who used to play basketball at the end of the street?"

"Yes, sir," Keith said, his voice cracking. "Good to see you again." He reached out his hand, but Mr. Slater ignored it, and it hung between them like a mannequin's lifeless limb.

"I see you turned into one of them long-haired hippies," Mr. Slater barked. "One of them war protesters."

Keith's face colored. "Uh, no, sir, I—"

"My son died in the war."

"Yes, sir. I know, sir."

"He would have turned twenty-one next week."

"I'm sorry, sir."

"You draft-card burning bastards ain't nothing but a bunch of cowards."

"Daddy!" Roanne pleaded. Her mouth trembled. She held onto Keith's arm. "He's not like that."

"How dare you bring this trash in here, dishonoring your brother." Mr. Slater jabbed his finger at Keith while he spoke to Roanne. "You're not going anywhere with this piece of crap."

Keith looked like he had been smacked in the face with a cold fish. Denny let go of me and backed toward the door.

"Daddy! It's my senior prom!" Roanne cried.

"I don't care if it's the goddamn Second Coming. You're not going!"

Roanne stood frozen for a moment with her mouth formed in an "O," then she burst into tears and ran down the hall toward her room.

"Denny, you and Keith should go," I said. "I'm going to check on Roanne."

"Are you sure?" Denny asked, already stepping out the door. I gave him a gentle push to send him on his way.

I ducked past Mr. Slater, not making eye contact.

Roanne was lying face down across her bed, bawling.

"Hey, Ro, I'm so sorry."

She sat up, her face streaked with mascara. Her perfect ponytail was frayed and twisted sideways. "I hate him! He had no right!"

I hugged her. "I can call Frank to pick us up. He's home on leave before he goes back to Camp Pendleton. We can meet Denny and Keith there, and if they don't show up, I'll be your prom date."

"I don't want to go anymore," she sniffled.

"Come on, Ro. It's our senior prom. We won't ever get to do this again." I brushed a damp strand of hair from her cheek, wet my thumb, and swiped a black smudge from under her eye. "And you look so pretty."

"I don't want to go. He's ruined it." She sniffed and swiped under her nose. "Let's do something else, just you and me."

"Do you want to walk down to Jim's and get a burger?"

"Like this?" She motioned to her crumpled, tear-stained dress.

"Grab your jeans. We can change at my house."

Roanne dug in a dresser drawer and pulled out a pair of

denims and a pink T-shirt. "He's so mean. I wish I had a dad like yours. He never talks to you like that."

"Yeah." My dad never talked to me at all.

- 2019 -

The limestone pillars stood like guardian giants on either side of the road into City Memorial Forest Park in Austin. To the right, inside the entry, I recognized a rock-faced house with a chimney, the original residence of farmers who owned the land before it became a public cemetery, the interior refurbished as a visitor center. Another historic, smaller building with a cupola bell tower atop a red-tile roof stood beyond, near a patch of woods. Across from the structures was a man-made lake. Benches were placed at one edge of the water, facing west toward the late afternoon sun. Near the center of the lake, four swans glided serenely.

It had taken me until three days after Xena's graduation to muster up the courage to drive here from San Antonio. It was late in the day since I had stopped in San Marcos to organize the final renovations of the addition to the cupcake shop there.

I parked and retrieved a gravesites map from a Plexiglas container bolted to a post at the head of the house's walkway. More than twenty thousand people were buried at Memorial Forest, the common folk among the historical figures, including a Confederate officer and descendants of one of Austin's founding fathers.

Back in the car, I unfolded and studied the map. More than a year had passed since my last visit, and I didn't trust my memory. The last place I wanted to be was lost in a graveyard two hours before closing time.

I circled through the mazes and cul-de-sacs, found the right section and the correct row, then parked and walked to the site. The tombstone was simple, pebble-patterned, gray granite topped with a cross, and it was placed next to an identical marker. I spread a blanket on the grass, sat down, and traced the inscription on the stone. "Francis Joseph

Canelli, Beloved husband and father, April 18, 1924–December 2, 2006."

Mourning doves cooed to each other from two rose arbors centered in the adjacent row of monuments. The wind stirred the branches of a nearby live oak, and the limbs cast a shadow that shuddered toward my narrow strip of sunny ground. Other visitors stood or knelt at other graves, but well in the distance, their remarks or prayers were inaudible to me and, hopefully, mine to them.

I sat silent for several minutes and took deep breaths to calm a surge of anxiety. What was I anxious about? He couldn't say anything mean to me or pull a gun or make me cry. I dove in to finish what I had come for in one visit.

"Hi, Dad." The doves paused their sad, soothing call, then started up again.

"I'm here because, well, let me try to explain. Do you remember that time you took me to the carousel? I must have been three. The painted horses were so tall. The ground was miles away when you set me on top of a pink-and-white one. The carousel operator lady tried to curl my chubby little fingers around the pole. I didn't know exactly what to expect, but the music started up, so loud, and the horse moved up and down. I thought you'd see how frightened I was immediately and snatch me off that contraption. But you didn't, and then I was going round, out of your sight. 'Where are you? Come get me, Daddy!'

"The horse came around to where it started, and there you were again. I wanted to reach out to you, but I was clinging to that pole for dear life. You were laughing and waving. You didn't come for me, and then the horse went round again and you were gone again, and I wanted to bawl, but the lump in my throat was so big, I couldn't get the cry out, and I peed my pants. I don't remember how many times that horse went round. It seemed like it would never stop. I cried all the way home, and you didn't say a word. You looked like you were annoyed.

"That's what you did, pretty much my whole life. You set me aside and left me, alone and scared while the whole time I was crying for you."

Hot tears tracked down my cheeks. Heaving sobs hurt my chest. I pulled up the tail of my shirt to wipe my eyes and nose.

"I wanted you to be interested in me. I wanted you to talk to me, tell me what it was like when you were a kid, where you went on your first date with Mom, what made you fall in love with her. Tell me about boys and how I should have self-respect and make them come to the door to pick me up instead of honking the horn and expecting me to run out. Tell me that my body was my own, and no one had the right to do anything to it without my permission. A girl needs a good dad to set the standard for the men who come later in her life. I think you'd have to admit you were pretty much MIA on that front."

I leaned my forehead against the cool granite. My fingers threaded through the grass beside the grave.

"I know you worked hard and long hours, but you know it wasn't about time. You showed up at all of Frank's and Joey's games. I had to get a ride with a friend to all my school plays.

"You said that all that singing and dancing play 'nonsense' wasn't your cup of tea, but it wasn't about the play, it was about me on the stage." I shook my head and smiled in spite of my tears. "It's funny, I would still look for you in the audience every time and feel crappy every time when I realized you weren't there."

I let my fingers again slip along the indentions of letters on the tombstone.

"I wanted to be worth something to you. I wanted you to notice me. I guess if I hadn't gotten in trouble that one time at senior career day, we wouldn't have interacted at all between the time I was ten and when I left for college. Except when you asked me to get you a beer, 'from the back of the fridge, Bunny.'

"I liked when you called me that, even if asking for a beer was the only occasion on which you used it. Bunny. Your special name for me. I shouldn't have minded so much when you stopped. I was fifteen, too old for cute nicknames. But you gave it to Christine. It hadn't been special after all, just a generic name for a little girl, like duckling or puppy or pebble or rosebud, an identifier for small things.

"Strange, isn't it, how some parents think that their kids no longer need them once they're grown up. They're out of the nest and good riddance. Scott made cracks all the time about Daniel, 'five more years,' when Daniel was thirteen, a countdown. I needed you."

A car cruised by, the man at the wheel hanging an arm out the window, squinting at the tombstones, perhaps looking for the one he intended to visit. The car turned in a tight loop and sped off from the direction it had come. The license plate was green and white, not Texas.

"I wasn't back home a lot when Scott was in the army, but you could have visited. You could have come over and eaten my pot roast and new potatoes and said it was as good as Mom's, even if it wasn't, and it definitely wasn't, just to make me feel good. You could have sat on the couch with me when Scott was out late and held my hand and asked if I was happy. A lot of times I wasn't happy.

"I should've never married Scott. I had no clue what I was getting into. The only thing I learned about marriage from you and Mom was that you weren't supposed to get divorced, not ever, no matter what.

"He treated me well most of our years together. He was a good provider. The bills were always paid. He was a good dancer. He played ball with Daniel in the backyard. Even the sex was good, before his drinking went out of control. Too much information? Well, we're both adults here."

I glanced at the matching tombstone beside Dad's, inscribed with "Rose Bernadette Zelinsky Canelli," like I was checking with her.

"Believe it or not, Mom is the one who told me this joke:

"'How does a woman tell when she's had good sex?'

"'She has time to fake the orgasm before he finishes.' Ha!

"Of course, I didn't know Scott was cheating on me from day one. I didn't want to see it, so I didn't. Would you have told me to leave him if you knew? Would you have given him a good talking-to? Would you have punched his lights out? I hope you didn't run around on Mom. Were you happy with her? Was she happy with you? Did that even matter?"

I paused for a minute and shut my eyes. I hadn't realized how intensely the pain would burn when I released it, how it would stab the insides of my lungs and rake at my throat.

"I was fifty-two when you died, and I don't remember one time that you said you were proud of me. I don't remember one time you said you loved me. Maybe you'd be happy to know you didn't pass that on to me. I tell Daniel I love him, a lot, as much as I did when he was a little boy. I never get tired of saying it."

I lifted myself to my knees, squared my shoulders to face the granite marker, and stretched out my arms, palms up.

"Hey, don't think I'm here to say everything bad that ever happened to me is your fault. At some point, we're grownups, and we have to take responsibility for our messed-up decisions, and I made my share of those."

I folded my hands in my lap and rocked back on my heels.

"What I'm here to say is you missed a lot, because you chose not to be there, not to be involved. When I took my bows as the Tin Man in *The Wizard of Oz,* in fifth grade, I got a standing ovation. I kind of stole the show with my freeze-up in the oilcan scene. Daniel turned out to be a great kid, and I have two precious grandbabies. I'm a writer of some small renown, not bestseller ranked, but I have a following, and writing gives me satisfaction. Christine's and my business is doing well. We're not performing rocket science, but if there was a Nobel for selling cupcakes, we'd be a shoo-in. I have a great relationship with my little sis. Of course, you remember Roanne, don't you? I had the truest friend in the whole world for fifty years. How many people can say that?"

I closed my fists and raised them in a fighting stance. "I've been knocked down and beat down and held down, but I found the courage to stand up and speak out and demand validation as a woman. We have rage that needs to be taken seriously, because, if it isn't, it could kill us; it has killed us, you know? You don't know.

"I'll just say this: I like what I've become, without your help, and what I'm still becoming, and I won't back away or back down."

The tears came again, not so heavy this time, and I swiped them away.

"Really, what I came to say is I wish it could have been different for you and me. But even though we'll never have that chance, I've found some measure of calm, and that's what I leave for you."

I stood, picked up the blanket, and folded it against my chest.

"Peace be with you, Dad."

The calling of the doves echoed in my ears.

I drove back to the entrance and was almost beyond the stone pillars when a whisper brushed my ear, and I froze. A breeze through the half-open window? But it sounded like soft breathing on the other end of a phone line, like on that last call from Roanne, the breath of something left unsaid, undone. I backed up, parked, and opened the glove compartment. The metal was cold and heavy in my hand.

I walked to the lake edge, cocked my arm, and threw the gun as far as I could. It plunked into the glassy water, disturbing its stillness with rippling circles. The swans lifted into the air, the tips of their wings tinged orange by the setting sun.

I climbed back into Mellow Yellow and maneuvered it onto the road. My body was so light, I could have flown home like a kite on the wind.

– 1995 –

"Hey, isn't that Roanne sitting at the end of the bar?" Scott asked. We had taken seats at a table midway between the stage, where a country rock band played, and the back wall of the No Drama Lounge, a dive in Harker Heights, about ten miles from Killeen.

The same cowboy memorabilia—branding irons, spurs, and tack—hung from the dingy walls as it had seventeen years ago when we had discovered the place. It even smelled the same, of stale smoke and excessive aftershave and something fried in day-old grease. Back then, Scott and Johnny had been stationed at nearby Fort Hood. Scott and I had lived in Austin, Johnny and Roanne in Killeen, and we had all been starry-eyed newlyweds. We had gone to the bar for the music, the company, and the cheap drinks.

On the summer night when the four of us had gotten together days before Scott and I left for Fort Clayton, Panama, the owners had let us stay past closing time, and the band played on for an extra half hour. Roanne had been seven months pregnant and had sworn off alcohol, but she sneaked a shot of vodka into her pink lemonade.

In the ladies' room, she had confessed to me, "Without that drink, I would be crying my eyes out. You're moving to the other side of the Earth. I'll be alone." She was the one who had uplifted me when I had first received the news of Scott's transfer. But I had stingily held back from soothing her that night in the bar, not telling her that she would hardly be alone, with Johnny and a new baby. I had been jealous of what seemed like her and Johnny's ideal family life.

Before Scott and I had returned from Panama two years later, Johnny had left the army with a sour taste in his mouth over a lost promotion, and he and Roanne had moved to

Round Rock. Scott and I had hopped from place to place, according to his duty stations, and our inseparable foursome was no more. We had talked often over the years about having regular get-togethers, us and our children, like the Slaters and Canellis back on Pecan Street when Roanne and I were girls, but that never quite happened.

The woman at the bar sat with her back to Scott and me, her blonde hair fanned across the collar of a white shirt tucked into slender jeans. She shifted her hips on the bar stool, turned to glance at the door, and I instantly recognized her profile.

"Yes, it's Roanne," I said. My mind flip-flopped between a sense that I was intruding on her and an assumption that she would be happy to see me. She looked toward the door again. Was she waiting for someone or hoping no one she knew would come in?

"What is she doing here, fifty miles from Round Rock?" Scott asked.

"If she saw us, she'd wonder what we're doing here sixty miles from Austin."

Scott and I had spent the day looking at houses for sale in Harker Heights, thinking of moving from Austin where we had been renting a two-bedroom apartment for the last year, since Scott had retired from the army. Daniel was a rambunctious five-year-old, and our living space seemed to be shrinking by the day. Scott and I had started taking Sunday drives through neighborhoods with single-family houses, staring longingly at cars backing out of private garages and listening fondly to the sounds of children playing in fenced yards.

A server came to our table and took our order for appetizers and drinks. The band finished "Friends in Low Places" and announced a break. As the last guitar strums faded, voices and clinks of beer bottles grew louder.

"I'm going to say hi to Roanne," I said.

Scott caught my wrist. "Hold on. Let's watch and see what

happens."

"Why would we spy on Roanne?" I scooted back my chair.

Scott still held my wrist. "Johnny told me she might be cheating on him."

"That's nonsense. She's not cheating."

"How do you know?"

"Because she would've told me."

"Oh, so she's done it before?"

I wriggled my hand free. "Of course not," I lied without so much as a blink or a stutter. I figured Roanne and Johnny must have worked things out after the incident ten years ago or they wouldn't have stayed together. "Never in a million years would Roanne cheat on Johnny." Again.

"Look," Scott said. "She's getting up."

Roanne slung a leather bag over her shoulder, walked toward the stage, and turned left into a hallway at the other end of the bar.

I stood up. "She's going to the ladies' room. I'm going to talk to her."

"Ask her if she's meeting some dude."

I rolled my eyes. "Shut up."

I was leaning against the cigarette-scarred vanity, staring at a travel poster of a beach when Roanne walked out of one of the two stalls. She stumbled a step backward at the sight of me, and I caught her elbow to steady her. "Sorry, Ro, I didn't mean to scare you."

"Con, what are you doing here?" she asked.

"Scott and I came up for the day to look at houses in Harker Heights. We saw you at the bar, but you were on your way to the bathroom before I could get your attention."

"Oh." She brushed past me, pumped soap into her hand from a wall dispenser, and turned on the faucet. "I didn't know you were thinking of moving."

"Yep, someplace not too far from Austin. Here or San Antonio. We liked it there when Scott was stationed at Fort

Sam. What're you doing here?"

Roanne tore off a sheet of paper towel and rubbed it between her palms. "Revisiting old times." She balled up the paper towel and tossed it in the trash can near the door. Her lower lip quivered. "Johnny and I had an awful fight. It scared Zoe to death. She hid under her bed, and she wouldn't talk to me."

I hadn't initially noticed that Roanne's eyes were puffy from crying. I gave her a brief hug and then held onto one of her hands. "I'm sorry, sweetie. What did you fight about?"

"The same thing we've been fighting about since he got out of the army sixteen years ago. I took an extra job, tutoring math three days a week in the evenings since the Post Office cut back his hours. Stella will be ready for college in less than two years, and we can use the money. But, according to Mr. Macho, I'm undercutting his manhood. I said something stupid, like someone has to bring home the bacon. You know Johnny's pride. He went ballistic."

"He didn't hurt you, did he?"

She shook her head. "He wouldn't, but he said a bunch of hurtful things, like 'How do I know you're teaching math when you go out at night? Maybe you're giving someone another kind of lesson.' That was totally uncalled for. I was so upset, I just got in the car and started driving. I was all the way to Belton when I remembered this place and how things were when we were all young and in love. I figured, what was another fifteen miles?"

"Seems like a long time ago." We hugged, and she sniffled on my shoulder. A young woman in a halter top walked in. I caught her reflection in the mirror, staring at us before she went into a stall. "You and Johnny will work it out, after you've both had time to calm down."

Roanne nodded, let go of me, wet a paper towel, and dabbed at her eyes. "I'm a mess."

I retrieved a wad of toilet paper from the empty stall,

handed it to her, and she blew her nose.

"How many drinks have you had?" I asked.

"Two White Russians."

"Are you okay to drive home?"

"I will be. I've been drinking water for the past half hour."

The woman in the halter top exited the stall, washed up, checked herself in the mirror, and pranced out.

"Come sit with Scott and me until you sober up," I said. "We haven't talked in a while."

"I don't want to talk about Johnny."

"We'll talk about houses, get your opinion. You can share my calamari. Scott won't touch it."

Roanne took a last glance in the mirror, shrugged, and we walked back to where Scott sat nursing a Bud Light. The band had started up again with "All My Ex's Live in Texas."

When Roanne reached the table, Scott jumped up and threw his arms around her. "Hey, girl, just like old times, huh?"

"Exactly. Old times," Roanne said, with a crooked imitation of a smile and much less enthusiasm than Scott.

"How's John—" I gave him the slashed-throat signal. He stood up and grabbed my arm. "We'll be right back," he said to Roanne. "Gotta take my girl for a spin."

Scott held me close, and I breathed in the starchy, crisp smell of his shirt. He wanted to know what Roanne and I had talked about in the bathroom. "Nothing much," I said and spun a story that Roanne and Johnny were stressed out over money problems. She had been in Belton earlier in the day checking out a job and afterwards had detoured to the bar, pulled by nostalgia, just like us.

Scott's hand attached solidly to my hip, but I was dancing separately, peering back at our table through the shifting crowd. I caught Roanne's eye and waved, letting her know I hadn't abandoned her. Scott kept me on the dance floor as the band launched into "Boot Scootin' Boogie," and the crowd spread out for a line dance. I whirled around, facing our table, and motioned for Roanne to join us. She stood up, raised a glass of water toward me, downed the contents, hooked her bag over her shoulder, and turned her face toward the exit.

"Roanne's leaving!" I yelled to Scott over the music while he made a step and a turn away from me, following the next movement of the dance. I lost a step and shuffled to catch up with the line. A wide-hipped woman in low-slung jeans had edged partway between us. "I'm going to talk to Roanne before..." I yelled when Scott's face whirled around again in my direction. I leaned around the interloping hips, and my toes dodged the woman's sizable Noconas. "...she goes!" Scott pointed to his ears, the signal for "I can't hear you."

I stepped out of the line, and the dancers slid past on either side, like a double-bladed saw. When I whipped my head around to look back for Roanne, a blank space hung there. I was alone.

"You wanna play Super Mario, Grandma?" Braden bounced up and down beside me as soon as I walked into Daniel and Amy's house in Dallas.

At least I recognized the name Mario from when Daniel had been six like his son was now, but that was the extent of my up-to-date knowledge of video games in the twenty-first century.

Charlotte echoed her brother's question, with my name changed to "Gwandma," in three-year-old speak. I bent to let her leap into my arms and held her perched on my hip.

Before I could answer Braden, Daniel saved me. "We'll see if Grandma wants to do that later."

"After the surprise?" Braden piped up. Daniel put his fingers to his lips, and Braden clamped both hands over his mouth.

Charlotte clapped a hand over her mouth in an approximate imitation.

"What surprise?" I said and squinted at Daniel.

"Later," he said, taking Charlotte, setting her down, and gently pushing Braden ahead with a hand at the back of his head. "Come on, guys, let's show Grandma the house."

A few steps in I could already see that the place was spectacular, if not a bit oversized for a family of four. The ceilings were worthy of a cathedral. A rock wall above the family-room fireplace rose past the landing on the second floor.

Daniel led me upstairs, Braden trailed his dad, and Charlotte scooted up the stairs like a puppy on her brother's heels. On the second level was the "entertainment" room, the millennial version of my generation's wood-paneled den. But instead of the recliners and the TV that required viewers to get up to change the channel, a curved couch, outfitted with built-in cup holders and snack trays and a control panel, faced a giant flat screen. Off to the side was a game station that resembled the bridge on the Starship *Enterprise*.

Beyond the entertainment area was a nook with a wall of windows where Amy's cello was propped in front of a music stand. A visit to Braden's and Charlotte's rooms came with a mini-course on Pokémon, a demonstration of a glittery, singing unicorn, and a litany of other games and toys and creatures that I had never heard of. Christmas shopping for the grandkids was going to involve some research.

Daniel took me up a second flight of stairs to the single space on the third floor. "The loft," he said, showing off the room with no windows but a huge skylight. The sparse furnishings looked temporary: a bed, a chair, a floor lamp, an area rug on the taupe tile floor, a poster on the wall. "It's a good place for a guest or whatever," he said.

"Oh, whatever." A third grandchild in my future? A surprise announcement later tonight?

At the end of the tour, and all that stair-climbing, I sat down at the bar that divided the dining area from the spacious kitchen. Amy opened a bottle of red wine and set a glass in front of me. The kids had traipsed off to another part of the house.

"That's some kitchen," I said and sipped my wine. "You have enough counter space to butcher a calf."

Amy smiled. "And I don't even like to cook. But it came with the house, so..."

"I love to cook," Daniel said as he came up behind his wife and put an arm around her waist. "On our mini-vacation to Santa Fe in October, I'm taking a one-day gourmet cooking class and running a half marathon. Amy's trying her hand at something called 'painting pioneer women.'"

"And playing a string concert on the plaza," Amy said. "If the details can be worked out."

"Good for you. And the kids?"

"We wanted to talk to you, ask you about that," Daniel said.

"Ah, and you're plying me with wine ahead of time."

"Yeah, well, we plan to be gone three days, Sunday through Tuesday. Braden and Charlotte will be in school and pre-school, and—"

"I'll do it."

"Only if you're really available and if you really don't mind. I know you have a book in the works, and that's a priority."

I waved my hand to dismiss their concerns. "I sent the final version of *The Pineapple Peril* and the first three chapters of my new series off to my editor yesterday. No book tour dates until November."

"No pressure, seriously," Amy said, "We know you have your own life."

"I do. I've signed up as a volunteer usher with a theater group. I'm restarting senior water aerobics at the YMCA." I had switched from the St. Mary's Y to the Blanco Road location to meet new people and avoid any former classmates I had shoved into the pool. "And I might have the occasional night out." Judd had left me a phone message on my drive up to Dallas.

"You're one busy lady," Daniel said.

"Yes, but I'm still free Sundays through Tuesdays for the foreseeable future. And do I mind being a full-time grandma for three days? I'm over the moon." I sipped my wine. "Was that the surprise?"

Daniel and Amy exchanged glances and ignored my question. "Thank you so much, Mom," Daniel said. "We'll talk details later." He came around the bar and hugged me around the shoulders. "We don't just want you up here on babysitting duty. Just because we're in Dallas doesn't mean we can't stay as close as always. We want you to think of this as your second home. Come up anytime, stay as long as you want."

"Seriously?"

"Absolutely," Amy said. "We certainly have the room. And the kids would be thrilled."

So, that was the surprise. I patted Daniel's arm as he released his hug. "I'd like nothing better." I took a long sip and let the liquid roll around on my tongue. "This wine is nice. I'm feeling quite relaxed."

"Well," Daniel said, "we're going to have a little bit of excitement soon." He took my empty glass and set it in the kitchen. I thought he was about to pour me a refill, but he put a stopper in the wine bottle and tucked it away in a cabinet. "We have a special guest arriving any minute now."

"Ah, the surprise," I said.

Braden ran in, hopped onto the stool next to mine, twirled it once, and grinned sideways at me. "Nope," he said. "That's not the surprise, Grandma."

Charlotte trotted into the kitchen, carrying a naked baby doll by its hair, plopped down on the floor, and kissed the doll on the forehead.

"Oh-kay," I said, then mock pouted. "I thought I was the special guest."

"You're the guest of honor, always," Daniel said.

"Do I know this person?" I asked. The doorbell chimed. "Is that Beethoven's Ninth?"

Braden and Charlotte darted to the front door with Daniel and Amy following at a less anxious pace. I whirled my chair a half turn to see who had arrived, but a wall blocked my view of the entryway.

Daniel's and Amy's low voices, Braden's and Charlotte's high-pitched shouts, and another, softer, female voice carried from the doorway. The door clicked shut. Something heavy thumped down on the floor. A suitcase? Footsteps shuffled in my direction. A face, framed in long, dark hair, and a pair of slim, rounded shoulders peeked around the corner.

I slid out of my seat and rushed to her, my arms spread

wide. "Zoe! You look wonderful!"

Her face was a bit plumper and aglow. I recognized the easy smile of the child who had played Mario Brothers with Daniel years ago. I pulled her to me, and joy flowed through me like blood rushing through a limb after a tourniquet has been released.

"Auntie Connie, I didn't know you'd be here," she gushed into my ear as she returned my hug. "Now I know I'm really home."

Daniel and Zoe caught me up. She had finished rehab in Virginia and was in an outpatient program in Dallas. She had to check in with her counselor weekly and attend AA meetings.

Daniel and Zoe had mapped out a three-month plan for her to find a part-time job, re-enroll at the university in Arlington in preparation for nursing courses in another year, and find public assistance housing. Meanwhile, she would live with Daniel and Amy.

"You have a great support system," I said, "including me, if needed."

We ate barbecue, not home-cooked by Amy or Daniel in their all-the-bell-and-whistles kitchen, but delivered from one of the top local smokehouses. I understood why the wine had been discreetly put away.

Zoe gnawed on a short rib. "I know Daniel and Amy won't put up with any bull...stuff." She caught herself in time to save Amy from explaining to Braden and Charlotte who was allowed and who was not allowed to use curse words. "And there's no way I'm letting Daniel down, after all he's done for me." She glanced up at him with a smile that he answered with a wink. "He even got my cell phone back from the San Antonio airport."

I smiled and nodded, hoping an old doubt had not flickered across my face and caught Zoe's eye. It had been less than two months since I had held her, sobbing and filthy, on the floor of Daniel's old house after a night of reckless drinking in the bars and alleys in San Antonio. I remembered too easily when Daniel was addicted, the many times that he had sworn he was clean, that he had promised he would never use again, steal again, lie again. And yet, he had. Hopefully, he would catch Zoe and turn her around if she started to stray.

Throughout dinner, Zoe threw me a series of furtive glances, apparently wanting to say something but not comfortable speaking in front of everyone else.

Toward the end of the meal, the children fidgeted like they were sitting on balloons that they were trying to burst. Daniel leapt up and turned off the light. I noticed Amy had left the table. In another minute, she was walking back into the dining area carrying a cake lit with a tall, pink candle glowing in the center.

"Surprise!" Braden yelled.

"Supwise!" Charlotte mimicked and busted into giggles.

Everyone but me started singing "Happy Birthday." I was breathless and snickering like a child.

"It's three days early," Daniel said, "but we had to get the jump on you so that you didn't bring the cake."

"You got me. What a surprise." I gasped and blew out the lone candle, thank goodness there were not sixty-four more. I blinked at the little wisp of smoke and looked across the table at an empty chair. Roanne should have been sitting there, beaming and clapping.

The dreams and night tremors that had bothered me after Roanne's funeral had dissipated since my visits to Scott and to Dad's grave. I had been sleeping more easily, waking astonished to find myself curled in the covers, not remembering the moments before I drifted off, having fallen into slumber quickly and deeply. The movie-like memories had not stopped playing in my mind. They went on and on, but they were no longer an inconvenience, they were simply part of my life.

Amy cut slices of the Oreo cake, made with white cake

batter with crushed Oreos mixed in and slathered with white cream frosting. I couldn't have done better myself. After the celebration, I walked Zoe up to the loft while Daniel and Amy took on the intensive ritual of bedtime preparation for Braden and Charlotte.

Zoe sat on the green coverlet of the bed, dug her bare toes into the furry white rug, and bit her lip. I sat down in a cup-shaped chair in a corner of the room. The moon shone through the skylight, illuminating our faces enough that we didn't need to switch on a lamp.

"What's on your mind, sweetie?" I asked.

She nodded, looked down at her fingers twisted together in her lap, then raised her chin to meet my eyes with hers.

"I know it's going to be hard. I have a safe place to stay and a plan to put my life back together. Daniel and Amy are great, but, Auntie Connie, you're the one who holds the key."

"Me? What key do I have?"

"The key to my mom." .

I waited for her to say more. The sounds of bath water running, little feet scuffling, and alternating childish giggles and whines sifted up from the lower level. A light down below flicked on, then off, then on again. Amy's singsong voice was reading a bedtime story.

"I wish we could be someplace completely away from everyone," Zoe said.

On the wall, behind her, hung a framed poster, foam-tipped turquoise waves meeting a sugary stretch of sand. Some exotic island, no doubt. Roanne and I had had our girls' weekends but never anywhere more exotic than the Texas coast. Still, what made those trips little paradises was being together, not where we went.

I sighed. "We'll come up with something." I gave her a hug. "Let's talk in the morning."

When the family noises had quieted, I padded down to the kitchen and fixed myself another slice of Oreo cake alongside a tall glass of milk. By the time I licked the last bit of frosting and crumbs from the back of my fork, I had decided on a plan for Zoe and I to make a getaway.

Ro, we can do this together. Please. Stay with me a little while longer.

The police detective couldn't hear the pleading inside my head. He had dragged a chair from Darla's dining room and set it at a respectful distance across from where I sat on the couch. He was a stocky, under-fortyish man in a navy suit and pale yellow tie, with close-cropped hair and pale, flat eyes. His broad shoulders and pasty color signaled a lot of time spent in the gym and meager time spent outdoors. What had he said his name was? Jenkins? Judson? He adjusted his lower half in the chair, opened a notebook, tapped the pad with a pen, and appeared to be scanning what was written there.

"You and me, Ro." My words escaped out loud.

The detective raised his head. "Ms. Canelli? Do you need a moment? Or we can do this later today if you're not up to it right now. I realize this situation is a terrible shock. You haven't had time to come to grips with all of it."

We were in Darla's living room. She had taken a tranquilizer and had lain down in her bedroom, Phil by her side, after they had returned from the morgue.

I had driven up to Round Rock after Roanne's last call. It was Darla's idea to check Johnny's house to see if Roanne was there. We found the street blocked at both ends with police cars. From there, the string of events had unraveled in a rolling nightmare that continued into the morning. The police had informed Darla of the "situation," and Darla had passed the scant facts on to me. The words were not information or explanation. They were a baseball bat to the side of my head that had beat me numb.

Two shots. Two dead. Too dead.

My mouth tasted of bile. My eyelids burned, tight and

swollen. My fingers were cold. The room was buzzing with an invisible fog. I stared at the chunky, gold class ring on the detective's right hand, tried to focus, get a grip, come to grips.

"Go ahead," I said to the detective. "I'm okay." We're okay.

He leaned forward slightly, the notepad sandwiched in his palms and dangling between his knees. "I'm sorry for your loss, ma'am."

The detective handed me a box of Kleenex. I dutifully took it and placed it in my lap, although my eyes were dry, having forgotten how to manufacture tears. I stared at my fingernails digging into my palm while I was unable to register the sharpness of the pain. Adrenalin or an involuntary force was holding me upright, and an emergency neuro-gear had kicked in, enabling me to string words together and mechanically issue them from my mouth.

"What you have to understand is that Roanne was a good person," I said. "She volunteered at the food bank. She would never do something like..." Roanne Slater, you didn't give me any warning. Do you remember that plane crash in Dallas? All on board killed, but also a man driving along the highway, struck by the plane's wheel. How could I have looked out for the unimaginable?

The detective laid the pad flat on his thigh. "I understand you and Ms. Slater were close. How long had you been friends?"

"Since we were fifteen." You were sitting on my bed, eating M&Ms. I put a record on the turntable. We were singing. "Fifty years."

"I understand you spoke to her last night on the phone." He scratched on the pad with his pen. "When was the last time you saw Ms. Slater?"

"Last week. We met at the cupcake shop my sister and I own in Austin. C Is For..." Christine. I have to call her, tell her about you. Did I leave my phone in the car?

"Did she appear out of the ordinary in any way?

Despondent? Hopeless?"

"Not at all. We made plans for our annual girls' weekend in June. We take a trip together every year in between our birthdays." The big six-five, now only me, not you, not fair. "She made reservations at a cabin at Lake O' the Pines in East Texas. We wanted to get away from the city." No sleeping in a tent for us, no hovering over a toilet in a campground bathroom.

"Nothing seemed off?"

"No. We looked at photos of the cabin on her laptop. We were excited." Pecan Praline was the special of the day. You ordered a dozen to take back home.

"What was her recent relationship with Johnny Kirkland?"

"Is Johnny—did she—" Did you?

"I can't confirm or deny Mr. Kirkland's status, ma'am. Next of kin notification procedure, you understand."

"Stella." Not Zoe. You wouldn't want that.

"Ma'am?"

"Notify her daughter, Stella." Do the police have Stella's phone number? In my phone. Where's my phone? They'd have your phone, wouldn't they?

I patted the couch, tucked my hand into the crevice between the cushions, then slid it out empty. No phone. And not one crumb. Cleanliness is next to godliness. That's your sister Darla.

"Did Mr. Kirkland and Ms. Slater have frequent contact?"

"No, they'd been separated since 1995, but they both stayed in Round Rock. They might have run into each other at Home Depot once in a while, but mostly they avoided each other." Home Depot? I meant to say Walmart. Where you bought the gun. No, they don't sell handguns at Walmart.

"The divorce was not amicable then?"

"It was horrible. She didn't want him to leave. She loved him, even after all he did."

"All he did?"

"In the middle of the divorce, she was accused of an inappropriate relationship with one of her students. There was no proof, some emails and an out-of-focus photo. She was certain Johnny had set her up with the school district."

"Did the district investigate?"

"The investigation was never completed. Roanne was so overwhelmed by the rumors, she resigned. Then Johnny brought up the accusations in their custody fight, tried to paint her as an unfit mother." Paint. From Home Depot. We had to buy more to cover up that disgusting word on your garage door. "The whole mess was taking a toll on their daughters. She let Johnny have custody, to end it all."

"And that was 1995," the detective said, his pen pausing over his notepad.

"1996 by the time the custody fight was over."

"Twenty-three years." The detective drew the pen across the page, underlining or crossing out. "That's a long time to hold a grudge. It looks like she had good reason to want to settle the score. Had she ever talked about getting even with Mr. Kirkland?"

"Roanne wasn't vengeful. She never talked of harming Johnny. After the divorce, she went on with her life. She and Stella mended fences before Stella got married and moved to Virginia. She was still working on Zoe, calling her every week even though Zoe never called back, but she wouldn't give up. She didn't hate Johnny." He called you gorgeous in that white bathing suit. "She still wanted him to forgive her." He sent you ten white roses on Valentine's Day.

"Forgive her? I thought he was the one who screwed her over."

"She cheated on him." All your exes lived in Texas. Stupid mistake.

"Did he cheat on her?"

"No. Johnny had a faithful streak a mile wide. With Roanne, his army buddies, his friends. I guess that's why he couldn't get over what she did."

"Had you ever seen Ms. Slater lose her temper and hurt anyone?"

I paused and took a deep breath. "Once."

"When was that?"

"Senior career day. She knocked Jimmy Hollister out of his chair and gave him a bloody nose." Blood. Girls bleed. Jimmy shouldn't have said those things to you.

"That was nineteen..."

"Seventy-two."

"Do you know of any recent incident between Ms. Slater and Mr. Kirkland that would have set her off?"

"Nothing." The detective looked up from his notes, his brows raised in a question. "She would have told me." Wouldn't you?

The detective tapped the pen against the notebook. "Ms. Canelli, you knew Ms. Slater for fifty years. Do you have any idea why she would harm Mr. Kirkland and apparently take her own life last night?"

I locked my eyes on the detective's. "She said she was angry."

"At whom?"

"At Tom and Dick..."

The detective cocked an eyebrow. "And Harry?" He started the upswing of an eye roll before he caught himself.

I nodded.

The detective sighed heavily and again tapped his pen against the notepad. "She had a bad track record with men. Was that the situation?"

"She was a good person."

"Volunteered at the food bank."

"She wasn't always treated well in return."

"Who were these men?"

"Her dad, for one. He forbade her from going to our prom. She was devastated." Your dress was the prettiest shade of yellow. And your date, what a heartthrob.

The detective's brows bent together. He cleared his throat. "Ms. Canelli, surely you're not telling me I'm here investigating an alleged murder-suicide because your sixty-four-year-old friend was angry about missing a high school prom?"

I shut my eyes for a moment, pressed my palms to my knees and took deep breaths. The cloth of the detective's slacks swooshed as he shifted in his seat. Impatient. "It wasn't just that one thing that one time." This guy had the situation all wrong. My hands crushed against the Kleenex box. "Detective, is it Jenkins?"

"Jergens, like the lotion."

My heart hammered. I looked down to see I had flattened the sides of the tissues box. Losing my grip. You were losing your grip. "Detective Lotion, I think she was trying to tell me that things had stacked up."

"What things?"

"All the unfairness. You smile through it, even when your teeth are set on edge. You pick up the kids, you make the meatloaf, you smile, day after day, year after year. " What did you say? You take it and take it until one day...

The detective heaved a loud sigh. "Ms. Canelli, I'm struggling. Help me out here, will you? I've probably pissed my wife off ten times a day for the past twelve years. She's on my case every time I don't change out the toilet paper roll. She gets over it. It's no biggie. She doesn't blow my head off."

"Until it is. Until she does." Until you did.

– JUNE 2019 –

During the two-and-a-half-hour drive from Dallas east to Lake O' the Pines, Zoe hardly said a word. She chewed at the edge of her thumbnail, complained that Mellow Yellow's interior smelled funny, buzzed the window up and down, and fiddled with the radio like a bored teenager.

Almost to our destination, we took a detour to Tyler to pick up the key to the cabin and a map. Until Zoe had talked about me having "the key" to her mom, it hadn't occurred to me that the girls' weekend reservation Roanne had made in February was still active.

Daniel had at first objected to me bailing on the family weekend and sent a pang to my heart by describing Braden and Charlotte's imminent disappointment when they awoke to find their grandma gone. I had appeased him, explaining that, although Zoe and I would be gone all of Saturday, we'd be back in Dallas before midday Sunday to salvage at least half of the weekend.

"Zoe really needs a retreat," I had told Daniel. "It's taken her so long to come out of her shell about her mom. I want to grab this opportunity."

Daniel had relented. "Okay, I guess you know what you're doing."

While Zoe stared vacantly out the car window, I had no doubt that I was totally winging it.

Eight bumpy, dirt-road miles from the highway, we arrived at the log A-frame nestled in a grove of pines. Zoe perked up at the sight of our accommodations.

"Awesome sauce," she said as she scooted out of the VW.

The heady evergreen fragrance and the trill-whistle-tweet of a wood thrush greeted us as we walked up the porch steps with our backpacks and a bag of groceries. A yellow butterfly lit on the back of one of two rocking chairs. A stack of split logs leaned against the wall.

Inside, the floor of the single room was made of pine planks covered partially by a red and black rug with a Native American design. The furniture was simple, a leather sofa, two side chairs, a rustic dining set, and a bookcase. We'd be sleeping in bunk beds. I flipped the ceiling fan and light switches to confirm that they worked, but windows in the back and front walls let in plenty of natural light.

The centerpiece of the room was a cast-iron woodstove with a stovepipe that curved up and through the ceiling.

"Do you know how to work that?" Zoe asked.

I opened the stove door. It groaned on its hinges. "Sure. You open the damper," I turned a knob on the front, "throw in some logs and start a fire." I looked around and spied a basket of kindling and a box of long-handled matches. "With those little pieces of wood and the logs out on the porch, but this time of year, I don't think it'll get cold enough."

Zoe spent the next few hours piddling around in the kitchen, looking through drawers and cabinets, nibbling on trail mix, slouching on the sofa with a bowl of ramen, shoveling the noodles into her mouth. Her headphones shut me and the rest of the world out.

I finished a turkey-and-Swiss sandwich, and, while I washed up our few dirty dishes, she walked out to the porch, leaving the door open, and plopped into a rocker. I had been patiently waiting for her to open the conversation, but evening was creeping up, and I was beginning to think the trip was all a big waste of time.

I took a short trek through the woods, walking slowly, thinking Zoe might follow me, and that, in the sanctuary of the trees, she would be more at ease. But, no footsteps crept behind me. When I returned to the cabin, she was in the same spot, slumped in the rocking chair that creaked to and fro, her left knee bent against her chest, her bare right foot tapping the porch. She studied her fingertips, pushed her cuticles back one by one with a thumbnail. I recognized her teal, cheetah-print phone as she bent intently over it and scrolled the screen.

I went inside, brewed some orange spice tea, then stood in the empty doorway holding two steaming mugs and a rolled-up pair of fuzzy socks. A wind had come up and put a touch of chill in the air. The evening sun hung low, glinting through the shaggy pine branches, slipping away like our time together.

"Zoe." She turned to me with a look of relief that washed through me, too. "Let's talk." I handed her a mug, tossed the socks into her lap, and sat down in the second rocker. I looked out into the woods beyond the road, while I blew across the surface of my tea.

An exhale of breath came from the other chair. The wood thrush sounded off again, and Zoe's words poured out like water from a breached dam.

"If she had let me have a few more days, if she had given me a chance. She'd been calling me since forever, every Friday, leaving me voicemails."

"I know. She said you never called back." I raised my cup and sipped.

"I didn't want to deal with her. I never listened to the messages. But, I had decided I was going to call her the weekend before Valentine's Day, maybe even go see her, I didn't know when, but soon. My car was in the shop, so I couldn't right away. Or maybe that was an excuse to put it off. I was a coward."

"You were thinking about it. That must have taken a lot of courage, after so long not speaking to her."

"I had so much to say. I didn't know how to begin. It wasn't just the time that had gone by. You see, Stella and I had talked only a few weeks before. Stella knew stuff. You know how she is, she would make the best spy. She's always watching and listening, and she takes everything in like a sponge. She knew what she was talking about."

I reached for Zoe's hand, but she curled it into her chest, behind her propped-up knee. She had slipped on the socks. "What did Stella tell you?"

"How Daddy kept those rumors against Mom going, how he refused to back her up with the school district, even added his suspicions. He didn't start it, but he threw fuel on the fire. I know he had his reasons. Maybe she even deserved it. She cheated on him. She broke up our family. But, I had chosen Daddy over her for all that time, and then I found out that he was just as horrible. When that sank in, I thought, 'I don't have any parents. They're frauds.' I didn't know how I would ever get them back, but I still thought there had to be a way."

Zoe's nails clicked against the side of her cup. She set the mug on the porch.

"You see, I had been thinking if I could face Mom, take responsibility for how I had hurt her, I could work up to confronting Daddy, demand that he own up to what he did. All four of us, Stella too, we all had a part in this, and we could repair things, be a family again. Then Mom crashed it, broke it to pieces. And there was no way to get them back, to get us back."

I reached toward her again, and this time she didn't flinch when I touched her knee.

"Why did she do it?" she pleaded. "Was it Daddy's fault? Was it my fault?"

"A wise friend told me that blame is a useless exercise." I pictured Judd's kind eyes, the familiarity with grief that lived behind them alongside the openness to joy. "Maybe, somehow, I could have held her back from the edge on that particular night, but I couldn't stop her pain. Your mom was a lover, not a fighter. She would put on a happy face and smile through the tears no matter what, but, I suppose, in the end, she couldn't keep up. The tears kept coming long after the smiles ran out."

My words seemed too small for the moment, but it was as much of an answer as I could give.

A series of whooshes passed above the roof of the cabin, large wings beating the air, and faded toward the trees. At the edge of the woods, the branch of a pine stirred. Zoe lifted her face to the sky. The curve of her cheek was pale in the gathering shadows.

"Mom was always so happy when Stella and I were kids. I can still see her out in the audience when she came to our school events, lit up with a smile, clapping, cheering louder than anyone else. How is that the same person who killed herself and my dad?"

The air nipped my cheeks. The sun had become a wavy slice of melon pausing behind the trees while I gathered my words before I spoke. "Even good people do horrible things," I said. Zoe nudged the mug with her toe. Her chin had fallen to her chest. For a moment, I wasn't sure she had heard me.

"I'm a horrible person for not reaching out to her when she was trying for years," she said.

"We're not always what we should be, including your Auntie Connie, but we don't start out that way, and we need to remember the good people we were and still can be. Hold close to that memory of your proud mom smiling and cheering. That's her, too. She loved you. Without pause, in her best and worst moments."

Zoe lifted her arms to shoulder height and let them fall again to her lap. "I don't know how I should feel about her."

I waited, counted a few breaths. What could I say? How to feel about Roanne was my struggle, too. "It's okay for you to still love her even though you might hate her at the same time."

Her shoulders bent inward. "I want her to know what it's like for me, her taking herself and Dad away, and I can't do that. It's like I'm dragging this great, angry weight around, and I can't figure out how to put it down."

"Your mom was carrying that weight, too. She had wanted to speak it, but she and I had both learned as girls what was permitted and what wasn't when you're female. It was okay to be upset now and then, but it was never okay to be angry. As my mother would say, 'Nobody likes an angry woman.'" I shook my head and slapped a hand down on my knee. "Oh, it was so important to be liked."

I set my mug next to the rocker. "Your mom did what she had learned to do, she held everything in—until she exploded. I suppose your dad was in the line of fire, or maybe she couldn't bear to go without him. She didn't want that for you and me. That's why she called you, week after week, and why she called me just before she died. She wanted me to put that anger down where it belonged."

A small creature scuttled through the shrubbery at the side of the cabin. Zoe shifted toward the sound, and her chair creaked as it rocked forward.

"Daniel told me how you went around to all those guys who hurt you and stood up to them," she said. "But what do I do?"

The heavy question shakily suspended in her trembling voice paralyzed me. This was the moment when Auntie Connie was supposed to snare the falling child. Panicky questions ping-ponged inside my head: What would Oprah say? What would Jesus do? What if I didn't get it right? What if I tossed a lifeline that fell a foot too short?

I offered what I had and hoped it would be enough. "Your Aunt Darla would say it's about forgiveness, but I think that comes later. You begin by allowing yourself to be angry as hell. With your mom and your dad and yourself. Sweat it out like a raging fever. Put it down where it belongs." I stood up and patted her bent knee.

She looked up at me with the eyes of a hesitant rabbit in the second before it bolts from the woods across a clearing. "Suppose I can't ever forgive them?"

"First, work on forgiving yourself." I stood and brushed the top of her head with my open palm. "That's what she wants for you."

I shivered, hefted an armful of logs, and walked back inside the cabin. I had been wrong about the night not being cold enough for a fire. I stacked the logs in the stove, piled on some kindling, and struck a match. The flames licked at the larger pieces of wood, but after a few minutes the orange and yellow tongues withered away. I checked the damper knob and listened for the metal plate to clank open at the top of the flue, then restarted the fire with another batch of kindling. Grabbing a poker, I prodded the wood, trying to coax it into a full-fledged blaze.

In the time it took for me to light four hurricane lamps scattered throughout the room, the fire had fizzled again. Extra quilts and wool blankets were stacked on the ends of the beds, and, under the bottom bunk, I spied a small electric heater. The owners had considered the fire-building incompetence of urban guests.

I set up the heater at the outlet nearest the bunks. The rods inside began a slow glow. Zoe still sat outside in the chilly night. I pulled a blanket off the bed and went to the front door to offer it to her. I had opened the door just a crack when a voice from the porch knocked me to my knees.

Roanne was speaking.

"Hi, sweetheart, I hope you did well on your finals. At least they're over with, right? Hang in there. It'll all be worth it in the end. I'll be so proud to see you walk across the stage in your white cap. Call me soon. Love you."

A pause, then, Roanne talked again. "Hi, sweetheart, what a day at the store, all those cute little Valentine knickknacks to put out. I'm going to your Aunt Darla's for dinner. She's making those awesome enchiladas you used to like so much. I'll take home leftovers if you want to come by this weekend. Call me soon. Love you."

Roanne's voicemail messages. Happy birthday wishes to her younger daughter three years ago. A recap of Stella's visit two years ago. A report on the removal of a patch of skin cancer from Roanne's face four years ago. Zoe hadn't listened to them, but she had saved them.

A whoosh and a crackle came from the center of the room. The logs had caught after all. The heat radiated out toward where I sat next to the door left ajar, my head propped against the wall.

Roanne's voice had gone quiet. I sensed a yet incomplete circle, hovering in space over the cabin, an arc of light in the darkness, the ends reaching toward each other, destined to meet. Zoe's lilt, floating into the brisk night, filtered through the crack of doorway.

"Hi, Mom, it's me. I'm sorry I never called you back. You see, I've been so angry with you for such a long time, and I..."

The fire popped and crackled, and an owl hooted, covering over the rest of Zoe's words.

I breathed in the perfume of the burning logs and let the blanket puddle around my hips.

"Hey, Ro," I said, barely out loud. "Don't you worry about Zoe. She'll figure it out. And me? I don't mind the memories anymore, the good times and bad, thrashing away in my head. I welcome them, I put my arms around them, pull them in, melt into them. We live together in those moments. You and me, Ro. Always. You and me."

The edge of a breeze reached into the sliver of doorway, stirred a strand of hair, curled into my ear. A swish, a sigh, a whisper:

"Exactly."

– ABOUT ATMOSPHERE PRESS

–

Atmosphere Press is an independent, full-service publisher for excellent books in all genres and for all audiences. Learn more about what we do at atmospherepress.com.

We encourage you to check out some of Atmosphere's latest releases, which are available at Amazon.com and via order from your local bookstore:

Twisted Silver Spoons, a novel by Karen M. Wicks

Queen of Crows, a novel by S.L. Wilton

The Summer Festival is Murder, a novel by Jill M. Lyon

The Past We Step Into, stories by Richard Scharine

The Museum of an Extinct Race, a novel by Jonathan Hale Rosen

Swimming with the Angels, a novel by Colin Kersey

Island of Dead Gods, a novel by Verena Mahlow

Cloakers, a novel by Alexandra Lapointe

Twins Daze, a novel by Jerry Petersen

Embargo on Hope, a novel by Justin Doyle

Abaddon Illusion, a novel by Lindsey Bakken

Blackland: A Utopian Novel, by Richard A. Jones

The Jesus Nut, a novel by John Prather

The Embers of Tradition, a novel by Chukwudum Okeke

Saints and Martyrs: A Novel, by Aaron Roe

When I Am Ashes, a novel by Amber Rose

Melancholy Vision: A Revolution Series Novel, by L.C. Hamilton

The Recoleta Stories, by Bryon Esmond Butler

– ABOUT THE AUTHOR –

Patricia Watts worked as a journalist for more than 20 years for newspapers in Texas, Hawaii, and Alaska. Following her news career, she tried her skill as a paralegal and then spent ten years investigating discrimination cases for the Alaska Human Rights Commission. Her novels include: *Ghost Light* and *The Big Empty,* crime mysteries co-written with Alaska author Stan Jones; *The Frayer,* suspense *noir*; and *Watchdogs,* a steamy thriller. Her home base is San Diego. She earned her B.A. in journalism at Humboldt State in California. She is the mother of a son and daughter and has seven grandchildren.

63606360R00194